Quoz

A FINANCIAL THRILLER

MEL MATTISON

A POST HILL PRESS BOOK
ISBN: 979-8-88845-202-8
ISBN (eBook): 979-8-88845-203-5

Quoz:
A Financial Thriller
© 2024 by Mel Mattison
All Rights Reserved

Cover design by Cody Corcoran

Post Hill Press
New York • Nashville
posthillpress.com

Published in the United States of America
1 2 3 4 5 6 7 8 9 10

To Dad, Mom, and Catherina

Banking establishments are more dangerous than standing armies.

—Thomas Jefferson, 1816, writing to John Taylor

Permit me to issue and control the money of a nation, and I care not who makes its laws.

—Attributed to Mayer Amschel Rothschild, founder of the Rothschild banking dynasty

Money is gold, nothing else.

—J. P. Morgan, from his 1912 testimony to the US Congress

PART I
All That Glitters...

According to official statistics, the largest holder of gold in the world is the United States at over eight thousand metric tons.

However, according to unofficial calculations, China holds not the two thousand tons publicly reported but closer to thirty-two thousand tons. As of 2007, China has replaced South Africa as the world's largest producer of gold.

Gold is the traditional way to preserve wealth in India. Citizens of the subcontinent hold an estimated twenty-five thousand tons of the yellow metal, over three times the amount held in reserve by the United States.

De-dollarization is a key policy of the Central Bank of the Russian Federation. Since the country's 2014 annexation of Crimea, its central bank has been on a massive gold-buying spree. Russia's true holdings are unknown.

CHAPTER 1

San Juan, Puerto Rico

MONDAY, NOVEMBER 1, 2027

DID I LEAVE IT AT El Loro Verde?

A scraggly wig hung precariously from the frond of a potted palm. Empty bottles of island-brewed Medalla beer crowded the frosted glass of a nearby coffee table. A wallet, keys, a bong, two remotes, and a half-eaten pizza also lay scattered across the room. But something was missing.

Though hard for many in San Juan to believe, Rory Augustine O'Connor possessed one of the most extraordinary financial minds on the planet. Until his abrupt departure from the ICARUS project last year, he was in charge of trading operations across six continents. He had managed eight direct and over two hundred indirect reports. Now, Rory couldn't manage to find his phone.

He continued to circle his luxury condo as remnants of last night's activities surfaced in his mind like fragments from some half-forgotten dream. Noticing the scraggy wig, Rory flashed back to his half-hearted attempt at a last-minute Halloween costume. *That's right, Sam Bankman-Fried.* He had merely added the tangled mess to his typical island attire—a T-shirt and shorts. The truth was, Rory's heart just wasn't into much of anything these days.

Screw it.

Rory abandoned the search for the missing phone. He approached a pair of open French doors that led to his expansive balcony overlooking the Caribbean. Located in the trendy Condado neighborhood, the condo was oceanfront with impressive views of Atlantic Beach. A soft breeze drifted past him and into the living room. He stood motionless for a moment, allowing the tropical warmth and humidity to gently caress his dehydrated skin. His bloodshot eyes tracked a brown pelican gliding effortlessly only inches above the water. Suddenly, the bird arched higher, then nose-dived lower to scoop up breakfast. As it landed softly on a placid sea, he couldn't help but think, *So easy, so free.*

Feeling a slight pang of envy as well as his hangover, Rory turned and walked a few steps through the living room and into the kitchen. He grabbed the stainless-steel handle of his $15,000 Sub-Zero, commercial-grade fridge and reached for a cold bottle of Medalla. As he twisted the cap, the sound of an electronic ring echoed from his office. From the tone, he knew at once it was not the missing phone.

Who the hell is this? Rory walked into his office and sat down at a desk overlooking a sweeping vista of turquoise-blue waters. He looked at the screen of his Mac. The incoming FaceTime was from Kota Nakazawa. *Shit, he definitely doesn't have my phone.*

But Kota was a good friend, and so Rory clicked the mouse.

"Rory, this Kota."

"I know. I can see you."

Kota wore a white button-down shirt and was seated at his desk in downtown Chicago, its imposing skyline visible in the background but dulled by hanging gray clouds. He said, "How are you doing? I am trying to speak with you all morning. You don't answer your phone."

The familiar sound of Kota's imperfect English combined with a strong Japanese accent managed to bring a smile to Rory's sodden face. Kota, however, was not smiling.

"I'm good," Rory lied. "How the hell are you?"

"I am well. We very busy here."

"That's surprising. I figured with the final phase of ICARUS coming online today, you guys wouldn't have much to do anymore. What's up?"

Originally from Tokyo, Kota had also been one of the chief architects of ICARUS. Like Rory, he left the project shortly after the launch of its first phase late last year but for different reasons. An expert in data mining and analysis who spent most of his career at universities before ICARUS, Kota wanted to cash in on some hedge fund money before that world became a thing of the past. Without too much trouble, he managed to land a job at Rory's old firm, Celtic Capital.

"We need your help," Kota said with a look of concern across his face. "I find some disturbing anomalies in market trading patterns. Milton want you here right away."

Rory considered replying, *I really don't give a damn what Milt wants. I don't work for that son of a bitch anymore*, but instead he lied once again.

"Look, Kota, I've got a bunch of stuff going on right now. I don't have time for this."

Rory sipped his beer as Kota ignored his disinterest. "The VIX is down well within parameters, just like we model."

"Yeah, so what's the problem? ICARUS is working like a charm."

"Overall, that is true. But ultra-short-term realized volatility is four sigma beyond what we predicted."

"Okay, I think I understand." Rory reached for a pair of binoculars atop his desk. He glanced around the Mac and out the window toward Atlantic Beach. His focus had shifted from four sigma to four young women dressed in thongs and working on their tans.

"I am not sure you do," Kota said firmly, clearly alert to Rory's inattention. "This is serious."

"No, I get it." Rory put down the binocs and refocused on Kota. "On a macro basis, prices are moving in our expected vol ranges, but on the micro or nano level, they're way off. There must be an issue with the volatility-suppression algo. Either that or there's some trader out there hopped up on Adderall and using HFT setups to monkey with fractional moves."

The rise of high-frequency trading had long since taken over the vast majority of transactions executed on world exchanges. Co-located servers, fiber networks, and complex algorithms had created a stock market run more by machines than by men or women.

"Yes, exactly," Kota confirmed. "Someone placing buy and sell orders for fractional shares, but they transact huge volumes in total. They just spread it out over tens of thousands of trades per second."

Rory came back curtly, "What the hell does this have to do with me? I'm not your mystery trader. You know that. And I sure as shit don't work for Milt anymore."

Milton McGrady was the boss at Celtic Capital. A master-of-the-universe type, the hedge fund billionaire had helped Rory get his start in the business some eighteen years prior. Indeed, Rory's relationship with the McGrady clan went back much further than that. Despite their long history, when Rory left Celtic to work on ICARUS, he and Milton did not part on good terms. Understandably, McGrady was not enthusiastic about his best trader heading off to create a quantum AI platform that would eventually render the hedge fund industry obsolete. Of course, that didn't stop him from hiring Kota, whose experience on the project offered an edge in an era where an edge was getting harder, if not impossible, to come by.

Kota brushed off Rory's shortness. "Milton thinks you are the only one who can verify the anomalies. He believe we can make a lot of money from them. All he wants from you is a few hours. In return, he will pay you fifty thousand dollars and fly you up on his Gulfstream; stay at any hotel you wish."

Rory considered McGrady's proposal. *A quick trip to Chicago might not be a bad idea, maybe grab an Italian beef from Portillo's. And like Nana said: never turn down free money.*

He took another swig of his Medalla as Kota's tone ratcheted up in urgency. "There is something else too. I model out all the data. I think there may be a big problem coming, a real crash."

"With the final phase of ICARUS going live today? You've got to be kidding."

"Rory, this is no joke. Please come. Something not right with ICARUS."

Kota was not a nervous man. In fact, he was one of the most composed people Rory had ever worked with, at least before happy hour Sapporo and sake. There was more to this than simply a few market anomalies. Kota was asking for help with something important, a potential crash involving ICARUS, the AI supercomputer designed to end all crashes.

Rory looked once more beyond his Mac, beyond the thongs and the sand and toward an endless horizon. The sea's tranquility was fading now as morning stillness broke under the mounting heat of day. He watched as another pelican, or possibly the same one, flew swiftly above the waves, then shifted his gaze back to the screen.

"All right, Kota. I'll come to Chicago."

CHAPTER 2

Nagpur Air Force Station, India

Monday, November 1, 2027

Both jets carried identical payloads: one hundred tons of .999 pure gold bullion. The two massive An-124 cargo planes had landed just minutes apart at the air force station in Nagpur. Indian military personnel moved quickly, preparing a football field–size hangar for the first jet. A company of armed air force MPs circled the second An-124 as it waited outside the hangar. It needed refueling before its next flight to Moscow by way of Qatar.

As the first jet slowly released its enormous rear door toward the hangar floor, the precious payload was revealed. At current prices, each plane's cargo was worth roughly $6.4 billion. At next week's prices, if the men receiving the shipment had their way, the glittering yellow bricks would be worth at least a dozen times that amount.

The bullion had been flown in directly from London after being released from the subterranean vaults below the Bank of England. The BoE, Britain's central bank, holds gold both for its own reserves as well as on behalf of other central banks. This particular gold was released upon demand of Arun Patel, governor of the Reserve Bank of India. For decades, the RBI had been keeping much of its gold reserves with the BoE for safekeeping and easy transfer to various counterparties, but the time had come for a sizable withdrawal.

Patel stood in the hangar watching as the young airmen unloaded the gold. Standing next to him were Zhao Hong, governor of the People's Bank of China, and Anton Golev, president of the Central Bank of the

Russian Federation. The three central bank chiefs all knew that their meeting in an Indian air force hangar on the outskirts of Nagpur was as uncommon as it was necessary. After years of planning, the time for action had finally arrived.

Zhao Hong—given name Hong, surname Zhao—was the youngest of the three men at forty-two years. He turned to Patel and spoke in only slightly accented English, "Did Sir Peter give you any trouble about releasing your reserves?"

"Of course the cheeky bastard did," Patel said with a grin. "And I loved every minute of it. Some of those Brits still see us as their bloody colony."

Arun Patel, gray-haired yet quite fit for a man in his late fifties, was small of stature with a gentle voice that evoked calmness in those who spoke with him. Nevertheless, his ruthless business acumen had garnered him a rather ferocious moniker. Nicknamed the Bengal Banker, Patel had his family origins in the state of West Bengal. After receiving his PhD in economics from Cambridge and serving for eight years on the faculty there, he transitioned to the private sector, where he worked his way up at Goldman Sachs. In 2006, Patel helped that firm open its first office in Mumbai. Eventually he served as the bank's managing director in charge of all Indian operations. Five years ago, the Indian government tapped the Bengal Banker to run the RBI amid global inflation in the aftermath of the COVID pandemic.

Anton Golev, the Russian, then spoke up. His voice was heavily accented, deep, and raspy. "Patel, spare us your tales of imperialist oppression. No one has suffered at the hands of Western Europe more than Mother Russia. Besides, I am here to ensure the other plane departs safely for Moscow, not discuss Indian history."

In his early fifties, Golev was muscularly built, around six feet tall with a belly growing ever so slightly each year. His slicked-back salt-and-pepper hair was medium length, and he wore a dark suit with a white shirt and no tie. The shirt's top button was undone, revealing a thin gold chain visible among the gray hairs on his chest.

"We have a history of culture and civilization here in India," Patel said, "that goes back long before your beloved Mother Russia was even a nation-state."

Golev did not reply with words, just an icy glare. Unlike his Indian counterpart, the Russian had not come to central banking from the posh universities of the West and with a résumé full of investment banks. Golev had begun his career in the Federal Security Service, or FSB, a successor agency to the Soviet KGB, and rose to some level of prominence there, including oversight of its vast budget. He also handled many of the personal financial affairs for a former FSB director who unexpectedly rose to the Russian presidency. Never one to let a good crisis go to waste, Golev had been the first to see the financial opportunity posed by Russia's status as a pariah nation. He realized there was a bright side to all those sanctions: it freed the Russian Federation from international scrutiny in its financial dealings, and Golev was a man who preferred to work in the shadows.

Patel ignored Golev's glare and said, "Let's just hope that Prince can hold up his end of the bargain."

Seizing upon the change in subject, Zhao added, "Do not worry, my friend. Everything will be in order soon enough."

The men stood in silence for a few uncomfortable moments as the final pallets were forklifted off the first plane. The gold was then loaded into armored trucks standing by for the short trip up Indian Highway 264 to the secure vaults of the RBI located in central Nagpur. Upon completion, Patel said, "Well, gentlemen, I must take my leave." He gave a respectful nod to his Chinese counterpart and a critical glance to Golev.

"Good night, Arun," Zhao responded, also with a respectful nod. Golev just stared at the departing Patel as he ducked into a waiting limousine, then turned his attention to Zhao.

Odd for a man in charge of China's central bank, numbers had never been Zhao Hong's strong suit, but he was a master of languages. Fluent in Mandarin, Cantonese, English, French, and Russian, his German, Italian, and Spanish were conversational.

As Patel's limo drove away, Zhao said to Golev in nearly perfect Russian, "We need India if this plan is going to work. Their gold and silver reserves are just too significant to ignore, and your beloved Russia needs a market for her natural resources."

"You really think so, Zhao? You think *we* need *them*?" Golev replied in his native tongue. Then, with a sweep of his hand toward the lights of Nagpur shimmering just outside the wide hangar door, he said, "These bastards need our oil and gas to farm, to manufacture, to work, to eat, to transport goods and people. We have them by the balls. If it weren't for the opportunity to get my hands on their gold, I would never have agreed to bring Mr. Patel into our little party."

"Perhaps. But remember, it will be better to have India as our ally when the dust settles. Their national obsession will pay off handsomely soon."

Zhao was referring to the Indian obsession for all things precious metals. Private households in India were estimated to hold around twenty-five thousand tons of the yellow metal. Their silver hoard, mostly in the form of jewelry, tea sets, and other everyday items, was immense. The coming surge in both gold and silver prices would increase the country's wealth by an astronomical amount. As for the hundred tons of gold that still sat in the cargo hold of the second An-124, that would be in Russian hands soon, India's down payment on construction costs for what would be the world's longest natural gas pipeline. The planned route ran from the frozen tundra of Siberia through the Himalayas and into northern India.

Golev turned and looked down with soulless gray eyes at the younger, smaller Zhao. "So, what progress have you made with the American senator?" he asked.

"I'm flying directly from here to the US to visit him personally. I'll make sure he gets the Phoenix Act passed into law this week." Zhao smiled and continued, "Soon the current global financial order will be a thing of the past, fodder for economic textbooks and the tears of Western bankers. Keep your eye on the big picture. With your resources and military strength, Europe will once again be Russia's playground, and not just the eastern half."

"Yes, and what about you, Zhao? What will be your playground? The rest of the world, I suppose. But you must keep your eye on the big picture as well. Remember, only we can truly deter the Americans."

Golev was referring to the massive stockpile of nuclear weapons still in Russian hands. Despite the buildup of the Chinese military in recent years, their nuclear arsenal was still just a fraction of what both the Russians and Americans maintained.

Zhao inquired, "Have you managed to get your hands on the source code yet?"

While it was the Chinese banker's responsibility to ensure passage of the Phoenix Act, Golev had been tasked with something more appropriate to his skills and background in the FSB.

"I have two of my best men working on it, both from the Zaslon unit of Spetsnaz. They are traveling to America as we speak. It is only a matter of time before I secure the code."

"I'm happy to hear that." Zhao made a quick glance at his watch and said, "I have a plane to board, but keep me updated. If Prince doesn't have the complete quantum AI source code by the week's end, he won't be able to restabilize markets after their collapse."

"*Da*," Golev said, then switched to English. "I will, how do the Americans say, keep you in the loop." He turned from Zhao and began walking toward the second jet, still laden with a hundred tons of what was now Russian gold.

"Just one more thing," Zhao added before heading to his own private jet. "Please have your men be discreet. The less attention we bring to our actions, the better."

Golev stopped mid-stride and turned, his gray eyes staring coldly back at Zhao. "My men are professionals. If there is any bloodshed, it will only be because it was necessary."

"Very well. And where, if I may ask, do your men expect to find the code?"

Golev smirked, his thin gold chain sparkling in the hangar lights. "That is two more things, Zhao." Before turning back toward the second An-124, he concluded, "But if you must know, latest intelligence indicates we'll find what Prince needs in Chicago."

CHAPTER 3

San Juan, Puerto Rico

THE HONK OF A HORN from Avenida Magdalena nine stories below could be faintly heard as waves looped rhythmically onto the nearby shore. Rory had concluded the FaceTime with Kota, making arrangements for his first trip back to Chicago in almost a year. He now stood on his balcony.

Rory brushed back his hair, took a sip of his beer, and sat down in a wicker chair. He could feel every bit of the fifteen or so pounds he had put on since moving to La Isla del Encanto. Normally in top physical condition, he had let some things slide over the past year, trading in his six-pack abs for twelve-packs of Medalla. Despite this slide, Rory still looked relatively healthy and fit, handsome even. At six foot two, 205 pounds, with penetrating blue eyes, he maintained a full head of jet-black hair with just a few grays filling in. He was by no means old at forty-three. Rory just no longer felt young.

He pulled a cigarette from a pack on the table beside him. A bad habit, he knew, but one, like so many others, Rory had struggled to break. Thoughts of regret seeped into his mind as the nicotine flowed to his brain. His exhalation was more like a sigh, the smoke slowly leaving his mouth and wafting up into the humid air. Staring once more into the horizon, Rory couldn't help but think back on that fateful night in Chicago almost one year ago: the night when Peter Costello, his best friend and longtime colleague, had an iPhone, seventy-eight bucks, and his life snatched away on the cold streets of the South Side.

Jolting Rory from his melancholy, a knock sounded from his condo's front door.

Now what?

Rory put out his smoke, grabbed his beer, and walked in from the balcony. He made his way to the door and glanced through the peephole. It was José Diaz, a twenty-year-old kid from the neighborhood who, among other things, bussed tables, cleaned cars, and occasionally served drinks at El Loro Verde, a bar off the nearby main drag of Calle Loíza. He wore a teal tank top, board shorts, and flip-flops.

Rory unlocked then swung the door open. "There's a buzzer downstairs for a reason."

"True," José said, an industrious smile on his face. "But Señora Jiménez was walking in just when I got here. Why? You busy?"

"Not really," Rory admitted. "Something to drink? I got water, Gatorade, and cerveza, but it's still a little early in the day for that last one."

José glanced at the Medalla bottle in Rory's hand.

Rory noticed the glance and said, "Medicinal purposes. Now, you want something or not?"

"Na, man. I got shit to do. I just come by to give you this."

José pulled an iPhone from his pocket and held it up in his right hand.

I knew that damn thing would show up. Rory took hold of his phone. "Thanks, José. I appreciate it."

"You were pretty blasted last night, bro," José remarked with a grin.

"Since I don't really remember what happened, that kind of makes sense. Anything interesting go down?" Rory flopped onto his couch.

"Let's see, you tried speakin' Spanish to Manny the whole night. You're getting better, by the way. You struck out with two honeys down from New Jersey, and then you almost got in a fight with Luis."

"Luis? What did that *gordo* do?"

José leaned against the kitchen island and faced Rory lying on the couch. "Well, he ate some of your pizza while you were talking to those two *gatas* from Jersey. You got in his grill about it, and he pulled that nappy-ass thing off your head." José pointed to the wig, still hanging from a

21

potted palm, then went on, "You two almost came to blows, but Manny broke it up before anything started. You just grabbed your wig and your pizza and left; must of forgot your cell. Some dude found it and turned it in at the end of the night."

"Yeah, that's right. I kind of remember now," Rory said as faint memories drifted back into his mind.

"Anyway, I gotta bounce." José pushed back from the island and headed for the door. He added, "But check your phone. It's been ringin' all morning. Someone's really trying to get ahold of you."

Rory shook his head as he looked down at his cell. There were four missed calls and as many voice mails, all from Kota.

"Hold up a sec." Rory stood from the couch and grabbed a couple of twenties from his wallet sitting on the coffee table. "Here, take this."

"You don't need to do that, man. You know I got your back," José said as he brushed away Rory's extended hand.

"I know. But just take it anyway. Go buy something for that young señorita of yours. And remember what my nana says."

"Your nana? What the hell are you talkin' about?"

"Forget it. Just remember: never turn down free money."

José took the forty dollars and left the condo. Rory returned to the balcony. He leaned up against the guardrail and stroked the stubble on his chin as thoughts of Peter and Chicago wandered back into his head. He was looking forward to the food, but not to the memories or to Milton McGrady.

Rory glanced seaward once again. The pelican had vanished, and so, too, had the morning's rhythmic, looping swells. They were now replaced by disjointed chop, whitecaps visible past the break. Taking a final sip of his Medalla, he wondered, *Maybe Chicago isn't such a good idea.* Then he placed the empty bottle on a nearby table and watched one last wave crash onto the sugary-white sand before turning to walk back inside.

There was something Rory needed to see.

CHAPTER 4

San Juan, Puerto Rico
Monday, November 1, 2027

RORY HATED TO DO IT. But like a car accident on the side of the road, he couldn't help but watch. He grabbed one of his remotes and turned on the TV. It came on to the channel it was almost always tuned to, FNN, the twenty-four-hour Financial News Network. Rory sat down on his leather couch just as the live coverage from Switzerland got underway.

ICARUS, or more formally, the project for the International, Central, and Automated Regulation of the Universe of Securities, was a groundbreaking quantum AI platform that revolutionized the world's capital markets. It promised the world a tamer, safer, and more stable economy—devoid of bank runs, bailouts, and volatile share prices. And thus far, it had delivered.

While much of the initial technology was developed at the Chicago Quantum Exchange—an intellectual hub based at the University of Chicago—the overall project was orchestrated under the auspices of the Bank for International Settlements. The fact that most people have never heard of the BIS is not an accident. Established in 1930 by international treaty and headquartered in Basel, Switzerland, it is *the* central bank for central banks.

Historically, the bank had kept a low profile despite it being the most consequential intergovernmental organization in the world. Unlike other global bodies like the UN or IMF, the BIS was a place where real decision-makers met and actually agreed on policy that would ultimately affect every human on the planet. Of course, once ICARUS came online, the BIS went from the shadows to the spotlight.

Suddenly, the world became aware of the bank and its activities. Many people who thought they understood the structure of global finance were surprised to learn that the leaders of the US Federal Reserve, the European Central Bank, and more than sixty other central banks all met discreetly and on a regular basis in Basel. Every two months, these powerful yet unelected men, along with a handful of women, came together to chart a course for the world economy. Cloaked in secrecy, these bimonthly conclaves are known as the AG or All Governors' Meeting.

The discussions and decisions made at the AG produce monetary shock waves that ripple, or sometimes rock, their way through society and impact everything from mortgage rates to the price of a gallon of gas. Despite the far-reaching ramifications of these meetings, no cameras are allowed and no minutes are released. In the name of discretion and confidentiality, the AG takes place behind closed doors with little or no press coverage.

Rory had tried to forget about both Peter's death as well as the BIS since moving to San Juan, but today was different: the third and final deployment phase of ICARUS was about to launch. Rory turned up the volume on his seventy-inch flat screen and listened as FNN commentator Jim Jacobs spoke dubiously of the AI platform but admitted it was a game changer.

"I mean look at this," Jacobs said as he turned toward his co-anchor, David Farley. "The VIX is sitting at 4.8. And this guy at the BIS thinks he can get it below 3. That's insane! It's not a stock market anymore. It's like watching paint dry. I feel like we're covering a horse race but in super slow motion. What the market used to move in a morning now takes a month."

The "guy at the BIS" referred to was Frederik d'Oultremont III, a Dutch financier, central banker, and part-time DJ with a fondness for EDM, electronic dance music. He was also the general manager in charge of the Bank for International Settlements.

"Yes, you're absolutely right about that, Jim," Farley commented. "My sources report another wave of hedge funds will be shuttering their doors soon. There's just no alpha out there to be had. Mr. d'Oultremont, our DJing central banker, has made quite a few enemies on Wall Street, that's for sure. If the VIX goes any lower, they're going to need bread lines for the traders. But for your average investor, it's a lot more comfortable knowing your 401(k) isn't going to crash three years or three months before retirement."

The commentators were not exaggerating. Since its Phase II rollout, ICARUS had consistently maintained market volatility under 5 as measured by the Chicago Board Options Exchange's Volatility Index or VIX. The VIX is the market's fear gauge, a measure of predicted volatility—how much the S&P 500 is expected to move up or down in the future—and typically held anywhere from 15 to 20, spiking much higher during times of extreme market stress. Before ICARUS, the lowest level ever recorded on the VIX was 9.14 in November of 2017. For it to go under 5 was like running a two-minute mile. It was unheard of.

To be clear, ICARUS had not removed the general upswing or downswing of an asset. It was just that it did not move that much. Before ICARUS, a stock might move from $22 to $30 a share one month and then down to $24 the next month, all with little fundamentally changed about the company or the economy. Most of the move would be noise—seasonal flows in or out of the market, the breaching of a key technical level, or simply a change in investor sentiment. After ICARUS, that same stock might move from $22 to $23 one month and then wind up at $24 the next, the same price as before, but with a fraction of the volatility in between.

And that was the key to ICARUS—its revolutionary AI-based volatility-suppression algorithm combined with unparalleled computational capacity and speed of execution. When large language models with deep machine learning burst onto the scene with ChatGPT in '23, people were blown away, but once predictive AI software merged with quantum hardware, it truly became a brave new world.

ICARUS was powered by a 4,096-qubit central quantum processing unit, allowing the platform to tap into and then process over twelve billion discrete market signals every second. It read every tweet, every news article and press release, every social media post, every 10-K, 8-K, and 10-Q. The entire internet was constantly surveilled in real time. All available sources of data and metadata were instantaneously aggregated and passed through a recurrent quantum neural network. This network acted as a predictive pricing engine and made use of quantum perceptrons in order to determine an asset's fair value. Then, the volatility-suppression algo took over. The VSA executed an expertly timed buy order here or a perfectly timed sell there, and voilà, ICARUS constrained the asset in a much narrower price range than would naturally occur.

Removing this volatility in the short term may not sound like much, but as the quantum neural network processed more and more data, it would get smarter and eventually squash long-term volatility as well. Indeed, the goal of ICARUS and the BIS was nothing less than to end the tumultuous cycles of the world's financial markets. No longer would multiyear bull markets run up the S&P 500 to obscene prices, only to be followed by a crashing bear market. The four steps up, three steps back nature of the market would be replaced by a slow and steady march, one step up at a time.

In the Phase I rollout, ICARUS adjusted only fixed-income securities issued in the major economies, a.k.a. developed market bonds—assets like Treasury bonds and corporate debt. In Phase II, developed market stocks like Apple and Airbus were added to the mix along with commodities such as West Texas crude, lean hogs, palm oil, and lumber. Phase III targeted the stocks and bonds of emerging markets. With today's launch of this final phase, every exchange-traded security and commodity in the world was now being massaged into its "correct" price by the long arm of ICARUS.

Only cryptocurrencies like Bitcoin and Ethereum were immune from its grasp. With no defined trading hours or exchanges to regulate them, crypto had proven to be the last bastion of financial volatility. It continued to make large moves up or down on a regular basis, offering a fertile market for those wishing to trade it either long or short. For that reason, Rory had started day-trading crypto, taking advantage of both the volatility and favorable tax treatment available under Puerto Rico's Act 22 capital gain exemptions.

The Medalla had helped to soothe Rory's hangover, but as he listened to the commentators drone on about ICARUS, the memories it brought back led to a different type of headache. Peter Costello's death had been too much for him to process. Now, watching the live coverage, Rory felt he was living that nightmare all over again. Still, he could not force himself to turn away. His old boss at the BIS, the man who had brought both Rory and Peter on board with the ICARUS project, was taking the stage.

CHAPTER 5

San Juan, Puerto Rico
MONDAY, NOVEMBER 1, 2027

THE CAMERA ZOOMED IN TO focus on Frederik d'Oultremont III. He stood on a platform erected outside the BIS headquarters building in Basel. At six four, he loomed tall in front of the makeshift podium, his piercing blue eyes beaming across the crowd of press and onlookers.

"Just eight days past, we marked the anniversary of a dark day in financial history," Frederik began in perfect English with only the slightest touch of a Dutch accent. "October 24, 1929, Black Thursday as it came to be called, triggered the Great Crash of world markets and ushered in a decade of depression, suffering, and economic power struggle that culminated in the worst war in human history. Today, almost a century later, the Bank for International Settlements is proud to announce an end to market turmoil, volatility, and the boom/bust cycles of the past. Never again will the world suffer under the yoke of manic markets, driving up prices and making the rich richer, whilst the poor get poorer. Never again will bank runs and crashes don the pages of the *Wall Street Journal*, the *Financial Times* of London, or the *Nihon* of Tokyo. Never again," exclaimed the banker, his voice climbing to crescendo, "will the world revolve around financial markets!

"Instead," Frederik stated in almost a whisper, as if he were declaring something sacred, "instead, financial markets will now revolve around the needs and desires and dreams of one humanity." And with that, an eruption of applause and cheers sprang, as if on cue, from the admiring crowd.

I hope you're right, Fred, Rory thought, though he had to admit, Frederik did put on a good show. He looked every bit the picture of success in a three-thousand-franc Swiss-tailored suit, a slight breeze blowing through his strawberry-blond hair. Not exactly a natural leader, Frederik was at times more comfortable with his music than with other people, but there was no doubt in Rory's mind that Frederik had led the implementation of the audacious project competently.

Of course, he didn't do it alone. Under Frederik, there had been a four-person leadership team arranged along functional lines. Rory ran what was sometimes referred to as open market operations, basically the trading department. Kota Nakazawa had been in charge of data science, all the trillions of inputs that ICARUS processed. The bank's treasury department, its money, was overseen by Sara Schnyder, an unconventional Swiss financier with a talent for cross-currency transactions. But the beating heart of ICARUS, its quantum AI source code, was all Peter Costello, the project's head of engineering.

Frederik concluded the address. "Ladies and gentlemen, this has been a long and difficult journey, but one more than worth embarking upon. The BIS, in conjunction with our central bank partners, has worked tirelessly and with an unprecedented spirit of international camaraderie to accomplish this amazing goal. However, it was not without loss or sacrifice. My one lament is that the software genius behind the magic of ICARUS cannot be here with us today. Perhaps more than anyone, Peter Costello believed in the ICARUS mission, and his—"

At the mention of Peter, Rory flipped off the TV. He had heard and seen enough.

And besides, he thought, *I've got a private jet to catch.*

CHAPTER 6

San Juan, Puerto Rico, to Chicago, Illinois
MONDAY, NOVEMBER 1, 2027

BEING A BILLIONAIRE HAS ITS perks.

Rory sipped on a Bulleit bourbon and Coke, relaxing before takeoff in Milton McGrady's Gulfstream G650ER. The G650 is a favorite among the world's elites owing to its long-range and high-speed capabilities. The typical four-and-a-half-hour flight time for commercial jets on the San Juan to Chicago route would be cut to less than three hours courtesy of the jet's powerful engines, capable of cruising at Mach 0.9. With a dozen customizable cabin layouts to choose from, the G650 was the jet of choice for everyone from Jeff Bezos to Oprah Winfrey, Elon Musk to Steven Spielberg. Settling into the soft Corinthian leather of his extra-wide seat, Rory relished the luxury but could not get Kota's words out of his mind. *Something not right with ICARUS.*

Shortly after takeoff, Rory unbuckled his seat belt and moved from his plush seat to an even plusher couch that nestled against the bulkhead. A rich mahogany table was conveniently situated along its length. Revolving captain's chairs sat opposite the table and couch. Moments later, Jennifer, the lovely and polite flight attendant, emerged from the rear galley. Wearing a formal yet undeniably attractive navy suit dress with mid-heel pumps, she brushed back her platinum-blonde hair as Rory wondered what he possibly could have done to deserve this.

"Now that we've reached cruising altitude, is there anything else I can do for you, Mr. O'Connor?" Jennifer asked.

Rory could think of a few creative responses to that question, but he said instead, "No thanks...and please, call me Rory."

"Okay, Rory, I'll be back in the galley if there's anything you need. Unfortunately, there's no chef on board this evening, but I could fix you something simple. A platter of cheese and crackers perhaps?"

"No, really, I'm fine. Maybe one more of these, though." Rory pointed to his drink.

"Of course." Jennifer's long eyelashes flashed a couple of times in front of her soft hazel eyes. She walked to the galley and came back a couple minutes later with another Bulleit and Coke. After placing it on the table next to Rory, she returned to the rear of the plane and closed the folding door that separated the galley from the main cabin.

Rory took a sip from his drink and then laid down across the couch, propping his feet just over the armrest. He looked at his watch, a Rolex Datejust with two-tone oyster bracelet made from stainless steel and eighteen-karat gold. It had been a gift from McGrady after Rory made his first million for Celtic Capital. The date window at the three o'clock position on the bright blue dial read 1. Rory stared at the number and could hardly believe that in four more days it would be a year since Peter's death. In one way, it seemed like yesterday, in another, like a lifetime ago. He sat up briefly and took another sip of his drink before lying back down, thoughts of that night seemingly getting more vivid the closer he got to Chicago.

The evening had begun normally enough at Hamilton's Pub. Hammy's was an old Irish bar on the South Side. Its high, flat ceilings were covered in ornate tiles fashioned from tin and rich with patina. The centerpiece oaken bar dated from the 1930s, and, at times, Rory questioned whether some of the stale beer that flowed from its taps did as well. Much like the bar, the surrounding neighborhood had seen better days, but it was located just a few blocks from the University of Chicago and convenient for a pint or two.

Peter had been struggling for months to complete the key volatility-suppression algorithm, or VSA. In particular, there had been one section, or "block," of code relating to the timing of transactions that Peter referred to as the Vega Block which had proven especially difficult. It was Rory's job to assign weights reflecting the market significance of various data inputs collated by Kota. From these weighted datasets, Peter could then build activation functions into ICARUS's pricing engine utilizing quantum perceptron technology. However, Peter not only needed to extrapolate the correct price based on Rory and Kota's work, he also needed to use the critical VSA to time open market operations perfectly and adjust the transaction size for optimal volatility suppression. As such, it was a team effort, and Rory worked closely with Peter on this vital component of the platform.

So, when Rory received a BIS-wide email earlier that afternoon from Frederik announcing that the Phase I launch was scheduled for the following month, it came as a surprise, almost a shock, to him. He demanded Peter meet him at Hammy's to discuss the matter. Beyond just curious about how Peter did it, Rory's pride was wounded. How could his best friend share his big breakthrough with Frederik before confiding in him? And to find out about it via an email blast only added insult to injury.

It had been one of those miserable Chicago fall days, dark and gloomy, just warm enough to stop the light rain that fell from turning to snow or ice. Rory arrived at the bar and sat down in a booth with Peter. He could tell his friend wanted to explain, discuss it more, but Peter insisted that he owed it to Frederik to explain the details of his breakthrough to him first. Frederik was flying in from Basel that night. Tomorrow, Peter promised, he would share everything.

Unsatisfied, Rory's temper flared, and he stormed from the booth. He refused to listen and acted like a child, turning his back on Peter, then sliding a buck into *Golden Tee*, a golfing video game. Peter knew it was useless trying to have a conversation with Rory when he was in one of his moods and walked out of Hammy's to catch a ride home.

Two minutes later, Rory heard the first shot, then a second and a third. By the time he got to Peter lying in a pool of blood on the sidewalk a hundred yards up the street, it was too late. An old-school Cadillac sped off in the distance as Peter slipped in and out of consciousness. He rambled nonsense, mumbling about the Chicago Bears, asking Rory if he remembered the longest distance between two places. Rory tried to understand, tried to help, but it was pointless. Before the ambulance arrived, Peter was dead.

Ironically, the last place Rory spoke with Peter was also where they had met. The two had struck up a random conversation at Hamilton's almost twenty years prior when they were both young doctoral students at UChicago. The chance meeting and intense debate they had that night about the impact of algorithmic trading on financial markets led them to become fast friends, though they disagreed on the role computers and AI would play in the evolution of finance.

Rory was a staunch believer in the organic nature of the market. It's a living, breathing organism, he argued, with a mind of its own that could never be tamed. Peter, on the other hand, believed that market outcomes were merely a function of understanding all the different inputs and their respective impacts on price—a closed system. He granted Rory that some of those inputs were sentiment-driven, even emotional at times, and reflected human nature. Yet Peter also believed their impact on asset prices could be quantified. Once data collection, AI, and computing speeds advanced enough, tradable patterns would emerge that would make sense of the chaos. Eventually this friendship led them to work together on various projects that sat on the cusp of finance and technology.

Rory and Peter made a formidable team. Rory was the driving force behind isolating data sets, assigning impact weights, and then understanding what those data foretold about market behavior. Peter was a virtuoso programmer. When they met in 2008, he had already completed a separate master's in computer science from MIT and was working on his PhD in applied mathematics at UChicago. His expertise was taking Rory's selected datasets and translating those inputs into actionable code for precise trade execution. When their work at the UChicago student-run investment fund showed tangible results, Rory brought it to the attention of an acquaintance from his old neighborhood on the North Side, a cop named Brendon McGrady with impeccable financial connections.

Besides being a sergeant in the tactical unit of the Nineteenth Precinct, Brendon was also younger brother to one of the world's hedge fund titans, Milton McGrady. The elder McGrady was impressed by Rory and Peter's work, and he tried to recruit them both immediately. Only Rory forsook finishing his studies. Peter stayed in the program and completed his PhD, but less than a year after graduation, he joined Rory at Celtic Capital.

McGrady became like a financial father to them both. He taught them how the game was really played. Over a decade later, when Rory and Peter walked into his office to tell him they were both quitting Celtic to work for some DJing central banker, McGrady felt betrayed. When he found out their mission was to create a quantum AI platform that would sap volatility out of the market, making it essentially untradable, McGrady nearly threw his chair out the window.

A gentle nudge to Rory's shoulder woke him from a light sleep.

"Sorry to disturb you," Jennifer said, a genuine smile on her face. "We'll be landing soon. You'll need to pick a seat for the final descent."

"Oh wow, I guess I dozed off," Rory said with a groggy voice, stating the obvious. He stood, grabbed his drink, the ice melted, and strapped into one of the available captain seat chairs. As the plane descended, it slipped below the cloud cover that had obscured the city lights upon approach. Rory took a sip of the watered-down Bulleit and Coke as he peered out the oval window of the G650. The beauty of the Chicago skyline came into focus just as a light rain began to fall, conjuring ghosts in Rory's head and evoking grim memories of a similar dreary night almost one year ago.

CHAPTER 7

Blue Ridge Mountains, North Carolina
Tuesday, November 2, 2027

ZHAO HONG NEEDED TO CALL his wife, but that could wait. It was a beautiful drive. The rolling hills were carpeted with fallen leaves in every shade of orange, red, yellow, and brown. It was early morning in western North Carolina. Zhao sat alone in the back seat of his armored SUV as it zipped around the tight mountain curves. He had flown all night from Nagpur to Charlotte with only a quick stop to refuel in Lisbon. Soon, he would arrive at the mountain retreat of Senator Matthew Whitlock. Despite some fatigue coupled with jet lag, a slight smile arched across Zhao's face. Unlike the mostly barren birch and maple trees of the Blue Ridge, his plan was beginning to bear fruit. Once the American Congress passed the Phoenix Act, all the pieces would be in place for the market to begin its collapse.

Zhao Hong did not rise to his post as governor of the PBoC by being a nice guy, nor was he the most brilliant and hardworking of scholars. Instead, the driving force behind his career had been his wife, Liling. While not the most beautiful blossom on the cherry tree, Liling carried herself with confidence and had an unflinching sense of ambition. She was, after all, niece to Wang Jun. Wang, besides being uncle to Liling, also served as president of the People's Republic of China. Marrying into such a powerful family came with perks for Zhao, such as acceptance at

Harvard Business School despite a less than impressive academic record. But along with privilege, it also came with pressure: Pressure to make a name for himself. Pressure to achieve and surpass Party goals. Pressure to help President Wang not just maintain his position as the most powerful man in Asia, but to help him become the most powerful man in the world.

Chinese leaders, like the Soviets before them, knew that a hot war with the United States was an unwinnable pipe dream that could have only one result: the destruction of China, if not the entire civilized world. The US had more than enough nuclear firepower to wipe the Asian superpower off the map. They had the greatest navy in the world, which could blockade the mainland and cut off China from commerce and resources. They had, in short, a powerful and devastating counterresponse to any military move the Chinese might consider. While China certainly had more warm bodies to throw at the possible conflict, any armchair general could see that it would be a fool's errand given the weaponry and technology of the Americans. What were the Chinese going to do? Storm the beaches of San Diego and Seattle like they were Normandy? Their armada would be a mile deep in the Pacific before it got within a thousand miles.

Decades of a long cold war would not suffice either. Like Stalin and Hitler in the twentieth century, Wang's power was that of an autocratic dictator wrapped in the flag of a party. And dictatorships, despite any outward appearances, are by their very nature fragile and weak, especially in the age of the internet. Despite the Party's best efforts to control freedom of thought, the people of China were connected to the outside world and becoming more informed every day. The Chinese Communist Party clung to power through a thin veneer of control, intimidation, and fear. There was only one path to sustained victory—global economic domination. Not a cold war but a gold war.

The linchpin of US hegemony had always been its economic might, an unmatched combination of natural resources, manpower, and money. That trifecta had shifted the balance of power in Europe twice, but China was not Germany. Combined with resources from Russia and Africa, China already had the manpower to threaten American supremacy. There was just one leg of the stool left to chop off: money. Or, to be more specific, the almighty dollar and its unrivaled position as the world's reserve currency.

Countries around the globe no longer hold the majority of their reserves in gold or even their own currency; they hold the US dollar. Moreover, almost all international transactions are conducted in USD. America represents less than 5 percent of the world's population, yet the nation issues and therefore controls the vast majority of the world's money. This unlimited supply of funding has allowed Uncle Sam to spend more on defense than the next nine countries combined. Zhao and Wang knew, to defeat America, they needed to destroy the dollar.

The plan was anachronistic and simple. China would follow in the footsteps of America during the World Wars, the British during the eighteenth and nineteenth centuries, and the Spanish before that. They would amass the largest gold reserves on the planet. Zhao was a modern-day Pizarro. And with the help of ICARUS, he would orchestrate the largest economic crisis in living memory, a sea of financial chaos so wild, global elites would recognize only one possible port in the storm: a return to the original money but with a modern twist. The world's new reserve currency would be on the blockchain yet backed by gold and silver. Los Conquistadores meet crypto. The dollar would be dead.

Zhao, Wang, and the Party had been laying the groundwork for years. According to published figures, the US held the world's largest gold reserves at around eight thousand tons. China came in a pathetic sixth place with roughly a quarter that amount. But like all financial data the Communist Party released for public consumption, those numbers were just what its leaders wanted the world to believe.

In 2007, China replaced South Africa as the world's largest gold producer, and the Party forbade export of any domestic production. China also became the world's largest buyer, purchasing much of its gold from Switzerland and Dubai while laundering even more of the precious metal via the Shanghai Gold Exchange. Once the world returned to a gold-based monetary system, it would become clear who the real economic superpower was. China's true gold hoard, in excess of thirty thousand tons, would make Fort Knox look like a cheap pawnshop window. And none of this even took into account the icing on the cake: silver.

Zhao continued to gaze out at the rolling hills as his SUV approached Senator Whitlock's retreat. Dealing with Americans had never been a favorite pastime for Zhao, and this senator was just the type he dreaded meeting with the most. *Oh well*, Zhao thought as he pulled out his phone, *at least I will get a look at Vanessa*. He punched in a short text to Anton Golev.

Any update on the code?

Zhao stared for a moment at the screen, hoping for a quick reply. None came.

CHAPTER 8

Blue Ridge Mountains, North Carolina
Tuesday, November 2, 2027

AFTER BEING "WELCOMED" BY THE senator's security detail, Zhao Hong was escorted to the back deck of the mountain retreat. Senator Whitlock sat in a cushioned chair of red cedar, a glass of Tennessee whiskey in hand. He stood as the leader of Asia's most powerful central bank walked through the door.

"Well, Hong, what do ya think? Beautiful, isn't it? That's Mount Mitchell over there, highest point east of the Mississippi. Not quite like the Rockies out west, but it's well over six thousand feet."

The two men shook hands, and Zhao gave a slight bow out of habitual politeness. The Chinese central banker wore a black suit with white shirt and no tie. Whitlock, in his late fifties, overweight, and sporting a head of dyed black hair, enjoyed playing the part of good ole boy. He had on a $300 flannel shirt, hand-embroidered cowboy boots, and designer blue jeans with a brass North Carolina–shaped buckle. While the buckle appeared well worn, its patina had been applied by the manufacturer at the factory.

The Whitlock family mountain retreat was situated on six hundred pristine acres off the North Fork of the Swannanoa River, about ten miles south of Burnsville. Traditionally a feasting ground for the Cherokee people, the land was later populated by Scots-Irish settlers and French trappers. James Whitlock, the family patriarch, originally surveyed the area when it was still part of the British Empire in the 1760s. Whitlocks had owned much of the neighboring land until they fell on hard times and were forced to sell most of it in the 1880s to a wealthy family from New York. George Washington Vanderbilt eventually bought up over fifty other farms and parcels to build his Biltmore Estate, the largest private residence in the United States.

The "Bear's Den," as Whitlock liked to call his abode, was a bit more modest than the Biltmore. However, it still reeked of privilege in a Daniel Boone meets Gordon Gekko sort of way. Animal skins carpeted its floors and hung from its rafters, most of them purchased from estate sales and auctions. Whitlock was not fond of getting his hands dirty. He was fond of modern art, though, and abstract canvases from some of DC's and New York's best galleries hung alongside the taxidermized heads of bucks, bears, and a mountain lion.

Matthew Whitlock grew up the son of a dentist in Charlotte, some two hours by car from the Bear's Den. He made a name for himself as a top partner in a law firm that represented large banks and financial institutions based in the Queen City. Before launching his Senate run in 2004, then congressman Whitlock had the 5,500-square-foot cabin built as a tribute to his family history and his success. Now, he rarely arrived by car but instead preferred private plane if traveling from DC or helicopter if from his primary residence in downtown Charlotte.

Continuing the pointless chitchat, Whitlock asked Zhao, "What's the highest point in China?"

"Everest."

"Yes, Everest, of course. How could I forget?" Whitlock replied, his slight southern accent a bit stronger than usual as he surveyed his ancestral lands. "Take a seat, Hong. Let's get down to business. But first, where's my hospitality? Can I get you a drink?"

"No, thank you." Zhao gave a quick glance at his watch. It was barely past 9:00 a.m.

"Suit yourself." Whitlock poured himself another whiskey from the outdoor bar and grill, then took a seat across from Zhao. "The missing code, whatever Prince needs to do his thing, do we have it?"

"I believe he refers to it as the Vega Block," Zhao said.

Whitlock took a sip of his whiskey, then said, "I don't pretend to understand any of that quantum AI mumbo jumbo. I just need assurances that Prince will be able to bring the markets back to life like Lazarus when the time is right."

So parochial, so American, Zhao thought. He ignored the senator's folksy airs and said bluntly, "Our Russian friend is handling it. Nothing for you to be concerned about. What concerns me, however, is the Phoenix Act. When will it be passed?"

"Don't get your fritters in a jitter. That bill is out of my committee and has the numbers to pass today, but I want this to be a big win. I'm just lining up a few last votes." Whitlock propped up his boots on a nearby empty chair and assured Zhao, "I damn well guar-an-tee Phoenix becomes law before the week is over."

The Phoenix Act would be the largest single expenditure in the history of government as well as pretext to the mother of all stock market crashes. At over $9 trillion in projected outlays, the act included something for everyone, from climate change activists to oil and gas drillers. There was an increase in Medicare and Social Security benefits, more money for social welfare and support programs, $175 billion to reinvigorate the US steel industry, and twenty times that amount for rebuilding bridges, airports, and other vital infrastructure, not to mention $1.1 trillion for student debt forgiveness. It was a lobbyist's wet dream and had more pork than a Chicago slaughterhouse. Indeed, there were so many handouts and giveaways to special interest groups on both sides of the aisle that—with a little shepherding from the senior senator from North Carolina—the bill was set to pass both the House and Senate with significant bipartisan support. Ostensibly, it was completely "paid for" through increased tax revenues projected from the growth it would create as well as modest tax increases on corporations and hyper-wealthy individuals. But everyone in Washington knew who would really pay for it—no one.

The tax receipts wouldn't come near the expenditures, but that hardly mattered. The US Treasury would simply issue trillions in debt, and the Federal Reserve would buy the lion's share of those bonds and notes with money created on a computer, ones and zeros punched into a server somewhere in Washington or New York. Since President Richard Nixon ended the gold exchange standard put in place at the post–World War II Bretton Woods Conference, the US had somehow managed to keep the dollar as the global reserve currency while at the same time printing trillions of greenbacks right out of thin air. It was the greatest financial confidence game in human history. Nothing else even came close. Uncle Sam made SBF and Bernie Madoff look like school kids shoplifting candy bars. The only thing that kept the house of cards standing was a shared international delusion in the value of the almighty dollar, that and a balance of power that suited all major world players...until now.

Despite the senator's theatrics, Zhao believed that Whitlock would indeed get Phoenix passed. He replied, "Wonderful to hear."

"And my gold?" prodded Whitlock.

"An armored truck with the first payment is making its way here as we speak," Zhao said as he soaked in the crisp, cool mountain air. "It should arrive within the hour. I had hoped it would show up at the same time I did, but it's not easy to transport ten tons of gold into these hills."

"Well, that is music to my ears, Hong. It's not easy to pass a $9 trillion spending bill through Congress either."

"Excellent, Senator. Once you succeed, as I'm sure you will, the remaining compensation will arrive here on your doorstep. You have my word."

The terms of their bargain affirmed, both men sat quietly for a moment. Whitlock sipped on his whiskey. The chirp of a cardinal could be heard as well as the rummaging of squirrels in the nearby leaves. The brief moment passed as the door to the cabin swung open. Vanessa Price, Whitlock's chief of staff, walked onto the deck in a pair of tight black jeans and a low-cut white silk blouse.

"Why hello, Governor Zhao, it is so pleasant to see you," Vanessa said as she gave a slight yet revealing bow of her chest in full view of the Chinese central banker.

"Hello, Ms. Price. You're looking exquisite as ever," Zhao responded as he admired Vanessa's flowing red hair, toned arms, curvy hips, and cleavage.

"I'm so sorry to interrupt you, but I need to steal the senator for just a moment." Vanessa shifted her gaze toward Whitlock. Her eyes, green as emeralds, made contact with his. Whitlock removed his boots from the chair, stood, and shuffled off the deck and into the cabin.

"How's it going?" Vanessa asked once the two were safely behind closed doors.

"I have him eating from the palm of my damn hands," Whitlock said with a giddy smile and a quick wink of his left eye. Then, more seriously, he asked, "Is the cave prepared?"

"Everything is in perfect order."

"Good. The gold will be here soon. Now what is it, sugar?"

"Something's come up back in DC. We need to fly back as soon as the bullion arrives."

"All right. I'll go upstairs and change. In the meantime, be a dear and divert Hong for a while. Just laugh at his dumb jokes and make small talk. He loves you, and I need him to get something out of this trip."

"Not a problem. I'll pretend he's handsome and interesting just like I do with you," Vanessa retorted with a wink of her own.

Back on the deck, Zhao looked down at his encrypted satellite phone. A text had just come in from Golev.

The trader is meeting with the Japanese data scientist this morning. My men are on it. Consider yourself in the loop.

CHAPTER 9

Chicago, Illinois
Tuesday, November 2, 2027

I KNEW I SHOULD HAVE brought a jacket.

Rory weaved his way south on the westerly sidewalk of State Street. He dodged rushing morning commuters and slow-moving tourists glued to their cell phones. It was just over a mile from the Peninsula Hotel to Celtic Capital, and the chilly but invigorating walk helped clear his mind. After checking in last night, Rory had decided to pay a visit to the hotel's sixth floor for a light dinner and perhaps one too many nightcaps at the trendy Z Bar.

This morning, Rory was dressed in gray business slacks and a fashionable Luigi Borrelli light green shirt with thin white pinstripes held over from his hedge fund days. Not only would he look presentable, but Rory would arrive on time for his 10:00 a.m. meeting with Kota despite the late-night drinks. *Not bad for a crypto-trading beach bum*, he thought. Rory had skipped breakfast, though, and his stomach growled as he crossed the Chicago River. Turning right onto Wacker, he looked up the street at 333.

333 West Wacker Drive is a thirty-six-floor high-rise office building that overlooks the bend in the Chicago River where its main branch meets its south branch. While not one of Chicago's tallest buildings, 333 is iconic in its own way. Its unique curving façade of blue-green glass shifts colors in the sun like a chameleon, always a slightly different shade. It was the perfect home for Celtic Capital and its leader, Milton McGrady. But there were no shifting shades of blue and green today. Though last

night's rain had passed, a thick blanket of heavy clouds still draped over the city, enveloping it in a sea of gray.

The sight of his old workplace quickly transported Rory back to the days of shorting the yen after Fukushima or buying long-dated puts on pandemic darlings like Zoom and Peloton in early '22. Rory's best trades had almost always been against the market, betting something he felt had been grossly overvalued would one day fall back to reality. Sometimes it paid off and sometimes it didn't, but Rory understood nothing can go up in a straight line forever. In the fall of 2021, he put on a large short position in Bitcoin when it traded around $50,000. As the price skyrocketed past $60K, everyone at Celtic thought Rory was crazy to leave the short on, let alone double up on it, but that's exactly what he did. By the summer of '22, he looked like a genius as Bitcoin broke below $20,000.

Rory entered 333 at precisely 9:52 a.m. He stopped by the lobby's security desk and received a visitor's badge before heading to the elevator bank. Stepping off the elevator, he took a deep breath, hesitated for just a moment, and then pushed open the frosted-glass door of Celtic Capital.

"What's cooking, hot stuff?" Rory said with a smile as he walked into his old offices.

Sally Davis, a mature woman in her early sixties, rose from her chair and removed her glasses before replying, "So, it is true. I heard you were coming in today but had my doubts. How are things?" The long-time receptionist and office manager moved from behind her desk to give Rory a welcoming embrace.

"I can't complain. What about yourself?"

"I *can* complain, but I won't," quipped Sally. "Kota is waiting for you in the conference room."

Rory walked past the small reception area and onto the trading floor. It was a large space that took up most of the half floor that Celtic now occupied. The firm had leased the entire floor when Rory worked there, but ICARUS had taken its toll. Most of the trading stations were empty. Double- or triple-monitor setups sat atop otherwise pristine desks.

The curving windows opened up on one end to northward-facing views of the city. On the east-facing side, Lake Michigan, its waters an uninviting muddled gray, loomed in the distance. A communal kitchen with a full-size fridge and freezer, cabinets, sink, and the office water cooler took up one corner of the floor. Next to the kitchen, Kota sat in a medium-size conference room outfitted with a large table, chairs, and flat-screen TV.

"Kota, how goes it?" Rory said as he walked through the door.

Dressed in sharply creased black pants with a crisp light blue button-down shirt, Kota stood from his seat and walked over to greet Rory. "So good to see you," he said as the two old friends exchanged a brief hug.

After some small talk and other pleasantries, Kota projected his laptop onto the flat screen and gave an impressive data-rich presentation. Thirty minutes later, the groundwork laid, he came to his conclusions.

"This screen shows last thirty historical trading days and observed minute-by-minute volatility." Kota scrolled through a large candlestick chart that displayed values for the open, close, high, and low price for each minute of market trading in the SPY, the most liquid exchange-traded fund that tracks the S&P 500 Index.

Unlike some newspapers and cable television programs, most professionals pay little attention to the famous Dow Jones Industrial Average. A relic of earlier times, the Dow is calculated from the price per share of each constituent rather than on the company's total market capitalization. Thus, some less-valuable companies in the Dow have much higher representation in the index than other larger companies simply because they have significantly fewer shares outstanding.

As Kota scrolled through the candlestick chart, it became clear that volatility had indeed been increasing. The "wicks" of each candle that extended to graphically display the intra-period high and low prices got longer and longer the closer Kota got to fresh data.

After giving Rory a moment to digest the chart, Kota said, "Based on stochastic pattern-recognition software, regression analysis, and Monte

Carlo simulations, I have produced a model for predicted increase in volatility."

The next screen used a layout that Rory knew well. Kota was famous at the BIS for his financial models and dashboards that showed key asset prices and a host of related charts as one moved through time. This model was laid out in the same way. Like a computer-generated weather forecast, the model ticked dynamically through the future. It was a time-lapse display of the markets based on Kota's predictions and showed price changes on key financial assets, everything from Treasury bonds to commodity futures and major equity indexes like the S&P 500, Nasdaq Composite, and Russell 2000.

The dashboard displayed on the flat screen continued to change before Rory's eyes, the picture getting bleaker with each frame. *What the hell?* Rory got up from his chair and walked closer to the TV. "You're showing the S&P down almost thirty-five, now thirty-eight percent. Oil is thirty-two dollars a barrel. Kota, this can't be right."

"Just wait, my friend. You see. There is more."

A minute later the model stopped, and the prices discontinued their downward spiral. All the major equity indexes were down almost 70 percent from current levels. WTI crude oil futures sat at twelve dollars a barrel.

Kota stood from his chair and joined Rory by the flat screen. "This is correct, Rory. Some deviation in outcome possible, but not significant. ICARUS volatility-suppression algorithm is not working right."

"The VSA? You mean this has something to do with the Vega Block?" Rory asked, referring to the key section of AI source code that he and Peter had argued about at Hamilton's.

Kota nodded.

"And you're confident about these projections?"

"I run over six million simulations; all predict a massive sell-off."

Rory looked back at the flat screen. *If these numbers are right, it'll make '08 look like a slight correction.* But he also knew that huge moves in major indexes take at least some time. Key support levels have to be probed first, then breached. Retracement bounces bump up against old support levels to confirm they are new resistance; then the process begins again. *Maybe this is just a glitch in the code,* Rory hoped. *Something Pete missed that can easily be fixed.*

He asked Kota, "When are these outputs predicted to occur?"

"Those are minute-by-minute changes displayed."

Not quite comprehending Kota's point, Rory turned his attention away from the flat screen and looked directly at him. "So how long we got? Next year? Next decade?"

"Not next year, Rory. This happen next week."

CHAPTER 10

Chicago, Illinois

TUESDAY, NOVEMBER 2, 2027

"RORY! FUCKIN'! O'CONNOR!" THE BOOMING voice rang out across the trading floor and into the conference room.

Still trying to process the implications of Kota's model, Rory turned his gaze from the dire projections plastered on the flat screen toward the conference room door. Ten yards away and closing fast was Milton McGrady. He walked at a brisk pace for a large man. His silver hair was a touch longer than Rory remembered, and his belly was definitely a bit rounder, but McGrady wore his usual $1,000 apiece hand-tailored white dress shirt with the sleeves rolled up, no tie. His slacks were creased, no cuffs, and made from a mostly gray plaid pattern with hints of pink and powder blue. On his left arm, a $90,000 Audemars Piguet Royal Oak model timepiece was wrapped tightly around his pudgy wrist.

Well, here we go. With half a smile on his face, Rory said, "Hey, Milt. How's it going?"

"Fantastic! Of course, I'd be doin' a hell of a lot better if that damn ICARUS wasn't around, but what the hell. I've already made my billions."

McGrady had come from humble beginnings. The son of a Chicago cop, he grew up in a hardscrabble neighborhood on the north side of Chicago, but his education was top notch. As a boy, he attended Loyola Academy, a prestigious prep school just north of the city that his father afforded only through extracurricular activities pursued while on "the job." Rumors were that McGrady's uncle, Patrick McGrady, ran an Irish criminal organization that dominated vice rackets in the community. Uncle Pat was found shot to death one night when McGrady was still a young man studying finance at Northwestern University in nearby Evanston.

The hedge fund magnate had received a deep education in the classics from Loyola Academy, an MBA in finance from Northwestern, and a PhD in the streets from his cop father and gangster uncle. It was a powerful combination that created a twenty-first-century Renaissance man with an attitude, just as comfortable quoting Homer, Aristotle, or Adam Smith as he was punching a guy's face in.

"So, you had a chance to review Kota's model?" McGrady asked Rory.

"I did."

"Good. Well, let's you and me talk in my office, then. Excuse us, Kota."

McGrady's office commanded a beautiful view of the river as well as the Merchandise Mart sitting proudly on the opposite bank. The Mart, a monumental and sprawling art deco structure, was the largest building in the world when its doors opened in 1930.

McGrady took his seat behind a large oak desk. Visible through the curved glass behind him, the Mart loomed below like a castle from a bygone era. Glancing around the office, Rory noticed the same plethora of Chicago sports memorabilia that had been hanging on the walls the day he and Peter marched in to tell McGrady their days at Celtic were over. The collection included a game jersey from the 1919 World Series worn by Shoeless Joe Jackson. A number of Chicago Police Department mementos completed the décor, tributes to McGrady's cop father and brother. McGrady kept close ties with the CPD and was one of the largest donors every year to their benevolence fund. Not coincidentally, Celtic Capital managed a good chuck of the department's pension assets.

"Please, have a seat," McGrady said in an uncharacteristically submissive tone. "It's so good to see you. How are things? Anything I can have Sally bring in? Coffee? Tea? I think there's some fresh scones out there somewhere."

He's laying on the bullshit already. Rory glanced to his right at a black leather chair and considered taking a seat as requested. But he did not sit down. McGrady's Mr. Nice Guy routine was not going to get Rory to drop his guard. *You may be ready to forget our last meeting, but I'm not.*

"Milt, last time I was in this office, you were a fuckin' asshole to Pete and me. We worked our butts off to make you more money than God, spent over a decade giving you all we had. Then, when we decided it was time to move on, you treated us like pieces of shit. I haven't forgotten about that. I doubt you have either. Which means there can only be one reason why you flew me up here: you need me for something. So, how about you drop the tea and crumpets routine and just tell me what the fuck you want."

"Rory, I forgot what a hard son of a bitch you can be." Unfazed by directness, McGrady leaned forward in his chair and said, "Look, I really think Kota is onto something. If he's right, markets are about to sink like the fuckin' *Titanic*. But I can't bet the farm and lever up short positions based solely on a computer model. That shit is fuckin' hieroglyphics to me. I need confirmation. A second set of eyes."

"So have someone else take a look at Kota's work. What do you need me for?"

"You helped to build ICARUS. If there's really a flaw in it, you're the guy who can sniff that out. Until I have more evidence that the market is truly about to fall off a cliff, I can't place any big bets."

Rory gave no response, unsure of what to say. On the one hand, the bad blood between him and the McGrady brothers went back long before Rory decided to quit Celtic, but yesterday in San Juan, the McGradys seemed like a distant memory. Now, in the flesh, Milton got under Rory's skin more than he anticipated. On the other hand, Rory wanted to be fair. After all, no one put a gun to his head and made him board the G650. After a moment's hesitation, he decided to take a seat and hear his old boss out.

McGrady softened his pitch. "Look, Rory, I'm a hedge fund manager without much to hedge these days. But if Kota is right, there's one last great trade out there for me, and I want to go out with a bang, something really big for the history books. Make sense?"

History books—yeah right. This guy is so full of himself. Rory sat back in his chair, arms crossed, as McGrady went on.

"It's not about the money. It's about the game. I don't want to ride off into the sunset and play pickleball or some shit. Can't you understand that? Or do you not give a damn about anything anymore, hanging out on the beach, drinking piña coladas, and trading fuckin' bitcoin? Talk about a pointless waste."

"You know what's a pointless waste, Milt? This fucking conversation. You and Brendon have been telling me what to do for way too long. Those days are over."

"What does my brother have to do with this?"

"You know damn well what."

"He kept you out of prison, didn't he?"

Rory gave no response. McGrady said, "Now calm down and listen to me. You have one of the greatest financial minds I've ever known. When you're on your game, it's a thing of beauty. I'm telling you, a lot of traders have come through that door, and you're the best natural talent I've seen. Raw and undirected for sure, but it's great, fucking unbelievable."

"What's your point?" Rory asked, a bit taken aback. In over a decade working at Celtic, McGrady never once praised Rory or told him what he thought of his potential, certainly not his "great financial mind."

"My point is that maybe you could be doing more with your life than trading crypto by the beach."

Rory took a deep breath. "I appreciate that, Milt. I really do. But I don't know what I can add here."

"Listen, I had Kota put all his work together on this." McGrady pointed to a new laptop lying on the desk in front of them. "I'd like you to go through it all this week, see if you can figure out what is really going on with ICARUS and the volatility anomalies Kota found. Make sure his model is solid. I need to know if I can really back the truck up on this one. All I'm askin' for is your opinion, nothing fancy or written. Is the market really set to crash or not? Then, when you're ready, the 650 is available for you to fly back to paradise." He concluded with a wink. "That Jennifer's not too bad, huh?"

He's got a point there.

Rory turned his glance from McGrady and looked out at the gray Chicago sky already knowing he would say yes. He could not shake the feeling that he owed it to Peter. *If ICARUS blows up, Pete will be the scape-goat. They'll say it was the VSA. That he fucked up.*

Rory took the laptop from the desk and stood. "All right. I'll take a look at it. But I want another fifty thousand on top of the fifty K for coming up here."

McGrady got up from his chair and stretched his right hand across the desk. "Done."

The two men shook hands, and Rory began walking toward the office door. But before he could leave, McGrady said, "That reminds me. Kota thinks this has something to do with the code Pete was working on before he died."

"Yeah. So what?"

"So maybe there's some stuff in his notes and things you should take a look at. Go pay his sister a visit. She's living in Pete's old house up in Roscoe Village. You know Mia, right?"

Rory did know Mia. He and Peter's younger sister had some history together. They dated on and off for a few years before Rory left Celtic to work on ICARUS.

"I don't know if that's a good idea, Milt."

"Just go see her. Okay?"

Rory wasn't sure how happy Mia would be to see him. He had been the last person to see Peter alive, and he skipped town to Puerto Rico without a word to her, didn't even attend the funeral. Rory never felt right about that. After further thought, he decided that an apology was owed.

"All right. I'll go."

Rory said his goodbyes to Kota and Sally before leaving Celtic Capital. Laptop in hand, he walked out into the cold Chicago morning and crossed Wacker. On the other side of the street from 333 was a park and green space called the Riverwalk. Rory punched up an Uber to take him to Mia's, then lit a cigarette. A honk from a nearby barge cut through the city sounds as a few gulls squawked overhead. Rory stared out at the slowly moving water of the Chicago River as it drifted opposite its original course. Somewhere in the back of his mind, he remembered learning that fact as a boy—that in the late 1800s, the river had been engineered to flow out of Lake Michigan rather than into the lake as nature intended. *Am I heading in the wrong direction too?* he wondered.

A moment later, a brown Toyota Camry pulled up along Wacker. Rory put out his smoke and threw the butt in a nearby trash can.

A hundred yards away, two Russians sat in a late-model Mercedes, both dressed in black. Just as Rory hopped into the Camry, the driver of the Benz threw his own cigarette butt out the window, placed his right foot on the brake, and hit the ignition button.

CHAPTER 11

Chicago, Illinois

TUESDAY, NOVEMBER 2, 2027

SANDWICHED BETWEEN TWO THREE-FLAT APARTMENT buildings, Mia's home seemed plucked from a simpler time. It had been her brother Peter's until his untimely death last year and was a midcentury, two-story brick structure with a wooden porch and two rocking chairs on either side of the front door. As Rory made his way up the front steps, memories flooded back of late nights, laughing with Peter, a beer in hand, sitting in one of the old chairs that now buffeted back and forth empty but for the wind.

Rory knocked on the door and waited, wiping away an unexpected tear that he told himself was from the cold wind blowing in gusts against his face. After a brief moment, he heard the scamper of dogs barking as they rushed to the door. The door opened. Mia stood with her best friends, Romeo and Juliet, two large akitas who sat obediently by her side.

Mia was in her late thirties with deep brown eyes, reddish-brown chestnut hair, and an olive Mediterranean complexion. She had on gray sweatpants and a matching sweatshirt embroidered with her nursing school alma mater, Loyola University Ramblers, in gold and maroon. She stood briefly in the doorway and looked into Rory's eyes. As another gust of wind came through, she stepped onto the porch. For a moment, Rory thought Mia was going to march forward and slap him across the face. After all, he deserved it. Instead, she hesitated, then, with a sincere yet detached voice, said simply, "I missed you."

"I missed you too," Rory replied as a train rumbled past on the nearby L tracks. His eyes met hers, and she stepped forward. They embraced one another for what must have been a solid half minute. Before letting go, Rory whispered, "I'm sorry," as tears welled up in his eyes. This time he was certain the wind was not to blame. As the rumble of the passing train died down, they both released their grip and quickly stepped back from one another.

"Well, come in. It's cold out here, and you're not wearing a jacket."

Rory stepped into the home, and after an awkward few minutes catching up, the two found themselves with coffee sitting at the kitchen table. Romeo and Juliet lay lazily on the old hardwood floor at their feet while Oscar, Mia's orange and overweight tabby cat, slept on one of the two empty chairs.

An emergency room nurse, Mia spent her days, or sometimes her nights, helping treat the most critical of conditions: a stopped heart, a gunshot wound to the chest, a child clinging to life after an auto accident. Rory had always been fascinated by her stories of the ER and was amazed at how this pretty, petite young woman managed drama and trauma with such a sense of peace. It was quite the contrast to the yelling and scream-ing neurotics who seemed to dominate the Chicago trading community.

Sitting across from her now, Rory felt worse than ever for leaving town so suddenly the day after Peter died. "I really am so sorry for every-thing, for running away and not being a part of Pete's funeral."

Mia took a sip from her coffee. "You don't owe me an apology, Rory. But it was hard after Pete died. I could have used a shoulder to cry on."

"I know, and I wanted to be here, but it just brought up such bad memories. My parents weren't much older than Pete when they were killed. I couldn't go through that again. Maybe I'm just a coward."

Rory knew it was a pitiful excuse even if it was true. His parents, both professors, had passed away in a tragic car accident twenty-five years ago. His father had been a thinker. He taught medieval philosophy and was apt to quote Aquinas or Augustine at the dinner table, the latter precipitating his choice for Rory's middle name. His mother was a genius with numbers, much like Peter. She held a PhD in applied mathematics, specializing in applying chaos theory to climate systems.

"You're not a coward, Rory." Mia stood from the table and asked, "Hungry? I can fix you something to eat."

"Starving, actually."

"Let me guess, you skipped breakfast."

"Guilty as charged."

Mia made some sandwiches, and the two talked about life, San Juan, and McGrady before the discussion turned to ICARUS. Rory explained that Kota had found some anomalies in market patterns and thought it might have something to do with the code Peter was working on before his death. Then he got down to the purpose of his visit.

"Is there anything of Pete's still here?" he asked. "Notebooks, an old laptop, anything?"

Mia rose from her seat at the kitchen table. "Follow me."

The two walked down to the basement, Romeo and Juliet following close behind as Oscar remained fast asleep in the kitchen. Peter had the basement fixed up when he bought the house shortly after starting work at Celtic Capital over a decade ago. It was his Batcave for algorithmic programming: half a dozen monitors, dedicated Bloomberg Terminal, a large flat-screen TV on the wall for market coverage, and his library, filled with everything from Nelson DeMille to the complete works of Tennessee Williams, his favorite playwright. As an undergrad, Peter seriously considered moving to Hollywood and becoming an actor but decided honing his mathematical and programming talents was the safer bet. Hanging on the wall were also his diplomas from MIT and UChicago as well as a large wooden clock Peter had handcrafted in high school shop class. In the shape of an oversize football helmet, it was navy, orange, and white with a big C painted behind the hands. Across the top, it read BEAR DOWN, and below the face, CHICAGO BEARS, both etched in with a wood-burning pen. Rory glanced at the second hand slowly ticking its way around the helmet and paused for some unknown reason, recalling how proud Peter had always been of that clock.

Mia walked up to Peter's desk. It sat buffeted against the wall in front of the clock with a large, comfortable gaming chair tucked under. "Take a look," she said.

Along with Peter's keyboard, mouse, monitors, and lamp, the desk was covered with an array of papers and notebooks. Rory quickly shuffled through the chaos but saw nothing referring to the VSA or Vega Block.

"Anything else?" Rory asked, disappointment apparent in his voice.

"Not really. Two guys sent by the BIS went through the office the night Pete passed. They took everything related to ICARUS. Said it was just a security precaution. They asked me if I knew of anything else work related, and I said no. Then a few months ago, I was doing some spring cleaning and found a box in his bedroom closet with some old notebooks and journals. That's what all this is."

Rory spent a few more minutes flipping through the notebooks on the desk. *Shit, this is all old stuff.* Then he gazed once more around the room. His eyes again became unconsciously fixated on the Chicago Bears clock hanging in front of him.

Was that what he was talking about?

Rory looked at Mia. "I never told anyone this, but right before Pete passed he mumbled some stuff, most of it incoherently. He mentioned the Chicago Bears, and he asked the strangest thing."

Mia took a step back from Rory. She had never heard exactly what had happened that night. She looked down at the floor for a moment, then said, "Go on."

"I honestly had no idea what he was talking about until just a second ago. Then I saw this clock and those old Tennessee Williams play scripts. Pete asked me if I remembered the longest distance between two places."

"I don't understand."

"I know. I didn't get it at first either, but think about it, Mia, 'the longest distance between two places.'"

Mia paused, a smile eventually coming to her face. She recalled Peter and his love for Tennessee Williams, especially *The Glass Menagerie*.

She quoted from the play. It was one of Peter's favorite lines. "'I didn't go to the moon, I went much further—for time is the longest distance between two places.'"

The two looked up at the clock. Rory leaned over the desk to pull it down. Once he had it in hand, Mia's mouth dropped open, and both her and Rory's eyes spread wide.

A safe with an electronic keypad had been built into the wall.

CHAPTER 12

Washington, DC

THE OFFICE OF SENATOR MATTHEW Whitlock was a tribute to his almost three decades in public service. It was also enough to make a cynical man gag.

After leaving his prestigious law practice in the '90s, Whitlock's first elected office was representative for the Ninth Congressional District encompassing suburban and rural areas around Charlotte. There were pictures of him with every president, Democrat or Republican, since the first George Bush. He had fashioned himself as a moderate, staying away from hot-button issues such as gun rights and abortion. Whitlock prided himself on his ability to work across the aisle. It played well in a purple state like North Carolina. Along with pictures of the senator shaking hands with various world leaders, his walls highlighted volunteer work with Habitat for Humanity and the many veterans' causes he affiliated himself with to make up for his own lack of service, as well as photos of his family, which included a lovely wife, twin boys, a girl, and their cocker spaniel, Toodles.

Whitlock sat behind his desk listening to some voice mails and sipping on a fresh whiskey. After the short flight from his Bear's Den landing strip to DC, he attended a last-minute security briefing and was now back in his office. Upon completion of the final voice mail, he slammed his glass on the desk, rammed the old-school landline phone back in its receiver, and roared, "Vanessa, get in here!"

His chief of staff walked into the oak-paneled office wearing more formal attire than her morning outfit. Gone were the tight jeans and low-cut blouse, replaced with a close-fitting beige pantsuit, Carolina blue silk top, and sparkling sapphire earrings set in eighteen-karat gold. Whitlock eyed the beautiful woman, over twenty years his junior, and asked her to grab a water for him from the mini fridge sitting in the corner of his office. He wasn't particularly thirsty and still had most of his whiskey left, but Whitlock enjoyed watching Vanessa bend down to grab the cold beverage. After placing the water on the senator's desk, she took a seat on its corner, crossing her legs and letting them dangle over the side.

"What's up, boss?"

"Madoch and Fischer have cold feet about the Phoenix Act. We need to figure out how to butter their biscuits." Whitlock reached for his whiskey, leaned back in his chair, and placed his boots on the opposite corner of his desk. He too had changed and now wore a white shirt, navy blazer, yellow tie, and black dress slacks; however, the boots remained.

Vanessa stood and grabbed a notebook from a locked filing cabinet. Taking a seat in a chair opposite the senator, she flipped through the pages for a moment, then stated confidently, "Madoch shouldn't be an issue. We have some iPhone footage of his son snorting lines between bong hits at a frat party."

"The All-American lacrosse star, Jeffrey? Will that be enough?"

"His name is Justin, but yes, it should be enough. Don't forget, Madoch's people are still busy doing damage control after rumors of the good senator's affair leaked this summer. He has no tolerance for scandal right now." Vanessa flipped through the notebook one more time, then concluded, "Fischer, unfortunately, is a bit trickier. Might have to use a carrot with her. She's squeaky clean so far as Darr knows. He's been unable to dig up any dirt, and his varsity squad isn't going to work with her."

Chris Darr was a former DC metro cop who now spent most of his time in strip clubs and bars, keeping an eye on politicians, lobbyists, judges, and anyone with a modicum of power in the capital. His varsity squad, adept at putting powerful men in compromising situations, consisted of a half dozen of DC's most seductive and dangerous women of the night. Darr had been on the senator's payroll for years and also served at times to help extricate Whitlock from certain "mishaps." These usually involved old whiskey and young women.

"Don't worry about Fischer," Whitlock said. "I know how to handle her. Just get her in here. Today! I'm heading out to meet with Cooper. I'll be back by five and expect to see Senator Kristin Fischer here with bells on when I return."

Whitlock had already drummed up enough support for the Phoenix Act that it could easily pass both chambers. Even the president had already expressed her support. However, the passage of this act would coincide with the collapse of the world's financial markets. Indeed, it would be the fuel added to the fire of wild spending that would precipitate the downward spiral. And so, it was imperative that it go into law with strong bipartisan support lest Whitlock and his party be blamed. With the addition of Madoch and Fischer, he would feel comfortable bringing the bill to the floor for a vote.

Whitlock completed his meeting with Mitch Cooper, the CEO of a large Wall Street firm that managed most of the senator's money. He returned to his office around 4:45 and poured himself yet another tumbler of whiskey. Whitlock had already had a busy day. Along with taking delivery of ten tons of gold earlier at the Bear's Den, he had just instructed his banker to make certain offshore moves with all his accounts. Whitlock sold out of his current stock positions to fund purchases of precious-metal mining companies, gold and silver futures, as well as related ETFs. By this time next week, the dentist's son concluded he should easily be the wealthiest senator in United States history.

Whitlock had always realized that the wielding of political power could be very lucrative. He saw how the sausage was made during his time as an attorney for large financial institutions in Charlotte. There were inside trades, sweetheart deals on real estate, and, of course, straight-up payoffs. But this move was taking things to the next level.

With his forthcoming wealth, he could afford to support any candidates he liked through backroom deals and the funding of political action committees. Hell, he could run Congress, run the country, and not even need to be elected president, though that was certainly a possibility as well. It was good to be rich, and it was good to wield political power. But it was unbeatable to have both.

At precisely 5:00 p.m., Vanessa Price buzzed her boss's phone, interrupting his political fantasies.

"Fischer is here," she said into the receiver.

"Let her in." Whitlock straightened his tie after hanging up the phone.

Fischer was an up-and-comer, a young and pleasant-enough-looking first-term senator from Illinois whom Whitlock hadn't quite figured out yet. On the surface, she clung to her ideals and seemed to genuinely believe in the system. But Whitlock had his doubts. He would find out what lay under the surface soon enough.

As the office door swung open, Whitlock smiled.

Senator Kristin Fischer had just stepped into a different type of bear's den.

CHAPTER 13

Washington, DC
TUESDAY, NOVEMBER 2, 2027

"KRISTI, HOW ARE YOU? HOW'S Dan and the kids?" Whitlock stood up and walked around from his desk. Shaking Fischer's hand, he continued, "Can I get you anything? Coffee, something stronger?" He pointed to the glass of whiskey on his desk.

"I'm fine, Senator."

Fischer carried herself with a professional demeanor and wore little to no makeup. She had on a navy long-sleeved top and plaid skirt, which may have been cut an inch too short for her comfort given the circumstances, but she had a dinner party to get to with Dan and wore something less formal than her usual wardrobe for the Hill.

"Please, call me Matt. Let's take a load off, shall we?" The senator grabbed his drink from the desk and moved toward a couch in the corner of his office. Fischer took a seat in a chair adjacent to the couch, a dark oak coffee table before them.

"So, why am I here?" Fischer asked, despite knowing full well why Whitlock wanted to see her.

"Where do you stand on the Phoenix Act? A little birdie told me you were a nay."

"Matt, I understand that with ICARUS controlling the markets it seems like we can spend like drunken sailors again here in Washington, but it's just not the right thing for Illinois or for America. The nine trillion dollars will still have to be paid for one way or the other, and the modest tax increases in the bill won't make a dent to offset those expenditures."

Whitlock took a sip of his whiskey and leaned in toward Fischer, his eyes clearly drifting down toward the young senator's shapely calves. "Kristi, I understand. Hell, I know it's a lot of money, but listen. I just had lunch with the CEO of one of the largest investment houses on Wall Street. He assures me that the Treasury can issue almost unlimited debt. Shoot, we've practically got a blank check since ICARUS came online. The market and the Fed will buy up our bonds like hungry pigs eatin' slop. Sure, yields may go up a few basis points, but that's good for the savers and pension plans that need our debt. This is a big win for everyone. What can I do to get you on board?"

"And what about inflation?" Fischer countered. "Have we already forgotten about what happened after the pandemic spending spree?"

Whitlock ignored her questions. "I know it's not easy for a first-term senator to raise campaign funds and manage the demands of our office. Maybe I can help, introduce you to some friends of mine from Silicon Valley and Wall Street. And don't forget about the big banks in Charlotte. I can make sure your coffers are full for that primary you have coming up." Whitlock took a short pull from his glass, then said, "We may be from different parties, but my guys like to butter both sides of their bread."

Fischer replied curtly, "I appreciate the offer, but I'm not going to change my mind. Besides, you already have the numbers. What does it matter how I vote?"

Whitlock leaned back on the couch and went on to tell Fischer what a brilliant young star of her party she had become, that her future was bright. He didn't want to see her defeated in '28 because she'd failed to support what was sure to become one of the most popular bills in decades. He, of course, was just looking for votes to cover his ass once the bill was revealed as the disaster it was destined to become.

But unlike other senators, when the markets collapsed, Whitlock would have his golden opportunity for redemption already teed up and ready to go. He would be standing by with legislation introducing US adoption of a new central bank digital currency backed by precious metals. Whitlock planned to be the country's savior from economic Armageddon, and he didn't want any threats to his limelight from the few senators who were against Phoenix from the start. Most were fringe players who never supported any expansion of the federal government, but Fischer had a growing national persona, and she could prove a challenge in the future. Whitlock would have to go for the big guns here and try to sideline the young senator for good.

"Kristi, do you like being in the Senate?" Whitlock asked with a genuine look of concern on his face. "It's a rough business, you know, dealing with campaigns and donors. And then there's the constituents. I swear they're a bigger pain in the ass than my hemorrhoids."

Fischer sat back in her chair. "Thank you for your concern, but I'm doing just fine." She made a nervous attempt to pull her skirt forward and cover her bare knees away from Whitlock's prying eyes.

"Well, I have it on good authority that Justice Baum will be retiring from the Supreme Court before the next election. That old coot is probably going to announce any week now so long as he don't fall over dead first."

"What are you suggesting?" Fischer wondered if this arrogant man was actually offering her a seat on the Supreme Court.

"Listen, I know that the law was your first love, not politics. It was my first love too, and many a time I have sat in this very office and wondered what my life may have been like if I didn't give up my practice to run for office. I'm too old a dog to learn new tricks now, but you, you could be one of the youngest justices on the court, sit on the bench for forty years.

I can make sure to let the president know who I think deserves that seat when Baum steps down. Hell, I'm the only one who can guarantee her bipartisan support and Senate approval for her nominee. And that nominee could be you...if I can count on your support for the Phoenix Act."

Fischer did not reply.

Whitlock leaned forward and locked eyes with her. "You know, Kristi," he said, the smile stricken from his face, "there's also an unhappy ending to this here story."

Fischer uncrossed and then recrossed her legs in the other direction, again adjusting her skirt. Noticing Whitlock's eyes shift downward once more, she felt uncomfortable both with his glances and this conversation. "What are you saying, Senator?"

"What I'm saying is if this bitch don't hunt, there's just not much use for her anymore."

Fischer moved to stand up, but before she could, Whitlock brought his hand quickly down upon her crossed and bare right knee. It was not a gentle touch. Fischer, paralyzed by Whitlock's audacity, stayed seated as he continued, "If you want to stay in the Senate, you *need* to support the act. I have a lot of powerful friends in this town, friends that can make *and break* a person."

Whitlock removed his hand from Fischer's knee, a smile returning to his lips. "I wouldn't want to see you make a mistake here and struggle with financing for your next campaign. I know that Jim Reynolds is considering challenging you in the upcoming primary. I can make sure old Jimbo throws his hat in the ring if we don't already have a junior senator from Illinois who knows how to play ball."

Fischer thought about slapping Whitlock in the face and threatening a host of ethics charges, but he was a powerful man, and it would simply be her word against his. She took a moment to process the choice in front of her. Could Whitlock really take away her backing and ensure a Jim Reynolds primary challenge? Probably. Reynolds was a god in Illinois, having made billions in the technology sector, bringing thousands of high-paying jobs to the struggling state when it needed them most. If the Phoenix Act was popular and she voted against it, she wouldn't have a chance against Reynolds, his notoriety, and his checkbook. She actually needed to think about this.

"Give me some time," Fischer said. "This is a lot to process." She stood and prepared to make her way to the door.

Whitlock sat back into the soft leather, his left arm draped open across the top of the couch. As Fischer turned to leave, he said, "Of course, Kristi, take some time, but not too long. The Phoenix Act goes to a vote this week."

CHAPTER 14

Chicago, Illinois

Tuesday, November 2, 2027

"Do you have any idea what the combination is?" Rory asked.

"Not a clue," Mia said, hands on her hips as she stood next to him.

They both stared at the safe that had been hidden behind the clock. It did not appear much different from a standard hotel safe. Rectangular in shape, about the size of a small shoebox, it opened with a ten-digit electronic key panel.

Rory thought for a moment. "Didn't Pete like to use street numbers from his old addresses as part of his passwords. I think at one point his iPhone unlock was 3612, his apartment number at UChicago."

Mia laughed. "That's right. It was." She leaned forward and hit in 3-6-1-2, then the Enter button below the keypad. Nothing. "What about 2217?" Mia suggested the street number for this home.

Rory gave it a try, but no luck. He said, "Hell, we don't even know how many digits we need for this safe. Maybe we should just call a locksmith."

Still preoccupied with street numbers, Mia said, "What about 1050? That was our address as kids on Euclid Avenue in Oak Park."

Rory reached his arm toward the keypad and punched in 1-0-5-0, then Enter. After a brief beep, the small safe cracked open. Rory couldn't help but shake his head. *Pete, programming genius, had his safe cracked in three attempts...*

...Or did he want us to find this?

Inside the safe were three items: an old Catholic rosary, a stack of hundred-dollar bills with a wrapper that read "$10,000," and a thumb drive. Rory handed the cash and rosary to Mia and said, "Christmas comes early this year."

"This was Gram's," Mia said, ignoring the money and holding the crystal and sterling silver rosary up to the light, the crucifix on the end dangling from her hand.

Rory excused himself and ran upstairs to grab the laptop he had received from McGrady earlier that day at Celtic Capital. Once back, he sat at Pete's desk and plugged the drive into the computer, then opened its directory. There was only one file folder on it. It was simply titled "Vega."

Rory took a deep breath and clicked on the folder. A pop-up appeared asking for another password. The folder was encrypted.

"Damn," Rory said after a few failed attempts trying to access the folder. "I don't think street numbers are going to work for this one. Seems like some pretty heavy-duty encryption going on here."

"Don't worry about it." Mia placed her hand on Rory's shoulder. "You'll figure it out. You always do. Besides, don't you know some hacker or programmer from your trading days who could crack it?"

"Milt might have someone at Celtic who could help. Maybe Kota could do it; just might take a little time."

Rory and Mia headed back up the stairs to the kitchen.

"Is there anything I can get you?" she asked.

"No, I'm good. I'm going to head back to the hotel and see if I can determine what type of encryption we're dealing with. Also, I need to take a closer look at Kota's work. I promised Milt. That's what's on this laptop here."

"So, you'll be in town for a while?" Mia asked hopefully.

"At least for the week."

"Well hold on, then." Mia opened a nearby closet door and pulled out a winter coat. "Yes, that should look nice," she commented as she held out the thick brown leather jacket. "At least take this jacket with you. You'll freeze to death in this city with no coat."

Rory recognized the jacket as Peter's old favorite coat, the leather soft and well worn. Grabbing the coat from Mia, he placed it on. "Thank you."

"Now, don't be running off without saying goodbye this time. And here, take this as well." Mia reached to the bottom of the closet and pulled out an old work bag of Peter's that read CELTIC CAPITAL.

Rory placed the laptop and the thumb drive in the messenger bag and slung its strap over his right shoulder. The two made their way to the door and hugged goodbye.

"Take care of yourself, Rory."

"I will. You know me."

Mia smiled. "I do know you. That's what I'm afraid of, Mr. O'Connor."

Rory exited the home. As he stepped off the porch, a narrow swath of sun managed to poke through the now intermittent patchwork of swiftly passing gray clouds. Rory cut down a back alley between Henderson and Roscoe, walking past scattered garbage cans, backyard garages, and small wooden decks jutting out from neighboring apartments and homes. Passing the light at Damen Avenue, he caught the Village Tap out of the corner of his eye.

What the hell. I could use a beer after a day like today.

Rory sent a quick text to Kota. He informed him of the thumb drive, including its encryption issues, then crossed the street.

Thousands of miles away, a cloned version of Rory's cell phone also received the sent message.

Anton Golev smiled.

CHAPTER 15

Chicago, Illinois

RORY BELLIED UP TO THE bar and ordered a house IPA. Often patronized by cops from the Nineteenth Precinct, the Village Tap offered standard pub fare with a local atmosphere. After taking a long swig of his beer, Rory removed Peter's leather coat and hung it on a hook below the bar. He placed the Celtic Capital bag on the floor, leaning it up against his stool.

Rory took a quick glance around the Tap. The five o'clock hour was fast approaching, and tables were starting to fill up. Two older men sat at the end of the bar a few stools distant. He could hear their thick Chicago accents discussing the Bears' chances at a playoff run. The front door then slammed shut, a common mistake of the uninitiated. Two men in their late thirties walked in, oblivious to the draft that swept into the warm bar on chilly days. In one corner, a handful of women chattered over a bottle of rosé. *Place is gentrifying*, Rory thought, then paid no more attention to his fellow patrons. Instead, his mind drifted.

Back in the city he had called home for most of his life, Rory almost felt as if his year in San Juan had been a dream, a place he had escaped to after Peter was killed. *Maybe I should move back*, he wondered, *at least for the summer?* He weighed Cubs games, street fairs, and the annual Taste of Chicago festival on the one hand and worried who he would have to share it with on the other.

Rory had no family left to speak of. Sure, there was a cousin or two out there somewhere. *Was it Tucson and San Diego where Rick and Adam lived now?* But he was an only child and spoiled rotten by his professor parents until an auto accident shattered his world like a vase dropped from 333 West Wacker. Sitting back on his stool, Rory ordered another round as a familiar track from Oasis came through the bar's sound system. He quickly forgot about Kota's model and the pending financial doom it predicted as the strong IPAs began to take effect. He was well into a third pint when a voice from the past rang out.

"Rory, holy fuck, is that you?"

Rory turned to face the man. He was leaning against the bar, standing between two open stools.

Jesus Christ, not both McGradys in one day.

"It is you. How the hell you been?" former sergeant, now captain Brendon McGrady said as he stepped around the stool that separated the two men and moved toward Rory. Tall, with a large chest, goatee, and wearing a gray blazer with a black polo and jeans, Brendon reached out his hand and rubbed Rory's hair as was his habit back when Rory was just a teenager.

Rory's relationship with the McGradys originally began with Brendon, not Milton. They had met at a bar called the Pumping Company. Located in an old Chicago firehouse, it was well known for its popular penny pitcher night, as well as for letting anyone in so long as they could see over the bar. Rory started hanging out there when he was a senior in high school, shortly after his parents died. A number of cops, including Brendon McGrady, also frequented the establishment and received free food, drinks, and a monthly envelope with cash in return for looking the other way regarding underage drinking.

Rory had turned eighteen just a month before his parents' untimely deaths, and despite still being in high school, legally he was an adult. As an only child, Rory inherited the house and his parents' savings. An uncle in Arizona offered him the opportunity to move in with them, but Rory saw no reason to leave Chicago just a few months before graduation. Given the tragedy, teachers gave him a pass in those final few months, and Rory found himself at the Pumping Company more nights than not. At first Brendon had been a friend, almost an older brother to Rory, but eventually their relationship led Rory into dark places that blurred the line between legal and illegal, right and wrong, all under the protection of the five-pointed star, the CPD shield.

Rory brushed his hand through his hair, a look of annoyance on his face, then replied, "I'm good. How are things?"

"Livin' the dream, my friend. Aren't you livin' in the Dominican Republic or some shit?" Brendon asked.

"Puerto Rico."

"Same thing, right, Jerry?" Brendon turned to the man standing next to him, and they both laughed. Just by his look, it was clear to Rory that Jerry was also a member of Chicago's finest, though he, too, dressed in plain clothes. Brendon directed his attention toward the bartender. "Hey, Kevin, we're fuckin' thirsty over here."

The bartender brought over a couple of beers for Brendon and Jerry. Brendon pointed toward Rory and added, "And another one of whatever he's drinking for my friend here."

"Thanks," Rory said, never one to turn down a free beer, even if it was from Brendon McGrady.

It wasn't so much that Brendon was a bad man. He was a man of his times and of his place, and Chicago was just one of those American cities where the police were expected to talk tough, act rough, and make a few dollars on the side. But as an impressionable kid who just lost his parents, Rory had taken the street-hardened attitude of the cops he hung out with and made it his own without really understanding the consequences. He got into mixed martial arts and began using his newly acquired skills on unsuspecting visitors to the Pumping Company. He likely would have just outgrown the phase and moved on to college, no harm done.

But one night, the summer after graduation and after a few too many penny pitchers, Rory nearly beat a guy to death for nothing more than a couple of belittling remarks about Rory's obvious youth. At the end of the night, Rory was in cuffs and the other guy was in a coma. It was touch and go for a while. Rory feared the worst: the man would die, and he would be brought up on a manslaughter charge or even second-degree murder. Fortunately, the man pulled through, but just barely. As it was, he still suffered a punctured lung, broken hip, concussion, and two cracked ribs. Rory later heard the man spent months in rehab for the hip and never walked the same way again.

Instead of being booked for aggravated battery or some other felony, Rory was told by Brendon and his buddies on the force to take a summer vacation. They'd handle it. Rory spent a few months with his uncle in Arizona, and when he came back in the fall to start college, no charges had been filed, not even a misdemeanor.

But Brendon wanted something in return: utter loyalty. For the next three years, until both the civil and criminal statute of limitations ran out, Rory was constantly at Brendon's beck and call, doing everything he asked, from participating in shakedowns to making collections on payoffs to bringing takeout to his tactical unit during stakeouts. At first, Rory felt lucky to get off with no charges, but over time resentment built. It wasn't that he hated Brendon, he just despised the cocky attitude and air of entitlement. Even after all these years, the time spent being Brendon's bitch still left a bad taste in Rory's mouth. The Chicago cop also served as a reminder—a reminder of a troubled and dark time, a time just after great loss, a time not unlike the past year.

Maybe I should just forget it, Rory thought as he finished off his IPA. *But if this guy rubs my hair one more time, I swear I'm gonna hit him.*

"Look, Brendon, thanks for the beer, but I gotta go," Rory said as he threw a couple twenties on the bar.

"No problem. Take care, man." Brendon turned his attention back to his conversation with Jerry.

As Rory stood from his stool and headed for the exit, the two men who had absentmindedly let the door slam shut also rose from their seats, their eyes glued on the Celtic Capital bag slung over Rory's shoulder.

CHAPTER 16

Chicago, Illinois
TUESDAY, NOVEMBER 2, 2027

CIGARETTE LIT, RORY GRABBED HIS cell, opened the Uber app, and summoned a car. With a slight sway from the four IPAs, he made his way around the corner and into a dimly lit alley. Rory needed to piss. Unzipping his fly, he looked up and managed to see a star or two through the light-polluted haze.

Or are those planes? Rory wondered as two men rounded the corner. *Perfect timing*, he thought with no alarm, aware that locals often used the passageway as a shortcut to Belmont Avenue. He continued his business but angled away from the approaching men, too buzzed to care if a couple of guys saw him pissing.

But they weren't using the alley as a shortcut. A tinge of anxiety ran up Rory's spine as he sensed the men standing behind him.

"Turn around, slowly," one of them commanded in what sounded like an Eastern European accent.

Russian, maybe Polish. Rory hurriedly cut off the stream of processed ale and zipped up his fly. He turned around slowly, a cigarette dangling from his mouth. The two men stood about two paces away; both wore dark leather coats with jeans. One of them was taller and slimmer than the other. The shorter man was stocky and powerfully built with a thick neck. In the dim light, Rory was barely able to make out a long scar that ran down his left cheek. The taller man held a suppressed .40-caliber SIG Sauer semiautomatic pistol in his right hand. It was aimed squarely at Rory's chest.

Rory opened his lips and let the smoking butt fall to the pavement. "You can have my money," he said. "I don't want any trouble."

The gunman did not reply. He held his position about two yards from Rory, far enough that no quick move on Rory's part could disarm him. The stocky man, however, stepped closer and said, "Hand over the bag."

Rory paused for just a brief second to weigh his options. The calculus was simple. *Two of them and one of me. I'm buzzed. They're armed. Not worth it.* He reached slowly for the messenger bag slung over his shoulder. As his hand grasped the strap, another figure rounded the corner of the alley.

Is that Brendon?

In an instant, Rory knew what had happened. He had left Peter's coat, the one Mia had loaned him, on the hook under the bar. Brendon McGrady held the worn leather jacket in his right hand. The Chicago police captain quickly processed the scene in front of him and dropped the coat to the ground. He reached for his 9mm HK P30 and trained the pistol on the taller armed man. "Drop it!"

Startled, the man quickly turned toward Brendon, his gun still raised in a firing position. Brendon did not hesitate. He fired two rounds into the man's chest. The gunman got off one shot as well, but his pistol discharged a fraction of a second after Brendon's first round struck him. The errant shot missed high and to the left. The second round from Brendon dropped him to the ground.

Rory did not hesitate either. As the shots rang out, the stocky one went to pull his gun, but Rory charged into him and tackled him to the ground. He shot an elbow to the man's chin, reflexes kicking in that hadn't been used in over twenty years since his days at the Pumping Company. He managed to grab the man's pistol, which had fallen to the ground during the initial takedown. Brendon quickly approached, his 9mm trained on the shorter man, who still lay on the pavement. Rory stood, gun in hand, and also put the stunned assailant in his sights.

Brendon glanced back at the taller man lying in a growing pool of blood, which appeared more black than red in the poorly lit alley. There was no movement. Brendon focused his eyes on the man's chest for a few seconds, looking for signs of breath. As he did, the shorter man made his move. He quickly reached to pull a snub-nose revolver from an ankle holster. Rory, his pistol still trained on the man's chest, saw his arm reach. As the jean leg moved up, Rory saw the hidden .38. Without thought or emotion, inhibitions dulled by alcohol, Rory squeezed the trigger twice, placing two rounds center mass. More blood flowed onto the alley, pooling in the cracks and crevasses of the broken-down asphalt.

Jerry, the other cop with Brendon, had since exited the bar after hearing the initial reports from Brendon's 9mm. Gun also drawn, he surveyed Rory, Brendon, and the two dead bodies lying in the alley. "What the fuck happened?" he exclaimed.

"I don't know," Brendon replied. "Ask Rory. I come out here to bring him his jacket. When I look down the alley, I see these two assholes have him dead to rights. So, I pull my piece and one of the motherfuckers makes a move on me, got a round off too, but I tapped him twice first. Looks like the other guy was going for an ankle holster when Rory capped him."

"Holy shit!" Jerry said.

"Rory, what the fuck is going on?" Brendon asked as Jerry moved toward the bodies and checked for vitals.

Rory remained silent, still trying to process everything that had occurred in what felt like a significant period of time but was in actuality about thirty seconds.

Jerry broke the silence and informed Rory and Brendon, "These guys are gone." Then he pulled out his phone to call it in.

Rory coughed, clearing his throat, and began, "I'm not sure, Brendon. Honestly. I walked around the alley to take a piss. That's it."

Brendon asked, "You know these guys?" as he pulled a small flashlight from his jacket and shined it on the corpses.

Rory looked closely at the men's features. He now vaguely remembered them entering the bar, but otherwise he couldn't place them. He stared at their lifeless faces for a few seconds longer, then it hit him.

I'll be a son of a bitch. Those motherfuckers.

Rory looked up at Brendon. "I don't know them, but I think I recognize them. I could be wrong about this, but I swear I saw these two guys last night." Rory had noticed them when he had his nightcap at the Peninsula Hotel's Z Bar. It was subtle, but he felt something was off with the two men from their occasional glances, visible to Rory in the bar mirror's reflection above the top-shelf liquors. *Maybe it's the scar*, Rory thought as he looked at the shorter man, dead by his feet.

"Oh really," Brendon said. "Sounds like there's more going on here than you've told us so far. After the cavalry comes, we'll take a trip to the station, get some coffee, and talk about all this. Okay?"

"Yeah, sure, whatever you say," replied a still shaken Rory, the gravity of what just occurred finally starting to sink in, including the fact that he now owed his life to Brendon.

Well, here we go again.

Rory dug into his pocket and pulled out his cigarettes. As the nicotine entered his bloodstream, his nerves began to calm ever so slightly. Suddenly, a black Buick sedan pulled up next to the alley. Rory dropped his cigarette to the ground, which extinguished immediately in a pool of blood. He raised his pistol toward the sedan, as did Brendon and Jerry. As if in slow motion, the driver's side window crept lower. The startled driver raised his hands, a panicked look on his face. With a slight quiver in his voice, he asked, "Did anyone order an Uber?"

CHAPTER 17

Chicago, Illinois

TUESDAY, NOVEMBER 2, 2027

OVER TWO LARGE CUPS OF coffee, Rory told Captain Brendon McGrady and Detective Jerry Wozniak of the Chicago Police Department everything he'd been up to since arriving in Chicago, including how this all seemed to coincide with apparent aberrations in market behavior and ICARUS. The last item seemed to go over the cops' heads, but they had to admit something didn't smell right. Still, could criminals be staking out luxury hotels and then following wealthy patrons around, waiting for a moment of vulnerability to swoop in for a robbery? Sure, it was possible.

Nothing was found on either of the two assailants' persons other than cash, pistols, extra magazines, and cigarettes. The serial numbers on the pistols all traced back to private sales made years ago. They likely entered into the black market shortly after that and changed hands an unknown number of times since then. Brendon had a weapons expert check out the suppressor. It was not of commercial origin. It was, however, made by a skilled professional and completely untraceable. Prints were being run through the FBI database, but the cops were not hopeful. No matches were found during the two hours Rory spent at the station, and it was doubtful if time would yield anything useful. The case was only a couple hours old, but it was already cold.

Rory had found it curious that his assailants seemed more concerned with the Celtic Capital bag than with his money or cell. After giving his statement, he made a quick call to Kota, filled him in on what happened, and warned him to be careful. If this had anything to do with the thumb drive and ICARUS, Rory reasoned, Kota could be in danger as well. Then Brendon offered to have a uniform cop take Rory to his hotel. Rory agreed but asked to first make a quick stop at the home of Mia Costello. He was concerned for her safety as well.

Rory rang Mia's bell twice. No answer, just the barking of Romeo and Juliet. He rang it a third time before the door opened.

"Rory? What's wrong?" Mia asked, peering past him for a moment and eyeing the marked squad car parked in front of her house.

"Can I come in?"

As Mia showed Rory into her home, he said, "I don't want to worry you about what could be nothing, but I think you, well we, could be in some danger." He filled Mia in on what had taken place. As he recounted the astonishing events, Mia brewed some coffee and began to fix a late-night breakfast of eggs, toast, and a few slices of microwave bacon.

"I can't believe this," Mia said, standing in front of the stove, a brightly colored hand-crocheted blanket over her shoulders. Romeo and Juliet sat on the kitchen floor next to where she stood, taking in the smells of the kitchen. Oscar, the orange tabby, was still peacefully asleep on an empty chair. "Rory," she asked, the concern evident in her voice, "what's this all about?"

"I'm not sure." Rory took a sip of his coffee as Mia popped some bread into the toaster. "But I think it may have something to do with this." He reached into the Celtic bag and pulled out Peter's thumb drive. "Kota's work forecasts a blowup in the markets. I'm talking about a market collapse the likes of which no one has seen in almost a hundred years."

"And you think Pete's work, the Vega Block or whatever, has something to do with this?"

"I'm not certain, but it could be the key to what's going on. Everything in Kota's models has to do with the volatility algorithm Peter completed just before…well, you know."

"Before he got shot to death. You can say it." Mia flipped the frying eggs.

Rory went on, "If whoever sent those men for me is interested in ICARUS, they could also be interested in this house. Might not be a bad idea to stay with your parents for a couple days."

"I've got the best security in the world right here." Mia pointed with the spatula at Romeo and Juliet still sitting patiently on the kitchen floor.

"All the same, be careful, at least until I fly back to San Juan, probably tomorrow or Thursday at the latest."

"What about the drive? Can you get it decrypted so quickly?"

"I'm going to drop it off at Celtic for Milt and his team to figure out. The encryption may take some time."

The bread popped from the toaster, and Mia placed it on a plate with the eggs and bacon. With an abruptness that startled Rory, she dropped, almost flung, the plate of food in front of him.

What the hell is she pissed about? I'm the one who almost got shot.

"Did I do something wrong?" he asked.

"So, that's it?" Mia took a seat across the table from him. "It figures, same old Rory."

"What does that mean?"

"Oh, I don't know. Maybe that when the going gets tough, Rory takes off," Mia replied cuttingly. "Let's see. You drop out of UChicago, quit ICARUS, disappear from this city and everyone who cares about you, and now—after apparently placing me in some kind of danger—all you can think about is heading back to Puerto Rico to do whatever the hell it is you do…I don't know, drink margaritas and trade cryptocurrency all day." Mia sat back in her chair, folding her arms across her chest. "I just don't understand you, Rory O'Connor. Don't you want to know what's on that drive? Don't you care about anything anymore…about anyone?"

This just isn't my night. Rory stood from his chair and addressed Mia. "Look, maybe that's fair, but—"

"But what? Go on. What's the excuse this time?"

He thought of rebutting Mia's little rant, then stopped, too exhausted to argue.

"I don't have any excuse," Rory admitted. He reached to put on Peter's old coat, the coat that saved his life, which now hung on the back of his chair.

Mia glanced at the coat and then at Rory. "What about him?" she said. "What about Pete? Whatever is on that drive must have been pretty important to him. For all we know, it wasn't some random shooting on the South Side that he got caught up in. This could all be connected. And like it or not, you're connected to it too. You're connected to it through Pete, through Kota, through ICARUS. You're connected to it through me."

"I told Milt I'd take a closer look at Kota's work. And that's what I'm going to do tomorrow. Then I'm heading back to San Juan. I don't know what else you want from me."

Rory donned Peter's coat, his meal sitting untouched on the kitchen table. Mia said, "You can do whatever you want, but I want to know what's on that drive. Give it to me."

"Why?"

She held out her hand. "So I can take it to Milton myself and find out what's on it. So I can see what my brother cared enough about to encrypt and hide in a safe. That's why."

Rory handed her the drive. "Is it okay if I borrow this jacket until I head home? I'll leave it at Celtic when I deliver my report to Milt. You can pick it up when you drop off the drive."

Mia shook her head and rubbed her temples with her thumb and forefinger, then said, "You can have the damn jacket."

Rory walked toward the front door and stopped for a moment before grabbing the handle to open it. He turned around and saw Mia standing about fifteen feet away in the arched opening that separated the kitchen from the living room. "Thanks for making breakfast," he said, unable to allow his eyes to meet hers. Rory opened the front door and walked down the old porch stairs toward the waiting squad car. He got in the back seat and made eye contact with the uniform cop via the rearview mirror.

"Take me to the Peninsula Hotel," he said. "I'm fucking tired."

CHAPTER 18

Chicago, Illinois
WEDNESDAY, NOVEMBER 3, 2027

THE NEXT DAY, RORY SLEPT in, ordered room service, and spent the entire afternoon reviewing Kota's model. All that remained was a trip to Celtic Capital. Then he could get the hell out of Chicago.

Although he would not admit it to himself, Rory was still shaken up by what had transpired outside the Village Tap. He had killed a man. And while the possibility of a total market collapse would normally be enough to get his Spidey-sense tingling, after last night, Rory felt numb to the world. There was no remorse, no second-guessing, just a perception of being on the outside looking in. At what, he really wasn't sure. Rory had wrapped himself in a cocoon of Medalla and soft tropical breezes. This trip to Chicago had jolted him back into a reality he had tried to forget.

Well, I'll be home soon enough, Rory thought as early evening faded into twilight. He packed the laptop in the Celtic bag, put on Peter's old leather coat, and made his way to 333.

"Rory, how the hell are you? Heard you had a close call last night," McGrady said as he opened the frosted-glass door to the Celtic Capital suite of offices. He had a cell phone to his ear and held up his hand to inform Rory he needed a moment.

They walked into his office as McGrady continued to speak into the phone. "Yes, Senator, I understand that ICARUS has changed the game as far as the amount of debt most economists now believe the Treasury can safely issue, but I still don't see the need to spend our grandchildren's birthright on a bunch of pork." He paused a moment and then concluded, "All right, then. Just remember, I warned you." He ended the call and put the phone back in his pocket.

"Drink?" McGrady asked as he walked to a small bar positioned under his Joe Jackson game jersey and poured himself a scotch.

"I'll have whatever you're having." Rory sat down in one of the armchairs that sat next to an oval coffee table and couch. The living room–like setup occupied one corner of the office, flanked by a Michael Jordan–signed basketball and a Walter Payton–autographed football. McGrady fixed the drinks and then took a seat on the couch.

"Trouble with a senator?" Rory asked.

"What? Oh, that. That was Kristin Fischer, the junior senator from our lovely state. She called to inform me, as one of her largest donors, that she's considering voting for the Phoenix Act." A look of disgust manifested across McGrady's face. "Fuckin' politicians will keep spending so long as the Fed keeps printing."

Rory was familiar with the act, which had been bandied about in the press for months. "I thought Fischer was one of the few politicians arguing against the bill."

"Yes, she is, or was at least. But the woman has it in her head that if she doesn't vote for Phoenix, it will leave her vulnerable. She's up for reelection next year. I guess she figured that by giving me a heads-up, I'd feel part of her 'inner circle' and keep the gravy train flowing."

"Well, she's probably right, isn't she?" Rory asked as McGrady sipped his scotch.

"Sure, but I don't have to like it. It's just that having a senator or two on speed dial can come in handy." In fact, Milton McGrady had more than just a senator or two in his contact list. At one point in the not-too-distant past, when McGrady talked, presidents listened. But thanks to ICARUS, his influence, and the influence of those like him, had been greatly diminished. It was a different world now, a quantum age dominated by AI and algorithms.

"Forget all that," McGrady said. "What's the story with last night? I couldn't believe it when Brendon called and told me what happened."

Rory assured McGrady he was okay and gave him a brief recap of the night's events. Then he removed the laptop from his bag and placed it on the table in front of them.

"I reviewed Kota's work all afternoon," Rory reported.

"And?"

"And there's not much I can say. It's a flawless piece of modeling. What's causing the increase in vol is anybody's guess, but it's there and it's growing."

"So should I start buying VIX calls and S&P puts tonight?"

You can buy or sell whatever the fuck you want for all I care. Rory stared out the window behind McGrady. A waxing crescent moon hung suspended in a lonely, dark sky, nearly starless thanks to the city lights below.

"Look, Milt, do what you want. The data and the model look right to me. It predicts a massive market meltdown. If the pattern holds, things should start bubbling up as soon as tomorrow, getting more serious by Friday's trade, and culminating in a catastrophic sell-off early next week. After that time frame, its predictions get hazier and more inaccurate, just like a weather report. As we both know, whether you're modeling the markets or the weather, it's always a game of probabilities." Rory paused and took a sip of his scotch. "As for me, I just wanted to stop by, give you my report, and return the computer. I'm leaving for San Juan as soon as possible, maybe even tonight."

"Tonight? It's too late for that now. I can't get the 650 fueled up for a run on this short of notice."

Rory was not worried about the Gulfstream. *Just get me back to my cocoon*, he thought.

"I don't need the 650. I'll fly home commercial. I'll leave tonight if there's a late flight. Otherwise, I'm out in the morning. And don't worry about the extra fifty thousand either."

McGrady rubbed his chin as if deep in thought, then said, "Look, almost getting fuckin' shot would mess with anyone's head. You must be exhausted. Why don't you take it easy? Stick around for a couple more days, and let's see what starts to play out in the markets. In the meantime, relax. Get a massage." He gave a quick wink and added, "You know I have a new woman who works on me. She's the best. I can send her to your room tonight."

This guy just doesn't know when to quit, does he. Rory had forgotten how much McGrady was accustomed to getting whatever he wanted. *Well, not this time.*

"Look, Milt, here's the deal. I almost had my brains blown out twenty-four hours ago. I'm tired. And frankly, I'm fucking fed up with anything to do with ICARUS. I just want to go back to my condo and chill out for a while, not get a fucking massage. Understand?"

"You were just here yesterday, and already I forgot what a son of a bitch you are." McGrady stood up from the couch. "Fine, go ahead, get the fuck out of here. You can head straight to the airport for all I care. Buy a first-class ticket on the next flight to San Juan and send me the receipt. But you know something?" McGrady approached Rory, moving into his personal space as Rory also stood from his chair. McGrady then inched closer, practically stepping on Rory's toes. He almost shouted, "You're a fucking pussy!"

Rory felt a few droplets of spittle land on his face. He had had enough. Rory took a step back with his right foot, then hauled off and punched McGrady right in his gut. The wind completely knocked out of him, McGrady bent over and tried to regain his breath. He managed to stumble his way to the couch and fell onto it like a 240-pound sack of Irish potatoes.

Rory just looked at the older man, regretting it almost immediately and well aware this was more about his own frustration and anger than McGrady's overbearing personality. He began to walk toward the office door, but before Rory could turn the handle, both men heard a knock. Rory glanced back at McGrady, still gasping for air. McGrady said in a muffled voice, "Open it." Rory pulled open the door. It was Mia Costello. She tried to make sense of the confusing scene before her with McGrady hunched over on the couch seemingly in pain and short of breath.

"Milton, are you all right?" Mia asked. "Do you need medical attention?"

"No, no, I'm fine," McGrady managed to reply. "Come in, come in."

Mia walked into the office. Brilliant chestnut locks fell softly around her face, which had just the right touch of makeup accented by a soft pink lipstick. She wore black slacks and had on a full-length red jacket with large brown buttons and a woolen green sweater underneath.

The three looked at one another for a moment. Then McGrady said, "I'd get up to give you a hug, but our friend here just sucker-punched me in the gut. I need a moment."

Mia turned toward Rory, an icy look in her eyes. "What is wrong with you?"

"Nothing. I stopped by to report on Kota's model, and we got into a little disagreement. That's all."

"So now you're going back to sun and fun, huh? You don't even want to know what's on this thumb drive?" Mia pulled the encrypted drive from her coat pocket and held it in her right hand.

McGrady, sufficiently recovered, rose from the couch. "Thumb drive? Rory, you never mentioned a thumb drive."

CHAPTER 19

Chicago, Illinois
WEDNESDAY, NOVEMBER 3, 2027

DAMN, NOW HE'S REALLY GONNA turn some screws.

Rory had purposely skipped over the drive in his earlier recap of events. He knew it would just be one more reason for McGrady to try and keep him in Chicago. Mia recounted for McGrady's benefit how she and Rory had located the hidden safe in Peter's office containing the drive.

McGrady took it all in and said to Rory, "Kota is still out there somewhere. I think he's planning on sleeping here tonight, afraid to go home ever since you were attacked."

"So what?" Rory replied.

"So, stick around. He may be able to access the drive in no time."

"Look, I'm sorry about the punch, Milt. It was unnecessary, but I'm heading back to San Juan." Rory turned to exit the office.

"Not so fast, you ungrateful son of a bitch."

I knew this was coming.

Rory turned back to look at the irate billionaire. McGrady said, "Brendon saved your ass last night. You owe the McGrady family a favor."

"I don't owe *you* shit."

But maybe I do owe Brendon. Rory was well aware of the rules when it came to the favor economy in Chicago.

As if reading his mind, McGrady said, "True, but you do owe Brendon, and Brendon owes me. Hell, I put all his kids through private school, for Christ's sake. Now, you do me this favor, stick around for a few days, and I'll wipe the slate clean between you and my brother."

Rory had to admit Milt's point. Brendon did save his life, and if he was being honest with himself, the drive had piqued his curiosity. "Let's see what Kota can do," Rory said. "Then we'll talk about paying back favors."

The three went out to the trading floor looking for Kota and found him brewing some tea in the kitchen area. He had on gray workout clothes and looked like he hadn't slept a wink since Rory warned him to be careful late last night.

Mia handed the drive to Kota. "Here's the drive we talked about," she said. Apparently Kota had been the one to grant Mia access to Celtic's offices.

Kota glanced toward McGrady and said, "You are okay with me doing this?"

McGrady nodded and they all walked over to Kota's desk.

Kota took a seat, adjusted his chair, and plugged in the drive. He spent a couple of minutes investigating the file folder as he sipped on his tea, then said, "This is not good."

"What's the problem?" Rory asked.

"This is not RSA."

"Okay. Go on." While not an engineer in any sense of the word, Rory did have some basic technical knowledge. He knew Kota was referencing a type of encryption.

Kota sat back in his chair. "Most files use RSA. You take two very large prime numbers, sometimes hundreds of digits long, and multiply them. This gives you even larger number. It takes a regular computer thousands of years to figure out first two numbers, but a quantum computer can use Shor's algorithm to compute the two primes. Pete understood that, so he did not use RSA."

"What did he use?" Rory asked.

"He use lattice-based encryption, maybe NTRU. It employ a truncated polynomial ring to—"

McGrady cut Kota off. "So, what you're saying is it's fuckin' Fort Knox, and we're not gettin' in?"

Kota shifted his eyes from Rory to McGrady. "Some think it possible to decrypt lattice-based, but no one know for sure. It is beyond my level. I am a data scientist, not an engineer."

"So, there's no hope?" Mia asked, unable to believe Peter would leave a drive that no one would ever be able to access.

"There may be hope," Kota said. "But you need a top engineer to create custom decryption program." He paused for a moment, took another sip of his tea, then added, "And there is only one computer in the world with any chance to open this."

Rory knew exactly what computer Kota meant. The data scientist from Tokyo did not need to finish his thought but did anyway.

"If you want to see what is on this drive, you need ICARUS."

CHAPTER 20

Blue Ridge Mountains, North Carolina

Wednesday, November 3, 2027

"Well, that was delightful," Vanessa Price remarked, removing the napkin from her lap and placing it on her plate.

Senator Matthew Whitlock sat across from his chief of staff at a rustic, century-old oak table in the dining room of the Bear's Den. Candles flickered, and the scenic majesty of the Blue Ridge was on full display through expansive floor-to-ceiling windows. The moon sat nestled in darkness over the eastern ridgeline, backdropped by a blanket of stars.

"You can say that again, sugar," Whitlock said, also removing the napkin from his lap. "Jamie ain't worth a damn when it comes to bar-be-que, but he sure knows his fish."

The two had just enjoyed a light dinner of rosemary and lemon salmon served with asparagus and paired with a full-bodied white Burgundy from the senator's extensive cellar. Both wore blue jeans and cowboy boots, the senator with a denim button-down shirt. The wide belt that looped around his expanding waist was held together with his favorite North Carolina–shaped buckle. Vanessa wore a tight black V-neck top. Made of lace, the fabric revealed tiny diamond-shaped pockets of her soft, delicate skin. Her red hair draped down around her shoulders, perfectly accented by her emerald-green eyes.

"So, did Senator Fischer get back to you yet?" Vanessa asked.

Whitlock put down his glass of wine and laughed. "What the hell do you think? Of course she did. She's now a big yes for the Phoenix Act."

"Really? That's great news," Vanessa said in a flattering tone, an admiring smile on her face. "How did you pull that off?"

Whitlock relished his role as DC puppet master. "Let's just say that some women find it hard to resist the charms of a true southern gentleman. She's been calling her top donors all night, letting them know of her change of heart."

"And did you discuss the Bullion Bill as well?"

The Bullion Bill was the next legislative challenge the senator would need to get passed in Congress as part of Prince's grand plan. Officially titled the Silver and Gold Exchange Act or SAGE Act, it called for the nation's return to a bimetallic standard, a standard based on the value of both gold and silver. Bimetallism was the original monetary system of the United States. Proposed by Treasury Secretary Alexander Hamilton, it became the law of the land with the passage of the Coinage Act of 1792. Bimetallism remained the cornerstone of American money until the Coinage Act of 1873. Known as the Crime of '73, it effectively removed silver—the common man's money—from circulation and placed the nation on a de facto gold standard.

The SAGE Act would also pull another page from US monetary history by confiscating all private holdings of gold. Just as Franklin Roosevelt did in 1933 by Executive Order 6102, SAGE would forbid the private ownership of gold, though silver would not be seized. The paper dollar, however, would cease to exist, phased out over time and replaced by a global CBDC.

CBDCs, or central bank digital currencies, are the holy grail for true economic control. For decades, governments around the world have lamented the fact that trillions in paper currency still circulate. Even worse, from their perspective, the ones and zeros that go back and forth among private crypto wallets, offshore banks, and failed states are also more or less untraceable.

Efforts to reduce the amount of cash money in the US date back to 1969 when the Federal Reserve discontinued its issuance of $500, $1,000, $5,000, and $10,000 paper bills, essentially necessitating that large transactions take place within the banking system. Now, with the passage of SAGE, Big Brother would plug into every transaction via a unified ledger through a network of highly restricted and specialized nodes. The blockchain, created to liberate money from governmental control, would instead be weaponized as the ultimate tool of economic tyranny.

"No, we didn't discuss SAGE," replied the senator. "We need the stock market to piss its pants a few days before I can start shopping that around."

"Of course," Vanessa said. "But do you really think Americans will sell their gold to the government freely?"

"Ha," Whitlock laughed. "Once people know we're offering twenty-five grand an ounce for gold, every stupid son of a bitch from here to California will be scraping through jewelry and safe-deposit boxes to get their new digital currency. What the hell else are they going to do? Holding gold will be illegal. They'll give it up just like they did in the '30s."

For gold and silver to adequately back the estimated one quadrillion, or $1,000 trillion, of global wealth, the price of gold would eventually need to rise to $100,000 an ounce, but for the initial confiscation, its price would be fixed at $25,000 an ounce. Silver would be fixed at a ratio to gold of sixteen to one, initially over $1,500 an ounce.

"What about the market?" Vanessa asked. "Will the economy be able to handle twenty-five-thousand-dollar-an-ounce gold?"

"It'll make some doomsday preppers and conspiracy theorists rich, but yes, the market can handle that kind of a rise. Hell, bitcoin went from under a buck to tens of thousands. If the economy can handle that, it can handle gold going up ten or fifteen times in price. But don't you worry your pretty little head about that."

Whitlock got up from his chair, taking one final sip of his wine before walking over to Vanessa. Changing the subject, he said, "I'll bet I know what you'd like to have a gander at." He hovered above her like a hawk and peered down at her well-ventilated cleavage, then grabbed her hand in his.

The pair made their way downstairs. The basement included a fully stocked bar, wine cellar, billiard table, and a home theater area complete with reclining chairs arranged on an upward-sloping section of the floor. The walls were covered with outdoor landscapes, mostly oil on canvas but some photography as well, including a few signed prints by Ansel Adams. One corner of the basement, however, was unfinished. It served as a small workshop. Hidden behind a rustic pine door, the area contained a drill press, lathe, and other woodworking tools that Whitlock had never learned to use.

The senator and his chief of staff entered the workshop area. "Come here, help me with this," Whitlock said, looking toward a large piece of plywood that was propped up against the back wall. He and Vanessa slid the plywood down the wall, revealing a steel door reminiscent of a bank vault. It was smaller than a normal-size door and had a digital lock activated by facial recognition. Whitlock bent down to show his face to the camera. He then spun the door open.

"Watch your head," Whitlock said as the two left the basement and entered what had originally been built as an escape shaft leading to an immense safe room of sorts. The shaft connected the basement of the main cabin to an abandoned mine about fifty yards away in a nearby hillside. The main entrance to the mine had been dynamited and sealed years ago. This was now the only way in or out.

Whitlock flipped a switch. A row of uncovered bulbs flickered on to light the way. The excitement was palpable. Whitlock and Vanessa walked down the corridor, which was narrow but high enough for them both to stand upright. It smelled like a long-shut attic. The sound of their boots echoed on the concrete floor in the cool, damp air.

"There it is, sugar," Whitlock said proudly. Before them was an open, cavern-like room built right into the rock. Ten tons of gold bullion sat in the center of the space.

"That's it? That's all the gold?" Vanessa said with a sense of jest, though it was indeed a smaller stockpile than most would imagine. Approximately eight hundred bars comprised the entire ten tons. It was stacked on two pallets, the bars arranged eight by five and piled ten high on each.

"That's it?" responded the senator with mock offense. "Those bars are worth over six hundred million dollars. And that's at today's prices. In a week, that little pile of yellow metal will be worth well over eight billion dollars. Hell, once we get the gold price to where it needs to be, that's probably thirty billion dollars easy. Soon, you'll be able to buy small countries for a few of those bars."

Vanessa walked closer to one of the pallets. She sat down on the gold and crossed her legs, the soles of her boots hovering a few inches above the ground. Then she flipped her flowing red hair back and ran her fingers seductively over the metal.

"Roman emperors might have died for some of that very gold," Whitlock said. "You know, more than ninety percent of all the gold ever mined is still out there somewhere, in a watch or a necklace or right there under your pretty little ass."

"Speaking of asses, why don't you shut up and get yours over here," Vanessa said as she removed her black lace top and slowly unclipped her silken bra. In the dimly lit cavern, the yellow of the gold radiated softly upon her pale white skin.

Whitlock moved closer to the gold and to Vanessa. Reaching for his belt, he fumbled to loosen it as Vanessa slowly uncrossed her legs and allowed her thighs to open. Eventually, Whitlock freed the North Carolina–shaped buckle, letting it clumsily fall to the cavern floor.

CHAPTER 21

Chicago, Illinois
WEDNESDAY, NOVEMBER 3, 2027

"MIA, CAN I GET YOU a drink?" McGrady asked.

Upon hearing Kota's revelation that ICARUS was the only computer possibly capable of cracking into the encrypted drive, Rory, McGrady, and Mia thanked him for his efforts and retreated to McGrady's office for a more private discussion.

"Why not," Mia said as she took a seat on the couch.

"So," McGrady asked as he pulled a fresh glass from the cupboard under the bar, "when do you leave for Basel?"

"Hold on a second here," Rory objected. He took a seat on the couch next to Mia and unconsciously rested his left arm on the backrest, close to her shoulders, then asked, "What makes you think Fred is going to let us walk into the BIS and start using ICARUS to get into some drive about which we know nothing?"

Mia answered before McGrady could reply. "Because Pete and Frederik got along well. If Kota is right and there is something wrong with ICARUS, he'll have to let us try. He might very well be worried about the same problems that Kota has identified."

McGrady spoke as he handed Mia her drink. "She's right, Rory. That record-spinning Dutchman is going to be just as interested in seeing what's on that drive as we are. Look, you may not believe this, but I care about you, just like I cared about Pete. I don't like it when someone goes after my people."

"Save the bullshit for someone who'll buy it," Rory said, standing from the couch. "Besides, it's the middle of the night in Europe right now, which means Fred is either sound asleep or off DJing somewhere. Either way, we won't be able to speak with him until morning. I'll tell you what, Milt. I'll sleep on it and call Fred in the morning. But no promises." Rory added just to be clear, "If I go, and that's a big if, it will only be because I owe Brendon."

He turned to look at Mia still seated on the couch. "Regardless of how we play this, it could be dangerous. There's no need for you to get mixed up in this mess."

Now it was Mia who stood in protest. "I'm going," she demanded, her right hand on her hip. "And by the way, Rory, don't you find it odd that two of the four team leads from ICARUS have been targeted by gunmen on the streets of Chicago?"

"It's a dangerous city," Rory replied, though he had begun to agree with Mia's theory that Peter's death may be wrapped up in all this.

"Why don't *you* save the bullshit," Mia shot back. "You were almost killed last night, and you know damn well it wasn't random. You told me how they zeroed in on the messenger bag. And Pete, well, if there's even a chance that his death has something to do with this, I want to be there."

McGrady said, "She's right again, Rory. And we don't have time for you to sleep on it either. You can contact d'Oultremont from the Gulfstream or upon arrival. From what I hear, he's a bleeding heart for lost causes. Better yet, if you both just show up on the doorstep of the BIS like two lost puppies, he'll have no choice but to help."

Rory considered the situation. He could not deny that he never felt 100 percent comfortable with the whole iPhone and wallet motivation for Peter's murder, not coming on the heels of his breakthrough with the VSA.

McGrady saw the wheels turning in Rory's head. "What's to think about? I can have the 650 fueled up and ready for you two tonight."

Rory looked at McGrady. "I thought there was no way you could get the 650 ready on such short notice."

"Anything is possible," McGrady replied dismissively. Then the billionaire played his trump card: money. "Look, Rory, how about I really make this worth your while? I'll pay you each two hundred and fifty grand to head over there. If you figure out what's on that file, you'll get another two fifty…each. That's a cool million plus an all-expenses-paid trip to Switzerland on a private jet. Hell, you can ski the Alps while you're there for all I care. Just find out what's on that drive. If I'm going to put down serious bets in the market this week, I need answers, not a weather report. And I need them soon."

Rory didn't know what to say. He'd seen McGrady do this before, offer some outrageous sum that meant nothing to him in order to get his way, whether the other person wanted to do it or not. Most times, in fact every time Rory knew about, it worked. He once saw McGrady pay $1,000 for the last dozen of his favorite cookies at a local bakery when the previous customer had already purchased them. When McGrady first offered a hundred dollars for the cookies, the man feigned insult at the offer. Then McGrady pulled out a wad of hundred-dollar bills and peeled off ten of them. He walked out with the cookies.

Mia stared intently at Rory. "Whatever is on that drive was very important to Pete. I promise not to get in the way, but I need to know if this has anything to do with his death."

Rory glanced out the window at the hanging crescent moon, a little higher in the sky than when he had arrived at 333. Perhaps he would regret it. Perhaps it was the scotch. Perhaps he just felt guilty for running out on Mia after Peter's death. Or maybe, if he was really being honest, it had something to do with the half million dollars. In any case, Rory turned his gaze back to Mia.

"I guess we're going to Basel."

CHAPTER 22

Chicago, Illinois, to Basel, Switzerland
WEDNESDAY AND THURSDAY, NOVEMBER 3–4, 2027

"HI, RORY!" JENNIFER SAID WITH a smile as he and Mia boarded the plane.

Milton McGrady and his oversize bank account were indeed able to assemble a crew for his Gulfstream 650ER on very short notice. It was just after 11:00 p.m. Chicago time. After a quick stop at the Peninsula Hotel and then Mia's home, the duo arrived just as the pilots were completing their preflight checklist.

Rory smiled back at Jennifer, who brushed back her blonde hair coquettishly. He turned toward Mia and said, "This is Mia Costello. It will just be the two of us."

"Hello," Mia said.

"A pleasure to have you on board, Ms. Costello, or is it Mrs.?"

"Mia is fine."

Rory noticed Mia's reply lacked her usual warmth of expression. *Is she jealous?* he wondered as they both buckled in.

"Can I get either of you something to drink before takeoff?" Jennifer asked.

"I'll take a Bulleit and Coke," Rory replied.

"Of course, how could I forget," Jennifer said as her left hand gently touched Rory's shoulder. This earned him a sideways glance from Mia, who requested a glass of white wine.

The jet was wheels up from Chicago's Midway Airport at precisely 11:17 p.m. Given the speed of the G650 and a strong tailwind, ETA at

EuroAirport just outside Basel was 12:13 p.m. local time on Thursday. That gave Rory approximately seven hours of flight time to take another look at Kota's work and try to catch some shut-eye before arrival. Upon reaching cruising altitude, he and Mia made their way to the rear of the cabin. Rory took a seat in one of the revolving captain's chairs and pulled out his laptop.

Mia stretched out on the couch. "I could get used to this."

Within ten minutes, she was sound asleep, the wine barely touched. An hour or so later, Jennifer popped into the cabin, a pleasant distraction from Kota's model.

"Rory," she whispered, seeing Mia asleep on the couch, "is there anything I can get you? I'm about to turn in for the night if that's all right with you."

"Could you fix me another drink? Hell, you know what? Just bring back the bottle, please. Other than that, I'm good. Sleeping beauty over there has been out like a light since takeoff."

Jennifer giggled in response as Mia shifted her position on the couch. The flight attendant left for the galley and came back a few minutes later with a fresh drink, the bottle of bourbon, and a plate with some cheese and crackers.

Rory recalled Jennifer's offer of the cheese and crackers from his last flight and joked, "I guess you really need to get rid of these before they go bad."

Once again Jennifer laughed, and once again Mia shifted on the couch.

Moments after Jennifer left the cabin, Mia sat up and yawned. "What's going on in here? I keep hearing your Marilyn Monroe of the skies laughing. Are you putting on a comedy routine or just flirting?"

She is jealous. "What can I say?" Rory said with a smile. "I'm a funny guy."

Mia stood to stretch and took a sip of her wine. "Anything interesting on that laptop?"

"Not sure if interesting is the word. More like apocalyptic."

"Well, that doesn't sound too good." Mia took another sip of wine, then sat down in an empty revolving captain's chair. She twisted it around with her feet to face Rory. "You know, I never could understand how you and Pete were so fascinated by the stock market. I'd say because of the money, but Pete wasn't that kind of a guy. Why did you get into it?"

"Because of the money."

"You really are a funny guy," Mia said, channeling her inner Ray Liotta. They both let out a chuckle. Then, more seriously, she asked, "What about ICARUS? That was a pay cut for you."

Rory sat back in his chair, sipped his drink, and thought for a moment. "Honestly, it had a lot to do with Pete...and Fred. They both were so enthusiastic about changing the world; I guess I wanted to be a part of it too. Did Pete ever tell you the story about how Fred recruited us?"

"He told me some of it. Fred was in town for a techno festival or something, right?"

Rory laughed as he recalled the night Frederik d'Oultremont III came calling. He was in Chicago for the annual Spring Awakening Music Festival, a vast multiday EDM extravaganza, not as a spectator but as a headline performer on the second day.

"Yes, exactly," Rory said. "We met him at Rosebud for dinner. He talked a good game to Pete and me. He described this unbelievable quantum AI tech that the BIS had only recently gotten access to, Lord knows how. He was convinced it would revolutionize the world's financial markets."

Mia sampled some of the cheese and crackers as Rory went on. "Fred told us about his horrible experiences during the Global Financial Crisis in 2008 and how it was nothing compared to the damage it did to everyday people. He discussed the impacts of post-pandemic inflation caused by massive fiscal stimulus and money printing and was convinced he had the solution. Finally, he said that Pete and I were just the type of people he needed to lead his financial crusade. Offered us jobs on the spot. Pete would be chief technical engineer, and I'd head up trading operations."

Mia took a sip of her wine, then asked, "And that was that?"

"Pretty much. I was a bit skeptical at first, but when Fred started quoting from Pete's PhD dissertation, 'Artificial Intelligence, Quantum Computing, and the Potential for a Truly Efficient Market,' I knew we were joining up. It was just too good of a fit for us. I did make Fred promise two things, though: no micromanaging and that Pete and I could spend at least half our time and build out teams in Chicago. It was good for a while, I guess."

Mia brought her hand to her chin thoughtfully. "For a while? What's that supposed to mean?"

"I don't know…it was a real tough slough there at the end. Frankly, it amazed me that Pete was even able to complete the volatility-suppression algo."

"Why?" Mia finished her wine and poured a bit of Rory's bourbon into her glass.

Rory took a sip of his drink, then explained, "The tough part about ICARUS wasn't accumulating the trillions of bits of information out there and then using AI to instantaneously analyze that data and fairly price stocks and other assets. Don't get me wrong, the pricing engine wasn't easy, but dampening volatility, that was the really tricky part. At the end of the day, the market just isn't naturally efficient."

"I thought it was the opposite. Isn't the market supposed to be efficient?"

"It's supposed to be," Rory said with a bit of a laugh. "That's the whole cornerstone of modern financial dogma, the efficient market hypothesis. But it's bullshit. All kinds of things cause prices to get dislocated—be wrong, basically—sometimes for significant periods of time. For example, when the Fed is printing money like crazy and the world is awash with cash, prices go way higher than they should. It's almost as if the market is drunk. Then the punchbowl gets taken away, and the market has a hangover. Prices get sold down and everything gets undervalued until the headache is gone and some sense of sobriety returns. That's the reality. In theory, markets are always efficiently priced, but Milt and guys like him have been proving that wrong for decades. It's like that old joke about the economist who finds twenty bucks."

"I missed that one," Mia said. "I guess I'm just not as up on economist jokes as I should be."

"Give me some of that bourbon." Mia handed Rory the bottle. "It goes like this: An economist convinced of efficient markets is walking down the street with a friend. His buddy stops, points to the ground, and says, 'Look, a twenty-dollar bill on the sidewalk!' The economist just keeps on walking as he replies, 'Impossible. If there were a free twenty-dollar bill on the ground, someone would have picked it up already.'"

Mia and Rory both laughed with more zeal than the joke deserved.

"You drink much bourbon?" he asked, beginning to notice some effect on Mia while seemingly not noticing its effect on him.

It's good to see her laugh, he thought.

It was good for Rory to be laughing as well. He took a closer look at Mia, still wearing the tight-fitting black pants and green sweater she had worn for her visit to Celtic Capital.

"Sometimes, but I prefer wine. Unfortunately, your little friend Julie seems to have gone to bed."

"It's Jennifer," Rory corrected, now staring directly into Mia's deep brown eyes. "I can go back there and see if I can find another bottle of wine."

"Don't worry about it," Mia replied faintly as her eyes locked with Rory's gaze.

The two both placed their drinks on the table. Mia got up from her chair and walked over to Rory. She grabbed his hand, and they moved together to the plush leather couch. Rory brushed back Mia's hair, away from her eyes and behind her left ear. They wrapped their arms around one another and began to kiss softly. Rory slowly leaned in, sliding closer to Mia and feeling the warmth of her breasts through the woolen sweater.

A few hours later, the G650 prepared for descent. As they strapped back into their seats, Mia asked Rory, "So, you think Fred will help us?"

"Damn," Rory said with a shake of his head.

"What is it?"

"I forgot to call him from the sat phone before we fell asleep."

"Well, we were a little busy," Mia said.

He returned her coy smile. "I'll call or text him once we land."

"Or maybe we take Milt's idea," Mia suggested, "just show up at the BIS like two lost puppies. He'll have to help us. We've come such a long way."

"Sure, let's give it a shot. We'll be there in no time anyways. It's not far from our hotel, and besides, no one should want to know more than Fred if something is wrong with ICARUS."

"I would think so," Mia agreed. She took a sip of some fresh coffee that Jennifer had prepared, then said, "That reminds me, I need to call into the hospital and ask my cousin to look after the dogs and Oscar."

Still thinking about Fred, Rory commented, "I just hope he's not off DJing in Monaco or Ibiza."

"Really? He still DJs?"

"So far as I know." Rory thought back to the first time he saw Fred mixing it up at a BIS holiday party. "He's pretty good, actually. When I worked on ICARUS, he would often be out of the office for a day or two, off in some exotic location for a gig or festival."

"That's interesting. What was his stage name? DJ Banker?"

"No, not DJ Banker." Rory laughed as he looked out the G650 window and caught his first glimpse of Basel and the Rhine. Situated in the north of Switzerland and nestled between both France and Germany, the medium-size city is bisected by the powerful river.

Then, almost as an afterthought, Rory said, "If I recall correctly, Fred goes by DJ Prince."

PART II
What Goes Up...

The Chicago Board Options Exchange (CBOE) calculates what is known as the fear gauge, or VIX. This volatility index says nothing about how volatile the current market has been. Rather, it is a prediction, the result of a mathematical equation that backs out implied volatility based on the price of S&P Index options.

The calculation of the VIX is grounded in the Black-Scholes equation formulated by Fischer Black and Myron Scholes. The relationship of the equation's various inputs to the price of an option can be described further by what traders call "the Greeks."

How sensitive the price of an option is relative to a change in price of the underlying asset is known as its Delta. Theta measures the option's price sensitivity to time. Gamma relates to the change in Delta with respect to a move in the underlying asset. Rho represents sensitivity to changes in the interest rate.

Option price sensitivity to a change in the implied volatility of the underlying asset is known as Vega.

CHAPTER 23

Basel, Switzerland
THURSDAY, NOVEMBER 4, 2027

"TAKE YOUR PANTIES OFF," FREDERIK said in a soft yet commanding voice as he turned up the volume on his $50,000 home stereo system. A mix from Belgian EDM artist Felix De Laet pumped through a pair of custom M1i monitors. Crafted from fine cherrywood by the Swedish firm Transmission Audio, they had come directly from the designer, whom Frederik considered a personal friend.

"Those are some killer speakers," Amber said as she dropped her panties and twirled in front of Frederik, moving her hips rhythmically to the beat. Around twenty-five with blue eyes and short blonde hair that stopped before reaching her shoulders, Amber wore nothing except a nose ring, two silver bracelets, and a Stetson cowboy hat Frederik had picked up last year before a performance in Austin, Texas.

"These aren't speakers," Frederik said, running his forefinger across the smooth cherry finish of an M1i as he admired Amber's curves. "These are monitors."

Amber laughed for apparently no reason, then asked, "What's the difference?"

"Speakers distort sound. They up bass or boost mids and highs. Monitors don't enhance the music. They deliver pure, clean sound. I need to use them when I mix."

"Oh right, cool." Amber reached for her champagne, then playfully placed the Stetson on the Dutch banker's head.

Frederik, who never drank alcohol, grabbed his Red Bull and the two toasted. Just as he was about to escort Amber into the bedroom, he noticed the shift in the light outside his home near Basel's old town. *Is it morning already?* He reached for his phone to check the time. It was 06:35, and Frederik had a train to catch in just over an hour's time. *Well,* he thought, *I guess this had better be quick.*

The home was two stories, originally built at the turn of the eighteenth century, and had a steep sloping roof made from wooden shingles. Its façade was composed of white stucco, and yellow shutters buttressed the windows. A narrow but long balcony opened up off the back of the second story and stretched across its length, overlooking a small but well-tended garden with a large sycamore maple at the center. The home was centrally located off Eulerstrasse near the Spalentor, a hulking eight-hundred-year-old gate that made up part of the city's original walls.

After a brief interlude with Amber, whom he had met the night before at Vice Club—a hip-hop dance spot located less than two kilometers from his home—Frederik showered, shaved, and dressed in a tailored charcoal-gray suit with faint chalk-like pinstripes and a crisp, freshly starched white shirt. Popping a purple silk pocket square in his breast pocket, he then took a quick glance in the mirror. *Looking good,* Frederik complimented himself.

He grabbed a bottle of cold milk from the fridge and a couple of power bars from his pantry, then left for Basel SBB, the city's main train station. Earbuds in, playing Beethoven's Piano Concerto no. 4, Frederik exited the house around 07:30. It was a short two-minute walk to the Birmannsgasse transit stop. After a seven-minute ride on the number one tram, Frederik entered the train station and made his way to track 6 for the 07:55 train to Zürich.

Ten minutes to spare. I could have spent some more time with Amber.

Frederik had a 13:00 meeting with Fritz Weber, chairman of the Swiss National Bank. They were set to discuss key agenda items for the upcoming All Governors' Meeting. Weber had also asked Frederik to update him on Project mBridge and how it might be duplicated in Europe.

mBridge was a successful CBDC platform the BIS had put in place with coordination from Asian monetary authorities. But Frederik's afternoon appointment with Weber was not the reason he needed to make the early train to Zürich. He had an 09:30 meeting that was much more important.

Frederik William d'Oultremont III was born in 1978 in the Dutch city of Maastricht. Tucked in the southeastern corner of the Netherlands between Belgium and Germany, it is a historically Catholic area and the capital of Limburg Province. Frederik grew up surrounded by the old families of Maastricht, and he could trace his roots there back generations. Indeed, family legend had it that Frederik was a direct descendant of the first king of the Netherlands, William I, Prince of Orange.

As a young boy, Frederik wasn't very good at traditional Dutch games like Sjoelen, a type of tabletop shuffleboard, but he excelled at counting and calculating the points scored in that game. As sliding disks careened into different slots on a box, each disk would be worth either one, two, three, or four points depending on which slot it landed in, and Frederik never forgot to double the total points from ten to twenty if each slot was full at the end of a player's turn.

His real passion, however, was music. In fact, Frederik was much more interested in electronic dance grooves than in economics when he went off to study at Erasmus University in Rotterdam. It was at university where he purchased his first turntables, mixer, and monitors. Everything was used but of good quality. It was also in Rotterdam where Frederik realized he was actually quite handsome. Having grown into his tall and lean frame, he caught the attention of quite a few co-eds. On weekend nights, he often DJed parties, and it was not uncommon for Frederik to leave with the most beautiful girl in attendance.

After building a fairly robust nest egg during the early 2000s as a derivatives trader at Lehman Brothers, Frederik subsequently lost his job as well as most of his wealth when markets tumbled in 2008. At this point, he gave up on the business world but not on his passion for finance. He completed a PhD in economics at the Wharton School in 2013 and went to work for De Nederlandsche Bank NV or DNB, the central bank of the Netherlands, quickly becoming its president in 2018. Three years later, Frederik resigned from the DNB to take the reins as general manager at the Bank for International Settlements.

His first two years at the BIS were relatively uneventful. But in late 2023, Frederik was contacted by Zhao Hong of the People's Bank of China. Zhao informed him of game-changing quantum AI technology to which China had recently obtained access. Zhao did not, however, mention that this access was a product of espionage conducted in America through China's secretive Thousand Talents program. While irate about the leak, eventually the US Senate Select Committee on Intelligence led by Senator Matthew Whitlock approved a colossal appropriations bill to support the transition of what had been a DARPA project from military applications to financial.

After months of multilateral diplomacy and on the heels of a particularly rocky period in the world's financial markets dominated by global inflation, volatile interest rates, and various bank collapses, it was announced in late 2024 that the world's central banks, under the auspices of the BIS, had agreed to work together to deploy newly available quantum AI technology. The official goal of ICARUS was to substantially reduce volatility found in the world's capital markets caused by manipulation, speculation, fraud, and the erratic sentiment of the global investor community. Now, three years later, that dream had come to fruition with the launch of the final phase of ICARUS.

Unfortunately for Frederik, ICARUS had never really been completed.

The cornerstone of the AI source code, the key to maintaining market stability, was the volatility-suppression algorithm. To say the VSA still had a few bugs was the understatement of the decade. Frederik had flown to Chicago last year to meet with his head engineer after Peter

Costello notified him of a major breakthrough concerning the code, but before Frederik could obtain details of the discovery, Peter's life was cut short in a tragic drive-by shooting. The subsequent search of Peter's home and computer had revealed nothing other than some notes that yielded only minor refinements to the quantum neural network.

Despite being incomplete, the source code still worked, but only partially. It required vast amounts of capital to manipulate assets in line with the AI pricing engine. Valuations were not being gently massaged into place with the occasional well-timed buy or sell order. Instead, ICARUS was acting like a quantum jackhammer executing thousands of transactions per second. The purpose of these high-frequency trades was not just to impact prices but also to obscure the enormous amount of capital being deployed. It was, however, an unsustainable process and on the verge of collapse. The money behind the operation was running dry, and Frederik's only hope of regaining control of world markets after their inevitable collapse was with a fully functional ICARUS.

Thus, he was counting on Anton Golev, president of Russia's central bank and former FSB operative, to deliver the missing piece of the VSA puzzle, the Vega Block. The two were scheduled to meet in Zürich at the world-famous Fraumünster at precisely 09:30.

Frederik was expecting progress.

CHAPTER 24

Zürich, Switzerland

Thursday, November 4, 2027

Frederik polished off his second power bar as he gazed out the window of his first-class cabin. The high-speed train had just passed the town of Baden and was hugging the turquoise waters of the Limmat River. A rising sun crested the rolling hills, its rays glistening off the morning dew. Frederik took a sip of his milk and then pulled out his cell. Before meeting with Golev, he first needed to speak briefly with Arun Patel.

"Hello," Patel answered.

"Sanjay, how are you doing this glorious morning?" A fan of spy novels, Frederik had embraced his role in this dangerous game with an almost childlike enthusiasm, insisting that each member of his plot have an alias. His fellow conspirators found it superfluous, but they typically indulged Frederik's eccentric nature.

Patel, a.k.a. Sanjay, replied, "It's actually the afternoon here in Mumbai, but to answer your question, Prince, I am doing well."

"I just want to make sure you have everything you need for Mexico."

"I am packing as we speak. My plane departs in two hours."

"Wonderful," Frederik said, imagining Patel neatly laying out fresh underwear and socks. "You have the paperwork, then? I want the silver shipments to start as soon as possible."

"Yes, yes, everything is in order." Patel paused for a moment, then asked nervously, "What of the Vega Block?"

Over the past year, Patel had initiated countless covert wires to BIS accounts. He had warned Frederik that his lieutenants at the RBI were getting suspicious. Some of them were starting to ask questions for which there were no satisfactory answers.

Using his code name for Golev, Frederik assured Patel, "I'll have news on that front soon. I'm meeting with Liev in an hour."

Patel replied sarcastically, "Oh capital! Tell that cheeky bastard hello for me."

"One last thing, I need you in Basel as soon as you're done in Mexico. We need to review our strategy before the All Governors' begins on Sunday."

"I was planning to spend a day or two back in Mumbai when my business is complete in Fresnillo. My son has a cricket match Sunday morning."

"Cricket match?" Frederik said with some annoyance. "We are crafting a new world economic order. I need you in Basel."

"Very well." Patel sighed, then said, "I'll head directly to Basel after Mexico."

"Excellent. See you Saturday." Frederik ended the call. His earbuds returned to classical music, now playing Bach's Sixth Symphony. A few minutes later, the train began to slow as it pulled into Zürich HB, Switzerland's busiest train station. He looked at his phone. *08:59, right on time.*

Frederik hopped out of the train and into the hustle and bustle of HB. Sharply dressed businessmen and women dashed about briskly. A Mideastern-looking man, possibly a refugee from Syria, played the accordion at the end of the platform. Frederik dropped a two-franc coin into his hat and then popped into Dunkin' Donuts for another jolt of caffeine, the Red Bull of earlier this morning wearing off.

Why does every train station in Switzerland have a Dunkin' Donuts? Frederik mused as the barista prepared his pumpkin spice latte. Exiting the station, he walked past a group of youths, the smell of cigarettes with just a touch of hashish wafting through the crisp autumn air. It was less than a kilometer from the station to the Fraumünster, plenty of time to walk before his 09:30 with Golev.

Frederik made his way south along the west bank of the Limmat River, passing little stores and cafés along a timeworn path of cobbled stone. Sometimes wide and open to the air, sometimes narrow and confined, the path follows the slight curves of the Limmat until reaching its nearby source, Lake Zürich. Framed with the Alps in the distance, the lake sparkled in the early morning sun. A few hundred meters shy of the lakeshore, just off the west bank of the Limmat, sits the Fraumünster.

Built in the thirteenth century above the remains of an abbey founded in 853, the Fraumünster is one of Switzerland's most famous churches. The structure itself is not overly impressive when compared to the great cathedrals of Europe, but Frederik appreciated the light in its choir area. Five large stained-glass windows designed by Marc Chagall had been installed there in 1970. The sun's rays pass through them in vibrant shades of red, yellow, orange, blue, and green. Each panel has its own color and design, depicting a distinct story from the Bible.

Frederik entered the church and paid the five francs entrance fee. *Used to be two*, he recalled. *Inflation.* He meandered his way to the choir area. There were no pews, but roughly a hundred chairs had been arranged for comfortable viewing of the heavenly light. Two old women stood nearest the southern wall and gazed upward at a vibrant blue Moses holding the Ten Commandments. In the back of the choir, a man with gray eyes and slicked-back salt-and-pepper hair sat quietly, almost in a state of contemplation. He stared intently at Chagall's yellow glass, an angel trumpeting the end of the world.

Frederik took a seat just left of the gray-eyed man, then said in a whisper, "Hello, Liev."

Golev laughed, then replied in raspy Russian-accented English, "Your love of cloak and dagger is admirable, but no one is watching us here. My men are outside and have been here since 08:00. The place is clean. And call me Anton or Golev. Liev is my brother-in-law's name, and he's a fat pig."

Frederik got right to the point of the visit. "Do you have the Vega Block?"

"No."

"That is unacceptable."

Golev did not reply. Frederik ran his right hand through his strawberry-blond hair anxiously, then said, "I really don't care what you do or how you do it, but I need the Vega Block. Can you search Peter Costello's old home again, see if there is anything we missed?"

"No."

"Why not?"

"Because his sister has two giant dogs, and my men in Chicago are dead, that's why. Killed in an alley Tuesday night by some gangster cop and that fucking crypto trader, Rory O'Connor."

"What! What happened?" Frederik twitched slightly in his chair and focused on his breath in a vain attempt to remain composed.

"Never mind what happened, Prince," Golev replied mockingly. Then, in a more serious tone, he said, "But I will tell you this: crypto-boy is not going to leave Switzerland alive."

Now Frederik was truly flustered. "Switzerland? Liev, what are you talking about?"

Golev looked intently at the Dutchman. "Listen good. I'm only going to say this once. Rory O'Connor and Mia Costello will be landing in Basel in a matter of hours. O'Connor has a thumb drive with Peter Costello's Vega files." Golev then pointed to one of the Chagall panels, adding, "And if you call me Liev one more time, I will throw you through that fucking window."

Frederik ignored the taunt, relieved to hear that the missing piece of his source code was en route to Switzerland. "That's excellent news. I'll cancel my meeting with Fritz Weber and head back to Basel immediately."

"Wrong. You'll do no such thing. Just go to your meeting with Weber as planned. You can meet with O'Connor tomorrow. First, I want my men to keep an eye on him, watch how he plays this. Besides, has he even contacted you yet?"

"No."

"My point exactly. If you go running back to Basel, what will everyone think? Where is your tradecraft, 007?"

Frederik had to admit, the Russian had a point. But he was worried this was getting more hazardous than anticipated. It was never Frederik's intention for anyone to get killed. He cautioned Golev, "Remember, this isn't Moscow or Chicago. If you or your men draw attention to yourselves by doing something to Rory in Basel, there will be consequences."

"What consequences?"

"An investigation, the canton police."

"Ha, canton police. You really do make me laugh. I spent twenty years in FSB. You think I'm concerned about canton police? But don't worry, I won't hurt the trader or his pretty little girlfriend. Not yet, at least."

"So, what is your plan, then?"

Golev leaned closer to Frederik, rays of light shimmering off the thin roped gold of his chain. With the odor of coffee and cigarettes strong on his breath, he began, "Listen very carefully. Here is what we are going to do..."

CHAPTER 25

Basel, Switzerland

Thursday, November 4, 2027

Basel is a city situated at the crossroads of empires. The third largest city in its historically neutral country, it straddles the mighty Rhine on its journey north from the resplendent Alps toward the North Sea. Quite literally sandwiched between France and Germany, Basel borders both nations directly. It was for precisely this reason that the city was chosen as home to the Bank for International Settlements. Originally created to streamline reparation payments after World War I, the BIS is heir to a checkered history, including the financial enablement of the Third Reich. Some theorize that BIS facilitation of Nazi gold appropriation during the war was a primary factor in Hitler's decision not to invade the alpine nation.

From Basel's center, one can take any number of its ubiquitous trams and be in either France or Germany within a matter of minutes. Indeed, the EuroAirport into which Rory and Mia flew has its runways in France but connects via a 2.5-kilometer, customs-free road to Basel. Jointly administered by both France and Switzerland, the airport is governed by a 1949 international convention.

After a quick stop to check in at Basel's world-renown Grand Hôtel Les Trois Rois, Rory and Mia boarded the number eight tram. The sun was shining in Basel, and at around sixty degrees, the warmer weather was a welcome change from cold and damp Chicago. Exiting the tram, Rory looked up across the street at number 2 Centralbahnplatz, headquarters of the Bank for International Settlements.

One of the tallest structures in the city, many at the BIS did not think it wise to move into such an ostentatious building and attract attention. From the 1930s until the late '70s, the bank had operated unassumingly out of the Grand Hôtel et Savoy Hôtel Univers in downtown Basel. But as the bank transformed itself from a reparations administrator to the central bank for central banks, it needed more space to spread its wings. A twenty-four-story, concrete, circular tower with rose gold–tinted windows and garden terraces that expand out from the lower floors was erected. To the less charitable, it evoked the unholy union of a nuclear reactor and a Chia Pet. Locals were not fond of the postmodern structure, which contrasted with much of the surrounding architecture, and it quickly got the moniker the Tower of Basel.

Four of the tower's twenty-four stories were built belowground. It was on sublevel three where the bulk of ICARUS's sophisticated hardware had been custom installed after its development in Chicago. The underground facility was equipped with strict climate controls and anti-seismic stabilizers. Special LED lighting, which emitted almost no heat, cast the entire floor in an eerie green glow reminiscent of the Emerald City. It was a wonderland of machine-learning majesty, powered by recurrent neural networks and state-of-the-art perceptrons, a quantum Oz, and Frederik was its wizard.

Located across from Basel's central train station, the tower's environs also included a nuclear bomb shelter, an infirmary on the second floor, and a triple-redundant fire-extinguishing system designed to ensure local authorities need never enter the building. Indeed, the entire BIS premises enjoyed embassy-like protections via its 1987 Headquarters Agreement with the Swiss government. Not even Swiss authorities were granted access to its grounds without permission. Staffers were also given the right to use diplomatic pouches free of customs searches, and—a favorite of the employees—both the BIS and its staff were made exempt from Swiss taxes. The building's aesthetics, however, did leave something to be desired.

"That's it?" Mia said upon seeing the tower in person for the first time. "Who designed that thing? It's awful."

"Some Swiss architect, I think," Rory said with a chuckle. "But it's not that bad. Kind of grows on you."

Security was comprehensive but not overbearing at the BIS. There were dozens of surveillance cameras, steel and concrete barricades near the entrance, and a staff of armed guards on duty 24/7. Rory and Mia walked through the front doors and into a small waiting area where a guard stood behind bulletproof glass. Two more guards, a set of steel turnstiles, and another set of doors leading into the building proper prevented them from going any farther. Rory approached the bulletproof window and spoke through the intercom.

"My name is Rory O'Connor. I'm here to see Frederik d'Oultremont."

The guard, dressed in a gray suit with white shirt and black tie, looked Rory and Mia up and down. They were dressed more informally than most visitors to the BIS. Rory had on a gray sweater, blue jeans, and a pair of running shoes. The Celtic Capital messenger-style bag was slung over his right shoulder. Mia had taken a quick shower and changed into a similar outfit at the hotel, except her sweater was red.

A handsome man in his thirties with blond hair and blue eyes, the guard replied with a Swiss-German accent, "One moment." He made eye contact with the two other guards near the turnstiles and then punched some keystrokes on his computer. "I'm sorry, Mr. O'Connor. I don't see that you have an appointment. In any case, Herr d'Oultremont is not on-site today."

So much for Milt's two-lost-puppies strategy. But Rory had anticipated Frederik may be out. Sara Schnyder, the head of treasury at BIS, was someone he had worked with closely and trusted implicitly. Rory hoped at least she would be available.

He spoke into the intercom, "I was the head of trading for two years on ICARUS, and we need to speak with someone today. It is rather important and urgent. Can you ring Sara Schnyder and tell her Rory O'Connor and Mia Costello need to see her?"

The guard displayed a none too convincing look of disappointment. "Again, I'm sorry, Mr. O'Connor, but Ms. Schnyder no longer works for the BIS."

Damn.

"What about Kartik Das? Is he available?"

The guard looked down at his computer, then picked up the phone. He spoke briefly. Rory and Mia could not hear the conversation, the intercom muted. A minute later, the intercom back on, the guard said, "Mr. Das will be down in a moment."

A few minutes later, Kartik Das walked through the large glass doors behind the turnstiles. Rory knew him fairly well. Born in Bengaluru, India, and educated at Cambridge, Das had been Peter's understudy. He was a brilliant programmer with a keen financial mind. After Peter's death, he took over as head of engineering. Das wore a light pink collared shirt with a pair of gray woolen pants. His stylish black leather dress shoes were slightly elongated and pointed at the toe box. Trim and in his late thirties, Das had shortly cropped black hair. A broad smile came across his face as he made eye contact with Rory.

"Hello, old friend," Das said, reaching out to warmly shake Rory's hand. He then turned to do the same with Mia, whom he had met at Peter's funeral. "Mia, it's a pleasure." Das continued, "Not that I'm complaining, it's great to see you both, but I must say I'm a bit surprised. What brings you to Basel?"

Rory took a couple steps away from the guarded reception area. Mia and Das shifted their positions accordingly. "Can we speak somewhere that is a bit more private?" Rory asked.

Das understood and arranged for Rory and Mia to have their digital pictures taken for BIS visitor cards, which were quickly produced. He then shuttled the pair up to a conference room on the twelfth floor that overlooked the city. A dozen black leather chairs circled a large table. In a corner, a cart was laid out with pastries, cream, sugar, assorted teas, and two carafes resting on warming plates, one with coffee, the other hot water. The Americans fixed themselves coffees and Das a hot tea. The trio took a seat around the conference table.

Rory filled Das in regarding his concerns about ICARUS. He gave an overview of Kota's work, highlighting the short-term hyper-volatility and mentioning that Kota's model predicted severe market turmoil without getting into too much detail. He did not tell Das about the thumb drive. Only Frederik had the ability to authorize the use of ICARUS for irregular operations, and the drive was something Rory wasn't prepared to share with Das yet.

Let's see what he has to say first, Rory thought, then concluded his recap, "...And that's what we've got. So, what do you think? Are Kota and I crazy?" He then sat back in his chair, curious to hear Das's response.

"You say Kota developed this model all by himself?" Das asked, reaching for his tea.

"I believe so."

"Who else knows about these concerns of yours?"

"Just us and half the traders on the floor of the Chicago Mercantile Exchange."

"I'm serious, Rory. Have you shared this information with anyone else?"

Das was being unexpectedly guarded. *Is he hiding something?*

Rory raised his voice slightly. "Why? What's with all these questions?"

Mia, who had been looking out the window in a jet-lagged daze, returned her attention to the conversation, apparently noticing the frustration evident in Rory's voice.

Das paused. His deep brown eyes glanced around the room as if he were confirming they were alone. Then he placed his tea on a coaster and leaned across the table. Almost in a whisper, he said, "This cannot leave this room. Understood?"

Rory and Mia both nodded.

"You and Kota are not crazy. Besides Fred and me, only Karl knows what I'm about to tell you."

Karl was Karl von Hoffman. A German, he had assumed Rory's role after his departure last November. Karl had not been part of the original ICARUS team, and while Rory had never met him, he knew who Karl was and of his reputation as one of the best tactical traders in Europe.

Das said, "ICARUS's pricing engine is working great. We know just where each stock, bond, or commodity should be trading. But the VSA is really struggling to keep assets at or near those prices. We've been burning through cash. At some point, the music will stop. We're worried ICARUS won't be able to contain the volatility much longer. It's like a ticking time bomb, and we have no idea when it's going to go off."

Rory was reassured by Das's candor. He reached for the Celtic Capital bag and pulled out his laptop. He placed it on the conference room table and booted it up. "I have something I want to show you."

After a moment, Rory accessed Kota's predictive volatility model, opened it up, and turned the screen toward Das. "I studied this on the plane last night. It shows thirty historical trading days and the observed volatility, then it extrapolates based on some stochastic patterns Kota had identified. It predicts the vol will break over simple minute-by-minute anomalies and start playing real havoc with the market soon, very soon, maybe even today." Rory looked at the bottom corner of the computer. It was the middle of the afternoon in Basel but only ten after nine in New York. The opening bell on Wall Street had yet to ring.

Das studied the model and associated Excel files. He searched through supporting tabs trying to grasp Kota's methodology. After about ten minutes of reviewing the work, he clicked it back to the predictive graph. Shaking his head, Das said, "I don't know what to say. This model is even more advanced than what we have here. It looks right to me."

Rory stood up and walked toward the broad rose gold–tinted windows overlooking the streets, alleys, and churches of Basel, then turned toward Das.

"Mia and I have something to share that can't leave this room either. Understood?"

Das again scanned the room as if assuring their privacy. After a moment's pause, he shook his head nervously in agreement.

Rory sat back down in his chair, reached once more into the Celtic bag, and pulled out the encrypted drive.

CHAPTER 26

Washington, DC

THURSDAY, NOVEMBER 4, 2027

ELIZABETH NORTON SAT AT A medium-size yet exquisitely crafted mahogany desk in the State Dining Room of the White House. Attached to the front of that desk was the official seal of the president of the United States of America. Flanked by at least a dozen senators and representatives, President Norton wore a camel houndstooth blazer and matching knee-length skirt with a black blouse and long strand of pearls around her neck. She looked pleased. Her rich gray hair draped luxuriously around a face that appeared much younger than her sixty-two years. Her smile, like something out of a toothpaste ad, beamed into the dozens of cameras all pointed directly at her.

"Today is a great day for the American people," she said, backdropped by multiple flags of the United States intermixed with those bearing the presidential seal. "Before I sign into law the Phoenix Act, the most consequential legislation since the New Deal, I want the world to know how proud I am of the truly bipartisan effort that has made this day a reality. I would like to thank each and every congressperson and senator, on both sides of the aisle, for their support of this bill, a bill that will ensure American growth and prosperity for generations to come.

"While it took hundreds of staffers and elected officials to make this dream a reality, I'd like to especially thank Senators Matthew Whitlock and Kristin Fischer." The president turned to her right, where both Whitlock and Fischer were standing, now also with beaming smiles on their faces and nodding into the cameras. The president continued,

"With their help and support, the Phoenix Act becomes law today. In the years to come, millions of Americans will reap the rewards of trillions in investment and infrastructure. This is exactly the type of comprehensive remaking of the American economy that I have hoped for since I myself was first elected to Congress." Pausing for dramatic effect, she concluded, "We did it!"

The band of politicians all began to clap and stared down toward the president's desk with approving admiration while President Norton signed the $9-trillion Phoenix Act into law with numerous pens, ceremoniously handing one over to both Whitlock and Fischer as well as other key congressional leaders.

After the formal and public part of the ceremony came to a close, the reporters and camera crews were escorted out of the large State Dining Room while the politicians and some of their staff stayed behind and made small talk, congratulating one another on their accomplishment. Senator Whitlock was able to get a moment alone with Kristin Fischer.

"You made the right decision, Kristi," he assured her.

"You didn't exactly give me much of a choice, Senator," Fischer said, managing to force a slight smile. "I'm not a fan of being backed into a corner, but I have to admit, there are some merits to this legislation." She wanted to add, *Not to mention I didn't want to end my career before it really started,* but bit her tongue.

"Smart as a whip," Whitlock quipped. "You'll go far in Washington. And don't forget about what we discussed. You'd look beautiful in the long black robe of a Supreme Court justice." With a wink, Whitlock walked away and found Vanessa Price sitting on a chair in a corner of the room pounding away on her cell phone.

"Ready?"

"Just give me one second." Vanessa finished her text message and placed her phone in her purse as she stood from the chair. She looked exceptionally beautiful today, her red hair done up with a slight curl, her form-fitting gray sweater and wool skirt accentuating curves in all the right places.

"I can't wait to send that bitch back to Iron Mountain, Minnesota," Whitlock commented as he and Vanessa left the White House and hopped into the back seat of their armored SUV for the ride back to the Hill.

"She's from Iron Mountain, Michigan. Upper Peninsula," Vanessa said with a slight laugh, not sure if Whitlock was joking or if he really thought the president's home state was Minnesota.

"Well, what do you think about the next president hailing from North Carolina?" Whitlock placed his left hand on Vanessa's thigh. She gave no response. He then told the driver to take the long route back to the Capitol and raised the privacy shield between the front and back seats. The two turned in their seats, leaned closer to one another, and began to kiss, Whitlock's hand moving ever so higher up Vanessa's skirt.

About 225 miles northeast of DC in Lower Manhattan, Wall Street wasted no time in reacting to the Phoenix Act. The market took a turn lower just as the senator's privacy shield moved up. It was ninety minutes into the trading session, and a plethora of red arrows flickered on the screens of brokerages across the country. Some of the most widely held names on the Street were breaching key support levels.

The new market, the ICARUS market, the unbreakable market, was starting to show some cracks.

CHAPTER 27

Basel, Switzerland
Thursday, November 4, 2027

"Maybe last night was a mistake," Mia said as she squeezed the lemon slice above her glass of sparkling water.

Rory sat back in his chair and took a sip of wine. *I guess we had to talk about it at some point.* He finished nearly half the glass.

The pair had left the BIS around 4:00 p.m. local time. Despite Das's best efforts, they were unable to get in contact with Frederik, whom they learned was busy meeting with the head of the Swiss central bank in Zürich. Das would be in touch as soon as he heard something. In the meantime, he would start work on a custom decryption program. Rory held on to the drive itself since Das was not authorized to allocate time on ICARUS without Frederik's express permission. As Kota speculated, Peter had indeed used lattice-based encryption. It was not going to be quick or easy, even with ICARUS. Rory and Mia planned on returning to the Hôtel Les Trois Rois, but after three cups of coffee each, they decided it best to fight their jet lag and forgo a well-deserved nap. Instead, they took one of Basel's convenient trams to a favorite pizza spot of Rory's, Spiga, located just a block from their hotel.

Rory placed his wine back down on the table and reluctantly responded to Mia's comment regarding last night. "Listen, I care for you. I really do. But we need to focus on the here and now. I had to shoot and kill a man less than forty-eight hours ago. It's all a bit much to handle."

"You didn't seem too rattled about things last night on the jet." Mia twisted a second lemon slice into her water with what Rory thought was exceptional vigor.

He glanced around the restaurant. Rory had chosen a corner booth from which he could survey the entire dining area, bar, and entrance. A handful of tourists and a young couple sipped on their drinks, enjoying both their pizza and a lovely fall day. After a moment's pause, he said, "I just think worrying about last night right now isn't the best idea, that's all."

"So, you do think it's a mistake, then?"

"I never said that."

"You said you didn't want to worry about last night right now. Why would you ever need to worry about it if it weren't a mistake?"

Do women go to some sort of law school to come up with these arguments? Rory wondered as Mia switched from her water to wine, also taking a rather large sip.

Their young waitress arrived and placed a plate of bruschetta on the table. "Your pizza will be out shortly. Is there anything else I can get for you?"

"No, thank you," Mia replied, and the waitress walked away to take the order from a nearby table.

An uncomfortable silence hung over the booth as both Rory and Mia reached for a piece of bruschetta. Each took a bite and then placed it on the small plates in front of them.

"Maybe you're right, Rory. Let's not 'worry' about last night. After all, we're in Switzerland enjoying a wonderful meal." Mia pointed down to her plate and added, "This is really good."

"Yes, they have very fresh basil in Basel." A smile returned to both their faces courtesy of the wine, good food, and Rory's bad sense of humor.

"How are the markets doing?" Mia asked.

Rory reached into his pocket and pulled out his phone. It was almost noon in New York, over two hours into the trading day. Rory double-checked what he was seeing just to make sure he wasn't reading the numbers wrong.

I'll be damned. It's really happening.

He put the phone down on the table. "Well, Kota was right. The market is starting to sell off, nothing huge yet, but still highly unusual. The S&P is down about a percent and a half."

"Is that a lot?"

"Pre-ICARUS, no. It would be considered run-of-the-mill profit taking ahead of the jobs number tomorrow. But post-ICARUS, this just shouldn't happen. Not on seemingly no news."

Rory paused for a moment, then checked a couple of the top financial sites. He looked up from his phone. "Actually, there is some news. Norton signed the Phoenix Act into law this morning. That could have something to do with it."

"What should we do?" Mia asked just as the waitress returned once again, this time with two small wood-fired pizzas cooked to perfection. She placed them on the table and then asked if she could get them anything else.

"We're good. Thank you," Rory said, then turned to Mia. "I'm not sure if there's anything to do. Until we get in touch with Fred, we can't access ICARUS. I guess we eat pizza, drink wine, and hope things don't get too bad too quickly."

"That's it?" Mia asked mockingly as Rory picked up his glass for another sip of wine while his pizza cooled. "We flew all night across the Atlantic to help stop a market meltdown that is starting right now, and you want to eat pizza and drink wine?"

"Point taken," Rory said as he cut into the pie. He held up a slice and gently blew on it to cool the steaming-hot cheese. "Maybe there is something we could do."

"What are you thinking?" Mia asked as Rory bit into his pizza.

Despite the burning sensation spreading across the roof of his mouth, a mischievous grin spread across Rory's face.

Rory and Mia discussed his plan and agreed that while risky, it was better than doing nothing. They finished their meal and walked across the street, stopping briefly at a small promenade overlooking the Rhine. The sun hung low in the sky as large barges made their way down the rushing river, water high on its banks after a wet October. Rory needed to update McGrady while Mia wandered off into one of the nearby shops.

"As far as the current head of engineering for ICARUS can tell, Kota's work is spot-on," Rory said into his cell as he puffed on a cigarette and gazed across the river.

McGrady, sitting in his office at 333, said, "That's all you got for me? Some tech guy 'thinks' Kota's work is spot-on?"

Before the opening bell, McGrady had put on some short positions, betting the market would move lower. They had worked out well so far, but from the tone of McGrady's voice, Rory could tell he was looking for more concrete verification that the market's move lower would continue.

"I don't know what to tell you, Milt. I don't have a crystal ball, but I trust this guy," Rory said, referring to Kartik Das. "He knows his stuff, and he can confirm that there have been unanticipated issues with ICARUS. That's all I got right now. If you're hesitant to make any big moves, that's your choice."

"I've got over twelve billion dollars available to allocate; a good chunk of that cash is mine. I need your honest answer. What's the fuckin' play here?"

Rory paused for a moment, his attention briefly distracted. On the other side of the Rhine, a street performer with a long gray beard was using a large wire ring to create beach ball-size bubbles. Rory remembered the man from his prior trips to Basel. He was always on one main thoroughfare or another, making bubbles and hoping for a few francs while blasting music from an outdated boom box.

Bubbles, the world is full of bubbles.

Good traders know the market, earnings expectations, Fed moves, macro head or tailwinds. But great traders have a feel, a gut instinct that experience has taught them to follow. Rory's gut told him that today's move lower was just the beginning.

He said to McGrady, "Keep the shorts on and sell some calls to finance more put buying, maybe get long the VIX. The market's going lower. I'll reach out once I have more information."

Rory ended the call just as Mia exited the nearby gift shop. She walked up to him, a smile on her face, both hands held behind her back. "I have something for you."

She presented Rory with a small box as a smile came to his face as well. It was a Victorinox Swiss Army knife. Rory pecked Mia on the cheek and said, "You shouldn't have, but I love it." He opened the box, examining the Huntsman model knife and pulling out some of the tools, including the corkscrew, scissors, and blade. "This is great," Rory commented. "I always meant to get one of these on my past trips here but never got around to it. Thank you."

He placed the knife in his jeans pocket and wrapped his right arm around Mia's shoulder. The afternoon warmth was fading as the sun drooped ever lower in the sky.

"Is everything all right?" Mia asked.

Rory's mind had once again drifted. After a moment, he said, "Everything's fine." But as his eyes refocused on the old man across the Rhine, Rory knew, *Everything's not fine. Everything is not fine at all.*

With all the action of the past few days, he hardly had any time to think. Originally nebulous, a situational awareness now began to take form and harden. There was more at play here than he understood. Rory watched a flurry of bubbles float up and then vanish into the crisp fall air as he realized the challenging truth. *I've got a puzzle to put together, but I don't even have all the pieces yet.*

CHAPTER 28

Basel, Switzerland

THURSDAY, NOVEMBER 4, 2027

KARTIK DAS WAS NOT A Brahman. He was the youngest son of a fruit vendor. His father's greatest possession was a small wooden cart that he toted around the busy streets of Bengaluru, the capital of the southern Indian state of Karnataka and formerly known as Bangalore. His father was also covered in burns over 70 percent of his body. He got them before Das was born while selling fruit at a local circus in 1981. Known as the Venus Circus Fire, over ninety lives were lost, most of them young children who had come to see trapeze artists and elephants.

Years later, Das was helping his father sell fruit one day in front of St. Joseph's College in Bengaluru. An elderly Jesuit priest took an interest in the young boy. He watched in astonishment as the young Das multiplied price times weight in his head more quickly than most grown men could do, more quickly than he could do. A professor of mathematics at St. Joseph's, Father David Ricardo, S.J., took a shine to the gifted boy, tutoring him free of charge in English as well as math. And when Das was older, Father Ricardo found a place for him in the all-male preparatory school attached to the college. With further aid from the priest, Das was later admitted to the main university, where he studied mathematics and developed an obsession for computers. After graduation, he attended Cambridge on a full scholarship, graduating summa cum laude with a master's in advanced computer science.

From Cambridge, Das went on to the City of London, Britain's famed financial district. There he experienced a life of wealth and privilege undreamed of as a child selling mango, chikoo, papaya, and banana on the streets of Bengaluru, but he never forgot his humble beginnings. He dedicated himself to giving back to those in need, just as Father Ricardo had given to him. The ICARUS project seemed like a perfect use for his talents, an opportunity to smooth out turbulent markets whose vagaries often had an outsize effect on those most vulnerable. Das understood that a spike in wheat or corn futures in Chicago could mean a child in Bengaluru would go to bed hungry the next week. Das had been that child. Without reservation, he committed himself wholeheartedly to ICARUS.

Rory was familiar with Das's background and understood his sense of commitment. Now, he was counting on it, hoping it was strong enough that Das would be willing to override protocol and begin the decryption process without express approval from Frederik d'Oultremont.

Rory and Mia stopped briefly at the Hôtel Les Trois Rois to freshen up, then put on their coats and made their way across the Rhine and to the apartment of Kartik Das. He lived in an old yet well-maintained three-story building near the iconic Messeplatz, less than a ten-minute walk from their hotel. Each floor of the building was a separate residence, and Das lived on the top floor by himself.

It was around 7:00 p.m. when they rang the buzzer to Das's flat. Das buzzed them in, and they proceeded up two flights of stairs, where Das awaited them outside his door. Rory had been to the apartment before. Along with Peter Costello, he had shared after-work beers with Das on the flat's small rooftop terrace when working at the BIS. It was a bit chilly for that tonight, and so Rory, Mia, and Das all took a seat in the living room. Rory and Mia sat on a modest gray couch that looked like it was from IKEA. Das sat across from them on a similarly styled chair.

"Did you see what happened today in the US?" Das asked. "S&P closed down over three percent."

"I know," Rory said. "And it's probably going to be a lot worse tomorrow if Kota's model is right. Could this all be because of the Phoenix Act?"

"I thought about that," Das said. "It definitely has something to do with it, a straw that's breaking the camel's back, but the suddenness and severity of the drop means there must be more to it."

"What do you mean?" Mia asked.

Das said, "ICARUS anticipates. It started pricing in today's signing the moment that bill started getting talked about in the press, probably earlier. The Phoenix Act was well telegraphed to the market. There's got to be more going on, probably with the VSA."

As Rory further explained to Mia why the day's action was so unusual, Das walked to his small kitchen and grabbed three Swiss-brewed Quöllfrisch beers as well as some European cheeses and fresh grapes. He still enjoyed at least some fresh fruit every day, a habit from his years helping his father on the streets of Bengaluru.

He placed the items on the living room table, sat back down in his chair, and gave Rory and Mia an update on his decryption program. "It's going to take some time," Das concluded, "but I think it's crackable."

"And where is Fred in all of this?" Rory asked as Mia reached forward to grab a couple of grapes.

"He texted me about fifteen minutes before you both arrived," Das said. "In fact, I was just getting ready to call you when my buzzer rang. Apparently, he had a dinner obligation in Zürich tonight that he couldn't avoid, but he would like to meet with both of you first thing tomorrow morning."

"Why the hell is he still in Zürich?" Rory replied in frustration. "Doesn't he realize what happened today in the US? If Kota's model is right, the markets will go into total meltdown mode tomorrow. By Monday or Tuesday, it could be game over."

Mia looked a bit quizzically at Rory. He turned toward her and said, "A three-percent move in one trading session just shouldn't happen anymore. It's practically a crash, the statistical equivalent of a ten-percent drop prior to ICARUS. Something is seriously wrong."

Das picked up the explanation. "And the entire world now knows it. If traders, pension plans, and other investors start to lose faith in ICARUS, they'll lose faith in the market. People will start to worry about the solvency of the banking system just like they did in '08. The credit markets will freeze up. Overnight lending will stop, and we'll start to see bankruptcies. At that point it will be too late."

Das paused to sip his Quöllfrisch. Rory concluded the lesson. "Right now, every money manager from here to Hong Kong is figuring out how much they can sell to de-risk at tomorrow's open. Nobody is looking to buy. Hell, there are no buyers. Except for Milt and the few opportunistic traders left out there, all the big money is already fully invested. There's no cash on the sidelines. This market is fragile as a Fabergé egg."

Mia, an incredulous look on her face, said, "I can't believe everything can go from roses to complete collapse in a matter of days."

"Markets take the stairs up and the elevator down," Rory said as he placed his beer on the table. "In today's world, bank runs go viral, traders move with lightning speed, and everything is interconnected. If this isn't stopped soon, and I mean by Monday, maybe Tuesday at the latest, we're looking at a global financial meltdown that likely leads to a depression, maybe worse."

This time it was Das who looked quizzically at Rory. "What's worse than a global financial collapse that leads to depression?"

Rory shifted his gaze from Mia to Das. Without a trace of hyperbole, he replied, "War."

Das shifted somewhat uncomfortably in his seat. There was something about Rory's gaze that sent a slight chill up his spine. "War? What are you talking about?" Das asked.

Rory pointed out the apartment window toward the BIS tower visible in the distance. "You know why that place was founded, right? Why the Bank for International Settlements was created?"

Das knew something of the bank's history, as did most who worked there, but he had never given it too much thought. He said, "Something to do with collecting reparations from Germany after the First World War."

"That's right," Rory said. "It was formed in 1930 after the crash in '29 to help ensure the payment of reparations from Germany to the UK, US, France, and Belgium, but the payments never really came. They were suspended just one year later because of a depression that started with a stock market crash in New York on Black Thursday."

"And how does that lead to war?" Mia asked.

"Before the crash, the Nazis were a laughable fringe party garnering less than three percent of the vote in the 1928 German elections. But once unemployment and inflation hit, they quickly became the nation's most popular party, winning almost forty percent of the vote in '32. Hitler was appointed chancellor the next year. The path towards World War II had begun."

"I guess I never really thought about it like that," Das said.

"Well, most people don't. But economics drives politics as much as the other way around, maybe more so." Rory stood from the couch and walked toward Das's window. "We've never really had a true financial collapse since the Great Depression. We came close in '08 and '09, but the financial system was more resilient then."

"How so?" Das asked, interested in hearing more of Rory's perspective.

"Back then, the system was prepared for shocks, or at least knew that they could happen. And the global central banks were able to swoop in and bail everyone out while the mess got cleaned up on companies' balance sheets. But now it's the Fed's balance sheet that is in trouble, and with the Phoenix Act, it will only get worse. The financial infrastructure simply isn't in place anymore to do anything about a real collapse."

Das conceded Rory's point. "It's definitely a scary proposition. I guess anything is possible."

"It is," Rory said. "It might not be Germany this time, but there are more than enough global hot spots that could act as the spark igniting the next major conflict." He pulled the thumb drive out from his right pant pocket and held it up. "But we may be able to stop it right here, right now. Every hour, every minute we wait, we get that much closer to financial Armageddon."

"What are you suggesting?" Das asked.

"What I'm suggesting"—Rory pointed with the drive in hand toward the window and the BIS headquarters—"is that we head over to that tower right now, upload this fuckin' thing into ICARUS, and get the encryption cracked ASAP. We can worry about explaining our actions to Fred tomorrow, if he even shows up."

The three looked at each other as Rory placed the drive on the table before Mia and Das. It lay flat between a bowl of grapes and three bottles of Quöllfrisch.

"We need you, Das," Rory pleaded. "We can't get in there without you, and I don't know the first thing about cracking any encryption, let alone a lattice-based one. What do you say?"

Das stood and walked to the window. He stared out at the BIS tower. Three floors below the monumental concrete edifice lay a sprawling sub-level, temperature controlled with the most advanced supercomputer the world had ever known. Das didn't think about money or the markets. Instead, he thought about Father Ricardo and his time at St. Joseph's. Das knew Rory might be right. This could get out of hand very quickly, and the people most hurt by it wouldn't be bankers at Goldman Sachs or JP Morgan. It would be people like Das's father, street vendors and the poor who toil every day just to put bread on the table.

He turned back around to face Rory and Mia. "What are we waiting for?"

CHAPTER 29

Beijing, China

IT WAS STILL THURSDAY NIGHT in Basel, but in Beijing, Friday's sun was due to rise in less than an hour. Zhao Hong had arrived at his office early to catch up on overnight market action in the United States. A knowing grin crossed his face as headlines from the Financial News Network scrolled across the flat screen hung in his office.

So, it has begun.

Zhao's office in the Xicheng District was sprawling but sparce. Hanging on the walls, along with the TV, were a framed Chinese flag and two portraits, one of Mao Zedong and one of his wife's uncle Wang Jun, the nation's current leader. Zhao muted the TV, picked up his secure office phone, and leaned back in his sturdy but unostentatious wooden chair, a gift from Wang that Zhao felt was also meant to be a reminder: don't get too comfortable in your role as head of the PBoC.

He punched in the digits for Anton Golev's encrypted cell.

"*Da?*"

Zhao replied in fluent Russian, "Comrade Golev, how are you this evening? It is still evening for you, correct?"

"Yes, Zhao, it is evening. I'm in Zürich and enjoying a late dinner of roast duck, which you are now disturbing. Now, what do you want?"

Zhao had become accustomed to Golev's gruffness and replied, "I'm sorry to disturb you, but we need to talk. Are you somewhere you can speak freely?"

"Yes, I'm alone in my suite at the Dolder Grand hotel. Speak."

"Very well. I'll dispense with the pleasantries, then. I want to know if you have the drive."

"Not yet."

"Well, what are you waiting for? That trader and his girlfriend have been in Basel all day."

With the market's recent drop, Zhao's anxiety was heightened. He knew that without a properly functioning ICARUS, the financial collapse that had already begun could quickly spiral beyond even their control.

"My men are on it."

"What's that supposed to mean?"

"We've searched their hotel rooms. O'Connor and the woman took the drive with them when they headed out for the night." Golev laughed, then added, "I thought the Chinese were supposed to be a patient people."

"We are, but in this case, time is of the essence. We need ICARUS up and running by Monday if we've any hope of staving off a complete meltdown."

Zhao heard some chewing sounds. *Must be a succulent duck.*

After a moment, Golev asked, "Have you ever snared a rabbit?"

"A rabbit? No."

"When I spent winters with my grandfather in northern Russia, we set snares every evening along all the paths that we knew rabbits liked to travel."

"What is your point?" Zhao asked in exasperation.

"My point is there is no need to go chasing after this rabbit. He will come to us. The trader is an American. Like you, he will not show any patience either. We know that he has the drive, and Frederik has not yet returned to Basel. Without access to ICARUS, he will surely try to break into the BIS tonight."

Zhao thought that sounded plausible but definitely not certain. "Are you sure?"

"*Da*, comrade Zhao. I am sure."

"How can you be so confident?"

"Let's just say I have set my snares in all the right places." Golev offered no more color or assurances. He simply said, "Now, if you'll excuse me, my duck is getting cold."

The phone went silent. Zhao looked out his window. An array of lights flittered on in homes and offices across Beijing just as the sun's rays began cracking open the darkness of night. He decided he would just have to trust Golev on this. He had delivered on his promises in the past, and there was no reason to doubt him now. Zhao was also confident Golev was not telling him everything, but that was to be expected when dealing with a man like him.

Not more than a minute later, Zhao's office phone rang, breaking him away from his thoughts and the silence of dawn.

He picked up the receiver. "*Wei.*"

"Is that you, partner?"

Zhao immediately recognized the unmistakable forced southern twang of Senator Matthew Whitlock. "How may I help you, Senator?"

"Zhao, Phoenix is now law. How did you put it when we last saw each other? Something about my remaining compensation arriving on my doorstep once the act is signed? Well, I'm in DC right now, but sure as shit I know that gold you owe me has yet to arrive at the Bear's Den."

Zhao had been expecting this call. In fact, he was surprised he didn't get it five minutes after the president signed the bill into law. "It will be there soon. I assure you."

Zhao lied. He had no intention of delivering ten more tons of gold to the arrogant American. Indeed, he loathed giving Whitlock every ounce of the first shipment just to get a bill passed that likely would have gone through fine on its own. But there was too much at stake to simply trust the American political process. *Better to hold it over his head*, Zhao thought, *at least until the SAGE Act is passed.*

Whitlock raised the tone of his voice, "Have you seen the markets here? They reacted quicker than we expected. The financial press is already connecting Phoenix to the sell-off today. I'm going to have a lot to answer for this. It's not going to be easy to turn this ship around and get Congress to support a precious metals–backed digital currency."

"Yes," Zhao said in a false, placating tone, "I understand. Your services are greatly appreciated. I have no doubt that under your leadership, the SAGE Act will pass. Now, is there something more you wanted, or did you just call to demand your gold?"

"Listen to me, Zhao. I may have led that bill through the Senate, but in my country, the president gets all the credit and all the blame for what happens, whether she deserves it or not. When the dust settles on this mess, Norton will be sweatin' like a whore in church. She won't have a prayer for reelection, but you know who does have a chance at the Oval Office? The man who is going to return this county to financial stability. It's still not too late for me to get into the race. Hell, the first primary is still three months away. I would be very careful how you speak to me. You might be talkin' to the next POTUS."

"President, is it? So, that's what you're after. You know, we tend to be very significant contributors to your elections via our networks of political action committees and wealthy donors. You could even get some help from Golev and the Russians on your social media campaigns. They're very good at that I hear."

"Touché, Zhao. Now just get me my fuckin' gold. Soon!" Senator Whitlock ended the call.

Well, Zhao thought, *an eventful morning already.* He unmuted the flat screen just as the sun began to shine in earnest, illuminating his office in a soft yellow glow. FNN's coverage had shifted from the United States to Asia. The opening bells in Hong Kong and Shanghai would be ringing soon.

CHAPTER 30

Basel, Switzerland

THURSDAY, NOVEMBER 4, 2027

THE BIS TOWER WAS NOT exactly the Emerald City, but Rory, Mia, and Das were indeed plotting a trip to Quoz. Still in Das's flat, they needed to map out a game plan if they were going to successfully access ICARUS without Frederik's permission.

Das asked, "Do you still have your visitor's badges, the plastic ones with blue stripes on the right side and your pictures on them?"

"Yes, I have mine here," Mia said as she pulled the badge from her handbag.

"I think mine is back at the hotel. Why?" Rory asked.

"Those badges are good for the entire day, until midnight. They'll still work to get you past the turnstiles. But that's the easy part. Getting all three of us into Quoz won't be as simple."

"Quoz?" Mia asked.

"Sublevel three, the core of ICARUS," Rory said, then reached for his Quöllfrisch.

Das elaborated, "The ICARUS mainframe takes up an entire sublevel, and it's quite the sight. Trust me, you'll see why we call it Quoz when we get there, assuming I can get us in without half of BIS security descending on us."

The trio left the apartment and headed to the hotel to get Rory's badge. The Hôtel Les Trois Rois sits perched on the Rhine in the center of Basel. A historic and well-known city landmark, there are records of a hotel on the site dating back to 1681. Everyone from Napoleon to

Queen Elizabeth II to the Dalai Lama has spent time at the Hotel of the Three Kings.

They entered the hotel through the main entrance. A large open space greeted them with a classic old-world chandelier overhead. Rory and Mia's rooms were on the second floor, and a sweeping grand staircase gave them easy access. The dimly lit hall had small wooden side tables every ten meters or so on which lamps, books, and the occasional bowl of complimentary potato chips sat.

What's with these chips? Rory thought as he approached his room, Mia and Das following closely behind. Suddenly Rory stopped short. Mia almost stepped on his heel.

"What is it?" she asked.

Rory pointed to the slender space that separated the old wooden door from the carpeted floor of the hallway. A shaft of light emitted from under the door. Rory then said in a whisper, "I didn't leave any lights on."

"Maybe a maid stopped by, turndown service or something?" Mia suggested hopefully.

"Possible," Rory said. But after what happened to him in Chicago, he wasn't prepared to make that assumption.

An old and heavy-looking brass lamp rested on a nearby side table in the hall. The stem of the lamp stand was circular, about the diameter of a baseball bat, and the base was hexagon shaped, approximately eight inches across. Rory wrapped his right hand around the stem and felt its weight. *Yeah, this should work.* He quickly unplugged the lamp from its socket and unscrewed the shade off the top. He then unscrewed the bulb and wrapped the cord around its base. Holding the roughly fifteen-inch-long lamp stand in his hand like a club, Rory felt comfortable that he could do some serious damage if necessary.

He held his credit card–like key up to the modern locking mechanism and slowly opened the door. Peering inside, it appeared as if no one was there, but signs that someone had been were obvious, and it wasn't the maid for turndown service. His clothes were strewn all over his bed.

His suitcase lay open and on its side on the floor. Various drawers had been pulled open but not shut.

Rory crept slowly past the threshold, lamp stand raised in his right hand. First, he checked the bathroom, then the closet. Finally, he glanced under his bed as Mia and Das peered into the room from the doorway.

"It's clear," Rory said. "Whoever was here is gone now."

Rory walked toward the double door connecting his room to Mia's. The door on his side had been closed and locked when he left but now was slightly ajar. The lamp stand cocked back in his hand, Rory pulled his door open and found the second connecting door, the one on Mia's side, swung wide open. He surveyed a similar scene. Lights were on, and Mia's clothes and personal belongings were scattered across her disheveled bed. Her suitcase lay open on the floor near the bathroom. After a check of the closet, bathroom, and under the bed, Rory sat the lamp stand down on an end table near Mia's bed and once again gave the all clear.

Mia walked over to her bed and began sorting through the clothes. "They went through my underwear. Fucking perverts."

Rory paced about both rooms, examining the shake-up and getting angrier the more he thought about thugs sifting through his and Mia's things. He stopped in the center of his room and called for Mia and Das. "Listen, guys, we now know that there's a group of people after Pete's drive. It wasn't just a couple random criminals looking for a quick score in Chicago. And whoever these people are, they are committed and have the resources to track Mia and me halfway around the world. We need to start being very careful with everything we do and say. Are you both sure you want to go to the tower tonight?"

"I think we have to," Das said. "Besides, the tower may be the safest place for us. It's protected by armed guards and under surveillance. There's no way anyone can get at us in there."

Mia thought for a moment, then responded, "I'm not sure we have a choice either. These people aren't going to stop."

"But who the hell are 'these people'?" Rory asked in frustration and exhaustion as he fell back onto his bed, jet lag and lack of sleep beginning to set in.

He got no response. After a moment, he sat up in the bed and turned his attention toward Das. "And here's another thing I just can't figure out. The market just had its worst day ever since ICARUS came online. Plus, Mia and I are here, in Basel, with what could be critical information, but Fred is nowhere to be found. How long could he be meeting with the head of the Swiss central bank? It doesn't make sense."

Das took a seat, cleared his throat, then said, "There's more going on here than just a glitch in ICARUS's code. I didn't say anything earlier because, well, I'm not really sure exactly what's going on. But I think you both need to know."

"What is it?" Rory asked, annoyed and angered that Das had been holding back.

"I don't think we should sit around here and discuss it. The people who did this could come back. Let's start heading to the BIS. I'll fill you both in along the way."

Rory conceded to Das's reasoning, and the three prepared to leave the room. Before Mia reached the door, she said, "Don't forget," and pointed to the dresser in Rory's room. Sitting on top of it was his BIS visitor's badge.

Rory walked over to the dresser, grabbed the badge, and took one last look around the room. More confused than frightened, he walked out the door and joined Mia and Das waiting in the hall. It was time to get some answers. It was time to break into Quoz.

CHAPTER 31

Basel, Switzerland
Thursday, November 4, 2027

Stars overhead, Rory, Mia, and Das walked in silence. They moved away from historic central Basel and into a more modern section of town. It was a kilometer and a half to the BIS, and cross-corner from the tower, they stopped at De-Wette Park. A small, rectangular-shaped green space, the park included a large memorial statue commemorating Swiss relief efforts to help French civilians during the Franco-Prussian War.

The trio found some seats. Das broke the silence. "Okay, this should be fairly simple. We walk in, and I'll wave hello to the guard. You two already have your badges, so we just stroll past and make our way through the turnstiles, no questions asked. Then, we head to my office on fourteen. From there, we can avoid elevator cameras and take stairs down to Quoz."

"Understood," Rory said. "Now, what about these suspicions you have?"

"I didn't say suspicions. They are more speculations," Das responded nervously.

"Whatever the hell they are, what is it?" asked Rory.

Das leaned in closer toward Rory and Mia, his breath slightly visible in the late-night chill. "When I took over as chief engineer, I started to learn more about the trade execution aspect of ICARUS, how the money actually moves and transacts in the market. In theory, ICARUS was supposed to intervene only occasionally, a few buys or sells made at key points such as when a stock approached an important moving average or trend line. But that wasn't what I saw happening. ICARUS was constantly buying and selling in huge amounts but spread over millions of minuscule trades."

"Exactly," Rory said, "very-high-frequency trading. Kota and I saw it in his data, but there was no way to know for sure who was behind the trades."

"Well, it's ICARUS," replied Das.

"So, what does that mean?" Mia asked, rubbing her bare hands together for warmth.

Das glanced over his right shoulder and took note of an older woman approaching with her dog, then said, "It means that at the end of the day, ICARUS has just been manipulating prices through brute force." Das paused for a moment as the woman and her dog walked past, then continued in a hushed tone, "I'm talking about an astronomical amount of buys and sells. By my rough estimates, ICARUS has invested at least a trillion dollars to control the markets. In the process, the BIS has racked up hundreds of billions in losses. I have no idea where the money is coming from. The bank has substantial reserves but nothing like what we've been losing."

After his afternoon meeting with Das, Rory had suspected that the BIS was behind the uptick in HFT activity but had no idea it approached such magnitude. "What does Fred say about all this?" he asked.

"He just refers me to Karl von Hoffman. Beside taking over your old post as head of trading, he's also been in charge of treasury operations ever since Sara Schnyder left."

"Interesting," Rory said. "That reminds me, what the hell happened to Sara? When Mia and I first arrived, the guard told us she was no longer with the bank."

"She quit months ago, working on some new crypto venture in Zug or maybe Luzern. I'm not sure exactly, but I know she's still in Switzerland."

Across the street from the park, a tram rattled across its tracks as Rory processed this new information. Things had definitely changed at the BIS since Peter's death, and Frederik's dallying in Zürich only looked more suspicious. *Can I trust Fred and Karl?* he wondered. *Can I trust Das? Hell, can I trust anyone?*

Rory turned his gaze toward BIS headquarters just two hundred yards from where they now sat and said, "We can't rely on anyone in that tower. Now, let's get going. It's fucking cold out here."

"You've been in Puerto Rico too long," Mia commented as the three stood to make their way to the quasi-sovereign territory of the Bank for International Settlements.

Minutes later, they entered the tower. All three scanned their badges and got through the entry turnstiles without a word from the guard. *Almost too easy*, Rory thought as they took the elevator to the fourteenth floor. They then entered the stairwell, mindful of avoiding security cameras where possible. After arriving at sublevel three, they entered a small hallway. On their right was a steel door with a sign above it that read RESTRICTED ACCESS.

Das led them to the door, stopped, and entered a series of numbers into the security panel. "Welcome to Quoz," he said as the three walked into the large, imposing space.

The circular design of the BIS tower lent itself perfectly to a hub-and-spoke design for ICARUS. In the center of the room was a large chamber completely encased in thick, bulletproof, and blast-resistant glass. It was hermetically sealed and kept at a constant temperature of 0 degrees Fahrenheit. Inside the chamber sat the CQPU or central quantum processing unit. The core of the CQPU was kept much, much colder, less than one degree above absolute zero, approximately minus 459 Fahrenheit. The super-cooled core needed the ultra-low temperature in order to maintain quantum stability. Its revolutionary quantum gates placed electrons in superposition and leveraged Heisenberg's uncertainty principle to run multiple calculations simultaneously.

It also required absolute stillness. While not a hotbed of seismic activity, Basel does have a history of earthquakes. Indeed, on October 18, 1356, the largest known quake to hit Central Europe had its epicenter less than ten miles from where the tower now stood. Known as the

Earthquake of Saint Luke, it wreaked havoc with fires and destruction from Paris to Prague. The city of Basel was completely destroyed. As a guard against such movements, the chamber that held ICARUS was built on highly sensitive stabilizers that could hold the compartment absolutely still through tremors via an automatic adjustment platform. It could counteract the slightest movement with shifts from a fraction of a millimeter to a dozen centimeters, all calibrated in microseconds.

There were also specially designed green LED lights that produced almost no heat and illuminated the entire sublevel in an emerald glow. Inside ICARUS, an amalgam of open-source and proprietary software combined with the latest in high-tech hardware to power a one-of-a-kind quantum neural network. Like tentacles from some AI-fueled kraken, eight thickly encased conduit pipes wired the CQPU to various server banks and conventional computing systems that encircled ICARUS's core.

Against the outer wall, in a gap between the server banks, sat another bulletproof glass–encased chamber—the Hive. It was the central control room where man met machine. Das walked up to the Hive's door and punched in another numeric code. With a slight hiss from the breaking of the airtight seal, the door popped open a fraction of an inch. As it did so, another set of green lights illuminated the space in the same eerie iridescent glow.

"This place is incredible," Mia said as she removed her coat and placed it on the back of a chair.

"It certainly is," Das agreed. "A real-life Emerald City."

Unlike the CQPU core, the Hive was kept at a temperature more pleasant to humans, precisely 72 degrees. It contained a large arching panel array with a combination of touch screens, monitors, and keyboards. Half a dozen USB ports had been built into the desk, as well as deep cup holders to ensure that no coffee mug or bottle of water accidentally tipped over and onto the plethora of diagnostic and operational hardware.

There were three chairs in front of the main control panel. A small refrigerator sat in the corner of the room with bottled waters as well as some sodas and energy drinks. Other than that, the room was bare and meticulously clean, free from dust or other contaminants. The air was devoid of odor and perfectly still except for a gentle draft emanating from temperature-controlled purifiers that had been built into the bottom section of the rear wall.

Rory pulled the thumb drive from his pocket, handed it to Das, and said, "Well, let's see what we're dealing with here."

Das sat down in the center chair, typed in some commands, and then inserted the drive into one of the available USB ports. As he worked, Rory and Mia watched the screens intently. After a few minutes, Das muttered something that they couldn't understand. Was that in Kannada? Rory wondered, referring to Das's mother tongue.

After a few tense minutes, Das finally spoke. Pressing his chair back from the control panel, he said, "It's not going to be easy, but I can do this." He then got up to grab a bottle of water, reminiscent of an exhausted runner after a long race.

"Well, how long?" Rory asked.

"With the best conventional supercomputers available, about 17.8 million years give or take a few millennia. With ICARUS, two, maybe three days. It's tough to be more exact at this point. Once the decryption program starts running, I'll be able to give a better estimate."

Das pulled the drive from its USB port and handed it back to Rory. "The folder has been downloaded into the mainframe. Don't need this anymore."

"So, what's next?" Mia asked.

Das said, "Now I spend the next few hours getting this thing to purr. It'll take some time. I need to complete and fine-tune the decryption program, then double-check for bugs. I'll do my best to bury its operation in the background, but if someone knows what they're looking for, they'll be able to tell the program is running. Then we get the hell out of here before anyone notices we're down here."

Rory found an empty spot against one of the walls. He slumped down to the floor, his back against the thick glass, and draped Peter's old coat over his knees like a blanket. "Don't be offended, Das. I'm sure you're about to perform some quantum AI magic, but I'm exhausted. Just wake me if you need anything."

"No offense taken," Das replied.

Mia got up from her chair as well and made her way to the same spot against the wall. She sat down next to Rory, closed her eyes, and rested her head on his shoulder. She slid her left arm behind Rory and wrapped her right arm tight around his waist. Rory closed his tired eyes and rested his head atop Mia's chestnut hair, the faint smell of coconut now discernible in the otherwise pristine air.

CHAPTER 32

Basel, Switzerland

FRIDAY, NOVEMBER 5, 2027

DAS NUDGED RORY AND MIA. "Rise and shine."

Completely knocked out by the combination of jet lag, lack of sleep, and stress, the two slowly raised their heads and opened their eyes, both appearing as if they needed a moment to get their bearings.

"Where the hell are we? The starship *Enterprise*?" Mia said jokingly.

"Precisely," Das replied. "Over there is the antimatter chamber, and I just got our warp capabilities back. Now, it's time to get the hell out of here."

Rory stood and reached his hand down to help Mia up, then pulled out his phone to check the time. It was almost 6:00 a.m. "Jesus, how long were we out?" he asked, looking at Das.

"Over six hours. It took longer than anticipated to rig this thing. I don't have a lot of experience with lattice-based decryption. In fact, nobody does."

"Good point," Rory said. "What about the timing? Can you give us a better estimate now?"

"I set up a progress bar." Das punched in a couple commands on the main access panel. A screen appeared displaying a nearly empty graphical bar. Below the bar, it read, "0.41% Complete, ETD: 64 hours, 44 minutes."

"ETD?" Rory asked.

"Estimated time to decryption," Das said. "It's running around one percent every forty minutes. Fingers crossed, we'll have access to the file sometime around 23:00 Sunday."

"That long?" Mia asked.

Das smiled. "I wasn't kidding earlier when I estimated 17.8 million years for a conventional computer. ICARUS is running that program at close to three hundred EFLOPS."

"EFLOPS?" Mia asked.

Das explained, "FLOPS are a measure of computing speed, floating point operations per second. One petaflop is a quadrillion operations per second. That's a one with fifteen zeros after it. The best digital super-computers in the world are lucky to break a thousand petaflops. An exa-flop or EFLOP is one thousand petaflops. ICARUS is running at close to three hundred EFLOPS. The fact it can crack lattice-based encryption at all is amazing, let alone in less than three days."

"I know you did your best," Mia said. "I meant no offense. And thank you. Finding out what Pete has on that drive means a lot to me."

"None taken." Das cleared out the progress graphic. The screens returned to their default state. The trio then put their coats back on, and Rory opened the control room door.

As they began to file out, Mia stopped in her tracks. "What's that?"

"Sounds like footsteps," Das said. Footfalls were clearly audible and getting louder with every step.

Before any of them could react further, a figure emerged from the green glow.

"Das, what is going on here?" a loud, stern voice with a thick German accent demanded to know. It was Karl von Hoffman, right-hand man to Frederik and current head of trading and treasury. He was dressed in a three-button, European-cut, forest-green tweed jacket with elbow patches, a white button-down shirt, and blue jeans. Karl was an imposing figure. Broad-shouldered and slightly taller than Rory, his dusty brown hair was perfectly parted to the side, his prominent chin covered by a well-manicured goatee.

"Ah, um, Karl, this is, uh, Rory O'Connor and Mia Costello, Peter's sister," Das replied.

"I've seen yesterday's visitor log. I know who they are. What I asked is what is going on. Why are they here, with you, at six in the morning?

You know visitors are not allowed in Quoz without express permission from Frederik, regardless of their past affiliations with the project." Karl's eyes stared disapprovingly toward Das and Rory. Then he turned to Mia and said in a slightly less condemning tone, "I don't know what these two told you, but this is a highly restricted area. I'm afraid I will have to detain all three of you until Frederik arrives."

Rory erupted. "Detain us? In case you didn't see yesterday's market action, ICARUS has some major fucking issues right now!"

"I'm well aware of the situation. Why do you think I'm here at this hour? Nevertheless, you are coming with me." Karl pulled his phone from his pocket and called up to security. He spoke for a moment in German and then placed the phone back in his pocket.

"You're a real asshole, you know that?" Rory said, stepping closer to Karl and considering a good punch to the gut just as he had done with McGrady.

Mia stepped between them. She placed her hand on Rory's shoulder and turned toward Karl. "We understand," she said and turned her face toward Rory and Das, giving them a look as if to say that now is not the time or place for a fight.

Karl walked toward the control panel. He began working the touch screens and punching in commands via the keyboard. Das nervously rubbed his right hand on his hip as he said, "Rory and Mia brought some data modeling from the States. Kota Nakazawa did it. You remember Kota, right, Karl? He was head of data science until Jean-Pierre took it over." Karl gave no response and continued his scan of the system. Das continued anxiously, "We were just trying to confirm some of the anomalies that Kota identified. It's quite interesting, actually."

Rory also wanted to distract Karl from the control panel. Trying a different approach, he said, "Look, Karl, I know us being down here isn't standard operating procedure, but what we've identified is very serious. We need to speak with Fred as soon as possible."

Paying no attention, Karl continued his investigation, then stopped and turned toward Das. "What the hell is this?"

Das looked over at one of the screens. It was the progress bar. Apparently, he had not done as good a job covering his tracks as promised. Karl had located the decryption program.

"Ah, oh that, that's just something I have running in the background. It's nothing," Das replied.

"It doesn't look like nothing, it says here, '0.69% Complete, ETD: 64 hours, 33 minutes.'"

Rory interjected, "Das, don't say anything. We'll talk to Fred about this once he arrives."

Karl quickly turned his attention away from the panel and snapped, "Don't worry. You'll be seeing Frederik soon enough."

A moment later Hans Guzman arrived at the door to the Hive. The head of BIS security, Hans had been with the organization for over a decade and immediately recognized Rory. The two had seen one another on various occasions but had never spoken beyond pleasantries.

Karl turned his attention from Rory to Hans and said, "Das brought these two down here without authorization. Please escort them all to the holding room until Herr d'Oultremont arrives."

As an autonomous compound, the tower maintained a small holding room. It amounted to a luxury prison cell that could be locked and unlocked only from the outside. It had no windows and was located on the lowest sublevel, one floor below Quoz. Other than as a place for exhausted BIS staffers to crash on late nights, it was rarely used.

Rory was furious but didn't believe resisting would help their cause. He and the rest of the group exited the restricted area. Their eyes, accustomed to the eerie green glow of Quoz, were assaulted by the bright fluorescent lights of the hallway. They made their way down one flight of stairs to sublevel four. Hans escorted Rory, Mia, and Das into the holding room. It contained a table, couch, two chairs, and a small, private half bath.

Fred will straighten this out, Rory thought as Hans turned and exited. But as the click of the dead bolt echoed against the concrete of the holding room walls, he began to wonder if that would really be the case.

CHAPTER 33

Fresnillo, Mexico
FRIDAY, NOVEMBER 5, 2027

FOUR HOUR'S DRIVE NORTH OF Guadalajara, in the Mexican state of Zacatecas, sits its capital and largest city, Fresnillo. A haven for cartel activity, Fresnillo often endures over a hundred homicides per month despite its relatively small population of around 140,000. Along with one of the highest per capita murder rates on the planet, Fresnillo and the surrounding area are also home to some of the largest silver reserves in the world. The Peñasquito Mine alone, located some thirty-five miles south of Fresnillo, has proven reserves approaching one billion troy ounces. Combined with the other mines in Zacatecas and surrounding states, the Sierra Madre mountains of central Mexico are the epicenter of modern-day silver production. Besides silver, the area also produces some of the finest mezcal on the planet.

Javier Delgado owned not only several large silver mines but also one of the grandest agave plantations in Zacatecas. Casa Luna, located on a sprawling twelve thousand acres just south of the pueblo of El Cristo, included his working farm, processing facilities, a large distillery, and a luxury hacienda replete with Olympic-size swimming pool, tennis courts, and a slightly undersized bull ring.

Sitting stoically at one end of a large wooden table located on a covered veranda just off the main hacienda, Delgado sipped on a fine mezcal as he tried to size up the studious-looking man opposite him, Arun Patel. The mild-mannered central banker from India was dressed in tan slacks and shirt, only missing the safari-style cap to complete the look of an English gentleman on the plains of Africa. A medium-size brown leather travel bag rested on the ground next to his chair. Delgado's men had searched the bag prior to Patel even stepping foot onto the grounds of Casa Luna.

"So, Señor Patel, how can I be of service?" Delgado stated in perfect English with just a touch of his proud Mexican accent. A handsome man in his mid-fifties with graying hair and a broad chest, Delgado could trace his roots back to Madrid. Hundreds of years ago, a royal land grant ceded to his ancestors a broad swath of central Mexico. Educated first in mine engineering at the Universidad Nacional Autónoma de México and then in business at Yale, Delgado was as unscrupulous as he was charming. With the suave presence of an urbane aristocrat, he also harbored a capacity for ruthlessness that rivaled his silent partners, bosses from CJNG and CDS, the Cártel de Jalisco Nueva Generación and Cártel de Sinaloa, respectively. Both cartels were currently involved in a bloody battle for control of the entire Zacatecas region, and Delgado played both sides, maintaining high-level connections within each organization.

"Thank you for seeing me on such short notice," Patel replied with his customary twinge of a British accent.

"Of course. It is my pleasure." Delgado reached for a finely crafted leather cigar case on the table and held it up in offer to Patel.

"No, thank you," Patel declined as Delgado pulled a hand-rolled Cuban from the case. Niceties exchanged, Patel cut to the heart of the matter. "I have the final paperwork here for you to sign."

As Delgado proceeded to snip and then light the cigar, Patel reached into his travel bag and produced a three-inch-thick binder. He explained, "Everything is in order, Mr. Delgado, just as agreed. Beginning next week, my buyer, through various holding companies, will become your sole customer. He agrees to purchase as much silver as you can produce at a price fifteen percent below the day's spot price in London at 15:00 GMT. In return for this potential discount, my buyer guarantees you a minimum rate of thirty dollars per ounce regardless of the spot price."

Why would anyone agree to such a contract? Delgado wondered. Silver rarely traded above thirty dollars an ounce. The only way this arrangement made sense would be if the buyer was very confident silver would trade above that level on a consistent basis.

"Yes, very well. I will have my attorneys review everything, which I am sure is in order, then sign the documents and have them overnighted to your offices in Mumbai. I am curious, however. Who is this mystery buyer? Surely you understand, I cannot make an arrangement of this consequence and not know with whom I am dealing."

"I'm sorry," Patel said, "but I am not at liberty to say."

"Ah, but you will say, Señor Patel." Delgado puffed once more on his cigar before gently cradling it in a nearby marble ashtray embossed with silver. He leaned forward and said, "Perhaps you do not understand. You will tell me the name of the buyer, or those documents will never be signed."

Patel took a nervous glance around the veranda. Three armed guards stood against the outside wall of the main hacienda. Two held assault rifles, the other stared menacingly with his pistol holstered.

Patel dipped into his travel bag once more. He pulled out a pen and small pad of paper, then hastily scribbled for a few seconds. Ripping the top sheet from the pad, he rose from his chair and asked Delgado in a congenial tone, "May I approach?"

Delgado took a sip of his mezcal, made eye contact with the man with the holstered pistol, and then nodded at Patel.

Patel walked slowly along the right side of the table. Stopping about a yard short of Delgado, he slid the paper down the table and in front of him.

Very interesting, Delgado thought as he read the name Patel had written. He then reached for his lighter and rolled the spark wheel, holding the flame directly below the small piece of paper. It caught quickly in the warm, dry air. Delgado laid the burning paper in the ashtray, then picked up his cigar and took another puff as the name Frederik d'Oultremont III went up in a cloud of dark gray smoke.

CHAPTER 34

Basel, Switzerland
FRIDAY, NOVEMBER 5, 2027

THE SUN HUNG LOW IN the November sky, and patchy clouds had begun to roll in from the Alps. Rory, Mia, and Das exited the twelfth-floor elevator, escorted from the holding room by Hans Guzman, head of BIS security. As they walked toward the same conference room where they had gathered the day before, Rory looked forward with some trep-idation to seeing Frederik d'Oultremont for the first time since arriving in Switzerland.

Hans held the door open for his prisoners/guests, then excused him-self. The refreshment cart still sat in the corner, fully stocked with cof-fee, tea, and assorted pastries. Unlike last time, however, the room was already occupied. Frederik sat legs crossed at the head of the table. He wore black pants with a checkered, red-and-blue button-down shirt. His strawberry-blond hair was meticulously parted to one side.

"Please, take a seat. But first, help yourselves to some refreshment," Frederik suggested as he rose from his chair and made his way to shake Rory's and Mia's hands.

Das prepared himself a tea, and Rory and Mia each poured them-selves a coffee. They then all sat around the table, Frederik with an orange Danish on a small plate in front of him.

"These are quite good, you know. Sure you won't have some-thing to eat?"

"I'm fine," Rory replied. "I think we have more to important things to discuss than pastries."

"Quite right," Frederik agreed. "Like a true American, ready for business. Very well, then, explain yourselves. Why were you in Quoz?"

"I'm referring to the market sell-off yesterday," Rory said. He looked intently, almost through Frederik and out the windows behind him. The clouds rolling in from the south were a dark gray, laden with precipitation. A storm system was making its way toward Basel.

Frederik did not reply. Instead, he reached for his Danish and took a small bite. Das used the pause to break the tension and respond to Frederik's original query. "Rory and Mia brought in some very interesting work done by Kota back in Chicago. Brilliant, really. We were just trying to confirm the findings with ICARUS."

"And Rory, you and Mia flew all this way just to share Kota's work?" Frederik asked.

Rory recalled hearing once that when being questioned it is best not to respond to the interrogator's questions. Rather, best practice is to deny everything and make counteraccusations. *Was that on the Discovery Channel, maybe a Bond movie?* In any case, he knew Frederik would not buy that he came all this way just to show Kota's model to Das.

Rory decided to place a couple of his cards on the table. "So, you want explanations, huh, Fred? Well, how about you explain this to me. Kota's model shows extremely elevated levels of high-frequency trading activity. I'm talking ten, twelve times the average daily volume. Everything I've seen points to huge positions taken by the BIS via ICARUS on both the long and short side. Can you explain this?"

Frederik didn't blink an eye. He said calmly, "There have been some difficulties keeping volatility in line with parameters. That much is certainly true. ICARUS has required, how should I say this, a bit more intervention in the markets than anticipated." Frederik uncrossed his legs and leaned forward across the table, staring directly at Rory. "We are changing the world here. You can't expect to do that without some hiccups along the way."

"So, a trillion dollars of buy and sell orders is now a hiccup, ah, Fred? Where the hell is that money coming from? The BIS can't float that much coin."

Frederik said nothing and took another bite of his Danish. Rory continued, "There's something else too. I almost had my head blown off barely three days ago. And yesterday someone broke into our hotel rooms. Do you know anything about that, *Fred-e-rik*?" Rory made certain to apply the full Dutch pronunciation to his name.

Again, Frederik said nothing. Instead, he pushed his chair back from the conference room table and walked around to the other side. "Mia, I should have said this when you walked into the room." Bending down on one knee to look her in the eye, Frederik said in a tone that sounded sincere, "I am truly sorry for your loss. Peter was instrumental in making ICARUS a reality. The world owes him a debt it will never be able to repay. I owe him a debt."

Standing back up, Frederik turned his attention back to Rory. "Did I ever tell you about my last day at Lehman Brothers?"

Now it was Rory's turn not to say anything. Frederik went on, "It was a beautiful September day in 2008. Two weeks earlier, I had my sixth anniversary with the firm—six years of blood, sweat, and more than a few tears. I woke up early that day, got to the office, and found a bankers box on my desk with a note informing me the firm had filed for Chapter 11. My services were no longer necessary. No warning, no thank you. They had a security guard watch as I, along with almost everyone else on the floor, packed up my belongings.

"Now, I don't expect you to shed any tears for me. The problem, the tragedy really, is that it didn't just happen to me and my colleagues on Wall Street. It happened to a million other people too, ordinary citizens, many of whom lost their homes, jobs, and most of whatever they were able to save up in their 401(k)s. It all happened in the blink of an eye. And why? Because after the dot-com bust and 9/11, a handful of careless politicians and central bankers felt it necessary to pump the system with way too much money for way too long. Then, to make matters worse, the

Federal Reserve—the very institution tasked to oversee the US banking system—failed to supervise. They allowed the banks to securitize and sell billions in mortgage loans that weren't worth the paper their prospectuses were printed on. And don't even get me started about the horrendous effects of inflation caused by the same ludicrous behavior during the pandemic. Rory, don't you see? Over the centuries, the boom and—"

"Enough with the boom-and-bust bullshit!" Rory interrupted. "I've heard it too many times before." *Maybe Fred saw the same show on how to handle interrogation.* Rory cut to the chase. "Did you or did you not buy a trillion dollars of securities to make ICARUS work? And did you have anything to do with the attack on me in Chicago?"

Frederik walked toward the tinted windows of the BIS tower and looked out over Basel, the sun now hidden behind the gathering clouds. He turned to Rory and Mia.

"Of course I didn't have anything to do with any attack. I haven't the faintest idea what you're talking about. And as for the transactions, yes, I arranged some sizable off-the-books lending facilities with a number of partner central banks. The capital was necessary to finance unexpected position sizes. But I had to, Rory. Otherwise, just like my years at Lehman, this all would have been for nothing."

Is he leveling with me here? Rory rubbed his temples as he tried to make sense of everything, but it was no use. His mind was mush after all that had occurred in the last week. *And what can I do anyway? Kota's model doesn't prove shit except for some increased volatility.* Rory knew it was impossible to run to FNN in the middle of a burgeoning financial crisis and claim ICARUS is a fraud without a shred of tangible evidence.

As Rory tried to figure out his next move as well as decipher if Frederik was friend or foe, his old boss walked back to the table and took his seat. "Now tell me," Frederik said, "what's this program running in the background on ICARUS all about?"

Try as he might, Rory was unable to see a path forward without Frederik on board. Reluctantly, he came clean. Rory explained the attack in Chicago and the hotel break-in, as well as the encrypted drive that precipitated their trip and Das's decryption program.

An apparent sense of concern flooded Frederik's face. "Those attacks are troubling," he said. "Let me help you. I know some people in local law enforcement. I can have some men from the cantonal police keep watch outside your rooms while you and Mia get some rest and a proper meal. We can meet back here tomorrow morning and discuss this further with clear heads. In the meantime, Das and I will review Kota's data. See if we can't shed some light on what exactly is happening."

Rory turned toward Mia. Her eyes looked as tired and lost as his own. She seemed to be looking for Rory to decide, but he asked anyway, "What do you think?"

"It's up to you."

Rory knew their options were limited. *If Mia and I want to see what's on that drive*, he reasoned, *we need Fred's help.*

"All right," Rory said with a tone of resignation, "we'll see you here tomorrow."

After the Americans left the room, Frederik turned to Das and smiled. "Nicely done. They walked right into the rabbit's snare just as our Russian friend predicted." Das returned a knowing glance as Frederik continued, "I am truly sorry for ordering Karl to keep you under lock and key. Dreadful, I know, but all part of the show."

Just as Frederik finished speaking, Karl von Hoffman entered the conference room. The three men, quite pleased with themselves, then enjoyed a light breakfast of freshly baked pastries and the finest Indian tea.

CHAPTER 35

Chicago, Illinois

FRIDAY, NOVEMBER 5, 2027

THE BLS JOBS REPORT WAS often a market mover. Milton McGrady sat at his desk on the thirty-first floor of 333 West Wacker. He looked at the clock, 7:28 a.m., two minutes until the release of monthly employment data by the Bureau of Labor Statistics. Since ICARUS had gone live, the average post-release move on the S&P had been around a tenth of a percent, much less than it had been historically but still a key event for the markets during this time of ultralow volatility. Wall Street analysts were expecting the report to show the U3 unemployment rate unchanged at 4.1 percent with approximately 310,000 new jobs created during the month of October. McGrady would use this Friday's report as a statistical litmus test. If futures reacted much more than a tenth of a percent, he would know that something was seriously wrong with ICARUS. It would be a greenlight to push his shorts and bet big on a move lower.

Many market watchers are familiar with Black Monday. On October 19, 1987, the S&P 500 shed a fifth of its value in a single trading session. Also familiar, Black Tuesday was the worst day of 1929's Wall Street crash. The crash had started four trading days earlier on what would become known as Black Thursday. Lesser known is Black Wednesday, September 16, 1992. On that day, speculators, including George Soros, "broke the pound." Soros's short of the British currency would go down as one of the greatest trades in financial history and, for better or worse, propel him to fame and astronomical wealth.

A day few know of, however, is Black Friday. Long before the name became associated with mad dashes for flat-screen TVs at bargain-base-ment prices, Black Friday referred to September 24, 1869. It was the cul-mination of a botched attempt to corner the gold market by acquain-tances of then president Ulysses Grant. The plot included financiers Jay Gould and James Fisk as well as Abel Corbin, a small-time speculator who also happened to be Grant's brother-in-law. The scheme eventually failed, but not before the price of gold plummeted, a result of Fisk issuing copious amounts of unbacked gold promissory notes into the market. It ended with the bankruptcy of numerous brokerage firms and a 20 per-cent drop in the stock market.

But it was ordinary farmers who were hurt the most as commod-ity prices fell in Chicago. Wheat plummeted 45 percent, from $1.40 to $0.77 a bushel. Corn, rye, oats, barley, and other agricultural products all had similar drops. In and of itself, the gold scheme wouldn't have been enough to cause such upheaval. The true root cause was overall market fragility. Not unlike modern times, this fragility was a direct result of massive money printing. The US had racked up enormous debt in order to finance the Civil War, but there still wasn't enough capital in the sys-tem. So, Lincoln did what the Continental Congress did in 1775—he printed money without the backing of gold. Known as greenbacks, this new currency quickly lost value as had the paper continental, which was printed to fund the revolution some four score years earlier. Eventually the economy would stabilize, but only after US bondholders were paid back in gold, not greenbacks.

Just as this first Black Friday resulted from a conspiracy reaching to the highest levels, which involved fiat currency, the gold market, large amounts of debt, and a resultant plunge in stock and commodity prices, so, too, would this new Black Friday.

November 5, 2027, would go down in history as the day the dollar broke.

McGrady sat back anxiously in his chair and listened. At precisely 7:30 a.m. in Chicago, 8:30 in New York, the FNN commentator exclaimed, "298,000. The economy created 298,000 new jobs in October." A moment later, it was announced that the unemployment rate remained unchanged at 4.1 percent, in line with expectations.

McGrady watched his screen and could hardly believe his eyes. While only slightly less than the 310,000 new jobs expected, the number resulted in a half percent drop in S&P futures, five times the typical post-ICARUS move. Commodities such as crude oil and natural gas also began to sell off. Bond yields fell slightly, but not as much as McGrady had expected given the decline in the S&P. Also odd, the dollar, normally a safe haven during times of market stress, actually fell a fraction of a cent against the euro, pound, and yen. Gold and silver both shot up around 3 percent.

Regardless of its eccentricities, the market had given McGrady his answer. Something was definitely wrong with ICARUS. He stormed out of his office and onto the trading floor, where Kota had assembled the troops. Approximately a dozen traders stood and awaited their marching orders.

"All right, here's what I want you to do," McGrady said with an echoing clap of his hands. "Start buying puts on the S&P, some for the front month with strikes around the twenty-day moving average and some down near the two-hundred-day expiring three months out. Go big. I want at least a billion in nominal exposure to the downside."

The room of traders looked at one another as if to check they were hearing right. But McGrady didn't pause for questions. He continued,

"And calls, VIX calls, buy as many as you can all along the curve but especially on the December contract. Got it?"

"Are you sure about this?" Kota asked, never having heard McGrady issue such a large and one-sided set of orders. By loading up on S&P 500 put options and VIX calls, McGrady was making a big bet the equity market was going down.

"Of course I'm fuckin' sure. I just told you to do it, didn't I? Now get to your desks and make it happen!" McGrady commanded before returning to his office.

As the clock approached 8:30 in Chicago, McGrady poured a shot of scotch into his coffee and took a seat on the couch in his office. He watched FNN as the commentators counted down to the opening bell. Looking out his expansive curved windows toward the Near North Side, McGrady could clearly see Goose Island, Cabrini-Green, and the Gold Coast. The Hancock Center reached one hundred stories up into a clear blue sky. To his left, the blue of Lake Michigan melded seamlessly into the horizon.

Almost looks like a perfect day for a swim, McGrady thought as he looked out on what appeared to be a beautiful summer morning from the warmth and comfort of his office. But he knew it was not summer. It was November in Chicago, and appearances can be deceiving. Separated by just an inch of glass, McGrady could hear cold gusts of freezing air as they buffeted against the windows of 333. A dip in the lake would have him dying of hypothermia in ten minutes. *Yep, going to be an early winter this year*, McGrady predicted to himself as the opening bell in New York began to ring.

CHAPTER 36

Basel, Switzerland

In Basel, the sun was definitely not shining. Gray clouds, pregnant with precipitation, still hung over the city. Hans Guzman had driven Rory and Mia back to the Hôtel Les Trois Rois. Once there, he escorted them to their rooms and performed a quick check to ensure no intruders had returned, then headed back to the BIS. Rory and Mia were tired but also hungry. They agreed on room service first, then get some rest. Rory called downstairs and ordered two Club Des Rois sandwiches for forty-six francs apiece.

A hundred bucks for two club sandwiches with fries, Rory thought as he shook his head. The prices were one thing about Switzerland that he definitely did not miss. In fact, right now he would have much preferred a ten-dollar pizza from El Loro Verde. As Rory hung up the phone, he felt a short pang of homesickness. He missed his condo, warm breezes off the Caribbean, and cold Medalla beer. About twenty minutes later, the sandwiches arrived along with some sparkling waters and two Budweisers. *It's not Medalla, but it'll do.* A dark oak table sat next to the window overlooking the Rhine in Rory's room. He and Mia sat down and began their late lunch.

"Budweiser? Missing home?" she asked insightfully.

"Maybe just a bit."

Mia twisted off the top of one of the beers.

"Hey, that one was for me too," Rory joked. They both tried to laugh, but their hearts weren't in it, not after what they'd been through and definitely not today.

Mia nibbled on her fries for a moment, then asked, "So, what do you think?"

"I think I should have stayed in San Juan, but it's too late for that now."

"Honestly, do you trust Fred?"

Rory took a bite of his sandwich, then said, "I wasn't sure at first, but after his little performance back there, no way."

"Performance?"

"That sermon of his, the one where he talks about the markets and their effect on the common man. It's a good line, don't get me wrong. Fred has a point. But it's his tell. Anytime he's trying to hide something, he breaks into it. Plus, now that I've had a chance to think about it, there's just no way the BIS could get the cash they've burned through in any legitimate way."

"What about those loans from central banks? Fred said they were off the books. Could that be enough?"

"We're talking about a trillion dollars. That would need to be disclosed somewhere, not by the BIS, but by the lending central banks." Rory dipped a handful of fries into a tiny hotel ketchup bottle and took a bite, then said, "The BIS is accountable to no one. No nation, no president, congress, or parliament has any jurisdiction over the bank. It's a law unto itself by international treaty. But other central banks are not set up that way. They release data regularly on the size of their balance sheet, operational activity, et cetera. They would need to disclose loans of that size. Unless they're in on it too."

Mia sipped on her Bud, then said, "Okay, but what about Chicago, the attack in the alley?" Then, with a look of sadness across her face, she added, "What about Pete?"

The mention of that name brought a somber expression to Rory's face as well. It was the one-year anniversary of Peter's murder. They both knew it, yet neither had mentioned it. Their eyes drifted away from one another and toward the window with its river view. As they both stared reflectively, the turbulent waters of the Rhine rushed past just a few yards distant. Then Rory turned his gaze back to Mia. He knew she was thinking of Peter. Her eyes were glossy, and her face looked forlorn and fatigued.

Finally, Rory replied to Mia's question. "Fred just doesn't seem like that type of guy. A hatchet job in a back alley? It doesn't fit. And as for Pete, it makes no sense. What good would killing him have done Fred? He needed Pete…still does, or at least his work."

"I guess," Mia said faintly, tears now welling up in her sad brown eyes.

Rory stood from his chair and walked around to comfort her. With his right hand, he brushed back her hair, then kissed her on the forehead. She stood and the two embraced. "I know, Mia, I know," Rory said, a lump forming in his throat.

At that moment, there was a knock on the door. "Kantonspolizei, open up, please."

What fucking timing. Rory released his tightly wrapped arms and walked toward the door. He looked through the peephole, then opened the door as Mia wiped away her tears with a napkin from their lunch. Two men dressed in suits, ties, and overcoats looked Rory over as they reached for their pockets and pulled out credentials showing they were with the cantonal police of Basel-Stadt.

The primary law enforcement agencies in Switzerland are the various cantonal police departments. Switzerland, officially the Swiss Confederation, is more a union of semiautonomous states, known as cantons, rather than a single country. Indeed, there is no official capital of Switzerland. Bern, centrally located in the middle of the country, happens to be where federal offices are maintained, but it is not recognized by the Swiss as their capital. The cantons, however, do have capitals, and Basel is the capital of its canton, Basel-Stadt.

"I'm Detective Meltzer and this is Detective Brunner," Meltzer stated as Brunner gave a quick nod.

"Nice to meet you," Rory said as he shook both their hands.

"Can we enter? We would like to look around and ask some questions if okay," Detective Meltzer said in somewhat disjointed English. He was a tall man, about thirty-five, with a fit build and shortly cropped blond hair. His partner, Detective Brunner, was about the same age but shorter, with medium-length dark hair and brown eyes. *Looks a bit like Roger Federer*, Rory thought, reminded of Basel's most famous native son.

Rory showed the men in. After introducing themselves to Mia, they surveyed both rooms, checking windows, closets, under the beds, and even opening the dresser drawers. Most of Rory and Mia's belongings were still scattered about where last night's visitors had left them. After about ten minutes, they asked if they could join Rory and Mia at the oak table by the window.

Detective Brunner spoke for the first time and gave Rory the distinct impression he was in charge. "Other than your rooms being broken into and searched," he asked, "has anything else unusual occurred during your time here in Basel?" *Good English*, Rory thought, barely noticing a slight accent, though it wasn't precisely Swiss German.

"Not really," Rory responded, unable to think of anything out of the ordinary other than the fantastic chain of events that had led him and Mia to this point. Both men sat silently, eying him closely. Rory felt they were looking for something more and added, "This was not an isolated incident."

"Herr d'Oultremont gave us a full briefing on the situation, including the attack on you in Chicago. Here in Basel, we take these matters very seriously, and your safety is our number one priority now," Detective Brunner said as he swept the room with his eyes. "Has anyone contacted you since arriving in Basel?"

"No," Rory said as he and Mia both shook their heads. "We arrived just yesterday and have only been here at the hotel, a local restaurant, and of course the BIS headquarters."

"And at the apartment of Kartik Das," Detective Brunner added.

"Yes, that's right. We were there for about an hour last night," Rory said.

How the hell does he know that? Did they talk with Das?

"Anywhere else you're forgetting to mention?" Brunner asked in what Rory now viewed as an accusatory tone.

"No."

"And no one has contacted you before or since?"

"No, I already told you that," Rory snapped back. *Fuckin' cops.* He took a sip of his beer and placed the bottle back on the table. "We're both very tired. Do you mind if we get some rest?"

"Of course," Detective Brunner consented. "We're just trying to assess the danger level here. But you are quite safe now." Both men got up from the table and headed toward the door. Before leaving, Brunner turned and faced Rory and Mia. "We'll be right here in the hallway. If you need anything or have any concerns, just let us know."

The men left the room. Mia turned immediately to Rory and said, "I don't trust them, but I'm not going anywhere until I know what's on that drive."

"I understand." Rory stood from his chair and flopped down on his bed, exhausted both mentally and physically. He stared up at the ceiling for a moment, then his eyes slowly drifted closed. Before falling into an uneasy sleep, he added, "And I don't trust them either, especially the Roger Federer lookalike."

A few hours later, lost in tropical island dreams, Rory was awakened by the muffled ping of his cell phone buried next to him in the sheets.

Who the hell is this?

He rolled over in his bed, fished around for the phone, and then looked at the screen. It was a text message from Sara Schnyder.

> LEAVE NOW!!! UR not safe. Go to SBB, take first
> train to Luzern. I'll be waiting for u, Sara.

CHAPTER 37

Basel, Switzerland

RORY DID A DOUBLE TAKE. After rereading the startling text, his first thought was to confirm it was actually Sara. He punched in a reply:

> What's your favorite song by the Clash?

Five seconds later, the phone pinged again.

> Bankrobber. Now get the hell out of there!

Yep, that's her.

The sound of the second ping had rung clear, unmuffled by the bed linens. Mia, who had been asleep in her bed, awoke and peered through the open double doors adjoining their rooms. Rory glanced toward her as well. They made eye contact for a brief moment when a strong knock echoed from the door.

Shit, they heard the phone. Rory hopped off his bed, but before he had time to react further, Detectives Brunner and Meltzer, who apparently had their own keycard to the room, walked through the door.

"Herr O'Connor, is everything all right?" Brunner said in a calm voice but with a menacing look in his eyes.

Rory quickly placed the phone in his pocket. "Detectives, may I see your credentials again?"

"Certainly," Detective Brunner replied as the two men simultaneously reached inside their suit jackets. But instead of creds, they both pulled out suppressed .40-caliber SIG Sauer pistols. Rory looked at the guns, quickly recognizing them as identical or at least similar models to the pistol pulled on him in Chicago.

"What's this all about, guys?" Rory asked, trying to stall for some time. Out of the corner of his eye, he could see Mia in the other room. She had quietly gotten out of her bed as well and was holding the weaponized brass lamp stand that Rory had left in her room the night prior.

"Give me that phone," Brunner demanded.

"What phone?" Rory said as Mia edged closer to the detectives. She was now just a couple steps away from striking range.

"The one you just put in your pocket. Hand it over."

Just as Brunner finished speaking, Rory could see Meltzer catch Mia's movement in the corner of his eye. He began to turn toward her but took too long. With every ounce of her strength, Mia crashed the lamp stand onto the side of Meltzer's head. He immediately collapsed unconscious to the floor.

Brunner quickly turned toward Meltzer and Mia just as the blow struck. He took a fraction of a second to register what was occurring and then fired a rushed shot at Mia. It missed the center of her chest but struck a few inches below her left breast. Brunner steadied himself and prepared to fire another round with more precision, but before he could get it off, Rory reached out with both hands and grabbed his arm and wrist. He twisted it behind Brunner's back, preventing a kill shot. But the damage was done. Mia fell to the ground, dropped the lamp stand from her hand, and began applying pressure to the wound with both her hands.

Still stuck in Rory's grasp, Brunner took his free left arm and blindly reached behind him, where Rory had positioned himself for leverage. Brunner found what he was looking for—Rory's crotch. He attempted to clutch and then twist the most sensitive parts but couldn't get a firm grasp through Rory's jeans. Rory quickly pulled away, trying to hold tight to Brunner's arm. He lost the grip eventually but not before stripping the SIG from Brunner's hand and onto the floor. He also heard a slight popping noise emanate from Brunner's shoulder as the man violently spun around to free himself from Rory's grasp.

Now facing one another, Rory struck first with a right hook to the side of Brunner's head. Appearing dazed from the punch and favoring his right shoulder, which Rory now believed to be dislocated, Brunner still managed to lunge forward and tackle Rory onto the floor. Spreading his legs over Rory's chest to hold him down, he attempted to raise his right arm for a counterblow, but his injured arm came down on Rory in an awkward manner with negligible effect.

Meanwhile, a few feet to Rory's right, Mia lay balled up on the floor, bleeding onto the beige carpet of the Hôtel Les Trois Rois. She continued to apply pressure to the lower left side of her abdomen in an effort to staunch the bleeding. However, she had been watching the struggle before her. She removed her right hand from atop the wound and grabbed the lamp stand. With a small toss, the bloody brass came to rest within arm's reach of Rory. He grabbed it with his free right hand and struck Brunner in the head, then reversed their position.

Now, it was Rory instead of Brunner who sat, legs straddled, over his opponent's chest. Rory raised the brass lamp stand up and then brought down another blow, but it only caught the side of Brunner's head. Once again, Rory raised the lamp stand, this time high above his head.

"Stop," Mia said in a weakened voice barely audible to the enraged Rory.

Ignoring her appeal, Rory brought the full weight of the heavy brass down with both speed and strength. This was no glancing blow. It landed directly on the square of Brunner's forehead, cracking it open like a grisly piñata. Blood and brains burst out in a shower of red and gray. Rory's breath poured in and out of his gaping mouth in labored gasps, but only one thought ran through his mind. *Mia.*

He moved from atop the lifeless body and crouched next to her. "How bad is it?"

"I'll be fine," she replied with a calmness developed from years of treating gunshot victims in the ER. "I think the bullet went straight in and out but may have clipped one of my ribs. It's not shattered, but it may be broken. There's some pain, but that's a good sign. I just need to stop the bleeding. Get the sheet from your bed."

Rory grabbed the top sheet from his bed and brought it back to Mia. "Now what?"

"Wrap it tightly around me, as tight as you can, like a cummerbund."

Rory folded the sheet once and then back over again. He gently lifted Mia to slide the sheet under her waist and then began to tie the ends together in a tight knot. Just as he cinched it with a final tug, he heard a groan from Meltzer.

Rory sprang to his feet from his crouched position above Mia. He turned to his right and kicked Meltzer's head like he was taking a World Cup penalty strike, then bent down and picked up the .40-caliber SIG lying on the floor. Rory stood over the man and raised the suppressed pistol into a firing position.

I'm taking this fucker out. Two to the body, one to the head. Rory started an even squeeze to the trigger, Meltzer's chest in his sights.

"No! Rory, stop!" Mia cried, louder this time and with a tone of command.

Rory released the tension on the trigger but kept the gun trained on Meltzer as he turned his head toward Mia. He did not reply, just stared at her with a rage in his eyes, the same rage that had brought the lamp stand down on Brunner.

"He's not worth it," Mia pleaded.

Rory took a deep breath. He stayed silent as a memory played in his mind. It was of the man at the Pumping Company, the man he almost killed over a wiseass remark and bruised ego. Rory had a rage in his eyes that night too, and he regretted his actions every day since.

He flipped the pistol in his hand and wrapped his fingers around the barrel. To ensure Meltzer was out, Rory drove the butt of the gun down onto his head, then turned the unconscious man over on his belly. He grabbed a long-sleeved shirt from atop his bed and tied Meltzer's arms behind his back, then removed the man's belt and used it to secure his legs.

"Thank you," Mia said as Rory once again crouched down next to her.

"I'm going to call an ambulance." Rory reached for his phone, then paused for a moment as the screen unlocked. Sara's text messages were still on the display.

"What is it?" Mia asked.

Rory turned the screen toward her. She looked at the message thread, then said, "I want you to go to Luzern."

"What? No way. I'm staying right here with you until help arrives."

"Don't worry about me. I've patched up worse wounds on my lunch break," Mia said as Rory dialed 112, the Swiss version of 911.

He requested the ambulance, then grabbed a pillow from his bed and gently placed it under Mia's head. "They'll be here soon."

"Rory, honestly, I'll be fine. You've called for help, now get out of here. Go to Luzern and find Sara. You have to figure out who's behind all this. Once the police arrive, it will be out of our hands."

Rory thought about that. *The Trois Rois isn't exactly some alley outside the Village Tap.*

Rory also recognized that he had no connections to the Basel-Stadt police and that once they arrived, he would likely be taken into custody. At best, he'd be stuck answering questions for hours, maybe days, and time was of the essence. At worst, there was a chance Brunner and Meltzer really were cops, albeit crooked ones. In that case, Rory had no idea how this would all go down.

"I'm going to come back for you, and we're going to find out what's on that drive," he finally said. "But you're right. If I stay here, we'll never get to the bottom of this. We need some answers, and Sara may have them. When the medics get here, tell them and the cops as little as possible. We don't know who's caught up in this."

"I understand," Mia replied.

Rory bent down and kissed her on the cheek. He then stood and briefly searched Brunner and Meltzer. They each had an extra magazine, and Rory placed them in his pockets. Before heading for the door, he quickly exchanged his now bloody sweater for a clean one, then grabbed his wallet and Swiss Army knife from the nightstand and put on Peter's old leather jacket. Just as he was about to leave, Mia said, "Rory, wait."

She sat up a few inches, and Rory could see a wince of pain as she struggled to raise her chest. Staring intently into Rory's eyes, she said, "Whoever is behind this, whoever tried to kill us and probably Pete, make them pay."

"I will."

"Promise me."

"You have my word, Mia. I promise."

Mia relaxed her head back down onto the pillow. Rory took one last look at her before reaching for the door. He turned and walked into the hall. The rage had vanished from his eyes, a new sense of purpose in its place.

PART III

Out of the Frying Pan...

CHAPTER 38

Amsterdam, Netherlands
Friday, November 5, 2027

FREDERIK BLASTED ONE MORE TRACK. He was wrapping up the final sound check ahead of his Friday night performance at Paradiso. Bass thumped through the rafters of the historic nightclub. A converted church dating from the 1800s, Paradiso was located off a canal near the Leidseplein in Amsterdam. Frederik had flown up from Basel after leaving the BIS and would be back in town early Saturday morning, but he needed this.

EDM was his release, his drug. Without it, nothing made sense, and Frederik wouldn't let the collapse of the world's financial markets stop him from spinning. After the complex sound system was configured to his precise specifications, he grabbed a cold Red Bull. *Time for some fresh air*, Frederik thought as he exited the legendary building and walked briskly into the chilly Amsterdam night.

It was late evening in Europe, but across the pond, the closing bell had just rung on Wall Street. The carnage was surreal. The S&P 500 had closed down 9.88 percent, the sixth largest daily percentage loss in the index's history, less than a percent shy of Black Tuesday's losses in October of 1929. Along with the massive sell-off in stocks, something else unprecedented was occurring. Tanking equity markets did not produce the usual flight to safety. Normally, a plunge in stocks causes buyers to rush into the US dollar and Treasury bonds, but their prices both fell. Some were questioning if the dollar's days as the world's reserve currency were over. Panic was taking hold in the global financial community, but not in its usual way.

If Monday saw a similar drop, that panic would spread beyond Wall Street and take hold on Main Street. The large banks and broker-ages would be the first to go under. Most of them had levered up under the expectation that crashes were a thing of the past, a relic of the days before ICARUS. Almost all available cash had piled into the market once it became clear that ICARUS could deliver on its unbelievable promises. Market pundits and professionals alike heralded a new era of low vola-tility and steady, positive returns. There was no cash on the sidelines, no buyers looking to swoop in and take advantage of fire sale prices. The old market was resilient and robust, full of liquidity, and positioned to han-dle dramatic moves. But this was the new market, and if it melted down on Monday, all bets would be off.

Frederik made his way across the canal adjacent to Paradiso and into Vondelpark, an expansive public space located near the Van Gogh Museum. The fresh air calmed his nerves, and a sense of peace swept over him.

The tranquil moment was broken by a raspy, mocking voice calling out from behind him.

"DJ Prince, aren't you due back at Paradiso soon?"

Frederik thought he recognized the accent, but it made no sense, not here, not now. He turned around hesitantly and was just able to make out a male figure emerging from the shadows. As he approached, the dim lights of Vondelpark finally provided enough visibility to reveal some detail. It was indeed who Frederik suspected. Anton Golev wore a black wool overcoat with black gloves and a Russian-style fur cap atop his graying hair.

"I hear it's going to be quite the show," Golev commented.

"I don't go on until 23:00."

"Wonderful. Then we have time for a chat."

The two men walked past one of the park's several sculptures. This one was locally known as Picasso's fish statue, though the artist actually intended it to be a bird. After a few more paces, they found a bench overlooking a small pond and took a seat.

"What are you doing here?" Frederik asked.

"I could ask you the same thing. DJing at an all-night club? I mean really, Frederik, shouldn't you be in Basel?"

Frederik considered rebuking Golev for use of his real name but sensed now was not the time. Instead, he responded, "Everything in Basel is under control. Your plan worked perfectly. The decryption should be complete by Sunday night. I'll be back early tomorrow morning. There's no problem."

"No problem in Basel, you say?" Golev pulled out a cigarette.

"Must you?" Frederik asked in annoyance. Beyond never touching alcohol, Frederik abhorred the smell of tobacco smoke.

Golev ignored the question and lit up. "Rory O'Connor just killed another one of my men and fled Basel. I think that is a problem, don't you?"

Frederik's eyes widened. "What? How could that be? Your men were supposed to just keep an eye on him, make sure we had him available in case Das needed his help to implement the Vega Block."

"True, but that bitch of yours contacted him, told him he was in danger and that he needed to leave Basel immediately."

Frederik knew to whom Golev referred. "Sara contacted him? How do you know?"

Golev blew a puff of smoke in Frederik's direction. "Must I keep reminding you that I spent twenty years in FSB before I became a 'central banker.' How the fuck do you think I know? We cloned O'Connor's cell phone before he even left Puerto Rico."

Frederik was impressed, but also nervous. Golev was proving harder to manage than anticipated.

"This is not good," Frederik said.

"Tell me something I don't know, like who will win Champions League this year."

Frederik, surprised at Golev's relaxed attitude, wondered why the Russian did not share his anxiety that Rory was on the loose and unavailable if required to help get ICARUS up to speed once the drive was decrypted. He warned Golev, "Even your beloved Russia will suffer if we don't get this figured out. A total financial collapse will result in global political unrest. I tell you, Liev, it will be devastating and—"

Golev reached out with his gloved right hand and grabbed Frederik's neck. "I told you, do not call me Liev." He applied an extra ounce of pressure, then added, "I know you think that you're in charge of this thing. You're not. I run this show, understood?"

Frederik stared into Golev's gray eyes, his pupils wide and open in the dim light. After a brief moment, he managed to respond a muffled, "Yes," as he nodded in agreement.

Golev released his grip. "As for suffering, the Russian people are used to it. If we can survive Hitler and Stalin, we can survive without ATMs, American Express, or even without Facebook...ha!" Golev laughed at his own wit.

Frederik coughed to clear his throat. "I really don't care what you do or how you do it, but I need Rory back in Basel and at the BIS by Sunday night."

Again, Golev laughed, then said confidently, "The American will be back in Basel soon enough."

"How can you be so sure?"

"Because I have the girl."

"Sara? Where?"

"You're not as bright as you think." Golev smirked, then took a drag from his cigarette.

Frederik thought for a moment. "You have Mia? But how?"

Golev threw the butt of his smoke onto the gravel path in front of the bench, then slowly clapped his gloved hands. After a moment of mocking applause, he said, "Mia Costello is in the back of a van parked outside the Basel Zoo right now, but I'd like to get her into the infirmary at the BIS tower if that's all right with you. She's been shot."

Frederik sat speechless on the bench.

The Russian stood and pressed his right heel onto the still burning cigarette butt. "Tell Hans Guzman to expect an incoming patient."

Frederik shook his head, shocked by one revelation after another from Golev. Finally, he said, "Yes, I'll contact Hans right away."

"Of course you will." Golev turned and walked away, his black attire quickly fading into the once tranquil Amsterdam night.

CHAPTER 39

Basel to Luzern, Switzerland
FRIDAY, NOVEMBER 5, 2027

THE PREGNANT GRAY CLOUDS FROM earlier in the day had given birth to a full-on storm. As Rory walked out the door of the Hôtel Les Trois Rois and into the Basel night, his phone pinged again. *Fuck, now what?* he thought as sheets of rain poured down upon him. Rory ducked under a nearby awning and looked at his phone: McGrady.

Where the hell are u? Call me! The fucking market crashed!

Sorry, no time, Milt.

Rory exited the messaging app and pulled up the online timetable for SBB. He learned that trains to Luzern departed Basel's main station about every hour on the hour. *No problem,* he figured, *I'll be able to meet Sara in less than two hours.* But as Rory made his way to the tram for SBB, he hesitated. Playtime was over. The rules of this game had changed. Mia was shot, and whoever was after him was not messing around.

Rory placed the phone back in his pocket and paused for a moment to gather his thoughts just as two valets came by, running frantically in the rain. *That's not a bad idea.* Rory scanned the area. Less than a hundred meters away, a now unmanned valet post sat next to the entrance of a posh restaurant. It was Friday night and prime dinner hour. At least a dozen sets of keys dangled in the wind.

Rory sidled up to the wooden valet box, grabbed a handful of keys, and continued his walk north up Blumenrain. It was the only nearby street wide enough to afford some parking along its length. Rory just hoped he was heading in the right direction. He alternated among the various key fobs until one of them momentarily flicked on the lights of a late-model Audi A5 coupe. Within minutes, Rory was cruising at 70 mph down Swiss Highway A2.

As he escaped the traffic of Basel, Rory familiarized himself with the car's layout, adjusted the power driver's seat, and quickened the wipers to a more appropriate speed for the steady and heavy rain that battered the windshield. It was a straight shot to Luzern, about sixty miles southeast of Basel. Rory settled into the right lane and reduced his speed. For the first time since arriving in Switzerland, he finally had some time by himself to think this whole thing through.

Some of the puzzle pieces made sense to him; others were a mystery. He understood the attack in Chicago. Someone wanted Peter's drive. But as for who or why, Rory had no idea. He sensed Frederik was involved, but couldn't see the motivation. After all, Rory brought the drive to him, not the other way around. And regarding Sara—what she knew and how she knew it—Rory was again at a loss.

He moved the Audi into the left lane to pass a slow-moving lorry. The rain was still coming down, but less heavy now. Rory was coming up on Lake Sempach. Homes dotted the shoreline, and some boats tied at docks bobbed in the wind. He knew from the lake it wouldn't be too much farther.

Gliding the Audi back into the right lane, he returned to his thoughts, but still the pieces just didn't seem to fit together. And then there was Peter's death. *Was that just a tragic accident or part of this fucked-up situation as well?* Rory wondered. *None of this makes sense. Unless...*

...unless there's someone out there who wants ICARUS to fail.

It was like a light bulb going off in Rory's head as he finally started to put it all together.

Cui bono? he thought. *Always start with who benefits.* He ran through a list of suspects in his mind: radical Islamic terrorists, the Chinese, Wall Street titans. They all had possible motivations, but the fact pattern didn't quite fit the MO of radical terrorists. As for the latter two, they both had too much to lose. *Too integrated in the current economic order.* And then it hit him like a ton of bricks.

The Russians. What do they have to lose from a total market collapse? The answer, of course, was not much. The Russian Federation had been suspended, sanctioned, or banned from every major global financial network since their move into Ukraine. They were on the sidelines looking in. Rory realized that if the Russians could bring down global markets, it would devastate the economies of both China and the US, while opening up a world of possibilities for Russia. Despite this epiphany, Rory still worried that he had more questions than answers. He hoped Sara Schnyder would be able to provide some of the missing pieces.

But first Rory had to find her, and after the hotel attack, he was hesitant to use his phone in order to arrange a rendezvous. Indeed, it dawned on him that his phone may be more of a liability than an asset at this stage of the game. He pulled over to the side of the highway and waited for a couple of cars to pass, then exited the Audi. He walked through some overgrown brush and down to the shore of Lake Sempach. After placing the phone on the ground, Rory grabbed a softball-size rock, preparing to smash the device before tossing it in the lake.

But he hesitated. Reality was setting in. For the first time since this wild week had begun, Rory felt scared—scared for his life and for Mia's. It took the drive from Basel to clear the cobwebs, but Rory now understood that this game he'd gotten involved in was for keeps. There would be no prizes for second place, just a cold hole in the ground.

He put down the rock and ran his hands through his wet hair and swept the rain from his brow. Rory looked down and saw what could only be small pieces of Brunner's brain mixed in with the blood-tinted water that now clung to his hands. He scooped up some water from the lake to quickly wash his face and hands, then looked up at the sky and opened his mouth, allowing some falling rain to accumulate on his parched tongue. If it weren't for the blood and brains he had just washed away, the splash of waves on the rocky shoreline might have reminded

Rory of Lake Michigan on a wet and stormy night. Two small wooden sailboats, their masts swaying violently in the wind, battered against a nearby dock.

Well, I could say fuck it. Head back to Basel, get Mia, and get the hell out of Dodge. The lorry he had passed a few minutes earlier careened down the highway, sending a blast of air and rain Rory's way as he imagined himself back in Puerto Rico, a Medalla in hand, scanning for pelicans from his perch overlooking Atlantic Beach.

Then, though it happened only an hour ago, the memory of the Hôtel Les Trois Rois and Mia's words flashed back as if long forgotten. *Make them pay*, Mia had said as she lay bleeding and wounded on the floor. Rory looked up once again to the sky.

One year, he thought. *One year since that night in Chicago.*

"Pete, I need some help down here," Rory said aloud, convinced his friend was listening.

Then he lowered his head, picked the rock back up, and brought it down hard against the phone. As Rory flung the shattered remnants into the dark, choppy waters, he knew what needed to be done.

Playtime was definitely over.

CHAPTER 40

Luzern, Switzerland
Friday, November 5, 2027

ONCE BACK IN THE AUDI, Rory considered how best to find Sara. She was expecting him by train. So, it would be up to him to locate her. With some luck, Rory hoped she would be parked in her vehicle somewhere near the station. An easy-to-spot classic, Sara's 1974 Series III Land Rover was mint green, souped up with oversize tires, and hard to miss.

Sure, she would still have it. Sara wasn't much into sports cars.

Indeed, Sara Schnyder wasn't much into following the rules either. Five foot five in height, she was an expert Alpinist, skier, and general outdoors woman. Her signature short blonde hair accented a button nose, sparkling blue eyes, and well-defined cheekbones. As beautiful as she was unconventional, Sara was also an adept financier. Her specialty was cash and liquidity management as well as cross-border multicurrency transactions.

During her time at the BIS, Sara worked hard and often all through the night, headphones in, pounding some punk rock anthem by the Clash or Ramones. She preferred to wear jeans or hiking pants to the office and carried herself with a relaxed attitude, but behind the carefree façade there was a serious businesswoman.

One area of life that Sara didn't take too seriously, however, was relationships. It wasn't that she didn't enjoy male companionship. On the contrary, she adored men, many men in fact, but never for too long. Easily bored, Sara had yet to be in a relationship she even remotely considered something with staying power.

After completing her MBA at the London School of Economics, Sara went to work in the treasury department of Deutsche Bank in Frankfurt. She worked her way up the ladder and became expert at moving all manner of financial assets and currencies around the globe, sometimes in ways not exactly aligned with industry best practices. When she heard about the ICARUS project, it was a temptation too hard to resist. How could she pass on the opportunity to help create a world-changing quantum AI platform with tremendous treasury-related challenges? ICARUS traded on more than forty exchanges in over thirty different currencies, and so, when Frederik came calling, Sara answered.

The two did not get off to the greatest start, but eventually Sara's skills and hard work overcame Frederik's prejudice toward hard-core punk. In fact, it was her love of music—albeit of a different genre from Frederik's beloved EDM and classical tastes—that led them to social outings at concerts and nightclubs. While not smitten with Sara at first sight, Frederik grew increasingly attracted to the saucy girl originally from Bremgarten, Switzerland. He hoped to grow their relationship into something more defined and exclusive, but Sara remained free-spirited and often went out with other men, including a couple of colleagues who also worked at the BIS. This behavior drove Frederik into fits of anger, but he couldn't break off the affair. He refused to believe that Sara didn't see something special in him that warranted a deeper bond.

Sara also became valuable to Frederik in other ways. She was willing to bend treasury guidelines and became instrumental in Frederik's ability to launder bogus renminbi, rubles, and rupees into BIS accounts spread across the globe in order to satisfy ICARUS's substantial capital needs. However, when Sara learned that there was more to Frederik's plan than just oversize trading allowances, she backed away from both the BIS and him, taking first an extended vacation to travel around Central America and then leaving the bank entirely shortly thereafter.

Sara had tried to forget the BIS, going to work for a nonprofit block-chain start-up based in Zug, Switzerland. Its goal was to create an interest-bearing stablecoin and use that interest to help end extreme poverty. The project was progressing nicely. Sara had moved on.

On Wednesday, however, she heard a very disturbing news report on Swiss TV. Apparently, a crypto trader who formerly held a prominent position with the BIS had been involved in a deadly shooting in Chicago. Sara was concerned and contacted a former colleague still working at the bank to see if he had any details. She received no reply until some two hours ago, at which time Sara learned from this highly placed source that Rory and Mia were actually in Basel. Though vague about the details, the former colleague urged her to warn the Americans that they were in danger, and so that is what she did.

Now, Sara Schnyder found herself parked outside the train station in Luzern, about twenty miles southwest of Zug. Sitting comfortably in her 1974 Land Rover, she cranked up both the radio and the heat, wondering exactly what danger Rory and Mia had gotten into and whether she may now be a part of it.

CHAPTER 41

Luzern to Sihlwald Forest, Switzerland
FRIDAY, NOVEMBER 5, 2027

A FEW STARS WERE NOW visible through the quickly moving clouds as Rory entered the lakefront city of Luzern. The rain had stopped. He decided to park the Audi a short distance from the train station and head the rest of the way on foot. Once parked, Rory partially pulled back the slide of his newly acquired .40-caliber SIG Sauer to make sure a round was chambered, then exited the car and walked toward the station.

The streets were quiet and mostly empty. Rory passed a young couple out on a romantic late-night stroll descending the steps of the Kapellbrücke, a landmark wooden bridge from the 1300s. As he approached the *bahnof* parking area, Rory began hearing a song by the Misfits. While not a fan, he had picked up on some of Sara's favorite artists during their time working together. Just ahead on the right, a handful of vehicles filled the lot, including one mint-green 1974 Series III Land Rover complete with oversize tires.

Rory rapped on the window. Sara, a startled look on her face, opened the door and climbed out of the vehicle. They both stared at one another for a moment, as if in disbelief that they were actually meeting in a Luzern parking lot. Then Sara leaned forward, giving Rory three quick kisses as is the Swiss custom, one on his right cheek, then his left, then back to the right.

"I was expecting you to be on the next train," she said. "How did you get here, and where is Mia?"

Rory looked at Sara. She was wearing a pair of tan hiking slacks with a blue fleece jacket and seemed not to have changed a bit. Her blonde hair may have been an inch or two longer, but other than that, same old Sara. She and Rory had become fast friends during his time at the BIS, and while he didn't share in her taste for music, they did share a common interest in blockchain technology and decentralized finance.

Rory glanced around the area to see if anyone was about, then replied matter-of-factly, "Mia's been shot. I had to leave her in Basel."

"What!"

Rory had no time for explanations. "I'll fill you in later. Right now, we need to get the hell out of here. People are looking for me. Do you have somewhere we could go, not your home, somewhere no one would look for us?"

Sara thought for a moment, then said, "Yes, I have a place."

They got into the Rover. Rory turned toward her. "I'd ask you to ditch your phone, but I know they aren't cheap. Taking out the battery should do the trick."

"Rory, what's wrong with you," Sara replied incredulously. "Mia's been shot, someone's after us, and you're worried about a few hundred francs." She cranked down the window and flung her phone into the Reuss River as they crossed the bridge on Swiss Highway A14.

"Do you remember that friend I told you about who works for Rega?" Sara asked.

Rega provides air rescue services across Switzerland. With helicopter bases throughout the country, they can reach anywhere in the nation within fifteen minutes.

"I think so. The rescue guy, right? Was Eric his name?"

"Exactly. I'm flattered you remember." Sara briefly took her eyes off the road and turned toward Rory. "Well, anyway, Eric has a chalet about fifteen minutes north of Zug in Sihlwald Forest. It's totally off grid. We'll be safe there."

Proving that the United States does not hold a monopoly on crazed gunmen, Zug, Switzerland, was the site of a 2001 mass shooting by a man named Friedrich Leibacher. He walked into the Zug cantonal parliament upset about some lawsuits that had been filed against him. Armed with an Stgw 90, the standard Swiss Army assault rifle, as well as a SIG Sauer pistol, pump-action shotgun, a revolver, and a homemade bomb for good measure, Leibacher proceeded to shoot and kill three members of the executive council and eleven members of parliament while wounding eighteen other politicians and journalists before blowing himself up with the bomb. A known paranoid, the gunman left a suicide note entitled "Day of Wrath for the Zug Mafia."

While the Zug massacre wasn't exactly the stuff that attracted wealthy outsiders, Zug's claim to fame as Crypto Valley did. Home to the Ethereum Foundation as well as other crypto-related ventures, Zug was a global hotspot for blockchain technology. It was also home to the nonprofit stablecoin project that Sara was now involved with.

Rory and Sara zipped through Crypto Valley and made their way toward Sihlwald Forest. The countryside became more rural once they got off the A14. On almost empty and pitch-black roads, the Rover wound its way through rolling hills and into the forest. The area had been set aside as a regional nature park in 2009, but the few preexisting chalets were grandfathered in and allowed to remain in the preserve. After a couple of left turns and a short drive on a gravel road, they reached the chalet.

Sara put the Land Rover in park and turned off the engine. As Rory opened the door to get out, an immediate awareness of silence overtook him, something that neither San Juan, Chicago, nor Basel could provide. The fresh air was thick with the scent of wet pine needles and fallen beech leaves after the storm. An owl hooted in the distance. Under different circumstances, Rory would have felt a sense of peace, but instead, it merely served to turn his focus inward. He felt his hand tremble as he turned to shut the Rover's door.

Sara fished a spare key from underneath a nearby bird feeder, and the pair headed into the chalet. It was rustic but included all the basic comforts of home. Sara flipped on the lights. The battery-based electrical system was charged by an array of solar panels stationed in the backyard. Primarily built from local beechwood, the chalet's walls were covered with photographs of some of the most spectacular peaks in the Alps as well as snapshots from the Sierras and Patagonia.

They made their way into the kitchen area. Rory sat down at a beechwood table surrounded by four chairs. Sara opened the refrigerator, grabbed a beer for herself, and then asked, "Would you like something to drink? Eric has beer in the fridge and well water from the tap. I could also brew some coffee or tea if you like."

"A glass of water, please, and I'll have one of those beers too. I'm parched."

Rory drank the water in one chug. Again, his hand trembled. "Can we head back outside for a bit? I need a cigarette."

A door to the rear of the cabin opened up to a small wooden-plank deck. It had hip-height fencing and sat about a foot off the ground. A small clearing had been made outside the perimeter of the deck where the solar panels sat. From there, the landscape faded into dark forest. With an unsteady hand, Rory pulled out a cigarette for himself and offered one to Sara, who accepted.

Sara's eyes shifted toward Rory's hand as she reached for the smoke. "Are you all right?"

"I'll be fine." Rory took a deep breath, then added, "I guess I've just been running on adrenaline. Think it's starting to catch up with me."

They stood in silence next to the deck fencing, resting their beers on the top board of the railing. The faint babbling of the nearby Sihl River was only interrupted by the occasional hoot of an owl. After a moment's respite, Sara turned to Rory. "So tell me everything. How did you and Mia wind up in this situation?"

CHAPTER 42

Sihlwald Forest, Switzerland
FRIDAY, NOVEMBER 5, 2027

RORY RECAPPED THE CHAIN OF events that led from his tropical condo in San Juan to Chicago then Basel and now a forest nestled between Zug and Zürich, Switzerland.

Sara ashed her cigarette over the railing and said in her slightly Swiss-German-accented English, "Holy shit, Rory. That's the most incredible story I've ever heard."

"I know. It almost feels like a dream to me." Rory paused to take a sip of his beer. "How did you know Mia and I were in danger?"

"A couple days ago, I reached out to Das after hearing about your incident in Chicago. Didn't hear back from him. Then tonight, just before I messaged you, he sent me some cryptic texts. Told me you both were in Basel and in danger. Said I should warn you right away."

"Das?" Rory said with some surprise. "If he knew Mia and I were in danger, why didn't he warn us at the BIS or send me a message directly?"

"I don't know. I do know that he has been part of this from the beginning. It was his connections at the Reserve Bank of India that helped get its governor involved. I guess he was some sort of mentor to Das when they were both at Cambridge."

Rory could see Karl von Hoffman mixed up with this, even Sara if he were honest, but he never figured Das would be involved.

I was hoping Sara would have some answers. Instead, Rory had more questions.

"What else do you know?" he asked as they transitioned over to a pair of deck chairs separated by a small table with a half-empty beer bottle on it.

They both took a seat. Sara looked Rory in the eyes. "I'll tell you everything I know, but I don't know everything. After Pete's death and your departure, we launched the first phase of ICARUS with few issues, but it wasn't long before we realized that limited intervention in the market wasn't going to cut it. At first we had adequate capital to move prices by blunt force, but as we expanded to cover more markets, there just wasn't enough money. One day, Fred and Karl came to me and said the BIS would be receiving massive infusions from the Indian, Chinese, and Russian central banks. At the time, I thought it would be legit, on the balance sheet type stuff, typical swaps or cross-currency lending facilities."

The Russians. I knew they had to be mixed up in this somehow.

"But it wasn't legit, was it?" Rory asked as Sara paused to take a final puff of her cigarette and then plopped it into the half-empty beer bottle on the table. Rory did the same.

"No, it wasn't. I processed hundreds of secret wire transfers."

"How much?"

"Over two trillion dollars in total."

The amount staggered Rory. It was double what he'd heard from Das. A sum so large could only mean one thing. The central banks involved were creating fraudulent, undisclosed currency. He paused to process this latest information for a moment, then said, "So ICARUS is a fraud, a pump-and-dump scheme?"

"More like a pump-and-keep-pumping scheme. Except on a scale that makes Frank Abagnale look like he floated only a couple bad checks."

"But how did you keep all that activity a secret?"

"The funds came directly from the central banks' internal clearing servers, completely covert. Their governors—Golev, Patel, and Zhao—are all in on it. This goes well beyond just Fred and the BIS."

This was more involved than Rory ever imagined. He asked, "But why? What's their endgame?"

Sara took another sip from her beer, then responded, "I'm not sure, but I know it has to do with gold and CBDCs. I spent a few weekends at Fred's house before I left the BIS. I managed to overhear a few things as well as see some reports he was interested in. They all had to do with gold reserves. And there was one other thing: crypto. He kept asking me all these questions about the blockchain and what would the rollout look like if the BIS created its own digital currency, Project Aurum type of stuff. BIScoin, he called it."

"Let me get this straight: Fred wants to roll out a CBDC backed by gold and controlled by the BIS," Rory said as suddenly the puzzle pieces started to fall into place.

"I believe that's his plan."

Thinking out loud, Rory added, "Well, the only way to get people to adopt BIScoin would be by manufacturing some sort of global financial crisis. The world would have to lose faith in the dollar, pound, euro, Swiss franc, everything."

"True," Sara agreed. "The whole system would have to basically collapse."

"Or be on the brink of collapse with no one to turn to except the BIS and Frederik d'Oultremont III." Rory paused for a moment, then asked, "When is the next All Governors' Meeting?"

"I can't believe you don't know," Sara said. "It starts Sunday. With the carnage in the markets this week, Fred has the perfect opportunity to plant the seed for BIScoin."

Rory followed things to their now logical conclusion. "And with the decrypted Vega folder, he can get ICARUS back on track, swoop in, stabilize the markets, and be the big hero he always dreamed of."

"That son of a bitch," Sara said with a tone of outrage. "I never would have fucked him if I knew he was such a *futzgsicht*."

"A what?" Rory asked as he looked more closely at Sara, his eyes adjusted to the darkness of the deck.

"Swiss-German slang," she replied, her button nose and the blue of her eyes now clearly visible in the moonlight. "Let's see, how best to translate that? Pussy face, I think."

They both let out a brief and uneasy chuckle. And for a moment, Rory considered leaning over to give her a kiss, but instead he stood and walked to the railing. *Maybe you're a futzgsicht too.* Rory reminded himself that Mia had been shot just a few hours ago. "What is wrong with you?" he mumbled softly while at the same time feeling an undeniable attraction toward Sara.

"What's that?" Sara asked. "Did you say something?"

Rory turned away from the railing and his moral dilemmas. He once again faced Sara. "Nothing," he said as they both stared at one another for a moment in the silence of Sihlwald Forest, a breeze ruffling the branches of a nearby beech tree.

"How about another beer?" Sara suggested as she, too, stood from her chair.

"I think right now I need some sleep."

Sara smiled. Then added somewhat leadingly, "There's only one bed."

With some hesitation, Rory said, "You take it. I think I saw a sleeping bag in there somewhere."

"Suit yourself."

They both headed back into the chalet. Sara took off her coat and hung it on the back of a kitchen chair. She walked slowly into the bedroom, leaving the door cracked open slightly. Rory forced thoughts of Sara out of his mind and located a sleeping bag in the corner of the living room. He unzipped it and laid it out on the couch like a blanket. After taking off his shoes, Rory wrapped himself in the warmth of the bag and took stock of the situation. *Off the grid, no phones, maybe I can finally get some rest.* Exhaustion settling in, Rory closed his eyes and quickly drifted into sleep, his hands finally still.

Outside the chalet, an owl hooted. Beech and pine branches rustled in the wind. And discreetly tucked under the Land Rover's rear bumper, a satellite GPS beacon silently transmitted coordinates through the moon and starlit sky.

CHAPTER 43

Basel, Switzerland
SATURDAY, NOVEMBER 6, 2027

HOPPED UP ON RED BULL and the energy from spinning boot-legs, dub mixes, and mashups at Paradiso, Frederik had not slept a wink on Friday night. After leaving the club around 06:00, he went straight to Schiphol Airport and was back in Basel before 09:00. Showered, shaved, and sipping on a locally fermented kombucha, he now sat at his desk on the seventeenth floor of the BIS tower. This was a big week-end for Frederik, the culmination of a life's dream and the realization of his destiny.

The world's most powerful central bankers convene on a bimonthly basis at the BIS. Held completely in secret with no cameras or press, the global banking conclave is split into three principal meetings: the Economic Consultative Committee, the Global Economy Meeting, and the All Governors' Meeting. As a matter of convention, the entire two-day affair is collectively referred to as the AG or All Governors' Meeting, taking its name from the third and final gathering.

It begins on Sunday evening in Conference Room E with the Economic Consultative Committee. Known as the ECC, this first meet-ing is the most exclusive. The ECC is a nineteen-member group, roughly the G20 minus a suspended Russia, currently chaired by Randolph Dower, head of the US Federal Reserve System. Other key members of the ECC include Sir Peter Tindall of the Bank of England, Zara Bernard of the European Central Bank, Makoto Fukai of the Bank of Japan, Zhao Hong of the People's Bank of China, and Arun Patel of the Reserve Bank of India. The group is rounded out by the less important central bank chiefs of a dozen other countries, including Germany, Switzerland, France, Italy, Sweden, Canada, Brazil, and Spain.

But the real work of the committee isn't handled during the formal meeting. After the ECC adjourns, the bankers retire to the eighteenth-floor dining room. No ordinary dining room, it was designed by the same Swiss architectural firm that created the Bird's Nest stadium in Beijing. With white walls and an ominous black ceiling, the guests dine on expertly prepared gourmet meals served with some of the world's finest wine as they gaze from their perch overlooking France, Germany, and Switzerland. It is at this dinner where the true global monetary agenda is set. Unelected officials, coordinating in secret, chart a course for the world economy over champagne and foie gras.

Monday's two larger and less exclusive meetings transmit decisions made on Sunday to the heads of lesser central banks, and thus, the clandestine global coordination of monetary policy is formalized. The Monday morning meeting is known as the GEM or Global Economy Meeting. Also chaired by Dower of the US Fed, the GEM includes the members of the ECC along with eleven additional participants. Observers from the lower tier of central banks, countries such as Algeria, Denmark, Kuwait, New Zealand, and Portugal, are permitted to attend but not participate. The third and final meeting, technically the actual All Governors', takes place after a delightful lunch served on the eighteenth floor. While attended by the chiefs of all sixty-three BIS member central banks, the AG is more a formality than a decision-making body, the real decisions having been made on Sunday night.

Arun Patel would be arriving soon for his Saturday afternoon rendezvous with Frederik, where they would review and hash out their game plan for Sunday. For now, Frederik rehearsed his reasoned and passionate plea for consensus around his master plan. His pitch was simple and comprised of only two primary objectives. First, the world needs to shift back to sound money policy, specifically a gold- and silver-based exchange standard. And second, the best mechanism to accomplish the first objective is via a global CBDC administered by the BIS, to be known as BIScoin.

Of course, two key members of the ECC, Patel and Zhao, were already on board as co-conspirators in the stratagem. Thus, given the geodynamics of central banking, Frederik recognized the entire arrangement essentially hinged on one man: Randolph Dower, leader of the most powerful central bank in the world: the Fed. If the American agreed to the scheme, Zara Bernard of the ECB and Makoto Fukai of the BoJ would have no choice but to join in also. And if the central banks of the US, Europe, Japan, China, and India were all on board, well, then the world would be on board.

Frederik's machinations were interrupted by an expected knock. He had messaged Kartik Das upon landing in Basel, ordering him to report in. After some brief pleasantries, Frederik provided Das with an update on last night's events at the Hôtel Les Trois Rois.

Seated in a chair opposite his boss, Das then asked, "So what do you want from me?"

With a sheepish grin on his face, Frederik slid a small silver fob across his desk. "This is the key to my Tesla. I have something very important for you to do. But first, you and I are going to take a little trip down to the infirmary. There's something, or rather someone, I want to show you."

CHAPTER 44

Sihlwald Forest, Switzerland

SATURDAY, NOVEMBER 6, 2027

RORY WOKE UP FIRST. HE found some coffee in the kitchen and brewed a pot, then pulled on his coat and stepped out onto the deck. The air was warmer, almost humid. *Maybe some rain today*, he thought as gray clouds moved in from the southwest. Morning songbirds chirped from nearby branches.

A few moments later, Sara, coffee in hand, stepped out of the chalet wearing the same hiking pants from last night, her fleece jacket unzipped.

"Is that Pete's old coat?" she asked.

"Sure is."

"I didn't notice it last night. Must have been too dark."

"Mia gave it to me when I showed up in Chicago without a coat." Rory had almost started to enjoy the quiet morning when Sara's question brought him back to the realty of the situation. "I'm worried about her. Maybe I should have stayed with Mia last night."

"I'm sure she's okay," Sara said. "You know the University Hospital is literally less than a kilometer from the Trois Rois."

"Yeah, you're probably right," Rory agreed.

They both sat in silence for a moment, enjoying the calm of the forest.

Suddenly, the peaceful silence was interrupted by the rustle of steps falling on pine needles and beech leaves. Rory reached into his jacket pocket and pulled out the SIG, then motioned for Sara to go inside. She hesitated briefly, then walked back into the chalet as Rory crouched behind a stack of firewood piled on the side of the deck. A moment later he saw a figure emerging from the woods.

Das? How the hell did he find us?

Rory crouched lower and peered through a crack in the stacked wood. There was a break in the railing at the rear end of the slightly elevated deck. A short staircase of three steps led down to the clearing that housed the solar panels. Das walked up the steps slowly. As he placed his first foot onto the deck itself, Rory stood up from behind the wood but maintained a slight crouch. He assumed a firing stance, unwilling to trust Das after Sara's revelations concerning his involvement in Frederik's schemes. *Time for me to do the interrogating.* Rory aimed the pistol directly at Das's chest.

"Hold it right there!" Rory said in a loud, commanding tone.

Das froze in his steps, then began to speak. "Rory, I'm here to—"

Rory interrupted, "Are you alone?"

"Yes."

"Put up your arms." Rory walked out from behind the woodpile keeping the pistol trained on Das while using his peripheral vision to keep an eye on the forest beyond. "Take off your coat and put it on the railing. I'm going to frisk you."

"Rory, it's not what you think. Really."

"Shut up and take off your coat before I put a round through those pointy-ass shoes you're wearing."

"All right. Anything you say." Das began to unbutton his heavy woolen coat. He placed the coat on the railing as Rory moved in slowly to pat him down. He pulled a wallet, cell, and key fob from Das's pockets, then ordered him inside. Rory followed a couple steps behind with the gun aimed squarely at the back of Das's head.

Upon entering the chalet, Rory saw that Sara was now standing across the living room pointing a Swiss Army assault rifle directly at Das. He knew that Swiss law mandates compulsory military service for all men who are also required to keep their weapons at their residences. Sara must have known where Eric stored his rifle.

Das stood still for a moment, the two weapons trained on him, then said, "I'm here to help. Really, I am. Please, hear me out."

"How the hell did you even find us?" Sara asked as she moved closer, the rifle's muzzle now only inches from Das's head.

"Fred has a GPS tracker on your Land Rover," Das replied.

Sara jabbed the rifle forward, poking its muzzle into Das's forehead. "What are you talking about? A GPS tracker? For how long?"

"I don't know. Awhile, I guess. The guy is obsessed with you, not to mention completely crazy. I mean he literally thinks he's a bloody prince of the Netherlands, for crying out loud. I'm telling you, Fred is dangerous and totally unstable. Why do you think I texted you to warn Rory and Mia? This has gone too far."

Rory had actually heard the wild claim from Frederik as well. He said that the first king of the Netherlands, William I, had married late in life and moved to Maastricht, where he fathered a son lost to history, a son Frederik asserted was his great-great-great-grandfather. Rory had always just chalked it up to Frederik's eccentricities. But he could see it now. Frederik was more than eccentric. He was nuts.

Rory moved from his position behind Das to stand next to Sara. Now facing Das, he said, "You're going to tell us everything you know about what's going on. I mean everything. Understand?"

"Yes." Das nodded.

Time for some answers. Rory sat Das down in one of the kitchen chairs. Then he and Sara took seats opposite him, maintaining their guns at the ready but no longer pointed at the clearly frightened Das.

Rory looked at his prisoner closely, watching Das's eyes as they drifted down onto the kitchen table in both submission and shame. "Well, let's hear it," he said.

Rory was correct: Das was both afraid and ashamed. He had debated in his mind what to say the entire drive from Basel. Now, glancing up at the two people who, along with Peter, had been his closest friends at the BIS, Das knew what he had to do. He needed to come clean, completely clean.

Das had originally gone along with Frederik because of India, because of Bengaluru and all the millions of kids there who, like him, had nothing. Frederik's plan would transform lives. Even relatively poor people in India kept some small amount of gold or silver. It was part of the culture. The tremendous rise in price for those metals would offer a better life for millions who kept their life savings in the form of a small silver necklace or a tiny gold ring.

But Das had never wanted anyone hurt, and now Mia had been shot. A line had been crossed. Das's blind allegiance to Frederik was gone. He resolved to tell his friends everything and hoped, if they were still indeed his friends, they would understand.

Rory and Sara peppered Das with questions for the next hour. Das explained that holding companies operated by the BIS held as much as 30 or 40 percent of the outstanding shares in certain companies. Oftentimes they were just trading with themselves, one holding company to another, in order to paint the tape with whatever prices they wanted. It was a juggling act with millions of shares, commodity contracts, bonds, and other financial instruments. With the passing of the Phoenix Act, they just couldn't keep all the balls in the air any longer. And once one ball dropped, it would be like a block pulled out from a Jenga tower. Everything was going to come crashing down on Monday.

The only hope to regain something like market stability was the encrypted drive Rory and Mia had brought from Chicago. ICARUS needed to be up and running properly before the markets opened in New York on Monday or it was game over, lights out for the global economy. Mass bankruptcies, busted pension funds, insolvent banks, and crashed retirement accounts would just be the start. By the end of the week, riots, looting, and general social unrest would sweep around the planet like a deadly virus.

Rory and Sara looked at one another as Das completed his mea culpa, their guns still at the ready. A lot of blanks had just been filled in, but there was still one important piece of the puzzle missing.

Rory sat up straight and tightened his grip on the SIG. "Das, I'm going to ask you this just once. What do you know about Pete's death?"

CHAPTER 45

Sihlwald Forest, Switzerland
Saturday, November 6, 2027

DAS DID NOT IMMEDIATELY RESPOND. Instead, he turned toward Sara. She followed Rory's lead and firmed her grip on the assault rifle. "Don't look at me," she said. "Answer Rory's question."

Das thought for a moment, tiny droplets of perspiration appearing on his brow and upper lip. Finally, he said, "As far as I know, Fred had nothing to do with it. He was counting on Pete to get the VSA up and running correctly. We were both in his office when the call came in with news of the shooting. He was shocked and horrified by it, just like me. But..." Das paused.

Any sympathy resultant from Das's sob stories regarding the children of India was gone as Rory flashed back to pools of Peter's blood coagulating on a cold Chicago sidewalk. He raised the SIG and pointed it at Das's head. "But what? Spill it or I swear to God I'm going to paint this kitchen red."

A drop of sweat dripped from Das's forehead onto the dry wood of the kitchen table. "But, if Pete's death is in anyway connected to this, Anton Golev would have to be the one behind it."

Sara then asked, "The head of the Russian central bank had Pete killed? But why?"

"I honestly don't know if Golev killed Pete, but I do know he's not a banker or economist by trade. He's former FSB. He got close to the Russian president and a bunch of oligarchs during the late '90s and early 2000s. The KGB stashed away billions of Communist Party funds after the collapse of the Soviet Union. Apparently, Golev's mentor at the FSB controlled it all, dolling it out to gangsters and thugs who eventually became the oligarchs."

"It makes sense," Sara commented. "I heard stories like this from my father when he worked in private banking, old KGB guys holding millions in numbered accounts."

"Yes, Sara, that's right," Das said. "A lot of those guys funneled Party funds into Zürich banks when the Wall fell. But if Golev killed Pete, I have no idea why."

"I have an idea," Rory said as he lowered the SIG and rested it on his thigh. "Russia is a financial outcast with little to lose. At the same time, China is rising. Replacing the US with China as the world's economic superpower doesn't move the needle for Russia, but you know what does? A total financial collapse. Think about it. Who would a complete breakdown in the financial system hurt more, or should I say least?"

"I see what you're saying," Sara said. "Russia isn't really part of the global financial system anymore, not after years of sanctions and asset confiscations. On the other hand, China, the US, Western Europe—they all rely on the global economic network."

Das chimed in, "And Russia has built out a black market for all its major exports. India and Europe get more oil and gas from Russia than they ever did before, except now it's all done through back channels and away from the global banking system."

"So, what you're saying is a financial collapse is a disaster for all of Russia's enemies, but business as unusual can continue for Russia itself, maybe even improve," Sara said, then added insightfully, "It's not so much about what Russia gains, but what everyone else loses. And that means Golev never wanted ICARUS to work. He never wanted the VSA completed. So, he killed Pete in Chicago before he could share his breakthrough with Fred, then made it look like some random gang violence so his partners in crime would have no idea what the real play was."

Rory stroked the stubble on his chin as he processed what now seemed obvious. It was the same conclusion he'd come to on the ride to Luzern, the only way this all made sense. *Russia wants to trigger a financial meltdown. Golev has no intention of letting ICARUS get up and running.*

"I think that's it," Rory said. He stood up from the table and placed his SIG on the kitchen counter, then opened the fridge and pulled out a bottle of beer.

As Rory twisted off the cap, Das added, "There's one more thing I need to tell you. And you're not going to like it."

Rory placed the beer on the counter, picked up the SIG, and walked back toward Das. He didn't know if he could take any more bad news, but what choice did he have? Placing the pistol flat on the table and under his right palm, Rory set his left palm on the roughly hewn wood as well. He leaned forward and stared directly into Das's dark brown eyes. "Go on."

"Fred wants you and Sara to come back to Basel and work to get ICARUS up and running. He's worried that I might need some help to get Pete's code up to speed before the markets open in New York on Monday."

Rory laughed bitterly at the suggestion. "You aren't kidding, Das. Fred is fucking unstable. Does he seriously think after all this that Sara and I are just going to waltz into Quoz and roll up our sleeves?"

Das was almost dripping in sweat now, clearly anxious, but he had to get it out. "Rory," he said, "this is the part you're really not going to like."

Rory leaned in closer, just inches from Das's face. "Spill it!"

"It's Mia."

"What about Mia?"

"Fred has her locked up in the BIS infirmary."

Rory could no longer contain his anger toward Das. Betrayal of their friendship in the name of India was one thing, but his complicity now bordered on the unforgivable. Rory lifted his hands from the table and shoved them squarely into Das's chest. The force pushed Das back in his chair, his head thumping hard against the wooden floor of the chalet.

Sara placed her rifle on the kitchen counter and quickly circled around the table to Das. She knelt down to attend to him, then looked up at Rory, who now held the SIG in his right hand.

"That's enough!" she said.

Rory shifted his gaze from Das to Sara, then turned and stormed out to the deck. He placed the SIG on the deck's railing and lit up a smoke. *This cannot be happening.* Rory paced across the weather-worn planks, clouds rolling in overhead.

A moment later Sara came out and handed him his beer. "Relax, Mia is going to be okay. We'll get her," she said as she laid a hand on Rory's shoulder.

Rory took a sip of his beer, then collapsed down in one of the deck chairs. Looking up at Sara, he said, "I just don't know if I can take this bullshit anymore. I'm losing my mind."

Sara walked around behind Rory and began rubbing his neck and shoulders. He took a deep breath and regained some composure. After a few moments of silence, Rory rose from his chair, grabbed the SIG from the railing, and tucked it behind his back. "Let's find out what the hell is going on."

Entering the kitchen, Rory looked at Das, who was once again seated in his chair, rubbing the back of his head. *He'll have a nice-sized bump there soon*, Rory thought as he leaned up against the kitchen counter and continued the interrogation. "You're sure that Fred has Mia?"

"I saw her myself. She was asleep in the BIS infirmary with Hans standing guard. So far as I could tell, she looked all right."

"Okay, so Fred has Mia hostage, and in exchange for her life he wants Sara and me to be there when the Vega folder is decrypted. That way, we can help get ICARUS up and running as soon as possible. Is that what you're telling us?" Rory walked over to the refrigerator and pulled out a bottle of beer for Das. *Maybe I overdid it a bit*, he thought as Das continued to rub the back of his head.

Das twisted the bottle top, took a sip, and then held the cold beer against the forming bump. "Yes, Fred's nervous about getting the code integrated. Karl is in charge of trading and treasury now, but you two were the ones who worked on the source code for those functions with Pete. He wants you both there and motivated to help as needed. When we're done, Fred says everybody can go home."

Yeah right, Rory thought as he sat back down at the table.

"What are you thinking?" Sara asked, turning to Rory.

"I'm thinking there's no fucking way that once we get ICARUS 2.0 online, Fred is going to let you and me just walk out of the BIS."

"But what choice do we have?" Sara said. "We can't just leave Mia in Fred's hands."

"I know, damn it," Rory replied. "But we need a way to get out of that fucking tower once we have ICARUS back online or we'll all be dead."

"But how?" Das asked. "Fred will have Hans or some other armed goon watching you the whole time. That place is like a fortress. All the exits and entrances will be guarded as well, especially with the governors in town."

A wry smile appeared on Sara's face. "Have you guys ever heard of the Swiss nuclear preparedness policy, Bunkers for All?"

A slight grin grew on Das's face as well. He was well aware of the Swiss obsession for digging. Along with long mountain tunnels and spectacular gold vaults, the Swiss had built out an extensive network of nuclear bunkers and fallout shelters across the country. Their stated national policy, Bunkers for All, required provisioned bunkers for the entire population. As a result, well over 350,000 shelters dot the alpine nation.

Das was also well aware that bomb shelter access existed from below the BIS tower, access that happened to connect to a larger fallout shelter built directly under the nearby SBB railway station.

Rory looked quizzically at his former colleagues, clearly unaware of the motivation behind their mysterious smiles.

CHAPTER 46

Washington, DC
SATURDAY, NOVEMBER 6, 2027

A SNORING SENATOR WHITLOCK LAY next to Vanessa Price in the bedroom of his Capitol Hill neighborhood brownstone. His groggy eyes opened at the sound of his cell. It was 5:30 a.m. in Washington.

Vanessa, dressed in a light blue silk negligée, rolled over in bed and picked up the ringing phone that sat on the nearby end table.

"Hello, this is Senator Whitlock's chief of staff."

"Ah yes, I need to speak to the senator immediately, please."

Vanessa responded, "And with whom am I speaking?"

"It's his friend in Switzerland."

Vanessa turned to Whitlock and handed him the phone. "It's Frederik d'Oultremont."

The senator took the phone, somewhat annoyed by the hour, and barked, "What the hell do you want?"

"Did you speak with Randolph Dower yet?"

"No, I told you I can't just ask the chairman of the Federal Reserve to agree to something he's not even aware is going to be proposed yet," Whitlock responded gruffly.

Frederik raised his voice and said anxiously, "You assured me that you would get the Fed on board."

"And so I shall. Jake Rosenthal is traveling to Basel with Dower."

"And?"

"And I own Jake Rosenthal. He's gonna be whisperin' sweet nothings about BIScoin into Dower's ear the whole time they're in Basel. BIScoin

216

is gonna happen. Don't worry about that. I'll have the Bullion Bill in committee by the time Dower gets back to DC."

Jacob Rosenthal, young, handsome, and greedy, was the president of the Federal Reserve Bank of New York, the most powerful bank in the Federal Reserve System. Before his public service at the Fed, Rosenthal had run a large private equity shop in Manhattan. Whitlock had been instrumental in getting the firm off the ground and continued to hold influence with all of the firm's largest clients. While Rosenthal was no longer involved in the day-to-day management of the firm, he retained a sizable ownership interest and would be returning as its general partner as soon as his term with the Fed was up. His time in the high-profile position would lend a patina of respectability and maturity to the ambitious young financier. Rosenthal expected to double the firm's assets once his stint as a central banker was complete.

"Are you sure Rosenthal can get Dower on board?" Frederik asked.

"Sure as shit, partner. Now I'm headin' back to sleep."

Whitlock ended the call, but he did not go back to sleep. Placing the phone back on the end table, he rolled over toward Vanessa and whisked away the top strap of her negligée. The senator had his own sweet nothings to whisper.

Frederik, on the other hand, was not interested in whispering anything to anyone. He looked at his watch: almost noon in Basel. *Where is Patel?* He stood from his desk to stretch his legs, walked over toward the window, and looked out over Basel and the surrounding tri-nation area. *I think we'll need a second tower*, he thought as a buzz sounded from his office phone.

It was security calling from downstairs to notify him of Patel's arrival. Frederik told the guard to send him up. A few minutes later, a knock rang out from his office door.

"Come in!" Frederik said impatiently.

Arun Patel entered the office, a bit haggard after his overnight flight from Mexico.

"It's about time," Frederik said, dispensing with his normal refinement. "Now, take a seat. We have lots to do."

CHAPTER 47

Sihlwald Forest to Basel, Switzerland
SATURDAY, NOVEMBER 6, 2027

RORY AND SARA CRUISED NORTH on Swiss Highway A3 in the '74 Land Rover. A light rain dotted their windshield. Das followed one car behind them, alone in Frederik's 456-horsepower Tesla Model Y Performance sedan.

"So, do you trust him?" Sara asked.

"Like it or not, we have to trust Das, at least for now," Rory said. "We have no hard evidence that Mia is being held at the BIS, and even if we did, that tower is essentially sovereign territory. Swiss authorities have no jurisdiction. Hell, no one on the planet has jurisdiction to enter those grounds without Fred's permission."

Regarding Swiss authorities, Rory and Mia had learned from Das that Detectives Brunner and Meltzer were not detectives at all. Rory had figured as much. Last he checked, cantonal police do not make a habit of carrying suppressed pistols. Das further explained that a back-up goon squad posted at the hotel by Golev had managed to evacuate Mia and the injured Meltzer—or whatever his real name was—before the actual police got to the room where they discovered his partner's dead body. Rory and Mia were presumed missing by the police and wanted for questioning as persons of interest.

Before starting out for Basel, Rory and Sara had successfully found and removed the GPS transmitter hidden under the Rover's bumper. They left it lying under a beech tree in front of the chalet. Rory had also made a quick call to Milton McGrady on Das's cell. He filled him in on the situation and requested that the Gulfstream be fueled up and ready to take off from EuroAirport at a moment's notice. After Rory's call, Das texted Frederik to let him know that the trio would be making their way to the BIS directly. However, they had one important stop to make first.

Sara flipped on the old-school radio and pushed in a cassette mixtape. "Anarchy in the U.K." by the Sex Pistols blasted out of the surprisingly good aftermarket Blaupunkt speakers.

"Mind if we turn that down a bit?" Rory asked, his mind focused on other things.

Sara turned down the volume as she merged the Rover onto the A1, heading west toward Basel. "I always love this part of the drive," she commented. "We pass back and forth over the Limmat River three times and then cross the Reuss and Aare Rivers as well."

Rory did not reply, though he had to admit it was a pretty drive. Rolling foothills and small farms dotted the landscape. A flock of sheep herded together for warmth under a large tree overlooking the fast-flowing waters of the Limmat.

Sara took note of his silence. "What's wrong?" she asked.

"Nothing really. It's just I can't help but think that somehow Fred and Golev are going to walk away from all this like nothing happened."

Rory was well aware of the diplomatic-like immunity that Frederik enjoyed as general manager of the BIS. So long as Frederik maintained that he committed his crimes while acting on behalf of the bank, there was a chance he would be immune from prosecution. Regardless, before leaving the chalet, the three had agreed that Das would use his access to compile documentary evidence of Frederik's actions in collusion with the central banks of China, Russia, and India.

"Fred may be able to be prosecuted," Sara said hopefully. "Das will get everything he can on him from the BIS servers. Fred had more than a dozen trading accounts opened in his name, or his holding company names, for illegal purposes. He'll have a tough time explaining those away as actions on behalf of the bank. As for Golev, I know it sucks, but he's former FSB. The Russian president himself must have given his blessing for these operations. The Kremlin will deny any involvement."

Rory did not reply. He knew Sara was right. Golev was untouchable. Even if their plan worked perfectly, and that was a big if, it would likely ruin Frederik, but Golev was a different matter entirely. Rory thought back to the promise he'd made to Mia, that he would make whoever was responsible for Peter's death pay for it.

I don't know how, but I'll find that son of a bitch one day. Now was not the time for revenge fantasies, though. Mia was in trouble, and Rory knew he needed his head in the game if they were going to pull this off. He tried to push Golev out of his mind.

"We should be in range of Basel stations," Rory said. "Put on some news if you can find it. I want to see if there's any reporting about what happened at the hotel last night."

Sara popped out the cassette and turned the dial on the radio until she found a local Basel station broadcasting in Swiss German. She listened for a moment, then said, "Nothing about the Trois Rois. FC Basel lost three–nil last night to Winterthur." She flipped through a few more stations but found nothing concerning Rory and Mia's eventful evening. Eventually, she located a BBC broadcast in English and left it there.

After a rundown of major geopolitical headlines, the anchor turned to the growing financial crisis. "The world's central bankers are on their way to Basel, Switzerland, this weekend for a previously scheduled meeting at the Bank for International Settlements. Normally these affairs receive little coverage, as no information is released to the media. However, we do have reports out of Reuters that some form of emergency action to stop the market collapse that began this past week will be discussed. The sources of these reports are unclear on the exact measures to be taken, but they suggest something significant is in the works. We'll have the latest updates as more information becomes available.

"In related news, finance ministers and treasury secretaries around the globe have stated their willingness to declare an indefinite banking holiday should the markets continue their free fall on Monday's trade.

Many financial institutions have already put limits or outright holds on withdrawals, fearful of widespread bank runs. Some market watchers are warning that if the situation doesn't stabilize soon, an economic calamity worse than the 2008 financial crisis could be in the offing."

"Maybe the news wasn't such a good idea," Rory said.

Sara popped the tape back in. "Sounds like there may be anarchy in more than just the UK soon," she joked nervously as the voice of Johnny Rotten filled the Rover.

Rory did not reply. He stared out the window at the rushing waters of the Limmat. With the recent rains, local rivers were starting to approach flood levels. Gone were the crystal-clear waters. A muddy brown torrent now charged violently between the river's banks.

CHAPTER 48

Basel, Switzerland

A LIGHT DRIZZLE FELL ONTO the gray city streets as the two-vehicle caravan arrived at SBB. Sara parked the Land Rover just a block away from the Basel train station. The bells of a nearby church tolled the hour. It was 5:00 p.m. Rory exited the vehicle and grabbed the backpack sitting in the truck's rear compartment. The pack contained Eric's Swiss Army rifle—partially broken down—the suppressed SIG Sauer pistol Rory acquired at the Trois Rois, extra magazines, and some paracord scavenged from the chalet.

Das, who had parked Frederik's Tesla behind Sara's Rover, walked up to Rory. "Do you have everything?"

Rory nodded as Sara exited the vehicle. The trio made their way into SBB. They turned right as they entered the station and proceeded down an elevator and past various tracks until reaching the end of the main platform. Tucked in a corner, with no signage overhead, was a sturdy-looking steel door protected with a punch-code lock.

"That's it," Das said as he pointed toward the door. He looked at Rory, then said, "That door leads to a shared fallout shelter with the BIS. It's one of only two exits, the other being off sublevel four in the tower. Because this door is the only way out if there were some issue on the tower end, the Grand Council of Basel-Stadt shares the code with the BIS." Das then punched in the code, and the three made their way into the bunker.

A musty, damp odor reminiscent of a moldy attic greeted them as they descended a dark stairwell lit only by the flashlight function on Das's cell phone. At the bottom of the stairs, Das found a switch and flipped on some incandescent lighting. The space was large, about half the size of a football field, with lofty ceilings crisscrossed by steel I-beams. The walls were solid concrete. Various crates and sealed boxes full of canned goods, water, and other essentials sat stacked in one corner. Rows of folded-up cots lined the two side walls.

Rory, Das, and Sara made their way across the bunker, their footsteps echoing off the concrete.

"This place is a little spooky," Sara commented as they approached the far wall where a small, dark tunnel led away from the primary space.

"No kidding," Das agreed, then pointed to the tunnel. "That passage is about a hundred meters long. It leads right to sublevel four."

Das led the way once again with the light from his cell. After a short walk down the mineshaft-like tunnel, they approached another steel door identical to the one through which they had entered the bunker. Their plan called for them to leave a weapons cache here, along with the paracord. Rory unpacked the bag's contents, then reassembled the rifle, loading a magazine and racking a round. He checked the pistol to make sure it, too, was loaded with a chambered round as Das shined his cell to shed some light. Rory double-checked everything then left the small cache just to the left of the door. If he could gain access to this space from sublevel four, they would be well-armed to do what was necessary.

Rory looked down at the weapons, magazines, paracord, and bag one last time, then dusted off his hands. "All set," he said.

Das swung the phone around to shine the light on the steel door. "See that code box? There's an identical one on the other side. They use the same code on both sides so anyone who gets in here can also get out. The code is eight digits. Hans updates it every year or so and notifies the other security officers as well as Fred, Karl, and me. A couple months ago he set it to the founding date of the BIS, 17 May 1930. I know, original, right? But it helps us remember."

Das continued, "Anyway, on the other side of that door is the clos-est restroom to Quoz. There's none on sublevel three. Rory, you will need to convince Hans or whoever is guarding you to take you to that restroom. From there, it's up to you how you neutralize him. Once you do, you can retrieve the weapons and paracord here, but you'll also need another code to get back into Quoz and access the decrypted folder. It's 0-1-0-1-2-0-0-2."

"What happened on New Year's in 2002? Did Fred DJ in Paris or something?" Sara asked.

"Funny," Das replied sarcastically, clearly anxious and unamused. "Actually, it was the official launch date for euro banknotes and coins."

"I got it," Rory said. "May 17, 1930, for the bunker, Jan 1, 2002, to get past the restricted access point into Quoz."

"Exactly." Das then concluded, "Once in Quoz, make sure you upload the Vega folder to the BIS cloud before going for Mia. A cloud icon on the right-hand control screen will give you access."

Mission accomplished, Rory, Das, and Sara were back on the side street outside SBB within fifteen minutes. Sara opened the Rover and placed the keys under the driver's side floor mat.

"All set," Sara announced after shutting the door. "It's about a fif-teen-minute drive from here to EuroAirport."

"Sounds good," Rory replied. "Hopefully the Gulfstream will be fueled up and ready to go."

"Now all we have to do is get to it," Das said as he looked up at the BIS tower standing ominously hardly a block away.

Rory was hopeful their plan would work, including the gathering of evidence on Frederik and a cloud upload of the decrypted Vega folder so they could work on fixing ICARUS from the safety of the G650, but in his mind there was only one real objective. One way or another, he needed to get Mia out of that tower. He took one more look at the BIS headquarters building, its sweeping façade rising up over a gray and gloomy Basel, then said, "Well, we better get moving."

The unlikely team piled into the Tesla. Frederik was waiting.

CHAPTER 49

Basel, Switzerland

SATURDAY AND SUNDAY, NOVEMBER 6–7, 2027

"SO GOOD OF YOU TO come," Frederik said with a smile as he stood next to his office desk, pomegranate kombucha in hand. Dressed informally, he wore blue jeans and an untucked purple button-down shirt with a gray T-shirt underneath.

"Rory and Sara have agreed to help get ICARUS up to speed as soon as the decryption program is complete," Das reported. "I told them Mia is being well treated, and they'll be free to go once the job is done."

"Yes, yes, of course," Frederik replied. "Please, take a seat."

There were three chairs arranged in a small semicircle opposite Frederik's desk. Das and Sara both sat down. Rory remained standing, his eyes piercing through the urbane front presented by Frederik. "Where's Mia? I want to see her. Now."

"She is doing quite well. Our medical facilities here are top notch." Frederik placed the kombucha on his desk next to his cell. He then picked up the phone and opened an app. "Here, have a look."

Frederik handed the phone to Rory, who could see what appeared to be a live camera feed from the infirmary. Mia was lying on a bed. The resolution was quite good, and he could make out Mia's chest moving slightly under her blanket. She appeared to be resting peacefully. Hans Guzman stood in the corner.

Rory handed the phone back to his old boss. "Fred, why the hell are you doing this?"

"Why?" Frederik replied in a tone of shock. "Why am I doing this? Let me count the ways. The Global Financial Crisis in '08 and '09; inflationary shocks in the 1920s, '40s, '70s, and '80s as well as in this decade; the Great Depression; the so-called Long Depression kicked off by the Panic of 1873. Need I go on? Humanity has suffered long enough under the current world economic order, don't you agree? I think it's time for a change."

"A change with you in charge of every transaction from Beijing to the Bahamas?" Rory replied rhetorically.

"Someone has to be trusted to manage things. Would you rather it be economically illiterate politicians subject to the whims of the electorate? Fools who spend trillions of worthless dollars, euros, and yen in order to buy votes and remain in power, enabled by their spineless central banks? You know, Rory, I thought you had more brains than that. This is a great endeavor, and you had a chance to play a part in it, but you ran off to Puerto Rico to trade worthless digital assets backed by nothing but ones and zeros."

"Just like the US dollar," Rory said.

"My point exactly."

Rory wanted to clock Frederik right there, bust his head wide open on the thick corner of his office desk, but now was not the time. Nor was it the time for a philosophical debate on monetary policy. He took a seat in the remaining open chair next to Sara, anxious to just get on with this dirty business.

"Good, now that's better," Frederik said, the smile of a psychopath beaming across his smug face. He sat behind his desk, then took another glance at his phone. "It's 18:00. The world's central bankers will be arriving in approximately twenty-four hours. Rory and Sara, I want you to use that time to refamiliarize yourselves with ICARUS. Karl will be arriving shortly. He'll get you up to speed. If, after a few hours of work, he assures me that you've cooperated, I'll allow you to visit with Mia. You both can sleep in the infirmary with her tonight. Hans will be your host. Any questions?"

"Yeah, I got a question," Rory said. "Were you responsible for Pete's death?"

Frederik turned in his swivel chair and peered out the office window for a moment. It was almost dark, and the rain had passed. A soft red and orange glow saturated a break in the clouds as the sun set on the horizon. After a deep breath, Frederik swiveled back and looked Rory in the eyes. "I have unfortunately been a part of some necessary unpleasantness in order to make my vision a reality. But I assure you, Rory, I had no part in Peter's death. It was a tragedy, a real loss."

Rory stared back at Frederik as he spoke. He saw no deceit in the eyes, just the delusion of a true believer, a madman.

No, Fred didn't kill Pete. Golev did, and now he's on a mission to stop ICARUS from succeeding.

"Where is Anton Golev?" Rory asked.

Frederik's eyes widened at the mention of Golev. "Only Golev knows where Golev is. That man can show up anywhere. But what's your interest in him? You know Russia has been suspended from the BIS."

Now it was Rory who peered out the tinted windows of the tower, the softening shades of red and orange disappearing into the darkness of night. "Never mind, Fred, let's just get this over with. I want to see Mia."

Rory and Sara spent the next three hours with Karl von Hoffman reviewing changes in ICARUS's operations since their respective departures. True to his word, Frederik allowed Rory and Sara into the infirmary once they were done. Mia was sound asleep and connected to an IV. Exhausted themselves, Rory and Sara decided to try and get some sleep as Hans Guzman kept a watchful eye from a chair located next to the door.

After a night of tossing and turning, Rory awoke abruptly, half hoping it was all a dream. But it was real. He lay trapped at the BIS. Mia was still asleep on the bed to his right as Sara slept in the bed on his left. Hans Guzman sat quietly in his chair, awake but with drooping eyes that betrayed his lack of sleep. Light streamed through the windows of the second-floor infirmary.

Hans looked up from his chair, alerted by the sound of shifting sheets. "*Guten morgen*," he said as his eyes locked with Rory's.

What's so fuckin' guten about it?

Rory got out of the bed. He approached the sleeping Mia, grasping her left hand in his.

Mia's brown eyes slowly flittered open. "Rory, is that you?"

"It's me."

"What are you doing here?"

"I'm here to find out what's on Pete's drive. Then we're getting the hell out of here."

"I don't understand."

"Don't worry about that now." Rory released Mia's hand and poured a glass of water from a pitcher on the nearby nightstand. "Here, drink this."

Mia sat up in her bed and took a slow, long sip of the water. Rory explained to her how Das found him at Sara's. Then he glanced back at Hans. Sara was awake now and standing by his side making small talk.

She's a smart girl. As long as Sara was distracting Hans, Rory could continue with his brief.

In a whisper, he told Mia, "Look, we have a plan to get out of here late tonight. Be ready. We'll come for you as soon as we can."

"I still don't understand. Why didn't you just call the police or the embassy?"

"We had no proof you were here, and these premises are sovereign ground by international treaty. The place is on complete lockdown with the central bank governors arriving tonight. There was no other way. Now, rest. You'll need your strength later."

Hans Guzman had apparently caught on to Sara's distraction tactics. He stood from his chair, straightened out his wrinkled gray suit jacket, then walked toward Mia's bed. "That's enough."

"Oh Hans," Sara said as she placed her hand on his shoulder, "give 'em a break. They've both been through a lot."

Rory looked at Hans and the way he looked at Sara. *Did she have something going on with Hans too?*

Hans looked into Sara's eyes almost like a lovesick teenager. "I'm to take you and Rory down to Quoz," he said in his thick Swiss-German accent. "Karl is waiting for you."

Rory said goodbye to Mia and kissed her on the forehead. Hans then escorted him and Sara down a stairwell and to the restricted access door for Quoz. Rory watched carefully as Hans punched in the security code, 0-1-0-1-2-0-0-2. It was just as Das told him, January 1, 2002, the official launch date for euro banknotes.

Once inside, the three paused for a moment, allowing their eyes to acclimate to the iridescent green glow. They made their way to the Hive. Karl von Hoffman sat in front of the central control panel and scrolled through lines of code. He wore a white button-down shirt with khaki pants and black leather loafers.

"*Danke,*" Karl said as Hans left the Hive and took a security position outside the glass walls of the control room.

Rory took a seat to the right of Karl. Sara sat on Karl's left. Karl picked up where they had left off last night, explaining recent code adjustments and their impact to trading and treasury capabilities. Rory listened half-heartedly as Karl droned on about new APIs connecting ICARUS directly to stock and commodity exchanges around the world. Once he completed the lecture, Karl flipped to the countdown screen. It read, "82.28% Complete, ETD: 11 hours, 31 minutes."

"So, now what do we do?" Rory asked sarcastically. "Sit here with our thumbs up our asses all day until this damn program is complete?"

Karl did not reply. He stood from his chair and opened the door of the Hive. "Hans," he called, "please escort our two guests to the holding room."

Rory and Sara made the walk down the stairwell to sublevel four. As they approached the holding room, Rory could see the bunker access door at the end of the hall. *So close.* For a moment, he considered attempting to take out Hans right then and there. But now was not the time, and the moment passed quickly. Hans and Sara exchanged a few words in German before the security chief turned and left them alone in the windowless room. Rory once again heard the click of the dead bolt, its sound triggering doubts that their plan had any real chance of success.

CHAPTER 50

Basel, Switzerland

LIKE SALMON COMING HOME TO spawn, the world's top central bankers had once again gathered in Basel. Frederik, still in his office, had a few minutes before the Economic Consultative Committee began its proceedings. He cracked open a Red Bull and turned on his stereo to a particularly bass-laden EDM track. *Nothing like some caffeine and a pounding mix to prep the mind.* After completing a set of breathing and visualization exercises, he shut off the music and made his way to Conference Room E. It was almost 19:00. The ECC was about to be called to order.

As Frederik entered the room, most of the other eighteen participants were already seated around a circular oak conference table with nineteen high-back black leather chairs spread evenly around its circumference. There were gold-embossed place cards at each of the spaces with the respective attendee's name and bank of representation. Frederik walked with head held high toward his appointed chair as he waved, nodded, and made eye contact with a number of his fellow ECC members. He paused for just a moment to share a knowing glance with both Arun Patel of the RBI and Zhao Hong of the PBoC before taking his seat next to Randolph Dower, chair of these proceedings as well as leader of the US Federal Reserve.

Officially titled the Federal Reserve System, the Fed was actually the third central bank in the history of the United States. The nation's first central bank was signed into law by George Washington in 1791 at the urging of Alexander Hamilton and contrary to the wishes of various other political leaders, including Thomas Jefferson. Such was the popular opposition, Hamilton was only able to get a twenty-year charter for what was known as the First Bank of the United States. When the twenty years was up in 1811, Congress refused to renew the charter. The bank died a quiet death.

But the issue was far from over. In 1816, President James Madison revived it with the formation of the Second Bank of the United States, again with a twenty-year charter. But still, the people of the United States were fundamentally opposed to the idea of a central bank. Shortly after his reelection in 1832, President Andrew Jackson pulled all federal funds out of the Second Bank and summarily paid off the entire national debt, the only president to do so. By 1836, the US once again had no central bank. Then, in 1910 a clandestine meeting was held on Jekyll Island in Georgia, where the nation's elite financiers and industrialists concocted their plan for the Federal Reserve System. The only problem—they couldn't get it passed into law with the current administration led by President William Howard Taft.

The financiers and industrialists were patient men, however. They made their support of the New Jersey governor's bid for president contingent upon his support of the Federal Reserve. Governor Woodrow Wilson agreed to encourage the creation of a third US central bank. With staunch support from those who attended the Jekyll Island meeting, Wilson was elected president in 1912. Less than ten months after taking office, the Federal Reserve Act was passed and signed into law by President Wilson. The act created the Federal Reserve System, including twelve regional banks, the most powerful of which became known as the New York Fed.

Randolph Dower came to lead the Federal Reserve System by way of Harvard, where he obtained his PhD in economics and made a name for himself as a leading academic authority on monetary policy. A student of history, Dower was a thoughtful man of sixty-two with a slim build and a gray beard trimmed to mesh with his slightly balding head. The consummate professor, he subscribed to academic-consensus views on monetary policy firmly grounded in current economic theory. Though loathe to admit it, Dower enjoyed the power of his position but eschewed the spotlight, uncomfortable under the camera's gaze. He often let his top lieutenant, Jacob Rosenthal, president of the New York Fed, act as his mouthpiece. The younger Rosenthal had a love affair with the camera, and his outgoing personality often overshadowed Dower both in public and private.

Frederik was counting on Senator Whitlock and his ties to Rosenthal in order to ensure Dower's support for BIScoin. However, he was less certain where Zara Bernard of the ECB and Sir Peter Tindall of the BoE would fall. European and British gold reserves were not as robust as those at the Fed, even when adjusted for the relative size of their economies. On the other hand, the ECB had been increasing its gold holdings almost continuously since its formation, raising the percentage of total reserves held in gold to over a third. Germany's central bank, the Bundesbank, owned some three thousand tons of gold, accounting for over three-quarters of total ECB member reserves. The Netherlands, France, and Italy also maintained substantial gold positions. *Yes, if the Fed gets on board, the ECB will fall in line.* He was almost certain of it. After all, Frederik knew the dirty little secret of central bankers around the world. For all their modern theories and focus on innovation, their balance sheets revealed the cold, hard truth. Gold was still the backbone of the world's most powerful central banks.

Sir Peter Tindall and the Bank of England, however, were another story. In 1999, in what had to be one of the worst gold trades in history, the then chancellor of the exchequer, Gordon Brown, decided that England's central bank should sell off most of its gold reserves. At the time, gold was trading at the absurdly low price of less than $500 per ounce. The yellow metal proceeded to go up fourfold in the coming years. The result of this ill-timed trade was that the UK held only around three hundred tons of gold, about 10 percent of Germany's total and less than 4 percent of US reserves.

Could Sir Peter live with those percentages? Well, I'll soon have my answer, Frederik thought as Dower gave a slight rap on the table with a small wooden gavel. The ECC had been called to order.

CHAPTER 51

Basel, Switzerland

Sunday, November 7, 2027

Randolph Dower preferred a more informal, American-style meeting. Unlike former ECC chairs such as Jean-Claude Trichet, he reveled in lively discussions, which reminded him of academic debates from his days with the Economics Department at Harvard. After some preliminary housecleaning such as reminding committee members of their obligation to privacy and confidentiality, Dower yielded the floor and opened it up to all members for discussion.

Frederik sat back in his seat and watched as Dower recognized the governor of the Reserve Bank of India. The prearranged strategy called for Arun Patel to present BIScoin as a radical but realistic solution, followed by Zhao, who would initially express skepticism but eventually come around to the idea. Once the other governors said their piece, Frederik would then close, and Patel would motion to put BIScoin on the Global Economy Meeting agenda. Zhao would reluctantly second. If China were seen as too eager for BIScoin, it might lead some governors to question whether rumors of vastly underreported Chinese gold holdings were actually true.

Patel wore a dark navy suit with a maroon-and-gold-striped tie. He sat up straight in his chair and looked across the table at the array of governors. "Ladies and gentlemen," he began. Including Zara Bernard of the ECB, two of the nineteen attendees were women, the other being Liz Peterson of Canada. Patel continued, "We are all well aware of the crisis facing the world at this moment. This is not a crisis of war or famine or natural disaster. This is a financial crisis that is economic in its nature. It demands an economic response, and not a timid one at that. The nineteen of us gathered here today represent over four-fifths of the global economy. Humanity is counting on us, the world's central bankers, to orchestrate a solution. We cannot disappoint them by presenting as panacea the very actions that have led to this calamity. By that I of course mean interest rate cuts combined with dramatic increases in our respective balance sheets. Those actions are precisely what has led us to this point. ICARUS has only managed to postpone the inevitable. Therefore, I would like to present an unconventional but necessary proposal."

Arun paused for dramatic effect and then continued in his Indian-accented English, peppered with hints of his Cambridge education. "The world must combine the latest in financial technology, the blockchain, with the most tested monetary instruments in human history, gold and silver. What I propose here is something old but also something new: a global digital currency backed by precious metals and administered right here in Basel through the Bank for International Settlements. What I propose, ladies and gentlemen, is BIScoin."

Shocked expressions appeared on the faces of many of the attendees. Liz Peterson actually gasped, and Sir Peter Tindall moved uncomfortably in his chair. Patel went on, "I have an executive summary prepared here." He passed around eighteen freshly printed color copies of a twenty-four-page slide deck, updated with the latest figures for gold reserve holdings. "In order for this to succeed, all of us must be on board. It must be seen as a global solution for a global problem."

Zhao was preparing to play his part when Zara Bernard of the ECB spoke up. She was wearing a blue pantsuit and yellow blouse, her long, dark hair wrapped tightly in a ponytail. Removing her glasses, she said, "Arun, you can't be serious. There isn't enough gold and silver in existence to backstop today's massive economy. It's impossible."

"On the contrary, Zara, if you look at what I'm passing around, there is actually more than enough. It's simply a matter of price. Only a few decades ago, the world still operated under Bretton Woods with a gold exchange standard fixed at thirty-five dollars an ounce. My projections show that by adding silver to the mix, we can encompass all the world's wealth with a fixed ratio of 16 to 1, pricing gold at $25,000 an ounce and silver at $1,562.50." Patel knew those numbers were still too low and only a quarter of what would eventually be required. However, courtesy of the magic of fractional reserve banking, those prices would suffice for the time being.

Lars Rooth of Sweden then spoke up. Sweden was the smallest nation represented on the ECC but had a long central banking tradition and substantial gold reserves. Formed in 1668, the Sveriges Riksbank was the world's oldest central bank.

"I say this not out of concern for my nation," Rooth began. "We possess sizable reserves on a per capita basis, but what about the world's poorer countries? Those who haven't had centuries to build up their gold position as Sweden has been able to do?"

Patel responded, "The plan does not call for this to happen in isolation. As noted on slide 17, this must be part of a grander strategy involving the IMF and the World Bank. Moreover, it will be a blessing for many of the world's poorer nations such as Ghana, Sudan, Peru, Bolivia, and Mexico, which currently mine much of the world's precious metals. And with relatively small contributions from the IMF, BIS, and larger central banks, we can completely capitalize smaller nations, swapping their dollar reserves for gold, silver, BIScoin, or some combination thereof. The details can be worked out in the days and weeks ahead, but to stabilize financial markets we must outline and agree to a solution at the Global Economy Meeting tomorrow. All I ask now is that we formally place it on the GEM's agenda."

Zhao Hong of the PBoC finally got his chance to speak. "Colleagues, China has the world's second largest economy, but we are not even in the top five when it comes to gold reserves. This would be quite a sacrifice for us. If China were to back this idea, there would need to be some concessions to account for our relatively smaller gold reserves. We currently hold over one trillion in US sovereign debt. That debt must be honored at least in part with gold and silver."

In reality, China's gold reserves were well in excess of those held by any central bank, including the Fed. And as for their US Treasury bond holdings, those were now well under a trillion. China had been covertly reducing its dollar exposure for years. And on Friday, when the market was selling off, Zhao had been taking advantage of the chaos to unload huge Treasury positions, exchanging dollars from those sales for euros, yen, gold, silver, and other USD alternatives. These dollar sales had helped weaken the US currency at a time when most market watchers had expected it to rise. On Monday, Zhao was prepared to dump even more Treasuries and then flood the foreign exchange market with USD.

The world's current reserve currency was about to implode.

CHAPTER 52

Basel, Switzerland

SUNDAY, NOVEMBER 7, 2027

"I SAY, SIRS AND MADAMS," Sir Peter Tindall piped up in the King's English. "Britain holds less gold than Portugal, less than Uzbekistan or Turkey or Kazakhstan, for heaven's sake. We cannot just accept that gold and silver will now be the coin of the realm. And what is this bimetallism foolishness, backed by both gold and silver? Have you not heard of Gresham's law?"

Tindall was referring to the time-honored monetary principle that bad money drives out good. It was true that attempts at bimetallic standards in the past had run into trouble when one metal became worth more in the marketplace than was accounted for by the fixed ratio of exchange. This was the case in the United States during its early monetary history. Initially, the gold-to-silver ratio was fixed at 1 to 15, the then current market ratio. However, over time, gold appreciated in the marketplace relative to silver, predominantly due to large silver discoveries in Mexico and South America. This brought Gresham's law into effect. Americans hoarded their gold, or it went into the hands of foreigners and out of circulation. Soon only silver coins circulated freely in the newly formed nation. But Patel and Frederik had anticipated this objection.

Patel retorted, "Sir Peter, we are all students of economics here and well aware of Gresham's law. But this is not the eighteenth century, where ratios need be fixed for years at a time. If a large amount of silver or gold were to unexpectedly hit the market, the BIS could quickly recalibrate the fixed ratio to the correct amount. What's more, much as central banks today can affect the money supply with the twin levers of interest rates and quantitative easing, the BIS will be able to adjust the money supply to the needs of the global economy by modifying the gold-to-silver ratio. If a looser monetary policy is desired, the BIS can decrease the ratio of silver to gold, thereby increasing the total value of money in circulation. Conversely, it can increase the ratio to tighten the overall money supply when warranted by economic conditions."

The debate continued for the next hour, with valid concerns being brought up and discussed from both sides. Tindall remained steadfast in his opposition, but Patel had thought of everything. When the Englishman criticized the ratio of 16 to 1 for being far from the current market ratio, Patel pointed out that over hundreds of years of history, 16 to 1 was fairly close to the overall average. Indeed, at times it was much less. China had held a 4-to-1 ratio for centuries. In ancient Egypt, the metals often traded 1 to 1. As a point of fact, Patel informed the committee that from a total-ounces-mined perspective, about eight times as many ounces of silver have been mined when compared to gold throughout human history. Thus, 16 to 1 was really much less favorable to silver than it deserved to be. In any case, Patel argued, the BIS would be the price setter in the world market, not a price taker. The market would adjust.

Silent up until that point, Randolph Dower finally spoke. "The Federal Reserve System would be willing to entertain this idea. However, we have been focused on the precious metal aspects of Mr. Patel's proposal. What about the blockchain and the role of the BIS? Mr. d'Oultremont, what are your thoughts on the matter?"

Frederik nodded in respect. "Thank you, Chair Dower," he began. "I have listened closely and with much interest to this lively discussion. And I must disclose having had some conversation on the matter with Mr. Patel earlier this weekend. When he first brought the idea to my attention, I was admittedly surprised by its boldness. But I have given the matter serious thought in the last twenty-four hours, and I must say, the Bank for International Settlements is uniquely qualified to administer such a digital currency should the central bankers of the world ask it of us. Our mission is clearly and prominently stated in the lobby of this tower: 'to support central banks' pursuit of monetary and financial stability through international cooperation, and to act as a bank for central banks.' I can think of no service that is more aligned with that mission than to, without fear or favor, oversee and administer a global digital currency. We have been working on the issue of CBDCs for years, going back to Project Aurum."

Indeed, the BIS had been working on this issue for years. Project Aurum, the Latin word for gold, was a sprawling joint venture between the BIS Innovation Hub and the Hong Kong Monetary Authority. It included a working CBDC technology stack complete with a wholesale interbank system and a retail e-wallet solution. The BIS had other CBDC joint ventures either completed or in the works as well, such as Projects Helvetia, Arena, Dunbar, Jura, Dynamo, and mCBDC Bridge. The bank's overarching vision for CBDCs had also been spelled out in various white papers and included a blueprint for the tokenization of both money and assets on a unified leger system.

Frederik continued, "We at the BIS believe that a single globalized currency would have immeasurable benefits for the world's population. No longer would dictators of autocratic countries be able to rob their citizens of their wealth by devaluing currencies to the point of hyperinflation. And for the wider global economy, the elimination of exchange risk in business transactions and the efficiencies to be gained by a single and constant currency would be immense.

"Ladies and gentlemen, the world is moving to the blockchain, but as recent events have shown, the current mix of cryptocurrencies can be extremely volatile to say the least. Scandals such as the FTX debacle in '22 have exposed their weaknesses. However, by combining the imprimatur of the world's central banks along with thousands of tons of gold and silver, the world would finally have a digital currency it could trust. For the first time in history, there would exist one legal tender for all debts, public and private, anywhere on the planet. BIScoin would be nothing short of revolutionary."

"Hear, hear," Patel said excitedly as he rose from his seat. It caught a few glances from the other attendees, and Frederik did not want him to oversell it, but what could he do?

Still standing, Patel declared proudly, "I hereby motion to end debate and vote on the issue at hand, specifically the addition of BIScoin to the GEM's formal agenda."

As Patel retook his seat, Zhao Hong said with a tone conveying grudging agreement, "China is willing to do its part. I second the motion."

"Very well, then," Dower replied. "As the motion only requires a simple majority, let's see if we can get this done with a voice vote." He stood from his chair and restated the motion. "All those in favor of placing the adoption of BIScoin onto the formal agenda of tomorrow's Global Economy Meeting, say yea."

Everyone except for Sir Peter Tindall of the BoE and Kim Seong-Ho of South Korea's central bank responded with a yea. Along with Britain, South Korea held the lowest per capita gold reserves at the table.

"All those opposed say nay."

Tindall and Kim murmured their nays.

"The yeas have it, then."

And with that, Randolph Dower smacked his gavel on the table. Frederik sat back in the black leather of his chair and, despite his best efforts, could not contain a smile.

CHAPTER 53

Basel, Switzerland
SUNDAY, NOVEMBER 7, 2027

TIME TICKED BY FASTER FOR Rory when he was sitting in the dentist's chair. It had been over eight hours since Hans had deposited him and Sara in the holding room on sublevel four. Rory paced around his windowless cage as Sara lay on the couch. His stomach growled and his mind raced.

Sara sat up on the couch. "I can't relax either. I'm nervous, Rory. How are we going to access the guns?"

Rory took a seat on the couch next to her. "I know. I've been thinking about that too."

In truth, Rory had also been thinking about that fleeting moment right before Hans locked them into the holding room, wondering if it was a missed opportunity. He worried the plan they had dreamed up at the chalet had too many variables.

Along with rescuing Mia, accessing the decrypted Vega folder, and gathering evidence on Frederik, they also tasked Das to complete a massive upload of the entire ICARUS source code to existing BIS cloud infrastructure. Once complete, the trio would theoretically be able to update the software from the G650's satellite connection. This way, there would be no need to stick around the BIS post-decryption. Or so went the plan, a plan that Rory was growing less confident in by the minute.

Still thinking of the moment before being locked up, Rory asked Sara, "What did he say to you?"

"Who?"

"Hans. Right before he put us in here, he said something to you in German."

"Oh that. He said he'd try to bring some food down for us during the post-ECC dinner. He's really not that bad of a guy, you know."

Rory wasn't interested in hearing about Hans's redeeming qualities. He glanced down at his Rolex. It was just after 9:00 p.m. *I'm not missing this opportunity.* He looked into Sara's blue eyes, then said, "That dinner should be going on right now. This could be our chance."

"What are you suggesting?"

"I think we have to go for it. We can't try to finesse this."

"But what about Das and the Vega folder?" Sara asked. "If you take out Hans now, someone will come looking before long. And it's likely the decryption program still needs a couple more hours. We can't just wait around and risk an entire security detail coming down here armed and alert."

"Right. And that's why we don't wait for the decryption program. Our main priority is Mia."

Sara thought for a moment, then said, "Fair enough. So, what's your plan? You know Hans wears a shoulder holster under that hideous suit of his."

"I figured he packed something. How do you know he uses a shoulder holster? He could carry on his hip."

Sara replied matter-of-factly, "Had a romp with him one year after the Christmas party."

So, they did have something going on, Rory confirmed to himself, then turned his focus back to the situation at hand. "Hans shouldn't be expecting us to pull anything until after the file is decrypted. Plus, he's got to be tired after spending last night on guard in the infirmary. I should be able to get the jump on him. I'm actually more concerned about Das."

"Das? Why?"

"Sara, I want to believe he's on our side now, really, I do. But I'm worried that he's already blabbed to Fred about our weapons cache in the bunker."

The two sat in silence for a moment as Sara reached out and grasped Rory's hand in hers. He could feel the perspiration on her palms. She then asked both nervously and with a note of concern, "Are you going to kill Hans?"

"I don't want to fire any weapons. If I can knock him out and leave him tied up in here, I will. But..."

"But you'll kill him if you have to."

"I'll do what needs to be done."

Rory released Sara's hand from his grasp. He stood and resumed his pacing. In a louder, more resolute voice, he said, "Fred can talk all he wants about necessary unpleasantness, but you and I both know damn well he's not going to let us walk out of here with Mia once we update ICARUS. We need to do what we came here to do—get Mia and then get the hell out of this fucking tower. You understand me?"

When he finished speaking, Rory stopped his pacing and turned to face Sara directly. With an almost imperceptible nod, she confirmed her agreement.

No more than fifteen minutes later, they both heard noises in the hall. Rory's body immediately tensed as adrenaline began pumping through his veins. *This is it*, he thought as the dead bolt clicked.

Rory moved quickly to the side of the door, awaiting Hans's entrance. He saw the rolling wheels of a dining cart cross the threshold, but no Hans.

"How's it going?" Das said as he pushed the cart into the room as if returning from a Sunday stroll.

Rory moved cautiously a few steps away from the wall and glanced past Das and into the hall. Now he could see Hans, but Das and his dinner cart blocked a clear attack angle. Within seconds, yet another opportunity evaporated. Hans shut the door behind Das, then locked the dead bolt. Rory stood infuriated and impotent in the center of the room.

"Well, I brought you both some food from upstairs," Das announced obliviously.

Rory dropped his head and rubbed the bridge of his nose as what may have been their best chance to execute an escape passed in the blink of an eye. Despite his anger and disappointment, Rory's body was begging for sustenance, and the scents emanating from the food cart were enticing. He stepped over and examined the two plates Das had pushed in. One held a gorgeous-looking rib eye paired with mashed potatoes and gravy. The other contained what looked like a perfectly grilled piece of halibut, accompanied by roasted potatoes and vegetables. Das had also brought down a couple of Quöllfrisches.

"Fish or steak?" Rory asked.

"Fish," Sara replied.

Rory handed Sara the halibut. They both took a seat at the small table and began gulping down the food.

After a few moments, the food had a mildly calming effect on Rory's nerves. "Thanks, Das," he said, a bit of steak still in his mouth. "Did you get what you need?"

Das pulled a BIS-embossed thumb drive from the breast pocket of his blazer. "This should be more than enough documentation to put Fred away for a long time."

"What about the source code upload?" Sara asked.

"Should be done in about an hour."

"Great," Sara said. "And the decryption program?"

"Over ninety-seven percent complete. It'll be ready around 23:00," Das reported.

Rory's mind, seemingly recharged by the rib eye, finally realized that Das's dinner cart may have been a blessing in disguise. Now, he even had silverware.

Rory motioned for Das to come nearer the table where he and Sara sat. In a hushed tone, he asked, "Is Hans out there waiting for you?"

"Yes. Fred needs me back upstairs. He's asked me to pull him from the dinner at 22:45," Das confirmed.

"Listen, this could be our best opportunity to access the weapons and get Mia." Rory locked eyes with Sara for a second, then refocused on Das. "When we're ready, you knock on the door for Hans to let you out. Then, I'm taking him down."

"Wait a minute," Das immediately objected. "There's still almost ninety minutes left on the decryption program. You can't wait it out down here. What if someone comes looking for Hans? There's an army of security up there."

"Fuck the Vega folder." Rory maintained his hushed tone but was growing more frustrated by Das with each second. "Mia is my number one concern. The markets will just have to collapse."

Again, Das objected. "Rory, I understand. We need to get Mia. But we need to fix ICARUS too. The world economy is on the brink."

Rory let out an exasperated sigh. His mind reeled as it tried to weigh Mia's rescue on the one hand and the consequences of a global depression on the other.

Das continued, "Look, wasn't it you who said this thing has the potential to spiral out of control, a repeat of the 1930s that could even lead to war? There is another way."

"Go on," Rory allowed.

"Okay, after I pull Fred from the dinner, he and I will head down to Quoz with Karl. But Fred has also ordered Hans to retrieve both of you around the same time. When he comes to take you guys up to sublevel three, that's when you take your shot. Once you subdue Hans, then you and Sara head to Quoz armed to the teeth, where we tie up Fred and Karl at gunpoint. We upload Vega to the cloud, get Mia, and exit through the bunker to avoid security. That was our plan, remember?"

Rory did remember, both the plan and the dire warnings he had made at Das's flat. A complete breakdown of the financial system wouldn't just lead to higher unemployment and tough times. The world was facing a real collapse, the end of a global economic order that had been in place since the 1940s.

"All right, Das," Rory agreed. "We'll do it your way. Now, you better get back up there before anyone gets suspicious. Just make sure that source code is completely uploaded. We're not sacrificing this opportunity for nothing."

Das turned and knocked on the door. A moment later, Hans released the dead bolt and swung it open. Das departed, and once again Rory heard the dead bolt click into place. He looked down at his rib eye and took another bite. His stomach had ceased its growling. But in his gut, Rory worried that this meal might just be his last.

CHAPTER 54

Basel, Switzerland

SUNDAY, NOVEMBER 7, 2027

FREDERIK WAS DOING MORE TALKING than eating at the post-ECC dinner on the eighteenth floor. The dining area had been drenched in opulence for the occasion with fine linen tablecloths and a dedicated server for every three guests. The soft sounds of classical music floated in the background, and the lighting had been dimmed to highlight views overlooking Basel and the surrounding countryside.

Frederik had arranged to be seated at the most exclusive of tables. He sat, a glass of Kopparberg non-alcoholic pear cider in his right hand, and regaled Randolph Dower, Zara Bernard, Arun Patel, and Sir Peter Tindall with tales from a time he DJed for forty thousand festival goers in Berlin.

Tindall placed down his fork and interrupted Frederik's revelry. Directing his attention toward Patel, he said, "You seem rather enthusiastic about this BIScoin idea. Could it have anything to do with the enormous hoard of gold and silver your people possess? I should think that the standard of living in India will increase significantly if we return to some sort of bimetallic exchange standard."

Patel took a sip of his wine and gently placed the glass on the table before responding. "It is true that the Indian people have long had an affinity for precious metals. But I can assure you that is not the primary motivation for my support. The hard truth is that the inflationary spending and lack of sound monetary policies undertaken in places like the UK and the United States have outsize effects on those in the developing world. If food prices rise in London, the people do not go hungry. They buy potatoes or chicken instead of beef, but they eat. However, we have a long history of famine in India, including some fifteen million deaths in just the last half of the nineteenth century alone, a period in which you Brits still managed to return profits for the East India Company."

Tindall stared at Patel as an awkward silence fell over the table. "Surely you can't blame the Bank of England for famines over a century ago."

"Perhaps not, but when the stock price of the East India Company fell sharply during the Great Bengal famine, the BoE did loan the company some one million pounds, a tidy sum at the time. It was used to violently keep workers at their posts, ensuring the company's net revenues met expectations. So, Sir Peter, would it really be so unfair if the people of India saw their station rise a bit?"

Frederik watched with interest Patel's attempts to shame Tindall into agreement with a plan that would clearly benefit India and harm Great Britain. He knew Sir Peter's mind would not be swayed. However, Zara Bernard, president of the ECB, was well known for her charitable activities in the developing world. Prior to being promoted to her current post, she had served as chief economist at the World Bank. She had worked ardently to improve standards of living around the globe despite the bank's history of what could only be described as predatory loan practices. Frederik hoped that Patel's remarks would tilt the bleeding heart of Bernard in favor of BIScoin. It was having its desired effect.

"Come, come, Sir Peter," Bernard interjected into the conversation. "It's not India's fault that the BoE sold all its gold at the worst possible time."

"Easy for you to say, Zara. The member countries of the ECB have some of the highest per capita gold reserves in the world," Tindall countered.

Well, mustn't let this go too far. Frederik interrupted. "Gentlemen and madam, please, let us keep this cordial." He turned toward the American, who had been noticeably silent at the table. "Randolph, what are your thoughts on the matter?"

The Fed chairman was an academic, and the thought of a gold and silver-backed currency went against his grain. He had been trained to believe there is nothing special about those metals. Over the course of history, everything from beach shells to tobacco had been used as money. And right now, the greatest monetary instrument in the world was under his control, the US dollar. But Dower also understood that the ridiculous amount of money printing at the Fed could not go on forever. He had often lamented the demands that politicians put on him to finance their next big spending bill. It would be nice to have that burden removed.

Of course, the Fed was supposedly independent. Theoretically, Dower could ignore the politicians and refuse to print money, but he was keenly aware that should he turn off the spigot, it would produce disastrous consequences for the US economy. Sky-high interest rates in the Treasury market would turn bank balance sheets underwater just as they had done to Silicon Valley Bank in '23. What's more, Dower knew that for every 1 percent increase in Treasury yields, the US taxpayer owed a quarter trillion more in debt service. Simply put, if he didn't increase the Fed's balance sheet and buy US debt by the truckload, the whole system would break. Certainly, the Fed had made efforts in the past to reduce its balance sheet, but they were always short-lived and mere pauses before yet another wave of bond purchases. With the passing of the Phoenix Act, Dower knew the Fed's balance sheet would once again begin expanding.

Dower also realized that there were other monetary chickens yet to come home to roost. The third rail of American politics was underfunded entitlement programs, and both the Social Security and Medicare trust funds were on the brink of insolvency. Combined, this issue made the Phoenix Act look like a rounding error. Upcoming shortfalls for both programs were in the tens of trillions. Indeed, the latest estimates out of the US Government Accountability Office predicted both programs would be bone-dry by 2033, just six years away. Something needed to be done, and a significant shake-up in the dollar-dominated global order may give Congress wiggle room to make necessary adjustments.

Dower faced a tough decision. He resolved to talk it over tomorrow morning with Jacob Rosenthal before coming to any final decisions. Peering across the table at his fellow central bankers, he said, "I think that Arun has made an interesting proposal, but for something of this nature, I can only recommend to Congress the appropriate action to take. Of course, I like to think I have some influence on the thinking of my political counterparts." He paused for a sip of wine, then concluded, "I'll need to consider it further before making my decision."

As a soothing movement from Beethoven's Ninth Symphony played in the background, Frederik took a moment to look around the room. He was not concerned about American legislators. With the Fed's backing, Senator Matthew Whitlock would be able to shepherd the SAGE Act through the US Congress with ease.

This really is coming together, Frederik thought as he glanced down at his watch. *22:43. Soon, Vega will be decrypted.* He could hardly contain his sense of anticipation. To calm himself, Frederik returned to his breathing. *Yes, that's better.* He took one final sip of his pear cider, appreciating the winds and strings of Beethoven melodiously floating through the night air. Then, from the corner of his eye, he caught a glimpse of Kartik Das entering the room and making a motion with his head toward the door.

So, Frederik thought, *it is time.*

CHAPTER 55

Basel, Switzerland

SUNDAY, NOVEMBER 7, 2027

RORY BEGAN TO SWEAT, FIRST under his arms and then on his upper lip. The blue dial on his Rolex Datejust showed 10:45. *Any time now, Hans should be here any time...*

As if in slow motion, Rory heard the tumblers click and the dead bolt slide clear. He took a deep breath from his position against the wall and just to the right of the door, an empty Quöllfrisch bottle cocked back in his right hand. Though his first inclination was to utilize the steak knife, Rory reluctantly conceded to Sara's argument that the bottle combined with the element of surprise should be enough to handle a fatigued Hans.

As he stepped through the door, Hans's eyes surveyed the room. Sara stood by the couch and drew his attention as she exclaimed, "Hans, how good to—"

Rory cracked the bottle hard into the back of the security chief's head, glass shattering like a firework on the Fourth of July. It was a solid blow, wobbling Hans's knees but not knocking him out. Dazed, he instinctively began to go for the pistol held in a shoulder holster under his suit just as Sara reported. Rory anticipated the move and jammed his right palm hard into Hans's nose, knocking him to the ground. Rory then reached down for the gun, but Hans was able to get a grip on his wrist before Rory could pull the pistol. He jerked Rory to the ground with him and managed to sneak in a quick left hook, but Rory's blows had clearly taken their toll. With his system pumping adrenaline at full throttle, Rory hardly noticed the weak hook as he reached with his left hand and grabbed ahold of Hans's medium-length hair. He smashed the security chief's head back onto the hard concrete floor twice, feeling Hans's body grow flaccid with the second blow. His resistance vanished. Hans had been knocked unconscious.

Rory retrieved the pistol, a compact 9mm Glock 19, and paused for just a moment to catch his breath. He stood up and looked down at Hans, obviously out, but for how long Rory had no idea. Sara, who had watched the brief struggle from across the holding room, walked over to Rory. He looked down at her right hand and noticed the steak knife gripped tightly.

"Just in case," Sara said as she tossed the knife onto the nearby dinner cart.

Rory presented the Glock to her. "Do you know how to use this?"

"Yes, my father used to take me shooting as a girl, rifle and pistol."

Rory partially pulled back the slide to check for a chambered round, then handed her the pistol. He said, "Keep an eye on Hans while I go to the bunker for the paracord and other weapons. I'll be back in a minute."

Rory exited the room. The bunker door was less than ten yards away at the end of the hall. *Date of BIS founding, May 17, 1930,* Rory thought as he rapidly entered the code, 0-5-1-7-1-9-3-0.

"Fuck," he uttered to himself when the door failed to unlock. He tried again, this time more slowly... 0 – 5 – 1 – 7 – 1 – 9 – 3 – 0. Again, the door did not open.

"Das!" Rory said out loud. *Did that son of a bitch backstab me again?* Rory tried the code one last time. Nothing. He ran back down the hall and returned to the holding room.

"Where is everything?" Sara asked.

"The damn door won't open. Das gave us the wrong code."

"Are you sure?"

"I tried three fucking times, yes, I'm sure. We don't have time to waste. If Das has turned on us, we're screwed. Let's get out of here."

Intensifying Rory's stress, he was conflicted about their next move. On the one hand, they could head directly to the infirmary and try to get Mia. She was likely under watch by another member of BIS security, but Rory felt confident that with the Glock and element of surprise on his side, he could overtake the guard. This course of action would leave it up to Das to get ICARUS on track, but in any case, he had apparently shifted allegiances once again. Rory couldn't give a damn if Das was left alone to avert a financial collapse. That was secondary. Right now, his primary concern was finding Mia, getting to the airport, and jetting off in the G650 as fast as possible.

On the other hand, Rory knew that without access to the bunker, the only way out of the tower would be the main entrance—highly guarded, under surveillance, and able to be locked down at a moment's notice. Perhaps the right play was to enter Quoz. At least Rory knew that code worked. There he could subdue Frederik, Karl, and Das if need be, maybe get some answers at gunpoint. It would also give him the opportunity to learn what was on Peter's thumb drive, which he knew was important to Mia.

Mia, Rory thought, *she'd want to see this thing through.*

Sara's mind was turning just as much as Rory's. She said, "I agree, let's get out of here, but where?"

Rory ran his hands through his hair and over the thick stubble that had grown on his face during the past week. "I think we have to head to Quoz. Try to get the correct code to the bunker exit, then get Mia. Otherwise, we'll have to leave through the main exits, and this place is locked down tight with the governors here."

"Right," Sara replied with a nod. She handed the Glock to Rory. He popped the mag and did a press check on the top round. Just a slight give. It was fully loaded as expected. He then tucked the Glock inside his jeans and against his back. Rory searched Hans and pulled a key chain from his right pant pocket. He and Sara left the holding room, locking Hans in behind them. They made their way to the stairwell, up to sublevel three and Quoz.

Rory punched in the digits, 0-1-0-1-2-0-0-2. The door clicked open. He slowly stepped through the entrance, gun drawn, with Sara two steps behind. They paused for a moment to adjust to the emerald glow.

Just as Rory's eyes began to focus, he felt a shooting pain as a pistol butt slammed down hard on his neck. He buckled to his knees. There was a scream from Sara and then silence as a hard-heeled shoe slammed into his back. Rory fell forward onto the smooth, cold floor, Hans's pistol falling out of his right hand and sliding a few feet in front of him.

It came to rest at the feet of Frederik d'Oultremont III.

CHAPTER 56

Basel, Switzerland
Sunday, November 7, 2027

FREDERIK REACHED DOWN AND SCOOPED the Glock off the floor. Towering above the prone Rory, he said, "A good effort, but not good enough."

Rory turned his head to the right and looked up at the smiling face of his old boss. Frederik pulled his cell from his pocket and showed Rory the screen. This time it wasn't of the infirmary but instead displayed a high-resolution video feed of Hans Guzman lying on the holding room floor. "I keep my eye on this entire building. Did you really think I would allow my global vision for the future to dissolve so easily?"

Rory did not respond. He craned his neck back and saw Karl von Hoffman. He was holding Sara in a tight bear hug, his right hand over her mouth. Rory also noticed that Karl was armed and wearing a holster similar to the one Hans had on.

"So, Karl," Rory said, "how does it feel to be Frederik's bitch?"

"Fuck you," Karl responded, then raised his big right heel for another blow to Rory's back. It struck square, and Rory's head slammed into the concrete floor.

"Enough," Frederik said to Karl. "We may need him. You weren't here when Peter originally put all this in place." He then turned his attention back to Rory. "Didn't you know? Karl is former KSK, Germany's elite counterterrorism unit."

"I don't give a shit what he formerly was," Rory replied, blood dripping down the corner of his mouth. "All I know is he's currently a fucking *futzgsicht.*"

Karl moved in for another kick, but this time Rory managed to roll to his right and avoid the strike. Frederik, still holding Hans's Glock, interjected, "I said enough. Rory, on your feet."

The group made their way to the Hive. Das was already seated in the center chair in front of the control panel. Rory gave a hard look at him, then glanced at the screen. It read, "99.92% Complete, ETD: 0 hours, 3 minutes."

"Just in time," Frederik commented. "Now we find out just how smart Peter truly was." He instructed Karl to stand guard in the corner of the Hive before turning back to Rory and Sara. "Please, take your seats and relax. You both will have a lot of work to do soon."

Sara took a seat to the right of Das as Rory remained standing. He and Frederik locked eyes. Frederik broke the tense silence. "Your bravado is getting boring. Must I pull out my cell again and show you Mia in the infirmary? Remember, no matter how terrible things get, they can always take a turn for the worse."

Rory did not reply as he begrudgingly sat in the remaining open chair just to the left of Das.

Frederik moved to a position directly behind Das and looked at the center screen. "Is everyone excited? Only one more minute until the mystery of the Vega folder is revealed. How do you think Peter did it?"

Rory and Sara said nothing, but Das replied, "Well, in his dissertation, Pete melded mostly traditional albeit very high-level mathematics with some of the latest thinking in deterministic chaos theory regarding closed systems to posit that—"

"Thank you, Das," Frederik interrupted. "What I really meant was, Do you think you will be able to integrate it into the ICARUS source code?"

Das said, "Until I see it, I can't say for sure, but Pete knew our system parameters better than anyone. I don't see why not."

The machine made a short beep as the progress bar hit 100 percent. Despite the circumstances, Rory couldn't help but feel some excitement as the contents of the drive would finally be revealed.

Das punched in a few keystrokes and moved the mouse to access the folder. It contained a docx file as well as an MP4. "Hmm, that's odd," Das said. "Two files here. One is a standard Word doc, the other a video file."

"Odd?" Frederik asked anxiously, staring over Das's shoulder.

"I was hoping there would be a .py, Python extension, some actual code here. Maybe I'll need to run a docx2txt program," Das said. He then clicked on the Word doc. "Hopefully we'll at least have a detailed road map of the work ahead."

As he scrolled through the document, Das's eyes grew wide. Rory stared at the screen in some confusion, the pages mostly a jumble of equations and other mathematical script.

"Well, what is it?" Frederik asked as he rubbed a sweaty palm against his thigh.

Das did not respond immediately but continued his scan of the pages. After a moment, he said, "It looks like a negative proof related to undecidability."

"A what?" Frederik questioned.

"It's along the lines of a Gödel incompleteness theorem, you know, like Turing's first proof, the halting problem."

Frederik, who had been trying to remain as calm and cool as possible up to now, began to show some frustration. "Speak fucking English, Das. What the hell are you talking about? Can you make it work or not?"

Das was unsure what to say next. He knew Frederik didn't want to hear it, but the more he scrolled through the pages, the more certain he was of what Peter had produced.

Finally, Das turned in his chair to face Frederik. Rory, Sara, and Karl also listened intently to his conclusions. "This is a negative proof. It's also what is known as a proof of impossibility. Basically, a negative proof demonstrates mathematically that a specific problem *cannot* be solved." Das paused for a moment, recognizing that his audience needed a bit more color, then explained, "For example, the irrationality of the square root of two. It's possible to mathematically prove that one cannot express the square root of two as a ratio of integers. That's an old one, but more recent negative proofs tend to deal with computational questions and are based on the work of Kurt Gödel. He was a twentieth-century mathematician and a true genius. Anyway, what Pete has here is a proof of impossibility for the ICARUS algorithm."

Frederik asked, "So what exactly are you saying?"

Das looked first in the eyes of Rory and then Sara. He sensed that they had understood the import of what he had just told them. Frederik's blue eyes, however, still had some glimmer of hope. Das realized he had to spell it out.

"Fred," he said, pointing back to the screen with his right hand, "this proves that ICARUS can never run as designed. It's a mathematical impossibility. It just won't work, at least not in any way that is sustainable."

Frederik took a step back, his face white as alpine snow. Grasping at straws, he asked, "What about the video? Can you play it? There's got to be some other explanation."

"I should be able to." Das turned back around in his chair and clicked on the MP4 file.

A moment later, Peter's face, like a ghostly apparition, appeared on the center display.

CHAPTER 57

Basel, Switzerland

Sunday, November 7, 2027

Rory felt like a levee inside his head had just given way. Seeing and hearing Peter released a flood of memories: their first meeting at Hamilton's, quitting Celtic to work on ICARUS, their argument the night he was killed, his dying words on the streets of Chicago. *For time is the longest distance between two places*, Rory thought as he tried to wipe the recollections away. But it wasn't working. Though he could hear Peter speak, Rory failed to synthesize the words. His mind floated from memory to memory.

Frederik and Das, however, were listening intently, and neither liked what they heard. Peter began by describing his progress, or lack thereof, on the VSA and the Vega Block in particular. He explained that as his work neared completion, he began back testing and running preliminary datasets through the VSA, obtaining results that made no sense at the time. After an all-night session, he went back to his dissertation and reviewed some of the core underlying equations behind his work.

Like Einstein's addition of the cosmological constant to his field equations of general relatively, Peter had needed to add a volatility constant to his equations in order to balance them out. He called it the Vega constant. Unfortunately, he had made a fundamental error in his original calculations.

The attached Word document, Peter went on to communicate in the video, was a negative proof regarding all possible values for the Vega constant. It demonstrated conclusively that the AI algorithm behind ICARUS could never work. Peter further explained that a number of recent incidents had begun to concern him. In fact, he suspected someone was following him. Worried he may be in danger, Peter had decided to create the encrypted drive and hide it in his safe.

Rory's focus began to return as the memories began to subside. He listened to Peter and started to comprehend what had transpired. He couldn't help but note the MP4's time stamp: 2026-11-04 21:42:16. The video was recorded the night prior to Peter's murder.

All eyes in the Hive were glued on the display screen as Peter concluded, "If someone is watching this, it's probably because something terrible has happened to me. Only one person would have been able to find this file and get it decrypted. Rory, if you're there, I want to apologize. I'm sorry that I got you caught up in this crazy project. I'm sure that if I hadn't been so excited about it, you probably would still be at Celtic with Milt and the gang, making millions, and not wasting your time on a lost cause. And I know that you won't like me keeping this whole thing a secret, but this is too explosive, too dangerous to let anyone know about until I feel it's safe. Please, tell Mia and my parents that I love them. I love you too."

The screen went black as Rory sat back in his chair. Sara and Das stared blankly as if expecting more, but that was it. Frederik stepped, almost staggered back, then sat on top of the mini-fridge located in the corner opposite Karl.

"That can't be it. Peter must be wrong," Frederik said in desperation. Rory spun around in his chair. "It's over."

Frederik did not reply. A tear ran down the left side of his face. His eyes had glossed over. The Dutchman was unhinged. He slowly raised the muzzle of Hans's Glock, but instead of pointing it at Rory, Frederik placed it to his own right temple.

Sara immediately stood from her chair. "Fred, what are you doing?"

Again, he did not reply. He just stared through the glass walls of the Hive as if viewing a ship disappearing into the horizon. Rory almost said, *Go ahead, do it,* but something in Frederik's eyes silenced him. He looked like a lost boy trying to find his way home.

Finally, Frederik broke the silence. "This is not my destiny. I am a Prince of Orange."

What the fuck is he talking about? Rory thought. "Look, Fred, ICARUS is over. Frankly, I'm not sure that's a bad thing. But this isn't the answer. Let Sara and I get Mia and leave. I know it wasn't you behind Pete's—"

Frederik interrupted, "Not a bad thing? Not a bad thing? ICARUS and BIScoin were meant to end the financial tyranny of corrupt politicians and worthless central bankers. They were to usher in a new world order and lift billions from economic oppression. And I was supposed to be the one who gave this gift to the world." Frederik paused, keeping the pistol to his head. "Rory, do you know the greatest trick ever played by bankers and economists?"

Rory played along, hoping that in such a state, Frederik might decide he didn't care if Rory, Mia, and Sara walked right out the front door of the BIS. "No, Fred. I don't."

Frederik smiled at Rory, the smile of a madman, the same smile Rory had seen on his face a hundred times before but never really understood until now. *Fred really thought he was going to save the world.*

The smile disappeared from Frederik's lips. "Rory, when you figure out the trick, then you'll know why the end of ICARUS is a bad thing."

Frederik's blue eyes were no longer glossy. Instead, they stared with intent toward the central core of ICARUS. His right hand tensed around the Glock.

"*Je maintiendrai,*" Frederik said softly, then pulled the trigger.

CHAPTER 58

Basel, Switzerland

BLOOD AND BRAINS SPRAYED ACROSS the Hive, primarily in the direction of Karl von Hoffman. Hans's Glock fell from Frederik's dead hand and rattled on the concrete floor. Rory sprang from his chair, grabbed the pistol, and immediately pointed it toward Karl. He kept the Glock trained on Karl's chest as the German furiously wiped away gray matter and skull fragments from his face. Eyes cleared, Karl reached for his pistol, but before he could pull it from his holster, Rory squeezed off a round. It struck him in the center of his chest. Karl reeled back, still on his feet. Rory squeezed off another round, striking him in the head and adding to the gore splattered against the bulletproof glass of the Hive. Rory then swung around toward the control panel and pointed the pistol squarely at Das, still sitting in his chair.

Sara shouted, "Rory, stop!"

Rory ignored her and kept the Glock trained on Das. "The passcode to the bunker never worked. The founding date of the BIS, ha, just another line of your bullshit."

Das reflexively raised his hands. "No, Rory, I swear, that is the passcode. You have to believe me. Maybe Hans changed it. I don't know. Please, Rory, you have to believe me."

"Shut up!" Rory commanded. "We don't have time for this. And I don't have the patience to listen to any more of your lies." Rory zeroed in the weapon on Das's head.

"Rory, don't," Sara pleaded.

Again, Rory ignored her, maintaining his focus on Das. However, he had no intention of shooting him, at least not yet. *I need that code,* he thought, concerned that without the okay from Frederik, guards at the front entrance would halt their escape.

"I'm going to ask you just once," Rory said, his tone measured. "If I hear another lie, I swear, I'm going to put a round right through your fucking head. Take a look around."

Das's eyes glanced toward the bodies of both Frederik and Karl, their heads smashed like rotten pumpkins after Halloween.

Rory said, "You're next, unless you tell me right now: What is the access code for the SBB bunker?"

"I told you. It's the founding date of the BIS," Das replied, a quiver in his voice.

Rory moved closer, pinning the Glock to Das's forehead. Das said, "I swear. That's it. 1-7-0-5-1-9-3-0."

Rory stepped back, the gun still pointed at Das but removed from his forehead. "What did you say?"

"The code. It's the founding date of the BIS. 17 May 1930."

"No, not that. The numbers, what are the actual numbers?"

"1-7-0-5-1-9-3-0," Das repeated.

You gotta be fuckin' kidding me. It dawned on Rory that Das had indeed given him the correct code, the founding date of the BIS, but unlike US convention, most of the world puts the day first, then the month.

Rory dropped the gun to his side. "I used the wrong digits," he admitted. "I was entering the date American style, 0-5-1-7-1-9-3-0. There had been no issue with the code to Quoz since the release date of the euro has the same month and day, January 1, 2002."

Das gave an audible sigh of relief as Rory reached out his hand to pull him up from his slouched and submissive position in his chair.

Rory turned and walked toward Karl's blood-soaked corpse. "Sara, take this," he said as he reached down and pulled a pistol off the body. He and Sara made their way to exit the Hive. But Das just stood in a stupor, staring first at the carnage creeping its way down the glass walls and then looking beyond, into the center of Quoz at the core of ICARUS.

Rory knew what Das was thinking. They both had once thought of this place as a modern-day Emerald City, a quantum Oz full of splendor. It had all been so bewitching. Now, in its creepy green glow, the Hive looked like something out of a horror film. Rory placed his hand on Das's shoulder. "I know, man. I know. But the dream is over now. ICARUS is dead."

After a brief moment of shared recollection, Rory said, "Let's go. We need to get Mia and get the hell out of this place before someone realizes what's happening down here."

Rory, Das, and Sara ran out of Quoz, into the stairwell, and up to the second floor. Rory stopped short in the hall just before the door to the infirmary. He looked back at Sara, then at Das. All three made eye contact. Then Rory swung open the door and burst into the room. He quickly scanned for a guard, the Glock raised in a firing position. Sara, Karl's pistol at the ready, crashed in behind him, but the room was empty except for Mia. She lay startled and awake, a set of stainless-steel hand-cuffs binding her to the railing of her hospital-style bed.

Das, unarmed, entered the room last. He surveyed the situation, then said, "Bloody hell! Now what?"

At almost the same time, Mia asked, "Rory, what's going on?"

"We're getting you out of here. That's what's going on."

Rory reached into his pocket and fished out the set of keys he had taken off Hans in the holding room. He fumbled in a few attempts to find the right key. Nothing worked. Then he tried to remove the railing with brute force, but it was bolted on tight.

Rory tried to put a smile on Mia's face. "Too bad that Swiss Army knife you gave me doesn't have a set of bolt cutters."

Mia didn't laugh, but she did look up at Rory with the hint of a smile. Her brown eyes looked tired but clear, like a polished piece of tiger-eye stone. *If I can just get her out of here.*

"Who locked you up?" he asked. "Was it the same guard in here with us this morning?"

"Yes, his name is Hans, I think."

"That's right, Mia," Sara said, then turned to Rory. "I know Hans. I think now that Fred is dead, he'll help us. Let's go down to the holding room and see if he has the key."

Rory agreed. After all, both he and Sara were armed, and after everything that had happened in the past week, Rory knew he wouldn't hesitate to put a round into the security chief if necessary.

Rory, Das, and Sara entered the holding room and found Hans right where they'd left him, unconscious and bleeding on the floor. Sara and Das moved him to the couch as Rory stood and watched, his pistol drawn. Sara grabbed a towel from the small private bath and ran some water over it, then brought it to Hans and wiped his brow, crusted with drying blood.

"Search his pockets," Rory said.

Sara found a small set of two dangling keys in the breast pocket of Hans's jacket. She handed them to Rory. From their size and shape, he knew instantly they would fit the lock on the cuffs.

"Let's go," Rory said.

"You go," Sara said. "I want to see if I can wake him. I don't want to leave him like this. Go get Mia, and then we'll meet back here and leave together through the bunker."

"Are you sure?" Rory asked.

Sara nodded, and against his better judgment, Rory left with Das to get Mia. But his concern turned out to be unfounded. The keys freed Mia from the bed. Within ten minutes, Rory was standing with her and Das back in the holding room. Hans lay awake but dazed on the couch. Sara had filled up the remaining empty Quöllfrisch bottle with cold water from the sink and was holding it to Hans's lips.

"Ready?" Rory asked.

Sara put down the bottle and stood. "I'm ready."

Hans looked up at her, regret and sadness in his eyes. "*Das tut mir so Leid*," he said faintly.

"What's he saying?" Rory asked.

Sara looked at Rory. "He's saying he's sorry."

Always a nurse, Mia bent down and elevated Hans's head with an extra pillow. She looked him over, paying close attention to the movement of his eyes. "He should be all right," she pronounced.

It's about fuckin' time.

"Come on, let's get the hell out of here," Rory said. "We've got a plane to catch."

PART IV
There's No Place Like...

Leonardo Bonacci, also known as Fibonacci, is considered by many to be the greatest mathematician of medieval Europe. He introduced Arabic numerals to the West as well as a sixth-century Indian sequence of numbers whereby each number is the sum of the previous two numbers. When begun with zero and one, the sequence flows thusly: 0, 1, 1, 2, 3, 5, 8, 13, 21, 34, 55, 89, 144, etc.

Market technicians, those who focus on chart patterns rather than fundamental inputs such as earnings estimates, place importance on ratios embedded within the Fibonacci sequence. 23.6 percent and 38.2 percent are just two of these key ratios. For example, 23.6 percent is roughly the ratio between any two numbers that are separated by two other numbers in the sequence, such as 13 and 55.

Known as Fibonacci retracement levels, these ratios suggest where an asset might change trend. Should a stock rise from $15 a share to $40 a share, it may then "retrace" a fraction of that $25 gain. For instance, a 23.6 percent retracement would consist of a decline of $5.90 to $34.10 a share, at which point the stock might resume its uptrend.

To the dismay of those who believe asset prices only reflect changes in fundamental inputs, these Fibonacci retracement levels are observed in market data with statistically significant frequency.

CHAPTER 59

40,000 feet above the Atlantic Ocean
MONDAY, NOVEMBER 8, 2027

AS PROMISED, MILTON McGRADY HAD the G650 fueled up
with a crew on standby. By 2:00 a.m. Basel time, the jet was flying across
French airspace at over 650 mph. Mia lay resting on the couch while
Rory, Das, and Sara all reclined in captain's chairs. Jennifer had dimmed
the lights and brought pillows and blankets for her exhausted passengers.
ETA in Chicago was 4:34 a.m. local time, almost four hours before the
markets opened in New York. In Asia, however, the major exchanges had
begun trade hours ago. It wasn't pretty.

Rory settled into his chair and placed the small pillow behind his
head. He closed his eyes and tried to get some sleep, but adrenaline continued to flow. His mind struggled to process the last twenty-four hours.

Just minutes later, Das's voice rang out above the low hum of the
engines. Apparently Rory was not the only one having trouble sleeping.

"Is anyone awake?" Das asked.

Rory did not want to respond, but after a moment's hesitation, he
replied, "Yes, Das, what is it?"

"I just synced up my phone to the Gulfstream's satellite Wi-Fi."

"Good for you. Now can we all try to get some rest?"

"Rory, all the breakers were tripped in Asia today. Hong Kong,
Tokyo, Seoul, Sydney, all halted multiple times. They had to stop trading
hours before the scheduled close."

After the US stock market suffered its largest ever daily percentage
decline on October 19, 1987—Black Monday—exchanges around the

world instituted "circuit breakers" to prevent such one-day calamities from ever happening again.

Das continued, "If the NYSE has to close early today, it could be game over."

New York Stock Exchange Rule 7.12 stipulates three levels that will halt trading on all US exchanges. They are known as MWCBs, or market-wide circuit breakers. The Level 1 MWCB is triggered by a 7 percent decline in the S&P 500. Level 2 is triggered at 13 percent. Both Levels 1 and 2 result in a minimum fifteen-minute halt, giving market participants time to literally take stock of the situation and assess if the sell-off is truly warranted or just algos gone wild. If trade continues lower after a Level 2 halt and hits Level 3, 20 percent down on the S&P, the market closes for the day regardless of the time it happens at. Since MWCBs had been in effect, only the 7 percent Level 1 breaker had ever been triggered.

Rory rubbed his thumb and forefinger over his tired eyes. "Das, it's going to be bad, really bad, but there's nothing we can do about it now."

"Maybe, but maybe not."

"What are you talking about?" Sara chimed in, clearly unable to sleep as well. "Are you saying Pete was wrong? He didn't negatively prove impossibility or whatever?"

"Pete's negative proof or proof of impossibility was spot-on," Das corrected. "But it was limited to long-term control. ICARUS can never moderate the markets as intended, but it has proved that for periods of time and with enough capital, prices can be significantly impacted. Just look at what we've been able to do at the BIS."

Rory turned in his chair. Das had un-reclined his chair, and his head was buried in his smartphone.

"Listen to me," Rory said.

Das lifted his head.

Their eyes met and Rory said, "I told you in Quoz, ICARUS is dead. The Hive looks like a war zone now. And we don't have access to any capital. What the hell can we do to stop the markets from crashing?"

"It's not going to be easy," Das said, "but if we could deploy enough money in just the right securities at just the right times, we may be able to stop US markets from hitting the Level 3 breaker and closing early. If we can do that, it may provide enough time for central banks to put together an emergency-relief plan that doesn't involve BIScoin or ICARUS."

Well, I'm not gonna be able to sleep anyway. Rory un-reclined his chair and flipped the light switch on above his head. He returned his gaze to Das. "You're serious? You have a plan for how the three of us can stop a global financial apocalypse as we fly forty thousand feet over the Atlantic?"

Das nodded. "I think we have to try. In some way, we all had something to do with getting this mess started."

Jennifer, hearing voices in her main cabin, entered the space. "Not so sleepy after all," she said with a smile and a glance toward Rory. "Is there anything I can get you?"

Despite the hour, Jennifer looked lovely as ever in her navy suit jacket and matching skirt with hose and mid-heel pumps. *What the hell,* Rory thought. "I'll have a Bulleit and Coke, please."

Rory, Das, and Sara got right to work. Rory's first order of business was a call on the sat phone to McGrady. If they were going to make this happen, they'd need cash and lots of it. Rory explained how they now had access to the ICARUS source code via the cloud. If the crazy plan worked, he promised McGrady that the potential upside was incredible. For good measure, Rory stroked the hedge fund billionaire's ego, convincing him that if they pulled this off, his place in the history books was truly guaranteed. McGrady was in.

Next, Rory called Kota Nakazawa. He told him to get to 333 West Wacker right away. He also asked Kota to arrange for transportation from the private terminal at Chicago's Midway Airport. Rory wanted two vehicles: one to take Das and Sara directly to Celtic and the other to rush him and Mia to the hospital. Rory was still worried about her. While Mia had been a trooper during their escape from Basel, she had lost a lot of blood and continued to look weak.

Rory's final call was to the switchboard at the BIS. At Sara's urging and on the off chance that no one at the bank had yet realized what had transpired on sublevels three and four, he agreed to call in anonymously and report that there may be an injured employee in the holding room. To Rory's surprise, when the operator patched him through to security, it was actually Hans who took the call. Sara's brief care had revived him enough to carry on with his duties. His hands were full given the night's dramatic events, but Rory seized the opportunity to influence the bank's damage control. He coached the still apologetic Hans on how to proceed, specifically how to spin Frederik's death to the central bankers expecting to see him at Monday's meetings.

Astonishingly, things were falling into place. *This might actually work*, Rory thought as he looked out the oval window of the G650 for the third time in the past week.

Sara, who could see that Rory was now off the phone, asked, "Is everything all right?"

Rory looked away from the window and into Sara's blue eyes. "Hans is fine," he assured her. "You and Das just figure out how much cash Milt needs to pony up if we want any chance at stopping that Level 3 breaker from tripping."

Rory turned his head back toward the window. There was just one thing that troubled him, a thought lodged in the corner of his mind like a pebble in his shoe. *It was too easy. We practically strolled out of that tower.*

Slowly sipping his bourbon, Rory stared into the emptiness of sea and sky, unable to discern the horizon. It lay cloaked somewhere between the darkness of the ocean and the cold, black night.

CHAPTER 60

Chicago, Illinois
MONDAY, NOVEMBER 8, 2027

MILTON MCGRADY BARELY HAD HIS seat belt buckled as he revved up his 444-horsepower and not exactly street-legal Porsche 959. The limited-edition roadster—only 337 were ever produced—purred down Lake Shore Drive. McGrady dispensed with summoning his driver at the late, or rather early, hour of 1:00 a.m. CST. He was too excited by the possibility of going down in hedge fund history as a true legend, perhaps the greatest of all time, not to mention making a boatload of money along the way. If everything went as planned, not since John Pierpont Morgan averted total financial destruction during the Panic of 1907 would a single financier play so pivotal a role in stopping a crisis from turning into total financial chaos. McGrady also stood to make millions, maybe even billions. But first he would need to muster all his resources—the press, politicians, bankers, institutional investors, and fellow hedge fund magnates—in order to inject enough capital into the system to prevent total collapse.

McGrady's first item of business was the rumor mill. He needed to spread well-placed rumors of key actions yet to be taken by the world's governments and central banks, rumors so well placed that once out in the ether, bankers and politicians alike would be forced to turn them into reality. McGrady would target key financial publications: Bloomberg, Reuters, the *Financial Times*, and, of course, the *Wall Street Journal*. The crux of the stories would be a repeal of the Phoenix Act combined with the assertion that a tsunami of sweeping central bank actions were currently being devised at the secretive All Governors' Meeting in Basel. If the release of the stories helped shore up US futures, policymakers around the globe would have no choice but to act in accordance with the unfounded reports lest they seem like the cause of financial doom.

McGrady also needed money, lots of money. In order to get it, he would have to convince his few remaining hedge fund allies to go all in no matter how much every bone in their body told them to sell. McGrady needed to assure them that the cavalry was on the way and the market was headed for a major rally. He just needed a little help from Rory, Das, Sara, and the ICARUS AI in order to make that prediction a reality.

As McGrady ran down in his head the list of reporters who needed to be contacted, he glided the Porsche off LSD and onto lower Wacker Drive. The deep purr of its engine reverberated off the walls of the tunnel-like structure. McGrady then exited the iconic double-level thoroughfare and pulled directly into the underground parking below 333.

It's gonna be a long day, but it's gonna be fun. Slamming the car into park and dashing for the elevator, McGrady felt twenty years younger. It was like the good ole days again. The markets were in turmoil, chaos reigned on Wall Street, and there was ample opportunity to make unfathomable amounts of money. He loved it.

CHAPTER 61

Chicago, Illinois

MONDAY, NOVEMBER 8, 2027

TWO BLACK FORD EXPEDITION SUVs were parked just steps away from the G650 when it rolled into the private terminal at Midway International Airport. Rory told Das and Sara that he would meet them at Celtic Capital once Mia was safe and sound at Rush University Medical Center, the Near West Side hospital where she had worked for the last ten years. After a quick passport check by immigration officials who greeted the party on the tarmac, Rory and Mia hopped into one of the SUVs and sped away from the terminal.

Less than thirty minutes after touching down, Das and Sara arrived at 333. Kota greeted them at the door. It was barely 5:00 a.m., over three hours until the opening bell on Wall Street, and already traders were buzzing around or talking with clients as if it were the middle of a trading day. Almost all the once-empty desks were occupied. After crossing the busy trading floor, Kota, Das, and Sara entered McGrady's office.

McGrady stood from his desk as Kota introduced his former colleagues. Kota also informed him that Rory would be arriving as soon as he got Mia to the hospital. Sally brought in some coffee. Then McGrady got down to business. "So, you're sure that none of yesterday's bloodletting will be leaked to the press?"

Sara said, "Rory spoke with Hans Guzman, head of BIS security, from your jet. He is taking full advantage of the embassy-like status of the bank. Hans will be able to keep Fred's death under wraps until later this week, once the markets have hopefully stabilized."

"Good," McGrady replied. "I've got a number of representatives and a few senators on board with repealing Phoenix. I've assured them all that if they want a functioning economy tomorrow, they need to announce the planned repeal today. I've also secured commitments from over a dozen of the world's largest hedge funds to start buying as soon as the opening bell rings. All their trades will be routed through Celtic. Now, what else do you need?"

Das spoke next. "I need access to your clearing platforms. Sara and I need to coordinate all trades and time them according to parameters we've put together based on the ICARUS AI."

With a laptop borrowed from Jennifer aboard the Gulfstream, Das had accessed the source code from the BIS cloud. It was hoped that by placing trades in conjunction with the flawed though still somewhat effective volatility-suppression algorithm, they may be able to stem the selling pressure and keep the markets from triggering Level 2 or 3 circuit breakers. It wouldn't be at quantum speed, but it was better than nothing.

McGrady responded to Das's request, "Sure, use whatever resources you need. Kota should be able to get you both access." And with that, Kota, McGrady, Das, and Sara stood from their chairs and exited the office.

McGrady was back in his element, barking orders and overseeing a motley group of traders. He had pulled in guys and gals who hadn't worked in the business since ICARUS went live, calling them at three in the morning and promising six-figure bonuses if they could get their asses into Celtic before 5:00 a.m. Now he had a full roster of some of the most experienced players in the business. They were snapping up futures contracts left and right and had begun buying individual equities in pre-market trading. The panic had gotten to such a fevered pitch that the babies were being thrown out with the bathwater. Blue-chip stocks with strong balance sheets were selling for as little as three times next year's earnings. It was a fire sale, and trading volume in the normally subdued premarket session had ramped up appreciably as dawn approached.

Meanwhile, Das and Sara settled into a conference room with Kota and began resurrecting a ghost. ICARUS was being born again.

At the same time that Das and Sara had departed the airport for 333, Rory and Mia settled into the back seat of their Ford Expedition as it sped off from Midway's private terminal. The sun had not yet risen, and an icy frost sat atop the windows of parked cars along Cicero Avenue.

"You're going to be safe and sound at your own hospital soon," Rory said to Mia as the SUV exited right onto the Stevenson Expressway.

"I can't believe we're back. This past week feels like a long nightmare."

"I know, Mia. But it's over now."

Within ten minutes, they were approaching Chinatown and the junction with the westbound Dan Ryan Expressway.

"It won't be long now," Rory said. He grasped Mia's hand and found it cold and clammy. *We're going to get to the hospital just… What the hell?*

Rory could not believe it. The driver was going the wrong way. He had taken the eastbound Dan Ryan instead of the west. "Hey," Rory said, "you went the wrong—"

Before he could finish the sentence, Rory heard the snap of an out-stretched cover in the rear of the SUV being released and rolling back up. There had been a black canvas cover at seat-height rolled over the rear compartment of the vehicle. A fraction of a second later, he felt the butt of a pistol crack him in the head.

The man who up to now had been hidden in the rear of the SUV then pointed his pistol at Mia's head while keeping an eye on Rory. He said, "Behave or the bitch gets shot."

The pistol strike was disorientating, but not enough to knock Rory out. *I knew it had been too easy*, he thought as the man behind him began to speak again, this time in Russian and to the driver. Rory turned to face his attacker, but as he did, another blow from the pistol smacked the back of his head. This blow was much harder, and a glimmering array of stars flashed in his eyes before slipping into darkness. As the SUV raced past Guaranteed Rate Field, home of the Chicago White Sox, Rory was definitely out.

CHAPTER 62

Washington, DC

MONDAY, NOVEMBER 8, 2027

IT WAS APPROACHING 7:00 A.M. in the nation's capital. Senator Matthew Whitlock sat in his oak-paneled office and hung up the phone after completing what must have been at least his twentieth call of the day. Word that BIScoin and his other plans were in shambles had reached him a few hours earlier via a frantic call from Jacob Rosenthal, president of the New York Fed.

Rosenthal relayed to Whitlock the latest from Basel. BIS security had just alerted the bankers gathered there that Frederik d'Oultremont III had tragically taken his own life on Sunday night. Upon commitment of complete confidentiality, the bankers were further told that the suicide was precipitated by the discovery of a fatal flaw in the ICARUS source code. Any discussion of BIScoin immediately ceased, replaced by heated debate surrounding possible next steps. An hour or so later, a report out of Reuters made its way to the bankers. It suggested, falsely at the time of its release, that the bankers had already agreed to enact substantial emergency measures. Importantly, these measures did not involve further expansion of the money supply via quantitative easing.

QE is the primary mechanism central bankers use to create money. They conjure the cash from nothing and then use it to buy their nation's bonds or other assets such as mortgage-backed securities. This new money inflates the existing money supply and leads to rampant speculation and inflation. Taking QE off the table would force governments around the world to recognize, at least until this crisis passed, the need to curtail deficit spending lest their bonds start trading at exorbitant yields. There would still need to be sizable interest-rate cuts, but at least the printing presses would be stopped.

As further unfounded reports emerged, the rumors gained traction in the market, and futures rallied from down 6 percent to down less than 3 percent. The central bankers decided it best to meet the expectations set by the mysterious press releases. As leaders from the most powerful banks worked out the details, they quietly authorized Rommel Gomez Cosio, governor of the Central Bank of the Philippines, to leak to the press confirmation that emergency measures were indeed forthcoming. Once again, the world's central banks were the proverbial dog wagged by the powerful tail of the market.

Faced with the prospect of a Federal Reserve unwilling to underwrite the massive debt necessary to fund the Phoenix Act, Whitlock revved his powerful spin machine into overdrive, anxious to quickly distance himself from the doomed legislation. With the help of his colleague from Illinois, Kristin Fischer, he also spent the morning drumming up bipartisan support for the immediate repeal of the act. Now, with most of the key decision-makers aligned to make repeal a reality, Whitlock was ready to start taking advantage of the turmoil. He called Vanessa Price into his office.

"What do you need?" Vanessa asked as she walked into the senator's office and shut the door behind her.

"I want to jump on this right away," Whitlock said. "Set up some media appearances for this afternoon after the market closes. If we can survive the day without a complete collapse, I want to be on the air taking the credit and pushing for a new ethos in Washington, one based on responsible spending and the reigning in of easy money and pork projects."

"Got it."

"And get Zhao Hong on the line."

Vanessa spun around on the red soles of her Louboutin shoes and made her way to the office door.

Despite the morning's action, Whitlock couldn't help but see opportunity embedded in the chaos. He rose from his chair and poured himself a whiskey, the first of what had already been a long morning. Just as he dropped two cubes of ice in his glass, the phone buzzed.

Whitlock walked back to his desk and grabbed the receiver with a burgeoning twinkle in his eye. "Hong, my friend. I have an idea."

CHAPTER 63

Chicago, Illinois
MONDAY, NOVEMBER 8, 2027

WHERE THE FUCK AM I?

Rory sat slumped on a concrete floor. He tugged to move his arms, but it was no use. His wrists were bound behind his lower back, while his upper back rested against something hard, flat, and cold.

A steel beam?

Rory's vision was blurred, but coming into focus.

This is some sort of warehouse. No, an abandoned meatpacking plant?

Rows of rusted metal hooks hung from the ceiling. Cracked windows let in no light, blacked-out by plywood boards nailed to the façade of the ramshackle building. Some old steel tables lay strewn about either upright or turned over on their sides. Rows of shelves storing large metal pans took up some space to Rory's left. Most of the ceiling-mounted fluorescent lighting was busted out or inoperable save a few tubes, including one shining directly over Rory's head.

Apparently sensing some life return to Rory, Mia asked in a whisper, "Are you awake?" She was also sitting on the floor, bound to the same steel beam, her hands near the base of Rory's spine and his hands near hers.

Picking up on Mia's subdued tone, Rory replied in a whisper as well. "Yes, where are we?"

"I'm not sure exactly. After you went unconscious, we drove about ten more minutes down the Dan Ryan and came here. You've been out for at least two hours. We're near UChicago, I think."

Rory continued his scan of the building as he struggled in vain to free his arms, his wrists wrapped securely with what felt like duct tape. There appeared to be two exits: one in the front between the cracked and boarded-up windows that apparently led to the street, the other a door in the rear that Rory imagined must open up to an alley or side street. Two men sat at a small wooden table in one corner of the abandoned plant, both their heads dipped down as they manipulated smartphones.

"Are those the guys from the SUV?" Rory asked.

"Yes, they've been sitting there glued to their phones ever since they finished tying us to this damn beam."

"Anyone else here?" Rory asked in a tone slightly louder than his previous whispers. His energy was beginning to return, dazed confusion replaced with anger.

"No, I don't think—"

"Shut up!" one of the men yelled.

"Fuck you!" Rory said impulsively. As the two men stood from the table, he questioned if his reply was such a good idea.

As they got closer, Rory immediately recognized the slightly over-weight driver of the SUV. His pudgy face was unforgettable, red with beady eyes and dominated by a bulbous nose. He wore his driver's uniform consisting of a black suit and tie with a white shirt. The other man, the one who had been hidden in the rear of the SUV, was shorter, but thin with an athletic build. His features were chiseled, including a firm jawline. His eyes were an icy glacier blue. Although relatively youthful in appearance, the crown of his head was completely bald. He was dressed in a navy tracksuit with red stripes down the side.

The two men hovered above Rory and Mia as they sat slumped against the steel beam.

"What the hell do you want with us?" Rory asked.

"Good question," the bald man replied. "All we know is that whatever you did, you really pissed him off."

"Who? Golev?" Rory probed, though he already knew this had to be the work of the former FSB operative-turned central banker.

"Very good," the driver said with disdain and only a trace of Russian accent. "The boss will be joining us shortly. He wants to deal with you personally. For now, just sit there and keep your mouths shut."

Again, Rory couldn't help himself. "Fuck you."

The driver walked closer to Rory and gave him a hard kick in his side, then bent over and spit in Rory's face. "That's for thinking I was going the wrong way," he said, apparently sensitive about his driving skills.

The bald man laughed as spit dripped down Rory's tired face. Then he turned to the driver, and the two men began to converse in Russian.

Rory managed to rub the spit off his face and onto the shoulder of his shirt. Then he interrupted the Russians. "Whatever Golev wants, I assure you it's with me, not her. This woman has been shot. She's weak and needs medical attention. Let her go."

Now both men laughed as Rory sat helpless on the cold concrete. He tried one last time, hoping these Russians had at least some sliver of humanity remaining, though he was doubtful. "Can you at least get her something to drink and eat? You wouldn't want her to die before the boss arrives, would you?"

The men continued to converse in Russian. Ultimately, Rory assumed they were either worried Mia might actually die before Golev arrived or else they were just plain hungry. In any case, after a couple minutes' conversation, the bald man walked back to the small table, grabbed his phone, and left.

"Is he going for food?" Rory asked hopefully.

The driver gave no reply, just another swift kick to Rory's aching ribs.

CHAPTER 64

Chicago, Illinois

The major European exchanges followed Asia's lead and closed early from tripped circuit breakers. All eyes shifted focus to the American open in New York. It was 8:30 in Chicago, 9:30 in the East. As the opening bell rang on Wall Street, consensus held that if the Level 3 breaker tripped—closing the markets early and down 20 percent—a majority of the Street's largest banks would be insolvent by the next morning. The world's financial infrastructure was on the brink of collapse.

Banks, institutional investors, pension plans, university endowments, and every other major market player had taken the smooth ride of ICARUS for granted. Many had levered up to heights greater than in '08, and unlike the SVB bank collapse in '23, the problem was not one of interest rates but of credit. Firms had gone way out on the risk spectrum believing that junk bonds and even common equities could be counted on for safe and steady returns. If the market in the US followed the pattern set in Asia and Europe, margin calls were going to come due. The liquidity to satisfy those calls simply did not exist. Balance sheets had been bled dry of any investible cash during the first two phases of ICARUS. Every available dollar was put into the "New Market," a market the world believed would never, should never, could never crash again.

The S&P opened down 5 percent, bad, but it was hanging in there. The buying efforts of McGrady and company combined with hopeful rumors led to what looked like a promising rally. The benchmark index quickly gained some footing down a mere 2.5 percent.

But the selling pressure carried over from Asia and Europe was too great. The rally quickly faded, and the 7 percent down Level 1 breaker was hit after less than an hour of trade at 10:23 a.m. eastern standard time. This automatically triggered a halt across US markets, and all trading ceased.

During this break, McGrady called Kota, Das, and Sara into his office.

"What the fuck! I thought you guys said we'd be able to stop the bleeding," McGrady bellowed. "And where the fuck is Rory? Shouldn't he be here by now?"

He got no response. Finally, Das spoke up. "More sell orders came in after the open than my models anticipated. We should be able to gain traction again once trading resumes. As for Rory, no one has heard from him."

"All right. Well, we don't have time to worry about him now," McGrady said in exasperation. "I have firm commitments for almost twenty billion dollars to be put to work. How much have we bought so far?"

"Almost twelve billion dollars," Kota reported.

"Twelve billion! We're not even an hour into trade! What the hell are we going to do if we hit Level 2?" McGrady slammed his palms on his desk as he stood up from his chair. He leaned over toward the sitting Kota, Das, and Sara. "I'll tell you right now, if we don't get this thing turned around, it's not just Celtic Capital that's going down. This whole fucking thing is going to blow up. They'll be picking up pieces of Goldman Sachs, Bank of America, JP Morgan, and every other fuckin' bank from Katmandu to Korea."

Sara stood from her chair. "We're doing everything we can. We just need more money."

McGrady replied, "I've called in every favor that I can. And I created a bunch of new favors, which I now owe. If there's a dollar or yen or even a fuckin' Swedish krona out there to get, I got it. You just have to make do with what you got." Then, almost looking like a defeated man, McGrady sat back in his chair with an uncharacteristic slump in his spine. The four souls sat quietly in his office, each beginning to doubt that they would be able to halt the slide given their available capital.

Das stood from his chair and paced around McGrady's office for a brief moment, then said, "What if there's one more large source of capital out there, untapped and sitting in cash."

"Bullshit! There's nothin' else," McGrady countered. "Pension funds, retirement funds, insurance companies, they're all fully invested ever since your damn ICARUS came online."

Das explained, "When Fred was planning BIScoin, he made certain arrangements to corner the production market for silver. Many of his business partners, particularly those out of Mexico, are known holders of large cash positions."

Kota, McGrady, and Sara stared at Das in confusion. Then Sara asked, "What the hell are you talking about?"

"I'm talking about the cartels."

"The Mexican cartels?" McGrady almost exploded.

"Yes," Das said, "but not directly, through a mining magnate out of Fresnillo. His name is Javier Delgado."

"And you know him personally?" McGrady asked, unsure why he was even considering the outrageous idea.

"Not exactly, but I know someone who does."

"Who?" Sara asked.

Das sat back down in his chair and spoke the name of his Cambridge mentor and the current governor of the RBI. "Arun Patel."

CHAPTER 65

Chicago, Illinois

MONDAY, NOVEMBER 8, 2027

WITH THE BALD MAN GONE, the pudgy driver returned to the small table in the corner. He sat down, picked up his cell, and placed a call. From the sound of his voice, Rory sensed he was talking to a woman, maybe his wife or girlfriend. Regardless, he appeared distracted.

Rory took the opportunity and whispered to Mia, "Can you wiggle your right hand into the left front pocket of my jeans?"

Their wrists had been bound tightly with the duct tape, but after over two hours of readjustments and micromovements, Mia had managed to gain some latitude with her hands. She shifted her body to the right a bit, away from the driver's view, and was able to position her right hand just inches from Rory's left pocket.

"That's good," Rory said, feeling Mia's fingers on his hip. "See if you can reach in."

"What am I looking for?"

A smile almost crossed Rory's face as he recalled Mia emerging from the gift shop nestled on the banks of the Rhine. He replied with a question, hoping it might bring a smile to her face as well. "Do you remember what you got me in Basel?"

"You have it?" Mia said, her tone clearly more upbeat than just seconds earlier.

"I sure do. Now try and get it."

With a stretch and some more wiggling, Mia managed to grasp the Swiss Army knife between her middle and index finger. She slowly attempted to slide it free from Rory's pocket. He felt the knife slip from her fragile grasp on the first effort. However, on the second try, she managed to pull the knife closer to the edge of Rory's pocket, at which point she was able to securely grip it in her hand.

"I got it," Mia whispered excitedly.

"Can you put it in my left hand?"

"I think so."

Mia shifted the knife into Rory's open hand. Rory wrapped his hand completely around the knife and readjusted his position a bit, trying to gain some separation between his hands and Mia's backside. The driver took a quick glance over at Rory as he shifted a few inches to the left. Rory kept still, hoping his tight grip around the folded knife concealed its bright red color. The Russian's attention waned after a moment, and his focus returned to his phone.

With his left thumbnail, Rory flipped open the roughly three-inch blade on the Huntsman model knife. He drew it back and forth against the edge of the wrapped duct tape. The first two passes were ineffective, but on the third attempt the blade caught and ripped enough of the tape that Rory felt the pressure release. He knew that with a tug of his hands, the rest of the binding would tear right through. He slowly turned his wrists, trying to avoid the sound of a rip. A moment later, the tear worked its way completely across the tape. Rory's hands were free.

"Done," he whispered to Mia.

"Now what?"

"We need to get him closer. Can you fake a seizure?" Rory suggested. "He knows you've been shot."

"There's no reason I should have a seizure at this point."

"He's not a nurse, Mia. That fat fuck doesn't have a medical degree. Can you do it?"

"I think so. When?"

"As soon as you're ready. We need to act before the other one gets back."

"Okay, here goes."

Mia began convulsing her body with repeated jerking muscle movements. She had seen seizures at various points during her nursing career, and her acting wasn't bad. She rolled back her eyes and let some saliva run from her mouth to mimic loss of muscle control and drooling.

The driver immediately looked over at her.

"Help!" Rory yelled. "I think she's having a seizure or something."

The pudgy man stood cautiously from his chair as Mia continued her convincing performance. He hesitated for a moment, looking around as if searching for someone to tell him what to do, but he was alone.

"Come on, man! I told you she needs to be in a hospital. Help her," Rory pleaded.

The driver walked closer to Rory and Mia, his cell phone still to his ear. When he was just a step away from Mia, Rory jumped to his feet and ran his right shoulder into the driver's sagging and exposed gut with a football-style tackle. The phone flew out of his hand as both he and Rory tumbled to the ground. With the wind completely knocked out of him, the fat man hardly put up a fight. In a series of quick, short, and powerful jabs, Rory repeatedly stuck the blade of the Swiss Army knife in, out, then back into the man's neck, sometimes missing and driving the knife through his cheek. Blood spurted out of his carotid artery like water from a garden hose. Rory grabbed his pistol, which had been holstered on the driver's hip, and then stood atop the man. The driver writhed in pain on the dirty factory floor and clasped both his hands around his neck in a futile attempt to stem the pouring blood.

"He's bleeding out," Mia said as she watched the scene unfold from almost eye level and just a few feet away, still bound to the steel beam.

"Good." Rory walked over to Mia and cut her free with the bloody blade.

Mia stood. Then both she and Rory watched as the pool of blood grew around the pudgy face of the Russian driver. Rory raised the pistol, another .40-caliber SIG Sauer, in his right hand and pointed it at the man's chest. But there was no need to waste a round. The man's hands fell limp from his neck.

"He's dead," Mia said, no sadness or regret in her voice.

Rory relaxed his right arm down by his side. The building was silent except for the occasional sound of a passing car emanating through the cracked and boarded windows. Rory tucked the pistol behind his back and turned to embrace Mia, but the moment was interrupted.

The sound of jingling keys rattled from behind the rear door of the abandoned plant.

CHAPTER 66

Chicago, Illinois

MONDAY, NOVEMBER 8, 2027

ANTON GOLEV DID NOT LIKE loose ends. He did not like men who killed or wounded his operatives. And he definitely did not like Rory O'Connor. As his private jet landed at Chicago's Midway Airport, Golev took one last look at his phone and realized that all was not lost. It appeared as if the financial collapse he had been hoping to engineer for years was finally coming to fruition. Replacing the US dollar with a gold-backed digital currency would have to wait, but every trapper knows not all the snares catch their quarry.

Golev had been aware of American quantum AI development long before ICARUS was even a glimmer in the mind's eye of Zhao or Frederik. The Russians had been keeping a very close watch on US technology ever since Hiroshima and Nagasaki. Even the Chinese, who considered themselves expert at stealing US innovations, did not have the deep and long-standing espionage network that the Soviet Union, and then Russian Federation, had built up over decades.

But there were holes. One of those holes was the contents of Peter Costello's encrypted drive. Golev had been worried that it contained a game-changing breakthrough that could fix ICARUS and end his plans for financial chaos. He had been tracking Peter's VSA development and had intercepted communications between the engineer and his boss at the BIS that described a breakthrough but gave little detail. The threat presented by this unknown breakthrough prompted Golev to order the death of the talented programmer, camouflaged as just one more act of American thuggery.

However, Zhao Hong and Frederik d'Oultremont had never given up on finding lost notes or files from Peter Costello. They were both convinced that a real breakthrough had been made and worried that Peter's best friend might just know something about it. As such, both Chinese and Russian agents had kept tabs on Rory O'Connor.

For the most part, it had appeared that Rory had given up on life, wasting it away in San Juan chasing women and trading crypto. But Golev understood the importance of keeping one's mind open to all possibilities, and so he ordered the cloning of Rory's cell phone ahead of the Phase III launch. The subsequent discovery of the encrypted drive was a wild card that Golev desperately wanted to remove from the deck. In the end, he found it almost comical that it contained exactly the news he wanted to hear: ICARUS was a dud.

Golev had watched attentively the debacle that took place on sublevel three of the BIS tower. Via hacked security feeds, he viewed the entire gruesome scene from his suite at the Dolder Grand in Zürich. Although his goal of dethroning the dollar and increasing Russia's wealth through a massive spike in the gold price had been thwarted, his primary objective—a complete meltdown in global financial markets—seemed well within reach.

There was just one problem: the pesky American, Rory O'Connor. Not only had he killed multiple Russian operatives, but he also knew too much. It was a loose end that required addressing, a loose end he would enjoy addressing.

So, Golev thought as he exited the jet and took his first breath of the cold Chicago air, *it will all end where it began.* He walked down the mobile boarding stairs, met briefly with two immigration officials, and stepped into a waiting SUV. There was no need to say anything to his driver.

CHAPTER 67

Chicago, Illinois

MONDAY, NOVEMBER 8, 2027

"OVER HERE," RORY SAID TO Mia as he quickly moved to take cover.

A twenty-foot-long meatpacking table, turned on its side, rested to the right of the rear door. Mia followed, and they both crouched down behind the table. Three seconds later the door swung open. It was the bald Russian, a bag of fast food in one hand and a cardboard tray holding coffees in the other.

Rory made no witty comment. He pulled his newly acquired SIG from behind his back and zeroed it in on the Russian. Then, without hesitation, he squeezed off three rounds in rapid succession. All hit their target. The Russian dropped to the ground like a felled buck. Rory walked over to the dying man, his navy tracksuit turning redder with every second.

"Where is Golev?"

"Fuck you," he replied, blood starting to drip from the corner of his mouth.

Rory stuffed the pistol behind his back and reached into his pocket for the Swiss Army knife. He flipped up the corkscrew and wrapped his fingers around the knife's base, still sticky with the driver's blood. An inch or so of corkscrew protruded from Rory's fist. He bent down and started turning its tip back and forth into the temple of the bald man's head.

"I said, where is Golev?"

"Fuck you," came the same response, this time with less defiance in tone.

Rory said nothing. He took the corkscrew and drove it into the man's right icy-blue eye. The Russian turned and jerked in agony as Rory removed the corkscrew. Rory stood up and away from the man. He put the knife back in his pocket and pulled the pistol from behind his back. Rory sighted it in on the suffering figure before him, but not at his head or chest. The SIG was pointed directly at the bald Russian's balls. "This is the last fucking time I ask. Where is Golev?"

"Okay, okay," the man said, evidently still able to see out of his one good eye.

"Tell me what you know," Rory demanded.

"He's flying in from Switzerland."

"When does he arrive?"

"I'm not sure, soon, anytime now. All I know is he said to take you both here and keep you alive. He wanted to handle this himself."

"And he's coming here directly from the airport?"

"That's the plan."

"With who else?" Rory pressed.

"His driver. I think his name is Sergey. That's all I know."

Rory had heard enough. It was time to end the bald man's misery. He raised his aim from the Russian's balls to his head and pulled the trigger. The pistol's report echoed throughout the plant, and then the space once again went quiet.

Rory and Mia stood in the silence and looked down at yet another dead body. The man's heart had stopped beating, but small trickles of blood continued to slowly ooze onto the cold concrete floor. As Rory stared into the lifeless and bloodied blue eyes, he inhaled a deep breath of the stale, dank air. Then he shifted his gaze from the body on the floor to the ceiling of the plant. But Rory wasn't looking at the rows of rusty meat hooks.

What do you think, Pete? he wondered. *Should I go for one more?*

After a moment's pause, Rory lowered his head and shoved the still warm muzzle of the SIG behind his back. He was getting comfortable with the gun, an obvious favorite of those in Golev's employ.

He turned toward Mia. "We have a choice now."

"What do you mean?"

"We can get the hell out of here and get you to Rush Medical. Or we can stay, wait for Golev, and see if we can end this thing."

Mia did not reply. She was exhausted and dehydrated. She walked over to the small table and chairs set up in the corner.

Rory followed, sat down, and asked, "Are you okay? If you need medical attention, we're getting out of here right now. Just say the word."

Mia was unable to hold it in any longer. "It's just too much," she said as tears began to run down her face. "I don't know if I can handle any more."

Rory had no words.

Ten feet away, the driver's cell phone lay on the floor. Mia's eyes shifted toward it. "Maybe we should just call the police," she suggested. "Let them handle it."

Rory stood and walked over to pick up the phone. "It's locked."

Mia got up from the table and grabbed the phone from Rory's hand. She walked over to the driver's dead body. His face and neck were slightly disfigured, but when she held the cracked screen of the phone in front of him, it unlocked.

She handed it to Rory, then said not softly but with a tone of anger and frustration, "I want Golev to pay for what he did more than anybody, but I don't want to see you get killed. I've seen too many fucking people get killed. And I'm not just talking about this week. I'm talking about Pete. I'm talking about all the kids who come into the ER with gunshot wounds or OD'd on fentanyl. I'm sick of it, Rory! I don't want to see any more people die."

Rory walked over to the now shaking Mia. It was finally time for that interrupted embrace. He looked into her brown eyes and then grasped her in his arms. Rory's ribs were still sore from the driver's kicks. His head pounded from the bald man's pistol-whipping in the SUV, but he didn't care. Rory could tell Mia was also in pain. Her gunshot wound had never been properly attended to. She was clearly weaker than she let on. Yet Mia gripped Rory tight. Neither wanted to let go.

Rory suddenly backed away. "Do you hear that?"

It was not very loud, but it was unmistakable. Through a cracked glass window, just beyond the plywood that separated the plant from the street, two men speaking in what sounded like Russian were vaguely audible.

"Yes, oh my God. They're coming."

Rory and Mia both instinctively rushed back to their ambush spot behind the overturned meatpacking table. They ducked behind it as Rory looked at the dead driver's phone, still in his hand.

Shit!

The phone had locked. Then, though he had probably seen it a million times before, Rory noticed as if for the first time EMERGENCY on the bottom left corner of the lock screen. He tapped his finger on it.

Come on, pick up!

"9-1-1. What is your emergency?"

"Someone has kidnapped us and is trying to kill us," Rory reported. "I'm not sure where they have taken us. Somewhere on the South Side. Can you locate this cell phone?"

"Okay, just stay calm, sir. Here's what..."

The front door to the plant slowly swung open. It was located opposite the back-alley door where the bald man's body lay and a good forty feet from Rory and Mia's hiding spot. Rory held the volume button down to mute the phone, then shoved it in his pocket. *Maybe they can get a fix.*

Rory reached for the pistol behind his back. At the door, a fat man dressed in a black suit and tie with white shirt walked into the abandoned plant. *Sergey, the driver*, Rory thought.

Sergey quickly scanned the space. His comrades' bodies were some distance from the door, and the plant was dimly lit, but Rory could tell that he noticed something was off.

Sergey took two guarded steps forward and called out, "Yakov? Vanya?" Then he drew a pistol from underneath his suit jacket. Rory could just make out an older man as he stepped over the threshold and followed Sergey into the plant. He wore a black wool overcoat. A Russian-style fur cap sat atop his head.

Golev.

CHAPTER 68

Chicago, Illinois

MONDAY, NOVEMBER 8, 2027

THE BEST THING I'VE GOT going for me is surprise. Don't waste it on a long shot.

Rory considered squeezing off a couple rounds, but the table behind which he and Mia hid was too far away.

Sergey paused and turned around. He said something in Russian to Golev, who immediately pulled his own pistol. Rory whispered to Mia, "Stay here." Then he moved silently and in a crouch toward a row of metal-frame shelves stacked with boxes and rusty meat pans.

Maybe I can get a round on target from here.

Golev and Sergey fanned out. At this point, Rory was sure they had seen the dead bodies. Their guns were held in firing positions, and they walked very slowly. *Damn*, Rory thought as Golev headed away from his position. But Sergey moved closer. Rory had a clear shot at a good angle from cover behind the shelves. *It's now or never.*

He squeezed the trigger twice, striking Sergey in his chest and right shoulder. Sergey stumbled back and then attempted to make his way toward the small table and chairs set up in the corner. Rory stepped from behind the shelves and lined up a head shot. He missed with the first attempt but connected with the next round. The bullet carved right through Sergey's skull. His brains discharged out the back of his head.

As soon as Golev heard the first shots, he had moved quickly to take cover behind one of the steal support beams in the middle of the plant. Rory could see his profile but had no angle for a good shot. He ran toward a different support beam, the one that he and Mia had originally been bound to. As he ran, Golev got a round off but missed far right. Now, the two men stood no more than ten yards apart. Both their bodies were barely protected by the steel beams. Each man sucked in his chest and tried to cut as slim a profile as possible, but toes and noses both stuck out wide of their respective beams. Golev had the better view, as one of the few working lights hung from the ceiling just above Rory's position.

"Give it up, Golev! The game is over!" Rory cried out.

"Ha, you make me laugh. The game is never over."

Rory did his best to project a confident, commanding voice. "Your men are dead. Frederik d'Oultremont is dead. The police will be here any minute now. Now turn yourself in and maybe one day your president will be able to get you out in a prisoner swap. It's your only hope. You lost."

Golev did not reply. Instead, as Rory finished his little speech, Golev took off in a sprint to another row of shelves adjacent to his beam. As he ran, he turned and fired off two quick rounds from a tough angle. Both shots missed but drew return fire. Rory had moved to the left of his beam and sent two rounds toward Golev and the shelves. After his second shot, the pistol's slide stop engaged and the SIG locked open. Rory was empty.

Fuck! Rory thought, ashamed he had never press checked the magazine, which apparently had been loaded a few rounds short of capacity.

The exposed barrel of Rory's pistol stuck out past his beam and, given the light above, was visible to Golev. Rory quickly noticed this fact and immediately pulled the pistol down to his right side, but the damage was done.

Golev stepped out from behind the shelves, his gun drawn. "What's wrong, Rory? Out of ammunition?" he said mockingly as he slowly crept closer. "How fitting. If it were only a few days earlier, on the anniversary, it would be so poetic."

It was very faint, but Rory could hear what he thought was a siren in the distance. *Did that dispatcher get a read?* In an attempt to stall, he said, "What are you talking about? What's so poetic?"

Golev returned a little laugh as he cautiously came one step closer. Rory understood why he was hesitant to rush in. Unable to see the SIG since Rory moved it to his side, Golev could not be entirely certain Rory did not have another magazine.

Golev said, "Oh, that's right. Yakov told me you were unconscious on the ride here. You don't know where we are, do you?"

"Well, I know we're not at your mother's house. I would recognize that place right away."

Golev could not help but chuckle at that remark, then said, "We're just off Fifty-Ninth Street. Hamilton's Pub is only two blocks away. I thought it would be fitting if you and Mia met your end so close to where I shot Peter last year. Where is his pretty little sister, by the way?"

That motherfucker. Rory fumed. He was furious at Golev and furious at himself for not paying attention to his rounds. But the sound of the siren grew louder. He had hope. "You hear that, Golev? She went for the police. They'll be here any minute now. Just put down your pistol and let's go outside."

Apparently Golev decided there was no more time for games. He quickened his pace and began closing the gap between him and Rory. One, two, three shots rang out, resonating through the stale air.

But they were not from Golev's gun. It was Mia. She stood, pistol raised, in the center of the plant as Anton Golev dropped dead to the floor.

Rory came out from behind the beam. He looked in astonishment at Mia, then down at Golev's cold and soulless gray eyes.

The Russian. She must've pulled a pistol off the bald Russian.

CHAPTER 69

Chicago, Illinois
MONDAY, NOVEMBER 8, 2027

THE CRAFTY BENGAL BANKER WAS more than happy to set up a call between McGrady and Delgado. After all, Arun Patel needed something to placate the cartel-affiliated mine boss. The silver purchase agreement executed only three days prior was clearly over, and he hoped this opportunity might soften the blow. He also needed an ace in the hole, something to use as leverage should his devious dealings with Frederik, Golev, and Zhao come to light. If Patel could threaten to leak a story detailing how Mexican drug cartels played a key role in stabilizing global financial markets, he may just be able to escape public prosecution.

For Delgado's part, the loss of the silver deal seemed more than made up for by McGrady's proposal. Not only did McGrady promise to deliver one hell of a quick return, but he also assured Delgado that when his capital was no longer needed, it would be returned smelling like roses. The aristocratic mine boss could not pass up this opportunity to launder such a sizable portion of his business partners' assets. In less than ten minutes, a deal was struck.

Sara Schnyder got straight to work. In rapid succession, she began initiating dozens of transfers from tax-haven nations around the globe. Once completed, the Swiss master of money movement would increase the trading reserves at Celtic Capital by over $8 billion. A special account was papered in the name Plata Grande Fund. Officially, its beneficial ownership was attributed to a consortium of global metals and mining companies. Unofficially, it was blood money. McGrady did not feel good about the transfers, but he did not rise to the heights of the hedge fund world without understanding that sometimes a deal with the devil was better than no deal at all. If markets collapsed, it would be chaos in the streets, with riots and looting likely to follow. Lives would be lost. Of course, if McGrady did not fulfil his promises to Delgado, one of those lost lives might be his own. He needed to deliver the *plata,* or he was getting the *plomo.*

As the gang at 333 sorted out transfers and tweaked AI algos, the trading halt imposed by the Level 1 circuit breaker ended. The market reopened. Without Celtic traders actively buying, stocks immediately resumed their free fall. The S&P was quickly down 10 percent on the day. As the index hovered just above the Level 2 breaker, reports began to surface out of Basel regarding emergency action by the world's central banks. A brief rally ensued, but there was no follow-through. The onslaught of selling continued. Around half past noon in New York, the market touched 13 percent down, triggering the Level 2 breaker. Trading halted once again.

The panic was not limited to the equity markets. Most commodities sold off dramatically as well, though gold and silver were on the rise. Interestingly, the US dollar and Treasury markets regained their flight-to-safety status. Any irregularities those markets had exhibited during Friday's trade were muted. Wall Street pundits brushed over the dollar's regained strength and attributed last week's declines to aberrations caused by Phase III of ICARUS coming online and diverting capital flows to emerging markets. Their attention was instead focused on plummeting equities. But what was truly threatening to the global economic order was not the stock market decline. It was the breakdown of credit spreads.

Corporate debt yields shot up as the revived safety trade drove Treasury yields down. The OAS, or option-adjusted spread, between high-yield debt and the bonds issued by the US government widened to over three thousand basis points. Soon, even investment-grade corporate bond spreads blew out. The enormous amounts of risky credit that had been built up on the balance sheets of the world's largest banks during the ICARUS-induced bubble were about to explode. Bankruptcies in these banks would have a contagion effect. Their overnight paper would be worth cents on the dollar. Money market funds, which held copious amounts of this very short-term bank debt, would "break the buck." Runs on brokerage and bank accounts were escalating.

Sara finally completed her transfers during the Level 2 halt. She informed McGrady that the Celtic traders were locked and loaded with new funds from the Plata Grande account. McGrady walked out of his office to the trading desks. He managed to get his hefty frame atop an empty desk and stood looking down on the small sea of traders. A hush fell over them as McGrady began to speak.

"Okay, listen up. We've got some more cash to spread around when this thing opens back up. Before it does, I want you to contact every prime broker, every bank, every possible source of capital you have. Margin that cash for every damn cent you can get. Lever up your fuckin' leverage. You understand me? I don't give a shit if you borrow money from your grandmother. Just take every fuckin' dollar of hard cash you've got to work with and turn it into ten, twenty, fifty times the nominal exposure. Then, when trading resumes, I want you to buy. Buy stocks, buy options, buy futures, buy whatever the fuck they're selling and then buy some more. We got one more crack at this thing. Now get to fuckin' work!"

As McGrady stepped down from the desk, there was no roar of hoots and hollers, just the sound of traders picking up their phones and using every relationship, every favor, every trick of the trade they knew, whether legally questionable or not, to juice their buying power.

Just moments before McGrady delivered his pep talk, another trader had walked through the frosted-glass door of Celtic Capital. It was Rory O'Connor. The sirens he had heard back at the meatpacking plant were indeed responding to his 911 call. When the police arrived, he and Mia did their best to quickly explain the situation, including the four dead bodies in the plant. Fortunately, one of the responding officers played softball with Brendon McGrady. Rory convinced the officer to call Brendon, and it was decided that formal written statements could wait. Mia was driven by ambulance to her emergency department at Rush Medical. Rory, meanwhile, received a high-speed police escort to 333.

"Wow, Milt. You missed your calling. Should have coached for Notre Dame," Rory teased as McGrady made his way over to him.

"Everything all right?" McGrady asked.

Not really, Rory thought. *My head is throbbing, Mia's in the hospital, and the world economy is about to collapse, not to mention I'm fucking exhausted and had to kill six men in as many days,* but he nodded a yes anyway.

"Good, then sit your ass down and start buying."

Rory smiled and found an available desk. *What the hell.* He picked up the phone to call one of his old prime brokers. *Let's see if I can still pull some leverage.*

Trading resumed just before 1:00 p.m. in New York. The market took one more swoosh down fueled by pent-up sell orders entered during the halt. But as the S&P approached down 18 percent on the day, the selling reversed.

Extensive buy orders from Celtic Capital flooded the market just as it hit a key Fibonacci retracement level. Since the decline began last week, the S&P had retraced exactly 38.2 percent of its gains since the March low in 2009 during the Global Financial Crisis. The shift was tentative at first, primarily powered by technicals and Celtic's relentless order flow. But after two key resistance levels were blown through to the upside, market sentiment fully reversed. Panic selling quickly turned to panic buying. Greed had replaced fear as the leading market driver.

At 3:04 EST, reports out of Washington indicating that a bill repealing the Phoenix Act was already out of committee added fuel to the buying frenzy. By 3:30, the market had turned positive. As the closing bell rang on Wall Street, the S&P had not only regained all the day's losses, but it also booked a gain of 3.4 percent. It was the greatest one-day reversal in market history, more than a 20 percent swing from low to high.

It had been a day for the record books at Celtic Capital as well. Rory, Kota, Das, and Sara regrouped with McGrady in his office. He ceremoniously sat them all down on the couch and chairs that surrounded his oval coffee table, providing them each with a tumbler of thousand-dollar-a-bottle scotch.

"So, how'd we do?" McGrady asked, knowing the firm must have made billions.

Sara punched up some numbers on a borrowed laptop. Sounding a bit like an accountant, she said, "As of the close, and I could be off by a billion or so on this, some of the positions haven't settled yet..."

"Yes, yes, give me a ballpark," McGrady interrupted anxiously.

"Well, including Celtic's proprietary accounts, client accounts, partner hedge funds, and the Plata Grande Fund, the total comes to thirty-eight." Sara then dropped her accountant-like tone and announced, "We made thirty-eight fucking billion dollars!"

At the sound of the number, the sixty-two-year-old McGrady had no immediate reaction. One by one, he looked around the room, making eye contact with everyone in turn as the enormity of the sum began to sink in. Then, with a clap of his hands, he jumped from his chair like a schoolboy. McGrady had been in this business for a long time. The rise of computers, algorithms, AI, and eventually ICARUS had sapped away most of the joy left for him. Now, all that was forgotten as a feeling of unadulterated capitalistic bliss washed over his aging body.

McGrady announced to the team that made it happen, "Each of you will be well compensated for your efforts. And I'm not talking six or seven figures; I'm talking eight, hell, maybe even nine."

"And we did stop the world from heading into economic Armageddon," Das reminded the ecstatic McGrady.

"Yes, of course," McGrady said as he sat back down in his chair.

Rory also took a quick look around the room. His gaze came to rest on Kota as he thought back to the FaceTime conversation that had started this entire odyssey. *Something had definitely not been right with ICARUS. Maybe something had not been right with me either.*

Rory shifted back to the moment and hoisted his glass. "A toast," he said as McGrady, Kota, Das, and Sara also raised their tumblers. "To averting the financial apocalypse."

They clinked glasses, but not before McGrady could add, "And to making one giant fuckin' pile of money."

As Rory brought the luxurious scotch to his lips, his eyes glanced briefly toward the ceiling.

And to you too, Pete.

CHAPTER 70

Chicago, Illinois

Monday, November 8, 2027

AFTER A SECOND CELEBRATORY ROUND, this time out on the trading floor with the entire crew, Rory left 333 West Wacker and made his way to Rush University Medical Center. He entered Mia's room—a double, with a glorified shower curtain separating each of the two beds. However, being a top nurse in the emergency department had its perks. The second bed was empty. As a precaution, Mia had an IV hooked up to ensure proper hydration, but she looked much better after a few hours' rest, the soft olive color returned to her skin.

"So did you save the financial universe?" Mia asked as Rory made his way toward her bed.

Rory brushed off the question, turning his attention to her. "How are you feeling?"

"I'll be fine. They want me to stay overnight for observation, but I should be able to head home tomorrow. I miss Oscar, Romeo, and Juliet."

Rory leaned slightly over the side railing of the bed. He reached down and held Mia's hand. "I'm glad. We were all worried about you."

"So," Mia asked, "what's next?"

"Well, futures are up nicely. There was a massive short covering rally at the end of the day. I think markets have stabilized."

Mia smiled and gave a little laugh. "Not with the markets. I meant what's next for you? For us?"

Rory hadn't had much time recently to ponder the subject, but he had a hunch it may come up. "Mia, you know that I care for you deeply."

"But…" she prompted.

"No buts," Rory said honestly, still holding Mia's hand. "I just don't know what to think about anything right now. My head is spinning."

"Mine too. It has been quite the week." Mia paused, then said, "Maybe give me some advance notice the next time you come to town."

"Will do," Rory replied with a smile. "Milt actually offered me a role as chief investment officer at Celtic, but I'm not ready to make any big decisions. Plus, I've got some potted palms back in San Juan that probably need my attention."

Mia returned the smile. Their eyes met, and she said, "You don't need to use watering your plants as an excuse to get out of Chicago. It's fine, Rory, really. I'm not sure what to think about anything right now either."

"You know," he said, "I've got plenty of room in my condo. Gorgeous tropical breezes come right off the ocean and onto the deck. When you're feeling better, come down and see me. Take a break from the Chicago winter."

"I'd like that."

Mia slowly released Rory's hand.

CHAPTER 71

Beijing, China

Tuesday, November 9, 2027

"So, tell me. What happened in Basel?"

Wang Jun, president of the People's Republic of China, rested his arms on his desk and interlaced his fingers.

Zhao Hong stood nervously in front of the large and intimidating desk of the most powerful man in Asia. Behind Wang, a panoramic painting of the Great Wall of China hung, flanked by oak bookshelves and a finely embroidered Chinese flag. On one of the side walls, a muted flat-screen TV streamed FNN. Although he had banned the network along with other Western outlets, Wang liked to keep his finger on the pulse of foreign reporting.

Zhao responded succinctly, "Things did not go as planned."

President Wang was not one to demonstrate his displeasure with loud outbursts or dramatic scenes. He leaned slightly forward in his chair and stared at Zhao. "I think that is an understatement. Wouldn't you agree?"

Zhao could tell from Wang's eyes that behind the calm demeanor, he was not pleased. Indeed, Zhao worried that his uncle by marriage was seriously considering a change in PBoC leadership, nephew or not. But Wang continued in a restrained tone. "Sit down, Hong. You must be tired from your long journey."

Zhao took a seat and proceeded to spin things in as positive a light as possible without sugarcoating his failures. Wang listened unenthusiastically as Zhao concluded his report, "While we sold some significant Treasury holdings on Friday, we refrained from liquidating our entire position during Monday's trade once it became clear that BIScoin was off the table. However, we still have the digital renminbi program in motion and are a global leader in central bank digital currency. Also, rumors have surfaced regarding our discussions at the BIS. Word of a possible return to bimetallism has caused a spike in both gold and silver prices. Our precious metal stockpiles are worth billions more today than they were just twenty-four hours ago."

It was true. Rumors of the BIScoin plan had made their way around the world's financial centers. Just the whisper of a global currency backed by gold and silver had triggered a short squeeze across the precious metal complex, causing prices to skyrocket. Gold was nearing $4,000 an ounce on the London Metal Exchange. Silver was up even more on a percentage basis at over one hundred dollars a troy ounce.

"That is all very well, Zhao, but what use are a million yellow bars sitting in our vaults? What can we buy," Wang asked, "with all our glittering gold?"

As Wang posed his questions, Zhao caught the scene unfolding on FNN out of the corner of his eye. Matthew Whitlock was giving an interview from the corridors of the US Capitol. The Breaking News caption read, SENATOR PROMISES NEW ERA OF FISCAL RESPONSIBILITY. PHOENIX ACT TO BE REPEALED.

Before departing Basel for Beijing, Zhao had completed an enlightening call with the senior senator from North Carolina. Their conversation provided an opportunity for the leader of the PBoC to redeem himself.

Zhao Hong stood from his chair and walked over toward the television. "What can we buy with all our glittering gold, you ask?" He raised an outstretched hand toward the image of Whitlock and suggested earnestly, "How about the next president of the United States?"

The End

ACKNOWLEDGMENTS

As is true with any novel, it takes more than just one person to bring it to publication. During my efforts to do so with *Quoz*, I have been helped by many along the way. While I considered an attempt at heartfelt, witty, and amusing anecdotes to say thank you in a way that highlights my prowess, or lack thereof, as a writer, I'm afraid it's not exactly my style.

Hence, I would like to acknowledge here simply but sincerely the following individuals without whom this book would either not exist or would exist in a form inferior to what lies before this page. For any lack of superiority the reader may find, however, I am responsible.

Much thanks to Jon Ford, my editor. Jon, your suggestions, input, and enthusiasm have been fantastic. To Anthony Ziccardi, Madeline Sturgeon, and the rest of the team at Post Hill, you have my deepest appreciation. Trey Radel, your help and support were invaluable. Thanks, bro.

Adam LeBor, your exceptional nonfiction work *Tower of Basel: The Shadowy History of the Secret Bank that Runs the World* provided me with inspiration and insight during my research phase. I am grateful for both your book and your interest in this one.

Though it could go without saying, to my parents and wife, thank you for believing in me even when I have given ample cause not to. Robbie and Oscar, you may not know it, but you are also individuals without whom this book may not exist.

Lastly, to my readers, much appreciation. I hope you found *Quoz* as entertaining, stimulating, and thrilling to read as it was to write.

ABOUT THE AUTHOR

MEL MATTISON IS A WRITER and financial services veteran. Leveraging over twenty years' experience in the realm of high finance, he brings real-world authenticity to his fictional narratives. Mel holds an MBA from Duke University and studied creative writing at Loyola University Chicago. Visit him at www.melmattison.com.